DESIRED BY DOOM

THE LAST RIDERS, OHIO CHAPTER

JAMIE BEGLEY

Young Ink Press Publication
YoungInkPress.com

Edited by CD Editing, Erin Toland,
& Diamond in the Rough Editing
Cover Art by CT Cover Creations

Connect with Jamie,
Facebook.com/AuthorJamieBegley
Instagram.com/authorjamiebegley
JamieBegley.net

'To Thine Own Self Be True'

CHAPTER 1
THE PROSPECT

"Are you joking?" Arden stared at her younger brother in disbelief. Usually, she knew when Luc was joking around. He was notorious for pulling pranks and filming their reactions as he grew up. What made her hesitate that he was serious and not joking was the change she had seen in him over the last year.

Luc had become more withdrawn. Her carefree baby brother had become a recluse, preferring to stay in his room instead of hanging out with their family or friends.

His jaw jutted out stubbornly. "I'm serious."

Looking toward her mother, whose face was pale as she stared back at her, she pleaded with her eyes to change Luc's mind.

Their mother took a seat on the couch next to him. "Why in the world would you give up a scholarship to one of the most prestigious schools in the country to join a motorcycle club?"

"I hate school. I've been telling you, but none of you have been listening to me." Dragging his hand through his brown hair, he gave her an exasperated scowl.

"We're listening now." Attempting to calm the tension between Luc and her mother, Arden stepped into the familiar role of peacemaker.

In hindsight, she had noticed his behavior had gone through a change since entering Skyline Conservatory. She had thought it was just the high expectations of the grades that were required to keep the scholarship awarded to him.

"Why do you hate Skyline?" she asked calmly.

"Why wouldn't I? Everyone makes fun of me for riding the bus at my age instead of driving, that my lunch is free, my clothes aren't designer. I don't belong at Skyline, and the rest of the students know it."

"You deserve to be there as much as they do," their mother protested. "I told you that they're just jealous. You're smarter than them, schoolwork comes easier to you—"

A sarcastic laugh came from him, which had her inwardly cringing, seeing the pain beneath the laugh.

Arden gave him a sympathetic glance. "I'm sorry, Luc. We've not been listening to what you've been trying to tell us. I didn't know not having a car was a big deal. You can take my car, and I can take the bus until I figure something else out."

"I don't want your car! Do you not get that their cars are status symbols to them? A Civic would have them laughing before I could park."

Not offended at having her car insulted, Arden sought for another alternative. "Then I'll pick up another few shifts and lease you a car. Which car would make you happy?" She would figure out the finances later. Right now, the most important part was keeping Luc in school.

"I don't want you to buy me a fucking car!" Luc shouted at her.

Cringing at the use of profanity directed toward her, she kept her cool. Anger wouldn't resolve what was making Luc determined to throw away his scholarship.

"I have a job. I'm going to buy a motorcycle when I have enough money and can get a license."

Him having a job was news to her. Glancing at their mother, she saw the same confusion on her face. Arden glanced back at her brother. "Where do you work?"

"The Last Riders are going to let me be a prospect until I earn my patch when I'm eighteen. Until then, they pay me to guard the door of the club or do any other jobs they want done."

"Like buying their drugs for them or stealing something?" Their mother started crying. "Are you trying to kill your father?"

"Calm down, Mom. Getting this upset won't do your heart any good either."

"Where is Dad?" Arden asked.

Luc threw himself down on the couch next to her. "He's at a doctor's appointment. I waited until he left before telling Mom."

"He wants me to be the one to tell Carter." Her mother's voice was shrill. "Carter has worked sixty-hour weeks to keep a roof over our heads, and this is how you're going to repay him? By joining a motorcycle gang instead of finishing school and becoming a doctor?"

"The Last Riders aren't a gang; they're a club," Luc protested, rising from the couch heatedly.

Arden broke into the heated exchange between her brother and mother, "Don't you want to become a doctor anymore?"

If her brother truly didn't want to become a doctor, then

she would back his decision to drop out of school—as much as she hated the thought.

A quick flash of pain before Luc could compose his expression told her the truth that he was trying to hide either from himself or them. "No, I don't."

Why was he lying to them? Arden had a sinking feeling she knew.

"Luc, I don't mind working the extra shifts to help Mom and Dad out until they get back on their feet."

"When are you going to realize this is our new normal? Dad's doctor told him that he won't be able to go back to work after this last heart attack. How can Mom work, tied to that oxygen machine? You expect me to pretend everything is okay and spend hours studying instead of pulling my own weight? Fuck, Arden..."

"Is this the behavior The Last Riders are teaching you? To curse at your sister?"

Arden winced at her mother's shrill voice. "It's okay, Mom," she attempted to calm her mother.

"No, it's not okay!" Her mother wailed. "You've been too good to Luc for him to speak to you this way."

Luc's face twisted in self-recrimination. "I need to get out of here. Tell Dad anything you want when he comes back, but I'm not going back to that school." Luc agitatedly walked toward the door and jerked it open. "I'm going to work. I'll find somewhere else to live if you can't accept my decision," he threatened over his shoulder as he went out the door.

Arden rose to try to stop him from leaving, but he slammed the door shut before she could reach him. Turning back to her mother, she hurried to kneel next to where she was sitting. "Catch your breath, Mom." Arden checked the oxygen machine to see if it was positioned on the right setting.

"You have to change his mind, Arden. This will kill your father."

"I'll talk to him when he calms down." Arden grabbed tissues from a side table and gently patted the tears coursing down her mother's cheeks.

"Tonight. The headmaster is planning on expelling him tomorrow. Luc hasn't been going to school like I thought he was. He lied to me... He's never lied to me before. Those Last Riders are a bad influence on him. This is going to kill—"

"Don't say anything to Dad. I'll get Luc to change his mind, and I'll straighten things out with the headmaster. There's no need to get Dad upset."

Her mom gave a sniffling nod. "I knew I could count on you. I'm going to take a nap. I don't want Carter seeing me cry."

Arden helped her mom stand up; it's becoming more difficult each day. Carrying the oxygen tank to the bedroom, Arden then helped get her mother into bed and situated.

"I'm going to leave, Mom. I'll call you in the morning after I talk to the headmaster."

Her hand was caught in a frail grasp. "All I ever wanted was for Luc to be happy. I thought he was. What have The Last Riders done to him?"

"I don't know, Mom, but I promise I'm going to find out."

CHAPTER 2

THE CLUBHOUSE

Arden took a sip of her coffee, trying to stay awake as she watched Luc stand watch outside the motorcycle club, which was going to destroy her family if she didn't find a way to convince him to go back to school.

It hadn't taken her long to find The Last Riders' clubhouse. Unfortunately, it had taken her longer to drive there, enabling Luc to get there first. She had planned to ask them *nicely* to discourage Luc from any further association with them. If that failed, she didn't know what she would do, but she was sure something would come to her if that bridge had to be crossed.

Tired, she blinked her bleary eyes. She had been sitting in the parking garage catty-corner to the bar The Last Riders called home. To pass the time, she had counted the motorcycles sitting outside and stopped counting at thirty, feeling her nerves getting the best of her. She had never been in this older portion of Ohio, and she wasn't thrilled at being there now. If she weren't afraid Luc would hate her, she would drive over to the bar and demand he get his ass inside the car. Fear of hurting their relationship was the only thing holding her back.

"Damn, Luc, how long are you expected to stand there?" she muttered out loud. All she needed was for him to leave for a few minutes, just long enough so she could get inside without him seeing her.

"How is this better than staying home and studying?" she asked, as if her brother had a chance of hearing her from the distance separating them. "This is ridiculous," she complained to the empty car.

Tempted to continue her search online about The Last Riders on her cell phone, she then decided against it. Most of the articles written about them were on their survival business.

The plastic coffee cup in her hand trembled when the club door opened and two men walked out, dressed in leather jackets. Arden was too far away to get a good look at their faces.

Placing her coffee in the cup holder, she saw Luc stride away with one of the men, getting on the back of a motorcycle and leaving the other man standing at the door. Pressing the ignition button, she started edging out of the parking garage after the motorcycle whizzed past. Her hands were sweating on the steering wheel when she pulled into the bar's parking lot. The biker standing guard at the door had his eyes fixed on her before she even parked.

Gathering every ounce of courage she had, Arden left the car when all she wanted to do was dive back inside and get the hell out of there. Using all her invented acting skills, she nonchalantly pretended as if visiting a motorcycle club was an everyday occurrence for her as she strode toward the door.

The biker raised a questioning eyebrow at her as he

firmly placed his back against the door to keep her from entering. "This is a private club. If you're looking for directions, there's a gas station down the street."

Only the thought of her father's reaction to Luc's drastic change of plans for his future kept her feet rooted to the spot at the biker's intimidating stare. "I'm not lost. I want to go inside."

"Fuck off."

Noticing the straining seams of the leather jacket, Arden knew she didn't stand a chance of forcefully moving the muscled biker from the door. Any appreciation of how handsome he would be if he weren't succeeding in intimidating her away from the club went up in smoke. His menacing expression, combined with the harsh look in his eyes, was meant to scare her away, and it was working.

She was about to take a step back when the memory of her mother crying into her pillow as she had left flashed across her mind. Instead of retreating, she took a step forward. Giving him a glare that matched his own, she jutted her chin out. "Listen here, I'm here to see whoever is in charge of this..." She raised a hand to motion at the motorcycles parked around the building. "Now."

The biker stared at her doubtfully. "You're here to see Wizard?"

"Yes, I am. Now, please move out of my way," she ordered huffily. Arden actually thought she might vomit at his feet she was so nervous. There wasn't a confrontational bone in her body. She wasn't a pushover, yet she would seek other avenues to get the results she wanted. Unfortunately, politeness was not going to get her inside the club before Luc returned.

"You want to see Wizard?" the biker asked again. "He isn't in the best mood tonight."

"Neither am I," she said grimly.

The biker opened the door without turning around, stepping backward as it was opened.

Arden was given a first look inside. Composing herself not to appear frightened, she was relieved to see several women sitting at some of the tables or moving around the bar area. The bar was larger than she had expected from the outside.

"Wizard!"

The shout from the biker who had opened the door nearly gave her a heart attack. Placing a hand over her heart, she looked to where he was staring.

A dark-haired biker turned his head to look over his shoulder. Blue-gray eyes met hers.

"What does she want?"

"I don't know. She said you were expecting her."

"I didn't exactly say he was expecting me," she muttered.

A fierce frown formed on the biker next to her. "You said you were here to see Wizard."

"I didn't say I had an appointment," she countered.

The crowded bar broke into laughter.

A large hand landed on her forearm. "Get your ass out," the biker ordered.

Arden jerked her arm away. "Don't touch me." She determinedly avoided the hand that reached out to grab her again and made it a couple of steps inside before a long leg came out to block her way.

She looked up at the owner of the black-jeaned leg, then wished she hadn't. Cyan-colored eyes caught her gaze, silently warning her that she wouldn't be able to shake his hand off if he touched her. She guessed him to be in his thirties, and his ruthless features set off yellow flags, urging caution. From the long length of his legs, she guessed his height to be over six foot three, if not more. If he was this alarming sitting down, she didn't want him getting up.

"Wizard, you wanting company?"

Wizard didn't bother turning around again. "No. Tell her to get lost. My appointments are filled for the rest of the night. Isn't that right, Margarita? Doom, take her number. I might have something available if Friday night is a slow night with Expo going on."

As the room broke out in laughter again, Arden was aware she had become the brunt of a joke. Disparaging laughter, she was used to. Contrasted to other women, she would never get men's notice other than how fast she could approve their surgery. Working in a medical office for four surgeons, she was surrounded by male coworkers and clients, and in the evenings, she moonlighted as a hostess at a local restaurant. At both jobs, she believed once she was out of sight she was out of mind.

"Friday won't do. I need to talk to you tonight."

Long Legs rose to his full height to tower over her. "Want to leave on your own steam, or you want me to offer my assistance?"

Arden didn't back down. She couldn't. "Fine, I'll leave," she snapped without making a move to do so. "I'll just call the police and let them ask to talk to *Wizard*."

Her belittling tone of voice had the whole bar going silent. A golden-red-haired woman standing behind the counter shook her head in warning.

"Doom."

The small hairs on her arms stood up at the way Long Legs's expression froze. Arden didn't have to be told how the man had earned the nickname. Every move he made was filled with lethal intent as she was snatched off her feet.

"Put me down!" she screamed, all the self-defense training she had taken flying out of her head. "This is assault!"

Raising her head from his back, she saw Doom wasn't carrying her toward the front door and frantically scissored her legs when he made a sharp left to carry her down a long hallway.

"I'll leave. Put me down right now!" she yelled, trying to throw herself off his shoulder.

The heavy sound of his boots striding down the dark hallway filled her mind with images from horror movies. Releasing a blood-curdling scream, she pounded on Doom's back. She didn't know what she had expected, but it wasn't seeing doors opening along the hallway and a variety of male faces staring at Doom inquiringly without saying a word to him or her.

"Help me! He's kidnapping me!" she screamed louder when they passed one doorway that was filled with a naked man grinning at her.

"I'll help if you want. I love dealing with screamers."

Arden snapped her mouth closed. The bearded man was covered in tatts and piercings in places that she had never imagined a man would want them.

"Back off, Buck."

Closing her eyes when they passed another naked man and a big-boobed woman who looked more envious than willing to help her, Arden quit struggling. Instead, she arched her back so she could lock her hands behind Doom's neck. Using all the anger she couldn't direct at Luc, she started strangling the biker carrying her.

His strides didn't falter, no matter how tightly she squeezed.

"Let go."

A firm grip on her wrist had her blinking back to awareness. Realizing her feet were back on firm ground, she released the stranglehold on his neck. Frightened, she looked around the room he had carried her to, finding it was an office.

Straightening her top and jacket, she gave Doom a haughty stare-down, which would have made her third-grade teacher proud. "Becoming physical was completely unnecessary," she stated firmly.

The giant standing just a couple of inches away from her cocked his head to the side. "I wasn't the one trying strangle the life out of someone." Reaching for the collar of his black T-shirt, he tugged it down to his collarbone.

Feeling the rush of blood fill her cheeks at the red marks around his neck, she instinctively moved closer to touch them, wanting to soothe the angry color.

"I'm sorry," she apologized, unaware he was staring down at her quizzically as she ran gentle fingertips over the rapidly darkening marks. "I'm not usually so physical, but you scared me," she confessed.

DOOM PULLED her hand from his neck and tugged his shirt collar back up. "You could have fooled me."

Mocking, cyan eyes had her taking a step back.

"Like I said, I was frightened." Making the excuse didn't make her feel better. She hated that she had hurt him.

"You're not now?"

"No, you aren't carrying me to God knows where."

He stared at her as if she had the IQ of a two-year-old. "Where did you think I was taking you?"

"I don't know... Outside, a back door to kill me, or..."

She felt her cheeks turning redder at the way he was looking at her.

"Or...?" he prompted, amusement entering his eyes.

She didn't answer, her own eyes moving around him to the open doorway.

"A bedroom?" His amusement deepened. "You thought I was going to rape you just because you threatened to call the cops?"

"I don't appreciate your humor. This isn't a laughing matter." Glaring at him, she pulled her shoulders back, trying to add another half inch to her height. It was hard to act high and mighty when she only came up to his waist. Sympathizing with how scared David must have been when he had confronted Goliath, Arden reached for her own courage to keep from making a sprint for the door.

"No, it isn't." He lost the humor he was regarding her with, making her comprehend the fact that she was still in danger. "It just blows my mind how you think that because I brought you to the office, you're safe from rape." He shook his head at her as if dumbfounded by her reasoning.

Arden took a tiny step to the side, preparing to run if he so much as moved a hair in her direction.

"Chill." Doom sat down in front of the desk, sprawling his legs out. "I was speaking figuratively. I've never been accused of rape, and to be blunt—"

"Please don't." She hastily shook her head at him. "I'm well aware of my lack of attractiveness." Wanting to smooth her short hair down and straighten her jacket again, she self-consciously didn't pull her gaze away from his.

"I was about to say, rape has never appealed to me, not even during role playing. I prefer my women willing and available."

Arden wanted to fan her face at the look he was giving her.

"I'm not." At least she only half-lied.

"No shit. I'd never guess that."

Her nostrils flared in anger. "Are you being sarcastic?"

He rolled his eyes at her. "Yes." Giving a frustrated sigh, he straightened his relaxed posture. "As much as I'm enjoying this conservation..." This time, she didn't have to ask if he was being sarcastic; it was plain to see. "What is so important you want to talk to Wizard?"

"Is he the one in charge of your club?"

"Wizard is the president of this chapter of The Last Riders." He nodded.

"Then he's the one I need to talk to."

"In case you missed it, Wizard has his hands full. You have two choices: tell me what has your panties in a wad enough to call the cops, or I can assist your ass out to your car. Keep in mind that every place in this club is monitored with video surveillance, so if you are planning on lying to the cops that anyone did anything inappropriate, we'll be the ones pressing charges against you. If you choose the first option, after you tell me what has you upset enough to come inside a motorcycle club without an invite, I will do my best to help with the problem. If I can't, I'll relay the info to Wizard. From there, I'll contact you as to what he wants done. If you choose the second option, which is what I *prefer*, then thanks for wasting my fucking time. This is going to be as good as it gets, so which do you choose?" He placed his hands on the arms of the chair, preparing to rise.

"*Since* those are my only options, I choose number one." She could be just as sarcastic as him.

From his malevolent smile, Arden didn't think he appreciated her sarcasm as much she had his.

"Then let's hear what we've supposedly done that deserves having the cops called on us."

"I think contributing to the delinquency of a minor is worth calling the police for. This place is considered a bar, isn't it? Unless I didn't see liquor being served out there?" Crossing her arms over a heavily beating heart, she gave him a superior smile. It was the highlight of her terrible day to swipe the arrogant wind out of his sails.

"I can verify myself as a fact that no one under eighteen is allowed on the grounds or in the bar."

"Really...?" she drawled. "Then can you explain how I saw my brother here? Oh and I can verify as a *fact* he's only sixteen."

She had to give Doom kudos; he didn't show concern at her revelation, but she did see a troubled expression enter his eyes.

"Who's your brother?"

"Luc Johnston."

"That doesn't mean shit to me. What's his biker name?"

"I don't know." She shrugged in bewilderment. "We only found out today he was planning on joining The Last Riders."

"Then he was just pulling your chain. No one under eighteen is allowed. Go home and call the little shit's bluff." He rose and motioned toward the office door. "I'll escort you out."

"Wait!" Arden dropped her arms from her chest in surprise that he was denying Luc being there. "I saw him with my own eyes."

"Where? Show me where." He reached out to take her arm, marching her toward the door.

"He's not here now," she argued, frantically pulling her arm out of his grip.

His detached façade did a one-eighty, turning brutal and making her legs feel like jelly.

"What fucking game are you trying to get over on us?"

"I'm telling the truth." She managed to articulate the words despite being terrified.

Her father's doctors had warned his next heart attack would make her mother a widow. If she had to fight the whole clubhouse to save her father's life, she would. He was the type of father other children wished were theirs. There wasn't anything he wouldn't do for them, and dammit, there was no biker, no matter how scary they were, that would stop her from doing the same.

Snagging her by the waist, Doom started dragging her toward the door.

"Luc was here!" she yelled, grabbing the doorframe. "He was standing outside, watching the door, before I was so politely escorted inside."

Arden was released so quickly that she found herself plastered to the doorframe.

"Are you talking about Blue?"

Turning her head to the side to look at him, she caught a stunned expression on his face. "Blue?" she asked, using the opportunity to tighten her grip on the wood.

"Describe what your brother looks like," he snapped.

"Luc has brown hair, is five eight, has a crooked pinky finger on his left hand from falling off his skateboard..."

The more she described what Luc looked like, the more furious Doom became.

"You can let go of the fucking door."

Arden nearly jumped out of her skin when he leaned behind her to roar out a name.

"*Puck*!"

Rapidly moving away from the door to the chair he had

been sitting in, she grabbed the arms, preparing herself for being forcibly removed. They might succeed, but she wasn't going to make it easy for them. The chair might be on wheels, but it wouldn't easily go through the doorway. She would hook her legs around the—

Her jaw dropped open when a man came rushing to the door, gaping at the naked man who didn't appear happy at having his sleep disrupted.

Did all bikers sleep in the nude? Arden glanced at her watch. At eight in the evening? No wonder Luc wanted to join. Hell, she wouldn't mind sleeping her evenings away instead of standing on her feet for seven hours until, if she was lucky, she would finally climb into her bed at one in the morning.

Lifting her gaze back to the naked biker, she found herself eye level to his penis. *Jesus, Mary, Joseph...* She started praying for celestial intervention.

"Where's Jesus?"

If she weren't already sitting, Doom's demand would have floored her. So help her God, she swore to herself, if a biker named Jesus showed up naked, she would kill her baby brother slowly—bit by bit, until the only thing left of him was a tiny blue dot.

CHAPTER 3

THE WIZARD

"Jesus left to take Blue home," the naked biker answered, gazing down at her with interest.

Doom pulled out a cell phone from his back pocket. "How fucking old is Blue?" He pinned the other man with narrowed eyes.

Arden relaxed her firm hold on the arms of the chair when she saw the conflicting emotions at the question.

"Uh... Who wants to know? Who's she?"

"Puck," Doom snarled with a curl of his sensuous lips. "How fucking old is Blue?"

"Eighte—"

"You better not lie to me." Doom nodded toward her. "She says Blue is her brother and he is sixteen. Is that true?"

Puck's face twisted into a grimace. "I can explain—"

"Where are you?" Doom cut him off, replying to something said to him on the cell phone.

Arden didn't feel the least bit sympathetic for whoever was on the other side of the call. At least the attention was off her for the moment.

"Come to the office."

Placing the cell phone back in his pocket, Doom stared at Puck as if he was considering tearing him to pieces, like she had sworn to do to Luc.

She cleared her throat, drawing the two men's attention.

"While we're waiting for whoever you're waiting for—" she made sure to keep her eyes upward, "can he get dressed?"

Puck started edging out of the room. "I can, but I don't think Wizard and Margarita would be happy. They're waiting for me. Doom, if Jesus is on his way, you won't need me any—"

"Go get dressed," Doom talked over him. "And bring Wizard with you."

Before Puck managed to make it out of the room, Arden yelled after him, "If he's naked, at least ask him to put on a pair of pants!"

She turned her eyes away from the empty doorway to see Doom staring at her as if she had lost her sanity.

"Why are you looking at me like that? Is it a club rule not to wear pajamas, or at least underwear? What if there were a fire and they had to evacuate?"

"It's kind of hard to fuck when you're wearing pajamas. Same for underwear—they get in the way."

Arden tightened her lips into prim line. "Then that's even more reason for them to get dressed before coming out of their rooms."

"Sorry to shock you, but nudity doesn't bother us."

Her blood began to boil at the way he was looking at her. It was the same way the workers at the restaurant did. She knew exactly what they thought of her after overhearing their comments one night when they had thought she had left.

"No joke," she said, wrinkling her nose. "No wonder

Luc wants to drop out of high school to join your gang. Why go to college to be a doctor when he can live in a frat house filled with grown men who wouldn't know what responsibility was unless it was court ordered?"

"You're talking a lot of shit when you know jack shit about us."

"I know all I need to know. I've been grabbed numerous times since I came here, just wanting to talk to someone in charge. If I were a man, would I have received the same reaction? Or would you have asked him to have a beer and have talked to him?" Her voice gradually increased in volume as she talked. "Today, I also witnessed a change in my brother's behavior, which I'm sure your gang is responsible for, considering how I've been treated tonight—cursing in front of our mother, who is in very frail health, and leaving her in tears to come here just to guard a stupid door. So, excuse me if I don't bow down to any of your overinflated macho egos and it bothers me to be subjected to seeing a man's penis whom I'm not on a first name basis with."

"The man or penis?"

"Huh?" Arden stared at Doom in confusion.

"Do you want Puck's and Buck's real names, or the names they call their cocks? I can tell you Puck's and Buck's real names, but I've never asked if they've given their cocks a name."

She was so enraged, Doom's taunts were like carelessly throwing more gasoline on the flames of her anger.

"By the way," she mimicked his taunting tone, focusing on his foreboding demeanor, "Puck and Buck? Really? Doom? Really? No wonder Wizard is the one in charge. He's probably the only one who can spell his nickname. Margarita must be a nuclear scientist."

"Finished?" a cold voice said from the doorway.

Arden swallowed the large lump of fear that had formed in her throat as Wizard strolled into the room, allowing Puck and another man to pass him before using the heel of his boot to slam the door behind them.

"Why is she still here?" Wizard came to stand over her.

"She's Blue's sister," Doom answered, resting a hip on the side of the desk.

"And why should I give a fuck who she is?"

"Seems our new prospect isn't eighteen."

Both Wizard and Doom stared at the man whom she had seen leaving with Luc. Up close, he seemed slightly younger than the other three men in the room.

"Explain, Jesus," Wizard barked out loud enough to have her jumping in her seat.

"I was going to tell you—" running a hand through his tumbled hair, Jesus gave them an apologetic shrug, "but I knew you would make him stay away."

"You knew he wasn't eighteen and let him hang out, anyway?" The casual way Doom asked the question belied the severe way he was looking at Jesus.

"Before you rip me a new a-hole, will you let me explain first?"

A small gasp escaped her when Wizard's foot came out and swiped Jesus's legs out from under him, leaving him prone on the floor.

Arden jumped out of the chair. "That was completely uncalled for."

Ignoring her, Wizard brushed past her to loom over Jesus. "I don't need an explanation. All the kid probably had to do was give you a sob story, and you said, 'Hey, don't feel bad. Come hang out with us.' It's the same ole shit you're always dragging back to the club for me to wipe up."

"My brother isn't—"

The word she was about to say lodged in her throat when Wizard angrily moved toward her. Arden hastily sat before he could knock her feet out from under her.

"Move," he snapped. "That's my chair."

"Of course... Excuse me." Neatly smoothing her jacket down, she read the violent atmosphere in the room. "Since we're in agreement that my brother shouldn't have anything else to do with the club, I'll leave."

"Doom," Wizard said coldly.

Doom moved to stand in front of the door.

"Puck, get her a chair from the other room."

Wizard hooked one leg over the other as Puck followed the order.

Standing still as Puck went to a side door, Arden watched as he went into another room, coming back with a chair that he placed directly in front of Wizard.

"Sit."

Arden sat. "Listen..."

"Shut up."

She closed her mouth, relieved when Wizard focused back on Jesus.

"I know I'm going to regret this—" giving an exasperated sigh, Wizard motioned for Jesus to get off the floor, "but give me one good reason, and it better be a good one, why you broke a club rule that automatically gets you thrown out?"

"Puck and I were hanging out at Pepper's place right after we came back from Treepoint. Her new place is right across the street from that stuck-up prep school. Puck and I saw five kids start tossing Blue around like he was a fucking frisbee. Blue took off running, and the five fuckers took off after him."

"Let me guess—you interfered?"

Jesus's face twisted into a grimace of anger.

"Would have sat back and watched if the kid had to take on two punks..." Jesus shook his head. "But five? Hell nah. Puck and I chased after them. Fuckers shit their pants, took off running as if their asses were on fire. The kid told us the fuckers had been beating him up since he started going to school there because he didn't belong."

"Why didn't he belong?" Wizard asked.

Jesus shrugged. "He wouldn't tell us."

"My father was a custodian at Starline. The pay isn't much, but it does give full tuition to children of their employees if they make the grades. His grades are so high that he's already been offered a full-ride scholarship when he graduates," Arden answered, her heart breaking at what Luc had been going through.

"He's that smart?" Wizard questioned.

"Yes."

"You go there?"

"No, it's an all-male college preparatory high school."

Wizard's focus on her made her feel as if she was under a microscope.

"Were you aware Blue was getting the crap beat out of him?"

"No. If I had, I would have spoken to the headmaster." She bit her lip to keep it from trembling.

Wizard caught the movement, using the wheels in the chair to turn back to Jesus. "Go on."

"Anyway," Jesus continued, "I gave him a ride home on my bike. He had me drop him off a street away so his parents wouldn't know he was being picked on. He asked me everything about my bike and The Last Riders. To make a long story short, either Puck, Buck, or I sit outside his school every day to give him a ride home.

"Couple of weeks ago, I noticed he was already outside before school was out, so I asked if he was ditching school, and he told me he had. Said he wanted to quit, that he would run away if he had to keep going there. When the kid showed me his back where they had punched him, I told him I would teach him to ride a motorcycle and how to fight if he stayed in school. When he still wouldn't go back to school, I caught him walking on the road near here. I took his ass back home. The next day, Puck caught him walking about a mile away.

"Wizard, he thought you would let him in the club if he asked. Said if you told him no, he would run away. I told him about the rule, and he still argued that he would ask first before taking off. What was I supposed to do? I knew you would say no. I didn't want the kid to run away. Fuckers out on the street would have a field day with him, and you know it." Jesus ran his hands through his hair again. "So, I told him he had to stay home, but he could guard the door a few hours a night. I didn't know what else to do to keep his ass at home."

"Basically, you let a sixteen-year-old railroad you into getting what he wanted," Wizard finished for him. "What you should have done was come to me."

"I should have," he agreed.

Ashamed at herself for misjudging The Last Riders, she was about to apologize for the things she had said when Wizard turned his chair back toward her.

"You can leave. I'll make sure none of the brothers give your brother the time of day from now on," he stated frostily, waving his hand for Doom to step away from the door.

Slowly getting to her feet, Arden didn't immediately

head for the door. Instead, she faced Wizard's unforgiving expression. "Please don't penalize any of them for helping Luc. None of us were aware of what he has been going through. I only found out today that they were making fun of him for not having a car. I have an appointment to speak to the headmaster to get him back in school. I'm sure once he's aware of what bullying Luc has been dealing with, it'll stop."

Wizard didn't respond, just stared pointedly at the door.

Turning, she left feeling two inches tall, without offering the apology she wanted to give. His attitude plainly showed he didn't want to hear anything else she had to say, and she couldn't blame him.

Starting her car, she blinked back furious tears as she drove away. Luc had planned to run away, and they had stopped him. Their dad would be home tonight, so she wouldn't be able to talk to Luc without him overhearing. She would call into work in the morning and tell them she would be a couple of hours late. She would take Luc to school herself. Once he knew the headmaster would help, he would return to the fun, loving brother she was used to.

Worry about Luc had her wanting to go home and curl up in bed, pretending this day never happened, instead of driving to work the last few hours of the shift she was late for. This day sucked. At least tomorrow would be better.

CHAPTER 4
THE OFFER

"Nothing is going to change."

"Yes, it will. You'll see," she promised a gloomy Luc, who was walking alongside of her with dragging footsteps.

Coming to a stop at the headmaster's office, she reached out to touch him, but he shrugged away from her touch. She let her hand fall back to her side.

"We'll talk after school. I'll be outside waiting."

"Yay."

Arden watched until Luc was out of sight before entering the office.

She was still in the main office an hour later when the secretary finally told her the headmaster was ready for their appointment.

Twenty minutes later, Arden returned to her car dispiritedly.

Inside, she tiredly laid her head on the steering wheel. She had only managed a couple of hours sleep before having to get dressed. Making no attempt to start the car, she sucked in deep breaths to keep from bursting into tears.

What was she going to tell Luc after school? Was she supposed to admit he was right? The headmaster had been informed by the staff that Luc was being mistreated, chalking it up to boys being boys and they would grow out of their misbehavior. If she did, there would be no way Luc would continue going to Skyline.

The only concession the headmaster was willing to make was to let Luc return to keep his scholarship, if he made up the work he had missed. When she had argued about taking legal action, he had turned the table on her, asking when her father would return to work. She had fled his office after lying by saying he was waiting for his doctor's approval.

Raising her head, Arden stared blankly ahead. What should she do? She couldn't take off work to pick Luc up from school every day. Even if she could, it wouldn't stop the bullying during school hours. She couldn't transfer him to another school without one of their parents finding out how bad it was at Skyline. Both parents were in extremely frail health, and neither would keep a secret of this magnitude from the other.

No, this problem was all on her, and she had no clue to what to do.

Giving a startled scream at a rap on the window next to her head, she turned to see Doom sitting on a motorcycle. She had been so lost in thought that she hadn't been aware he was there.

Starting the car, she rolled the window down.

Doom leaned his head closer to the window so she could hear him over the purr of his motor. "Wizard wants a talk."

"Where is he?" she asked, glancing around.

"At the club."

"I have to go to work," she protested.

"It won't take long. Go first." He gave a curt nod of his head toward the road. "I'll follow." Then he straightened back on his motorcycle without giving her a chance to reply.

Arden debated whether to take the left to work or the right to The Last Riders' club. She still owed them an apology. Coming to the decision, she took a right.

She found it hard to keep her eyes on the road and not on the rearview mirror. Doom on a motorcycle was a spectacular sight. He handled the bike with ease. She could understand Luc becoming so enthralled with the bikers at sixteen. At twenty-seven, she was having a hell of time with it herself.

They gave off an air of danger, confidence, and of being untamable; all of which would appeal to the teenager who was too young to have acquired those qualities yet. There wasn't a woman alive who wasn't attracted to a bad boy. It was hotwired into their DNA. They would fall for them every time.

You couldn't live in Ohio without having heard of The Last Riders. She had seen them riding around the bustling city occasionally and had passed the club a few times on the way to Kentucky. If she wasn't mistaken, one of the nurses on staff had even dated a Last Rider for a brief time.

Haven was a couple of years younger, outgoing, and had quickly made friends among the staff when she had been hired. Many of the staff, male and female, would often go with her after work, even have gatherings on the weekend. When Mondays would roll around, Arden was treated to listening to what a great time they all had and plans for their next get-together. Then, one Monday, the gossip mill was filled. Haven had met someone at a bar they had gone out to. It wasn't long before the details had filtered down to her low-level job that the man she had met was a Last Rider. Those who had been with Haven all talked about how good-looking he was and how envious they were of her. The gossip began to shrink week by week about her new love interest when Haven stopped going out with their coworkers and spent more and more of her free time with The Last Riders. Then her friends in the office started complaining they never got to see her anymore, even begging her to bring him along when they invited her out. Invariably, she would make one excuse after another. Soon, they had quit asking. Haven hadn't appeared to mind. She seemed to be walking on cloud nine.

A couple of months later, Arden had noticed a change in Haven when she would escort patients down to schedule their surgery. She was no longer walking on clouds. Her feet seemed to have landed with a thud.

Arden's heart started beating faster when she arrived at the club. Nervous, she got out of her car and waited for Doom to park and get off his bike. She fell in step behind him as they strode toward the bar. The Last Rider then opened the door for them without a word.

Regretting coming here instead of going to work with every step she took, Arden promised herself she would listen to what Wizard had to say, give the apology she should have given yesterday, then get out as quickly as possible without making a fool of herself.

Entering the bar during the morning was much different than last night. It was nearly empty, with only three bikers sitting at a round table. They glanced toward them then resumed talking among themselves.

Assuming they were going to the office, Arden bumped into Doom when he turned in the direction where the bikers were sitting.

"Excuse me," she apologized for bumping into him. "I thought we were going the other way."

She quickly moved away from him, and her regret at not going to work shifted to overdrive the closer they came to the table where the three bikers were sitting. The men had stopped talking at their approach.

"Have a seat. I'll get Wizard."

Arden sat down gratefully, afraid they would hear her knees knocking. She self-consciously gave them a tentative smile as Doom deserted her at the table.

"Good morning," she greeted them tentatively.

None of them returned the greeting.

Coming to the decision that there was no reason to let The Last Riders continue their steamrolling behavior, she said, "My name is Arden."

The one sitting across from her broke his menacing silence, but didn't return the favor of giving his name. "We know who you are."

Forcing herself not to look away, she kept the friendly smile pasted on her lips. "And you are...?"

"Why? So you can figure out how smart I am by how many letters I have in my name?"

Suppressing the desire to turn tail and run, she gave all the men an apologetic glance. "Yesterday, I was having a really bad day, and I said things I shouldn't have said. I'm sorry. That's why I actually came here when Doom asked me to—to apologize to him and Wizard for being so rude. I truly appreciate Puck and Jesus for watching out for Luc..." Her apology trailed off when she saw the men's eyes move over her shoulder to stare behind her. Turning her head, she saw Wizard, Doom, Jesus, Puck, and Buck come filing out of the side hallway.

She turned back around and anxiously waited for them to reach the table.

This isn't good, she told herself. *This is going to be very, very bad,* her self-preservation instincts warned.

The four men took the remaining chairs, and Arden looked at Wizard expectedly for him to begin.

"How did talking to Skyline's headmaster go?"

Arden politely refused to give the information as best she could. "That's a private discussion for Luc and our parents to have this afternoon."

"In other words, he's not going to do jack shit."

She dropped her eyes from Wizard's harsh expression.

What could she say? The headmaster had callously refused to intervene without proof that Luc was being bullied.

"Are you going to transfer him to another school?"

"My parents..." Arden hesitated. She didn't want to go into the details of her parents' health in front of so many strangers. "That's a hard question to answer."

Wizard gave a sharp glance. "How hard could it be? Let me make it easier, then. Yes or no?"

Arden nibbled on her bottom lip nervously. "Probably not."

"Probably not? Does that mean you're just going to let the kid run away?"

"Of course not!" She had to blink back furious tears, determined not to break down in front of the hardened biker. "Luc and I will talk tonight, and we'll come up with a solution that will make him happier."

"The only thing that is going to make Blue happy is telling that headmaster to kiss his ass when you unenroll him from that fucking ass-kisser school."

"I can't be the one to unenroll him; one of my parents

has to."

"Then have them fucking do—"

"We will discuss it this afternoon when Luc gets out of school."

"Blue isn't in school," Doom revealed frostily.

"Yes, he is," she argued. "I walked him inside myself."

"Then he must have taken off through a back door, because I caught him about two blocks from the school," Doom disclosed with a hard edge to his voice.

Arden took their cutting attitude toward her because she saw underneath their biker veneer that they were concerned for her brother.

She pressed her lips together to keep them from trembling, hurt that Luc hadn't believed in her enough to wait and talk to her before heading to The Last Riders.

"You brought him here."

Wizard nodded. "He's in the office."

"Did you tell him not to come here anymore, like you said you would?"

"I told him to do his fucking homework while I took care of some work."

"Is there a back door he could slip out? What if he tries to leave?"

Wizard gave her an intimidating stare, which had her twisting her hands in her lap.

"Never mind," she rushed on, embarrassed. "So, you asked Doom to ask me to come here to drive him home after you talk to him?"

"Yes." Wizard rose, gazing across the table at her disparagingly. "Or I can offer you another option."

Arden frowned, her instincts screaming that she wasn't going to like whatever the offer was.

"Let Blue become a Last Rider."

CHAPTER 5
THE COUNTER

Arden gaped at him. "No."

Wizard cocked his head to the side, his arms crossed over his chest in an intimidating stance. "What shit Blue has been experiencing isn't going away unless it's dealt with full stop. The one being bullied needs to be removed from the situation, or the bullies need to learn what it feels like when the shoe is on the other foot, preferably when the shoe is shoved up their fucking ass."

She thrust her chin out angrily. "Violence won't solve—"

"What do you think Blue has been dealing with? Those fuckers aren't playing patty cake with him. They're beating the fuck out of him. Kid can't even take a piss unless they're drowning him in their crap. Those pampered asses don't take him on man to man; they gang up on him four or five at a time. The only way it stops is if Blue learns to fight. Are you able to teach him that?"

"No, but I can hire someone who can."

"Anyone you hire will teach him basic self-defense. With Blue, it's gone past that point. They've made him into their bitch. Anytime they get pissed off, regardless of who or why, they take it out on him. What he needs is what we can give them without us having to lay a hand on their punk asses. All they would need is to see Blue has a show of force standing behind him, coupled with a few techniques we could teach him, and they'll leave him the fuck alone without any of us having to raise a hand to them."

There was no way she wanted Luc to join The Last Riders, yet she didn't want him being continuously beaten by his classmates.

"What do you mean by *a show of force*?"

"The whole club could be there after school instead of just Puck or Jesus. He could point out who fucked with him that day, and a few of us would trail them home. It'll scare them shitless."

"You wouldn't touch them?" she asked, trying to decipher if Wizard was being truthful.

"We wouldn't have to."

Arden licked her dry lips. "The Last Riders could do that without Blue having to join your club. You could also teach him how to fight—"

The group of men started laughing.

Arden stared at them, not understanding why they were laughing at her.

Wizard clued her in with a mocking smile.

"And how would that benefit The Last Riders?"

Arden flushed, darting her eyes away from Wizard to see why Doom wasn't laughing out loud at her. She could see he was just as amused as the others.

She tried another tactic. "On television and in news articles, I've read stories about motorcycle clubs helping out bullied kids."

Arden gave Jesus and Puck pleading glances. Both men

maintained their focus on Wizard. She brought her eyes back Wizard's unsympathetic expression.

"Yeah, well, that wasn't The Last Riders," he said with a sarcastic curl of his lips. "Maybe you should look into one of those clubs and ask them for help."

Wizard dropped his arms back to his side. "I've got more important shit to deal with. This is a waste of club time." He moved around the bar counter. Expecting him to pour a drink, she was surprised to see him take a coffee cup and fill it with coffee from a pot sitting to the side.

"Doom, get Blue."

The chair Doom was sitting on scraped across the floor as he rose.

"Wait. What are you going to say to him?"

"I'm going to throw his ass out of the bar and tell him not to come back. He has no value to me as a Last Rider, and if I catch him on club property again, I'll call the cops and have him arrested for trespassing."

Arden jumped up from the chair to approach the bar counter, standing across from Wizard. "If you do that, Luc will run away as soon as my back is turned."

"Why should I care? I made the offer to make him a Last Rider," he said nonchalantly before taking a drink of his coffee.

"Please. I could pay you..." She wasn't above begging, not where Luc's safety was concerned. He had threatened to run away, and she believed it wasn't an idle threat.

"We're too lazy—remember?" Doom said as he moved behind her, heading toward the hallway.

Arden grabbed his arm. "I'm sorry. I apologize. Is that what you want to hear me say?"

Doom shrugged his arm out of her grip then leaned

against the bar next to her. "We don't need your apology. Do we, Wizard?"

"Speak for yourself." Wizard shot her a glare from over his coffee cup. "I wouldn't mind hearing it."

Arden gave Wizard what he wanted. "I apologize. Luc wanting to drop out of school and join The Last Riders threw me for a loop. I reacted by saying things I deeply regret. Please don't take your anger toward me out on Luc."

Wizard set his cup down. "How is me wanting to keep Blue off club property me taking my anger out on you? You're the one who doesn't want him to be a Last Rider. We don't need your money. Believe it or not, we have a business that generates enough money that we don't need yours. The Last Riders only offer protection to club members and their families. Each and every member somehow brings something to the table to benefit the club as a whole. Blue, once he becomes a doctor, would eventually benefit the club. You refused. We don't need to be told twice. Doom, get—"

"You said family members?" Anxious, Arden didn't let him finish.

"Yeah, so?" Wizard reached for the coffee pot for a refill.

Arden swallowed hard. Was she seriously going to say what she was thinking? Glancing toward Doom and the other men at the table, she didn't find one ounce of sympathy.

"Yesterday, I saw several women in here." Arden felt as if her throat was coated in clay. "Were any of them members?"

Wizard nodded. "A couple."

"Would you protect Luc if *I* were to become a member?"

CHAPTER 6
THE PLAYER

Arden kept her gaze on Wizard, seeing Doom turn more fully toward her from out of the corner of her eye. Despite feeling a heated flush rush to her already red cheeks, she managed to maintain her composure.

Wizard cocked his head to the side. "Are you seriously asking?"

"Would you help me with Luc?" Nervous about what she was about to ask, she grabbed the edge of the bar to keep herself from falling. "With the fighting stuff, making him stay in school, and the bullying?"

"Depends."

"On what?"

"What you bring to the table."

"I'm free weekend days until six p.m. I can work at the bar for you, clean tables. I can watch the door like Luc was doing."

Wizard stared at her as if she had lost her mind. "Are you serious?"

Arden nodded eagerly. "I work as a hostess at Spaghetti Mama. I've never missed a shift. Call and ask them."

"We'll take your word for it."

Arden turned her head to give Doom a dirty look at his strangled response. "I'm a very good worker, I'll have you know."

"When do you work there?" Wizard questioned.

"Every evening from five to twelve, during the week and the weekends."

"I thought you worked at a doctor's office?"

"I do, from eight in the morning until four-thirty." Arden didn't offer for them to contact the office for a reference. The surgeons frowned on their employees moonlighting.

She could see Wizard's and Doom's amusement fading.

"Listen, joking aside—" Wizard dumped the remains of the coffee into the sink before reaching for a bottle of bourbon to pour himself a shot, "the women members do more than serve drinks and clean the bar. They—"

"I know. I read you run a survival business. I'm very good on a computer."

Doom dashed that hope, propping his cheek on his hand on the bar. "We got that covered."

Arden chewed on her lip. What else was she good at that could benefit The Last Riders? Her mind furiously turned over ideas to convince them to let her join.

"I can cook and bartend." She couldn't, but they didn't need to know that. "I can take inventory, run errands. I can paint," she said, glancing around at the peeling paint on one wall. "Clean the bathrooms and bedrooms."

"Chill." Wizard screwed the top back on his bourbon. "We don't need a maid."

"Speak for yourself. All that stuff sounds pretty good to me," Jesus spoke up from the table.

"Jesus!" Doom barked out, taking a seat at the bar.

"This is ridiculous. We change our own beds, don't need our meals cooked, or the bathrooms cleaned. To put it bluntly—"

"Please do." Arden gave him a thankful smile, laying her hand on the arm he had resting on the counter. "I'm late for work, so any suggestions about work I could do around the club would be helpful."

Doom jerked his eyes away from hers and slid his arm from underneath her hand. Shaking his head as if to clear it, he looked toward Wizard, as if giving him the chance to talk.

Wizard gave Doom a smirk she couldn't understand the meaning of.

Doom tightened his lips in a hard line. "I will." He gave Wizard a scowl before turning back to her. "We have plenty of women to do the chores around the club. The men do them, too, or we take turns. The system works fine for us—"

"Says you," Puck interjected. "None of us says that, which is why we all jump at the chance to go to Treepoint when Viper needs us."

"Viper coddles you fuckers." Wizard glared at Puck until he lowered his head.

Arden gave Puck a sympathetic smile. "There's nothing wrong with getting chores done for you so you can concentrate on things more important."

Puck perked up, as if he was a mistreated puppy being stroked for the first time.

"Cut it out, Puck," Doom warned so softly that Arden wasn't sure she had heard him correctly.

"Cut what out?" Arden asked.

"Nothing." Doom glared daggers at Puck. "Going back to what I was going to say—"

"I wish you would," she urged. "I still need to take Luc home and get to work."

Arden saw a muscle start to bulge under the corner of Doom's eye.

"We don't need a housekeeper. What the women members do is take shifts at the warehouse."

"I could take weekend shifts—"

"Let me finish," he ground out.

"Okay." She gave him another smile.

The muscle under his eye began to pulsate again. Should she tell him that he should have that tic checked out by a doctor?

"Work at least two shifts here at the club a week—"

So far, she didn't have a problem with anything Doom was saying.

"And fu..." Doom cleared his throat. "Provide companionship to any of the brothers who want it."

Arden's eyes widened at the revelation. Staring around at the men's expectant faces, she felt a surge of sympathy for them. She gave each of them a bolstering grin.

"I can do that." Her gaze became pitying. "I can understand being homesick and lonely in a big city. I get lonely, too, sometimes. Anytime anyone needs someone to talk to, I would be more than happy to be there for them. As long as I'm not working," she hastily clarified. "I love talking. I'm really good at it once I open up. I can talk forever. My friend says I could talk his head off when I'm in the mood."

Glancing toward the table, hoping to earn Puck, Jesus, and Buck's trust, she noticed the pained expressions on their faces.

Terrified that she had just talked herself out of a job, she sought to correct their misunderstanding.

Raising her hand in the air, she tried to win their

support back. "I promise anything we talk about will stay just between us. I work in a medical office—I totally get you wanting our conversations to remain private."

Turning toward Wizard, she gave him a hopeful glance. "Do we have a deal?" Worried sick about her parents and Luc, she gave Wizard an imploring glance, unaware her bottom lip was trembling. "Please. Once a week, I'll even bring over a pan of Mama's baked spaghetti."

Wizard lifted an eyebrow at Doom. "It's up to Doom. He's my Sergeant at Arms. He'll be the one training you."

Arden turned to give Doom the same look that had worked on Wizard.

"Fine. You can become a prospect."

Arden jumped off her seat. "Does that mean I'm in The Last Riders?"

"It means we're considering it."

"But, until then, you'll help me with Luc?"

Doom gave her a curt nod.

"Thank God." Arden glanced at her watch. "Can we go over my shifts some other time? I really need to get to work."

"Please do," Wizard said with his hand on his chin, watching the interaction between her and Doom. "I can save you some time and give Blue a ride home."

"Thank you. I'd appreciate it." Her smile turned into a frown. "There's just one thing... Do you have any helmet he could wear? Last night, I saw him riding with Jesus, and he wasn't wearing one."

Wizard narrowed his eyes at her. "I'm sure there's an extra one around here somewhere. I'll even help Blue put it on before I buckle him on my bike. Safety first, as I always say."

From his expressionless face, she couldn't tell if he was mocking her or not. Giving him the benefit of the doubt, she slid the bottle of bourbon farther away on the counter so he wouldn't take another drink.

"I'll leave you men to it, then." She smiled as she glanced around the room, her gaze ricocheting off Doom's and Wizard's deadpan faces to center on Jesus's more welcoming one. Deciding to leave before they reconsider letting her join, she left, feeling their stares on her every step of the way.

She received a strange look from the biker outside guarding the door at the sigh of relief that she couldn't hold back any longer. Then she hurried to her car.

Today wasn't so bad after all. With The Last Riders' help, Luc would get back on track with his studies and their parents wouldn't have their health jeopardized by their son becoming a runaway.

As soon as the wheels of her car turned away from the club, Arden couldn't prevent herself from rolling her eyes at the act she had put on at the end.

"Really?" She gave a disgusted snort at the men. Did they really believe she was so naïve that she hadn't known exactly what "companionship" Doom was inferring? She hadn't been born last century. Who knew reading historical romances would come so useful? All she needed was for them to believe her long enough for Luc to learn how to defend himself and for the bullies to be stopped.

She could play a naïve innocent until then. All she had to do was dodge and prevaricate when anything turned sexual. It wouldn't be hard. Where men were concerned, she had always been out of sight, out of mind. The key to her success would be to remain out of their sights and limit their interactions. How hard could it be?

CHAPTER 7
THE DOCTOR

Doom watched the door close after the exasperating woman calmly left as if it was settled for her to become a Last Rider.

"Since when is Doom Sergeant at Arms?" Puck asked belligerently from the table.

Wizard stared him down. "Since you fucking knew Jesus was lying about Blue's age. You're no longer over new members—you've lost my trust."

"No church meeting? Nothing?"

Wizard raised an intimidating brow at Puck, which he shared with a mute Jesus. "Would you rather I call a formal church meeting and involve Viper? What punishment do you think he would give? Viper leaves the decision on who I want to fill the ranks, but concerning hardcore infractions, we all follow the same fucking rules." Wizard's cold voice gradually rose in volume. "You fuckers broke one of the main hard and fast rules of the club, which automatically has you losing membership. Not only did you knowingly and willing abet a minor in coming to the club, you fucking lied to me and everyone in here that Blue was eighteen. You should be fucking thanking me that you are just losing your title rather than handing your bike keys over."

Puck lowered his gaze to the table.

Jesus and Buck waited mutely for Wizard's punishment as he strode from behind the counter to place his hands down on the table in front of them.

"Jesus." Wizard raised one of his hands. "Bike keys."

Jesus paled as he numbly reached inside his pocket. Handing Wizard his bike keys, he then stood up and started taking off his jacket.

"Sit your ass back down. You're still in the club, but you're going back to probate. I'll return the keys when my trust is earned back. Let me down again, and your ass is fucking gone!" Wizard snarled at him.

Jesus sat back down, nodding his head.

Doom went behind the bar to pour himself a bourbon. So far, the brothers had gotten off better than he'd expected. Wizard, unlike Moon, who used to be the president of The Last Riders' Ohio Chapter, ran a tight ship. Wizard was a hard-ass where the club rules were concerned.

"Buck, I expected more from you. You usually keep these knuckleheads in check."

Buck shrugged. "I never could stand a kid getting picked on. I didn't want to see him on the streets." A kid living on the street had always been Buck's weak point.

Wizard just shook his head at them. "You three have more heart than is good for you. How many times have I told you that we do what we can, but never do anything that could jeopardize the club?"

Wizard gave a heavy sigh. "You can keep your bike, only because Jesus has to have someone cart his ass around. As punishment, you and Puck can be the ones to teach Blue how to keep from getting his ass handed to him. Each day of school that Blue misses is a Friday night party you fuckers will miss by standing guard duty. So, it would benefit you two to make sure his ass is where it's supposed to be."

Doom took a drink to hide his smile. The three brothers were thick as thieves. It wasn't the first time the three men had gotten into trouble, and despite Wizard's punishments, Doom was certain it wouldn't be the last.

Moon had been the one to give Jesus and Puck their rank in the club when he was president here. Wizard hadn't changed the ranks Moon assigned, hoping Moon would return once the trouble he was embroiled in Ohio was solved. Unfortunately, Moon had made a powerful enemy, whose anger seemed to be getting worse the longer Moon stayed out of his grasp.

Taking pity on the brothers, Doom sought to distract Wizard. "You do know she was yanking our chain, right?"

"You think?" Wizard turned to him and rolled his eyes.

"I don't think so—"

Jesus snapped his mouth shut when he drew Wizard's attention.

"Don't think," Wizard said scornfully. "Just don't. Take it from me, she was bluffing."

Doom refilled his glass. "What we going to do about it?"

"What I'm going to do is go talk to the little fucker in my office before I decide."

After gulping his drink down in one swallow, Doom followed Wizard to the office.

Blue turned frightened eyes to Wizard when the men entered the room.

Doom almost felt sorry for the teenager. Wizard could scare the shit of men much older and more experienced than him.

"Stand up when I fucking enter the room," Wizard

snarled, moving to stand in front of him. "You finish the assignments you missed?"

"Yes, sir."

"Good. Now grab your shit. I'm taking you home. Tomorrow, your ass is going to be in school, and you're going to stay there until the end."

Doom had to give the kid credit when Blue shook his head. "I'm not going—"

The next second, the kid was staring up at the ceiling with Wizard's boot on his chest.

"What did you fucking say?"

Blue grabbed Wizard's foot as he tried to struggle out from under it. "I'm not going back. I hate it there!"

"You're going back. You want those punks to know they won? You never give a fucking win without making fuckers like that pay with their own blood."

"I can't take them all on!" Blue stopped struggling under Wizard's pitiless regard.

Removing his boot, Wizard grabbed Blue by the front of his shirt and lifted him to his feet. Then, moving around him, he took the chair to stare intently at the teenager. "Did Jesus explain how to become a Last Rider?"

Blue looked toward where Jesus was uncomfortably standing.

"We hadn't gotten that far yet," Jesus answered for him.

Wizard gave Blue an unamused smile. "Then let me enlighten you." He took out his cell phone. After a couple of swipes of his finger, he turned the phone toward Blue. "You have to take on six of the original members, one at a time. Take your pick."

Staring at the picture that Wizard was showing him, Blue turned pale.

"That's what I thought." Wizard lay the phone down on

the desk. "How did you think you became a Last Rider if you can't even take on five punk-ass bitches?"

Blue gave Jesus a pleading glance.

"Don't look at Jesus to save you. The only one who can save your ass in this room is me. You know why?"

"No."

Doom saw the kid was practically shaking in fear.

"Because I'm the president of The Last Riders, and when I say something, I can back it up without asking for any help from them. I've earned that honor by being willing to spill my fucking blood and endure any pain for The Last Riders. I benefit the club with my military experience." Wizard then narrowed his eyes on the boy. "Now, listen to me closely... You still want to become a Last Rider?"

"I do."

"You sure about that?"

"Yes."

"How are you going to earn the right to wear a Last Rider jacket?"

"By going back to school."

Wizard gave him a curt nod. "All the brothers can fight. How are you planning on benefiting the club? There are no free rides here."

The kid looked confused, as if he didn't know what to say. Wizard helped him out.

"Doom is Sergeant at Arms. It's his job to make sure the club has everything we need. Doom, what does the club need?"

"Ever since Train and Evie moved to Kentucky, our chapter has been short someone with medical experience. Evie was a combat nurse, and Train was a military medic. Having a doctor in our ranks would one-up us from the other chapter."

"You want me to become a doctor?"

Doom didn't give Blue false hope. "You'd still have to fight for a spot after you graduate from medical school."

Blue didn't seem happy with the stipulation. "I'd have to wait until then?"

"You need Wizard to show you the picture again? You wouldn't make it past one of the original members, much less take on six. I did two tours in the military, had been in more bar fights overseas than I can remember, and worked five years as a captain of a commercial fishing boat. The men who work on those boats work hard and play harder. I wouldn't have lasted two fucking seconds if I couldn't beat the shit out of any man on my boat." Doom gave Blue a twisted smile. "I still wasn't prepared to take them on. I did win the right to become a member, but I had three cracked ribs, a broken nose, jaw, and a fractured arm when it was over. You have to withstand a beating that would maim or kill another man. They want to know, when you go to battle, you can depend on the man standing next to you to protect you if you go down. How can you protect anyone else if you can't protect yourself first? Defeat isn't in The Last Riders' vocabulary. When we go to battle, the last one standing *will* be a Last Rider."

From the kid's expression, Doom saw he was getting a grasp on what it would take to be a member of the club.

"You want to change your answer about joining?" Wizard asked.

"No."

Blue's mutinous expression mirrored his sister's, Doom thought.

"Then guess what you need to do," Wizard stated.

"Go back to school."

"Cool. We're in agreement." Wizard leaned back in the

chair. "Then grab your shit. Buck and Jesus will drive you home. Your ass will be at school in the morning, and when the brothers and I pick you up after school, be the first one out. I want you to show me who's been using your ass as a bobbing apple in the toilets. We're not going to fight any battles for you, but since you're considering becoming a doctor to protect the brothers' health, the least we can do is level the playing field until Buck and Jesus can teach you how to take them on and give them a taste of their own piss."

Wizard looked toward the men standing to the side. "Buck, Jesus, take him home." Wizard waved them away.

"Blue." His expression went back to grim. "I better not catch your ass within a five-mile radius of this clubhouse again until you can sign Dr. in front of your name. Get what I'm telling you?"

"Yes, sir, I do."

"Good. Then get the fuck out of my club."

Doom handed Blue his backpack, hiding his smile until the brothers and the kid had left.

Wizard used the wheels on the office chair to swivel in his direction. "Damn, I need another drink. I'm not used to being so nice."

Doom couldn't hold back his laughter any longer. "For a second, I thought you were going to burp him."

Wizard made a face. "It would be nice to have a doctor on call to stitch us up and dig the bullets out."

"Yes, it would," Doom agreed.

Wizard's expression grew more serious. "So, what are we going to do about the sister's offer?"

CHAPTER 8

THE MILK

"Let's play her game." Resting his hip on the side of Wizard's desk, Doom gave him a cunning smile. "It could be fun."

Wizard rolled his eyes at him. "Or not. You still pissed at her for questioning The Last Riders' intelligence?"

"You're not?"

Wizard gave him a smug smile. "According to her, I'm the smartest one here."

Deadpan, Doom stared back at him.

"Jeez, Doom. Give it a break. She apologized. I'm good with her."

Doom shrugged. "I'm not pissed."

"You look pissed. But what do I know? You have the same expression on your face all the time. I'll leave it to you. I really don't give a fuck."

He didn't believe that for a millisecond. "Then why didn't you tell her no?"

"I was too busy admiring her acting ability. If she had bigger tits, she would make a hell of an actress."

"Her tits were fine."

"Too small for my taste." Wizard shrugged.

"Which is why I have better taste in women. Your problem is, you always judge a vase by the handles."

"And how is that a problem for me?"

"Not for you," Doom agreed with him. "For the rest of us, it gets boring."

"You didn't seem bored last night when we were fucking Celeste."

"I'm just saying, it might be nice to have a change of pace. One that wouldn't give me a fucking concussion when she comes."

Wizard tiredly rubbed the back of his neck. Standing, he stretched his back. "Do what you want to do. You might be right; it could be fun. I needed to find someone to replace Siren, anyway. You can give whatever-her-name-is Siren's schedule."

"Her name is Arden," Doom informed him.

Wizard glanced at his watch. "Don't care."

"I thought Celeste wanted Siren's schedule?"

"She does, but those are the times when Blue's sister can work. Besides, I prefer Celeste more on her back than working behind the bar." Wizard rubbed his neck again. "I need to put in a couple hours at the warehouse. When Celeste gets her ass out of bed, you can break the bad news to her."

"Fuck no! You do it."

Wizard smacked him on the shoulder. "That's why I made you Sergeant at Arms. Puck sucked at doing the dirty work while you excel at breaking hearts."

From the way he raised his brow at him, Doom could tell Wizard didn't want to argue with him. Arguing with Wizard was a wasted effort, anyway. It was his way or the highway. Both he and Viper had that same infuriating trait.

Seeing he wasn't going to get the argument he was waiting for, Wizard started to leave.

"Who are you going to pick for your enforcer?"

Wizard turned back to face Puck, his good humor vanishing.

"Don't give me that look. You made your bed, now lie in it," Wizard snapped harshly. "Call Burn and tell him to come to the warehouse in thirty minutes. I'm going to give the rank to him."

Both he and Puck gave Wizard the same surprised look.

"He'll tell you no."

"He'll try." Wizard nodded. "In that case, he can hand over his jacket, bike, and pay the money back he owes the club. I'm tired of pampering him. Burn isn't the only one who Taylor fucked over. Rider tried to warn him about that bitch, and so did I. He's had long enough to get his head out of his ass." Wizard shook his head. "I went by his house a couple of days ago, and he was waiting there for Taylor to drop his kid off. She never showed. Taylor only lets Burn see him every other Sunday while she's draining him dry."

Doom shook his head. "He has a custody hearing on Monday, to increase his visitation. He won't jeopardize losing—"

"He's had two hearings already. Nothing is going to change with this one." Wizard gave him a rueful look. "His chance of getting more visitation is between little or none. Meanwhile, he's draining himself dry paying for lawyers that aren't getting results done, and forking cash over every fucking time Taylor says she needs it for his kid while she's using it to buy a penthouse in Louisville."

Doom cocked his head to the side. "How you find that out?"

"I called in a favor. Hawk checked it out for me after I

saw Burn, and he told me he had given Taylor ten grand to hire a fucking nanny. I knew it was bullshit. Hawk found out she used the money to put down the deposit on a penthouse."

"How's Hawk doing? I haven't talked to him in a while."

"You can ask himself tonight when you pick him up from the airport," Wizard told him. "He put his fifteen years in with Homeland and booked a flight here."

"He's staying?"

Wizard grimaced. "For now, unless Viper tries to steal him away. I need to get going. Chaos is waiting for me."

Doom knew Wizard didn't give a fuck if he kept Chaos waiting. "You just don't want to be here when Celeste wakes up."

Wizard didn't deny it. "That too. Later."

Puck sat down in Wizard's chair after he left. "He's going to make Burn his enforcer."

"Do you care?"

"No." Puck grinned. "I just don't want Wizard to know."

"I'm pretty sure he knows," Doom scoffed. "You've done everything you could do to get busted down in the ranks since Moon gave you the position."

Puck shrugged. "What can I say? I'm a simple man."

"You're a randy fucker who prefers getting laid to being on call when Wizard needs work done."

"That too," Puck laughed.

Doom left Puck to grab something to eat. He headed into the small kitchen situated behind the bar, but found slim pickings when he opened the refrigerator.

"Fuck." His growling stomach prevented him from being too picky. He closed the door to the nearly empty fridge and opened a cabinet to take out a microwavable macaroni cup, which he put in the microwave before he made himself a peanut butter sandwich. Chewing on the stale bread, he poured himself a glass of milk and took a drink, which he had to spit out in the sink.

"Fuck this." At least one benefit of becoming the Sergeant at Arms was that he would be put in charge of supplies. While Buck made sure the brothers had enough firepower to weather the apocalypse, where it came to feeding the crew, he sucked.

Doom was rinsing his mouth out with tap water when Kat breezed into the room.

"Wow." Kat wound her arms around his waist. "You came out of your cave while the sun is still out? I always wondered if you would melt in the sunlight. Now I know." Rubbing her cheek against his shoulder, she dipped her hands into the back pockets of his jeans to squeeze his ass.

Still tasting the spoiled milk, Doom didn't let the woman sidetrack him from his anger. "I thought you and Puck were supposed to go to the store last night?"

Kat lifted her cheek from his shoulder to pout up at him. "We got distracted."

"There's nothing to eat," he complained.

Plastering herself against him, she ran her tongue along her bottom lip. "I got something you can eat," she moaned suggestively into his neck.

"Cut it out, Kat. I'm serious."

She wiggled her hips against his. "I am too." Looking up when he remained stiff under her touch, she gave a regretful sigh and stepped away. "Okay, okay, I get the message. I'll go this afternoon."

"You'll go now."

"Fine. See if I suck your dick anytime soon." With a

sassy flip of her hair, she turned toward the doorway leading back into the bar area.

Casually reaching around her waist, he hauled her backward. "Don't forget milk. I'm tired of going to the convenience store when you forget it. They don't have the brand I like." Doom released her before she managed to distract him like she had Puck. "Take my car. The keys are under the mat."

With another pouting look, Kat left.

He moved toward the microwave and pulled out the macaroni. Staring down at the unappetizing glob, he added the cheese.

He was choking the last bite down when Celeste poked her head through the open doorway.

"I was beginning to think I was the only one awake." Yawning, she walked further into the room, wearing an overlong baby-pink T-shirt. "Where's Wiz?"

Doom gave her a disapproving stare. "He told you not to call him that."

"My bad. I'll make sure not to say it in front of him."

"I wouldn't," he warned. "It'll put him in a bad mood for the rest of the day. He was called into the warehouse."

"Oh, did he leave me my new schedule? Did Siren have a shift tonight? If she did, I'm going back to bed—"

"About that. There's been a change of plans."

Celeste narrowed her eyes on him. "Those plans better not involve me not getting Siren's schedule."

Doom knew only one thing that would settle Celeste down when she was about to erupt in a tirade. Grasping the front of her T-shirt over her stomach, he pulled her into his arms.

"We'll make it up to you," he promised in a low voice.

Celeste folded her arms over her generous breasts to

prevent herself from being drawn closer. "The fucking asshole. He promised me I could have her schedule."

"There's a new prospect who only has those hours available."

"He's giving a prospect the best time slot, and I've been begging for it for two years?"

"She won't last three days. When she taps out, the spot is yours."

"What makes you think she'll tap out?" she asked doubtfully.

"Arden doesn't even know all the club rules. Once she does, she'll run so fast a K-9 wouldn't be able to track her."

"You sure?" Celeste raised her arms to circle his neck, snuggling against him.

"Have I ever been wrong?"

"No..." she slowly drawled out. "But that doesn't mean there won't be a first time."

"Maybe so, but she won't be the one to prove me wrong."

Doom lifted her into the air until her legs wrapped around his hips.

Celeste gave him a calculating glance. "What is this? A pity fuck because Wizard screwed me over?"

Doom opened a drawer containing misplaced items that had been left in the bar. Taking a condom, he walked to a small table, where he used his boot to pull out a chair and sat down with her on his lap.

Tugging her nightshirt up to her waist, he stared appreciatively at her bare pussy sitting on top of his straining cock. "Does that look like I feel sorry for you?"

She licked his bottom lip. "No." Then she reached for the snap of his jeans as she slightly lifted herself up to pull his hard-on out of the confines of his jeans. Taking the condom from his hand, she tore it open and slid it on his dick.

"There isn't a man alive who would consider you a pity fuck." Pulling her down on his cock, he latched on to one of the ruby-red nipples pointed at him.

As she slid her wet pussy up and down his cock, he grasped her breast in his hand to keep it from bouncing upward. The drastic difference between her large breasts and tiny waist had long since lost appeal to him.

From her eyes, Doom could tell she received no pleasure from having her breasts touched. Releasing her nipple, he gripped her waist to lift her off his cock. Then, easily turning her around, he sat her back on his cock. Celeste's calves wound his to brace herself as she ground herself on him. Low moans turned to shrieks as he rubbed the pad of a finger over her vulva.

"If she doesn't quit in three days, I get to spend the whole night in your bed. Just you and me."

Doom pounded his climax out into Celeste, not worried. He never let any of the women in his room, much less spend the night with him. Preferring to keep to himself once he went inside.

There were only five bedrooms in the back of the bar, and once the night wound down, most of the women would search for any empty spot rather than return to their various homes, if none of the brothers wanted them to stay. Margarita was the only female who had earned one of the scarce rooms.

Celeste and Doom were walking out of the kitchen when Kat came in with two bags of groceries.

"Let me wash up. I'll get the rest of the groceries from the car," he offered.

"No need." Laying the groceries on the bar top, she told him, "This is all of it."

Doom stared at the two lone bags. "There's no way all of the items on the list I texted you are in two bags."

"Oh... I forgot to look at the list until after I checked out, but I'm sure I got most of them."

Doom glowered at her. "Then where's my milk?"

CHAPTER 9

THE TALK

Jeez. She was beginning to despise mornings.

Glaring up at the sun as she approached The Last Riders' club door, she would rather jump from a 747 midflight than meet Doom, who was already waiting. The tall asshat had texted her that he would be there to make sure she was on time. Unfortunately, The Last Riders were fulfilling their end of the bargain, and she was going to, too, even if it killed her. And if she didn't manage to get more sleep soon, it just might.

At least she recognized the guard standing out front.

"Good morning," she greeted Buck with an enthusiasm she wasn't feeling. Would it kill one of them to smile? So far, all The Last Riders whom she had met had the personality of a wasp. Well, except Jesus, she clarified. He had saved Luc.

"Go on in. Doom's waiting."

Arden rolled her eyes behind her dark sunglasses. She bet the asshole was. They had been arguing back and forth about when she would work at the club. She had managed to come up with different excuses until Saturday morning, but he had warned her that, if she was so much as a minute late, any interactions with The Last Riders would end for Luc.

The change in Luc had her mother and father over the moon at how hard he was working on his schoolwork. When she had gone by her parents' home, Luc told her school was getting better and went on and on about how The Last Riders had shown up after school. From Luc's expression, she could tell how much he admired them.

It might be a no-win situation for her, but for Luc, he was winning against the bullies who had been tormenting him.

She opened the door and saw Doom sitting at the bar, facing the door with a cup of coffee in front of him, looking like death warmed over. From his disappointed expression, he hadn't expected her to show.

A woman behind the bar gave her a curious glance as she removed empty bottles from the counter.

Sliding her dark glasses to the top of her head, she gave Doom a sunny smile. "I'm here, and I'm not late."

Doom lowered his eyelids as his eyes went from the top of her head, where she had pinned her hair into a top knot, to the white, frilly blouse, going lower to the plain black slacks, and ending at the black flats on her feet.

"I hope this is acceptable dress." Arden couldn't help but to serve that dig. When he had texted her what time to be here, she had asked him what she should wear. He had responded with a "whatever." So, she wore what she wanted.

Doom's dire expression didn't change, but Arden noticed the muscle under his eye started twitching.

"Siren." Doom stood up, gesturing to the woman behind the bar. "Arden."

He slid his cup toward Siren, and Arden noticed he didn't look at her again after his initial gaze.

Siren came to where he was standing when he motioned her closer.

"She's in your hands. She stays until six. I'll be in my room, if you need me."

When he turned around, he wasn't able to avoid seeing her. The muscle tic became more pronounced.

"You might get a pad of paper and pen from the office," he told Siren. "You might need to draw pictures."

The dig found the mark he had intended. Doom was never going to get over her insulting the club's intelligence.

"Wow, that wasn't off to the best start." Siren gave her a mock ferocious glare, mimicking the one Doom had given her. "What did you do to get on his bad side?"

"Apparently, just breathing."

The woman burst out laughing. "I've been waiting for someone to give Doom a hard time."

Arden frowned. She had screwed up again. Her best bet was to lay low, not to antagonize the man. Her tiredness had her acting irrationally.

Yeah, right. She rolled her eyes at herself. The man had set her off since he had carried her into Wizard's office.

She was going to have to be the bigger person and try to heal the rift between them that she had caused.

"Come back here, and we can get started. Doom has a shitload of stuff he wants me to show you before The Last Riders start coming back."

Arden walked to the end of the bar then stepped behind the counter. Siren treated her with the same once-over that Doom had given her. The woman's face grew worried.

"Hon, those clothes aren't going to cut it. Doom said you're wanting to be a Last Rider?"

As Siren was talking, two women came out of the hallway that led to the office and bedrooms. They had been heading for the front door, but overhearing what Siren had said, they made a beeline to the bar to take two stools near them.

"Y-yes," she answered self-consciously.

All three women were basically in the same type of slim-fitting jeans. The only difference in the clothes was Siren's top was scrunched at the side of her purple top, allowing the thin material to show the bare expanse of her stomach. The other two women were wearing regular sweatshirts.

Siren flicked the starched bow at her throat with her fingers. "The only votes you're going to get in those duds is them voting against letting you join."

"Votes?" Arden asked.

"Votes," Siren repeated, giving the women sitting at the bar reprimanding glares at their snickers. "Kat, Lola, aren't you supposed to be going to the liquor store to restock?"

"We will. There's no hurry. The brothers won't see the light of day for a couple more hours." The woman who spoke gave her grin. "I'm Kat, by the way." Nodding her head to the side, she introduced the other woman, "She's Lola."

"It's nice to meet you."

Kat smiled back. "Same. All the women love to meet newbies. Well, except for Celeste. You stole the shift Wizard had been promising her."

"Oh... I'm sorry." Arden didn't know what else to say. The hours she had settled on with Doom were the only hours she could work.

"No biggie for me. I hate working mornings or late at night. The fun is just getting started then."

Lola elbowed Kat in the ribs. "Quit interrupting. Siren was explaining the votes."

Kat frowned. "Doom must have told her about the votes."

Arden shook her head. "No, he didn't mention votes."

"He asked me to tell her." Siren leaned against the counter. "There was a miscommunication that the brothers want me to straighten out."

Widening her eyes, Arden pretended innocence. "Miscommunication?"

"They didn't tell you about the votes you have to get before a woman can become a Last Rider."

The two women broke into laughter. "That's a *big* miscommunication." Lola rolled her eyes. "Since when have any of the brothers been shy about explaining them?"

Siren gave Lola a harassed glare. "Are you going stop talking or not?"

Lola pretended to zip and lock her mouth.

Arden could tell Siren wasn't buying her look of pretend innocence.

"Hon, I don't know why you're wanting to become a Last Rider, but if you're just looking to get back at an ex, or wanting to spice up your love life, this isn't the place. Why don't you check out ladies' night at Wily Goose Ale House on a Saturday night? The action isn't bad there, and your coochie won't take a couple of days to recover."

"It took you two days?" Kat seemed impressed. "Hell, it took me a week to get the hang of it."

Siren threw a bar rag at Kat. "Shut the fuck up."

Kat grabbed the rag and started to get off her stool.

"What're the rules?" Arden put an end to the budding fight she could see was about to take place from Kat's furious expression.

Kat sat back down, and then both women's arms went to the bar top to prop their face on their hands to watch.

Siren ignored them.

"You need six votes to become a member. It used to be from the original members, but since they're all in Treepoint, Kentucky, in the other chapter, they let Wizard, Puck, Buck, Jesus, Doom, Moon, and Nickel give votes. You'll have to catch a ride with one of the brothers to go to Kentucky for Moon's and Nickel's votes unless you manage to get them while they're here. Nickel comes here about every couple of months, Moon just whenever he doesn't think he'll get caught. The mayor's daughter wanted to be a Last Rider when Moon was the president here. Needless to say, he's been dodging the law ever since."

Arden filed that piece of information away as she continued to listen.

"I miss Moon," Lola lamented.

"Anyway—" Siren gave Lola a threatening glare, "to earn the votes, you have sex with six of them any way you want, as long as they come. For example, Buck can watch Puck do you, and if Buck comes, you basically get a free vote."

"They watch?" Arden could tell Kat and Lola were enjoying her embarrassment, while Siren was giving her a sympathetic glance.

"Depends. If you're in this area, anyone coming into the bar can watch. Hon, none of us are shy. But if they take you to their room, the brother gets to choose if the door is to be left open or closed. Most of the brothers let you choose. Wizard doesn't give a fuck who watches. The more, the merrier. That brings me to another point Doom wanted to make sure you're made aware of."

"How nice of him," Arden grated out between clenched teeth.

Siren's gaze became more sympathetic. "If the door is open, anyone can not only watch but join in if the brother gives them permission."

Arden felt the bile beginning to churn in her stomach. "Are we talking about a threesome?"

"Or a foursome, or a fivesome," Kat choked out laughingly.

Lola wasn't about to be outdone. "I had a sixsome. How I finally got my last two votes. I get my tattoo next Monday. The girls and I are going out afterward. You can come."

"I'm working." Arden was thankful she had skipped breakfast this morning. Her anxiety from what Siren was telling her would have had her barfing on the counter.

Lola made a moue of disappointment. "That sucks."

Arden looked at Siren to show her Lola wasn't distracting her.

"A few of the brothers will hang back from giving you their votes to spread them out so they can gauge how well you fit in with the club and how well you get along with everyone. You also don't have to limit yourself from fucking the regular members who don't vote. You can fuck anyone in the club as long as they are a Last Rider. Who you can't fuck is someone who isn't a Last Rider. You get what I'm saying?"

Arden nodded. "Loud and clear. I'm expected to have sex with six of The Last Riders who vote for me *after* I have sex with them, have sex with anyone else in the club I want to just for funzies, and get refills at the same time."

Siren shook her head. "No, if you're working the bar, that's your only job. No one wants to check if you washed your hands after giving Puck a hand job. It wouldn't be very hygienic."

They were just discussing sixsomes, and they're worried about hygiene? Their lack of inhibitions showed the vastly different ways between how they regarded sex and how she did.

"Since we're on the topic of hygiene, the brothers have to wear condoms. There are plenty around the club. Wizard makes sure there's a supply in the pantry. I'll show you the pantry when we're done talking."

Siren pulled out a cardboard box from under the counter then took out a handful of condoms, placing them in what Arden had thought was a straw box at the end of the counter. Coming back, she took the whole condom box she had pulled out and carried it back to the end of the bar to dump the contents inside.

"Last night was busy. Hawk came back from San Francisco. All the brothers came to welcome him back."

Lola and Kat nodded.

"Plus, it was a Friday night."

"Fridays are normally busy?"

"Fridays are special around here. We allow inside anyone over twenty-one who wants to party and get their foot into the door to become a Last Rider," Siren explained. "I don't know how you managed to get invited to become a member without coming to one of the parties..."

Arden opened her mouth to tell her about Luc, but Siren put her hand up to stop her.

"Normally, the only way to become a prospect is being friends with a Last Rider or having attended one of our Friday parties, and one of the members asks if you want to join. Men can become a prospect at eighteen, women at twenty-one. You need to keep in mind that the men are looking to get laid, not to fall in love. You get possessive over one of the brothers, it will be the quickest way to be shown the door. All of us here want the freedom and excitement of fucking who we want to fuck, when we want to, and how we want, without anyone standing on the moral high ground, casting judgments. If you don't want to fuck a certain Last Rider, you don't have to. You don't even have to fuck for votes, if you don't want to join. You just won't be privy to club business. The Last Riders want you to earn their trust, and vice versa—whatever goes on in the club stays in the club. We have church meetings once a week where we discuss and settle shit. Wizard doles out the punishments, so beware—you don't want to piss him off by breaking the rules." Siren gave a long-winded sigh. "Which you would already know if you hadn't skipped the line and came to one of our parties."

Arden opened her mouth to explain, but Siren clutched the rag in her hand tighter with a glare.

"I do not need to know," she said slowly and distinctly. "I'm leaving after this shift is over." Siren turned her other hand to show her engagement ring. "I'm getting married."

"Congratulations."

"Thanks. I've had a blast here, but when Vandal gets off work, he wants me raring to go, not fucked out from the other brothers."

Arden ran her finger across the bridge of her nose between her eyes, closing them, wishing she were in an Amazon rainforest, not here. She wished some poisonous bug would just put her out of her misery. How was she ever going to get out of this mess she had talked herself into?

Arden opened her eyes and pressed her dry lips together. "Is there anything else I need to know?"

"I don't think so. Wait... Did I mention you need to get

an all-clear from your gyno that you don't have anything catching?"

"Catching?" Arden focused her eyes back on Siren.

Even Kat's gaze had become pitying. "Any sexual diseases. Until you get a blood test stating you're clean, none of the brothers will touch you."

At least there was one bright spot. It would take her at least a month to get an appointment.

Siren went to the mirror where the liquor bottles lined the wall, grabbing a small card tucked into the side then handing it to her. "This is the gynecologist most of the girls use. She parties here every so often. You can call her on Monday. She'll fit you in."

"Thanks." Arden gingerly took the card.

"Make sure you put the card back after you write the number down. It's nice to have handy."

"I bet it is," Arden said drily.

All three women smiled at her attempt at humor.

"Do the men get tested, too?"

"Oh yes." Kat's smile widened. "Of course, their tests come free of charge."

Arden knew what she wanted to do with the card. She wanted to wad it up and shove it down...

"I guess that's it, other than for me to show you around and where everything is." Siren gave her a considering look, making no attempt to move from where she stood. "So, are you staying, or am I waking Doom?"

Stubbornly, Arden stared back. "I'm staying."

CHAPTER 10

THE ACCIDENT

Doom left his room and walked down the hallway, prepared for Siren to tell him that Arden had left ten minutes after her shift had started. He'd have to remember to ask Siren at what part did Arden say she quit, or if she had just left without a word.

Turning the corner, however, he came to an abrupt stop at seeing the woman he would have sworn wouldn't have lasted half an hour, much less the whole day.

Taking the same stool he had sat on this morning, Doom glared at Arden as she gave Puck a beer before turning toward him.

Siren broke off talking with Buck to stand in front of him. "Can I get you something?"

"Beer," he told her curtly.

"Looks like Celeste is winning the bet she made with you." Siren wasn't fazed by his bad mood.

He wasn't surprised Celeste had told the other woman about the bet. Siren might be a hell of a bartender, but a secret-keeper, she wasn't. It wouldn't matter if Siren told anyone else; Celeste wanted bragging rights if she accomplished something no other woman in the club could say they had done.

Staring around the bar, he couldn't figure out what was different.

Siren grinned, noticing his frown. "It's the lights."

He returned his eyes to hers. "What?"

"Everyone's been asking what's different. It's the lights over the bar. Arden fixed them when she noticed they weren't working. They haven't worked since Rider fixed them the last time."

He looked to Arden, who was still talking to Puck just a couple of stools over, within hearing distance of his and Siren's conversation.

"Arden's dad works for the school district. When she was little, he would take her to work with him on the weekends. He repairs things around the schools, and she learned how to do odd jobs by watching him."

"Was working on bar lights one of those jobs?" he said, raising his voice to make sure Arden could hear him as he twisted the cap off his beer. "I thought you said he worked at a school, not a bar."

At his snide remark, Arden turned her head in his direction. "Someone needs to go back to bed and get up on the right side."

Siren eyed each of them interestedly. "Don't mind him. Doom's normal persona is being a grumpy asshole."

Doom glared at Siren from over the lip of his beer.

"Yeah? He has that down pat. Maybe he should try something new." Arden gave him a mocking smile. "Have you tried cheerful yet? Or—" Arden moved away from Puck to lean against the counter, as if she wanted to share a secret with him, "sociable?"

Surly, he wanted to drag her over the counter and give

her something to think about other than the humor she was regarding him with.

Lifting the beer bottle to his lips to buy time to get the attraction, which had just hit him with the force of a four-by-four between his eyes, under control, Doom saw he had missed a couple of other details since he had left to sleep.

Arden's hair, which had been sitting sleekly on the top of her head, was now a hot mess. Several wisps had escaped the bun and were drooping to the side. Her frilly bow was dirt stained and as flat as a tire, and the pristine white blouse showed several drops of what appeared to be bloodstains.

Lowering the beer bottle, he narrowed his eyes on her, checking her face and hands. "Is that blood on your shirt?" Becoming disturbed at the thought that she had hurt herself, he caught himself when he saw Puck and Buck turn their gazes from the television mounted on the far wall, watching him.

Arden made a face, glancing down at herself. "Yes."

"Are you hurt?" Doom didn't take his eyes off Arden when he asked the question. Fuck, even Siren straightened from leaning against the counter at his harsh tone.

"No." Arden waved the question away. "It isn't my blood."

Making sure to use a deliberately neutral cadence in his voice, Doom was able to mask the lethal intent he was unexpectedly feeling. "Then whose blood is it?"

"I didn't catch his name." Arden shrugged.

"Legion," Siren supplied helpfully, lowering her mirth-filled gaze when he turned his head to look directly at her.

"What happened?"

"It was an accident," Arden explained. "I was reaching for more glasses on the top shelf. Siren was busy, so I climbed up onto the counter." Arden pointed to the wooden counter behind the bar. "I didn't see him coming up behind me, and as I was climbing back down, my elbow *accidently* hit him on the nose."

Her innocent expression was just a tad bit too innocent for his liking.

"His nose bled like a geyser." Siren made no attempt to hide her laughter. "Jesus had to drive him to the ER."

Arden grimaced. "I feel terrible."

"I can tell." He wasn't buying that bullshit for a hot second.

At his narrow-eyed stare, her hand went to pat her hair in a failed attempt to restore a bun that had given up trying to hang on.

"Wow. Look at the time. I need to hit the road, or I'll be late for my shift at Mama's."

Doom noticed the high flag of red on her cheeks as Arden gave Siren a bright smile.

"Thank you again for all your help today. I hope just because you won't be working here anymore after today, doesn't mean you won't still stop by to see me."

"Hon, wild horses couldn't keep me away."

"Good, then I guess I'll be seeing you soon," Arden said enthusiastically before switching her gaze to him. "I'll make sure I'm on time again in the morning. Have a great night," she said less enthusiastically.

After he balefully watched her scurry from behind the counter to the front door, he turned back to Siren, who had a sudden interest in wiping down the bar. "What really happened?" he asked curtly.

Siren paused mid-wipe. "Let's put it this way... Legion's record is broken."

He clenched his jaw, and any amusement Siren felt evaporated.

"He was helping her down by putting his hand on her ass to steady her, and her elbow caught him."

"Deliberately?"

Siren reluctantly nodded her head. "Pretty sure."

Doom slid his empty bottle forward. "Give me another one."

Siren reached into the cooler. "What you going to do?"

"Nothing. I'll tell Wizard. The punishment will be his to determine." Doom grabbed the bottle Siren handed him and quickly took a drink. "Where is everyone? The place is dead."

Usually, on a Saturday, the club was hopping, with the brothers blowing off steam and the women aiding on the blowing.

"The brothers are out running around with Hawk. He's picking out a new bike. The women don't think I know, but they're out getting me a cake."

Doom didn't miss the sheen of tears in her eyes. "You can always change your mind."

"Nah, I'm good. I'm ready to settle down and become a one-man woman. At least until Vandal wants us to come to a party on Fridays."

Doom snorted. "I don't see that happening anytime soon. Vandal has been trying to get you to marry him for a while."

"He'll get bored, and when he does, we can come out to play."

"I wouldn't count on it."

Siren gave him the sultry smile she was known for. "You going to miss me?"

"You know it."

She made a face at him. "You're lying, but thanks for making the effort." She went back to wiping down the counter. "I like the new girl," she said offhandedly.

"She won't last."

Siren shook her head. "I think Arden will surprise you. She's got a hell of a backbone." She braced her elbow on the bar. "The girl is a worker. She went to the refrigerator to get some milk for her coffee, and instead of saying how disgusting it was, she cleaned it. When she noticed the bar lights weren't working, she didn't stop until she found the reason."

"She was telling me the fuse box is overloaded," Puck piped into the conversation. "She warned me that I should tell Wizard the wiring is for shit, and he needs to hire an electrician to install a bigger box able to handle the load we're putting on it. She said don't use the lights while we're using the microwave. Even made a note to go on the microwave in case we forgot to tell the other members. She said we're one nuke away from a catastrophe."

Doom frowned. He would call an electrician himself on Monday. He didn't want to chance a fire with any of the brothers or women sleeping out back.

Siren gave a moue of disgust. "When she went to the women's restroom, she came back out with brighter lightbulbs and cleaning supplies. Cleaned the whole room from top to bottom then ran to the convenience store and came back with air fresheners. I felt like royalty when I went to take a piss."

"She wasn't hired to clean the bathrooms or fix shit."

Sounded to him like the cagey woman was using every opportunity to keep from interacting with the brothers. While the bar workers were working, they weren't expected to get up close and personal with the brothers, yet she could have used the opportunity to get more comfortable with them. The actress had no intention of earning any votes like the rest of the women did. She was biding time until Blue didn't need their protection.

His nickname might only have four letters, but he was smart enough to recognize a con when he saw one. She might have gotten away with it today, but tomorrow was going to be a helluva different story.

CHAPTER 11
THE TWINS

Yawning, Arden pulled up in the drive-thru. She glanced at the clock on the dash and saw she had fifteen minutes to spare. She was wasting precious minutes, but she couldn't take another day of the swill the coffeemaker at The Last Riders' clubhouse spit out. Not only was the coffee pot older than her, but the coffee it put out tasted like it was, in fact, old.

She placed her order and moved ahead in the line. Giving a smile to the barista, she grabbed her coffee then drove off.

Would she be the only one working today, since yesterday was Siren's last day, or would there be another woman to help out? If it was as slow, maybe not. One person could easily handle the bar on her own. Siren had also mentioned that the men had been out motorcycle shopping for a member who used to belong to the club, so it was up in the air if today would be slow or busy.

Either way, she had dressed down. Wearing a plain gray sweatshirt, which was as roomy as it was comfortable. With matching gray pants, she looked more like she was on her way to the gym than to tend bar.

She had made sure to watch Siren when a few of the men had trickled in for a mixed drink, but if anyone asked for anything other than a beer or a shot of something, she was going to be screwed.

The closer she drove to the club, the more nervous she became. With Siren gone, she wouldn't be able to come up with an excuse to leave the bar area like she had the day before.

By the time she pulled up to The Last Riders' clubhouse, her stomach was tied in knots. At least her nervousness had woken her up. At this point, she was basically going on the steam coming from the coffee cup in her hand.

Locking her car, she made her way to the door. "Morning, Legion. How are you doing today?"

"Been better."

His bloodshot eyes and grayish complexion told her he might be having a terrible morning, but he must have had a hell of a night.

When she opened the door, she was surprised to see the bar was completely empty and a complete mess. She went behind the bar, rolled her sleeves up, and got to work. Pulling out the trash can sitting under the bar, she started swiping all the debris over the side, leaving the bottles and glasses. She then made a circuit around the length of the bar before she put the trash can back where it belonged and started dealing with the glass items.

Her arms were elbow deep in the dishwater when Buck came down the hallway, bare-chested, wearing only blue jeans. He hadn't even bothered to put shoes on.

"Have you made coffee yet?"

"Yes. Want some?"

Buck nodded, taking a seat. Then he reached over the counter and nabbed the television controller to turn it from *Unsolved Mysteries* to a football game. "Why you watch that shit? It'll just give you nightmares," he commented.

"Why you watch the shit you watch? It'll just give you an inferiority complex."

Buck's dour expression turned appreciative. "I used to play football."

"Really?" Arden went back to washing the glasses. "What position?"

"Offensive lineman."

"How long did you play?"

"Until I graduated from college."

"You still play any?"

"Not for a while."

"The school Luc attends needs a new coach. The one they have is leaving in two weeks. His wife got a job in another state."

"Hmm... I might check it out. Would be something to do in my free time."

Arden dried her hands off then started drying the glasses. "You should. All Luc does is talk about you, Jesus, and Puck. You must be good with kids."

He gave her a strange look. "You not worried I'd be a bad influence on high school kids?"

She shook her head. "Not at all. How could I be? You kept Luc from getting beat up by bullies. You got involved more than most of the parents at that school."

After asking him if he wanted a refill on his coffee, she went to get the broom and started sweeping the floor. She had just finished when Puck and Jesus showed up with Kat and Lola. All four seemed to be in the same condition Legion had been.

The two women gave her friendly smiles as they took over one of the round tables in the middle of the room.

"Mind bringing us some beers?" Puck called out.

Arden took them their drinks.

Kat made a face. "I hate this brand. I'm regretting not splurging for my own when we went to the liquor store."

Lola wasn't any happier.

Arden left the table with the women still complaining about their choices.

As the hours went past, she made small talk with the men when they sat around the bar. The nerves she had started the day with had eased, and she was gradually relaxing her guard.

She was washing more glasses when Kat sidled up to Buck, who was still at the bar. Hooking an arm around his shoulders, she pushed her breasts against his side. "Why don't you come over and sit with us?"

"I'm watching the game."

"How come you can't be as much fun during the day as you are at night?"

Buck removed her arm to lift her onto his lap. A happy squeal had Arden raising her eyes to see Buck nuzzling between Kat's breasts. Kat's legs had gone around Buck's hips so she was straddling him.

"You didn't get enough of me last night?" he muttered, using his mouth to tug her low-cut top even lower.

Arden kept her eyes on what she was doing. *Just six more hours, and I can leave*, she kept telling herself. She could do this.

As she turned away from the sink, her eyes were caught by Doom's as he turned the corner from the back, followed by Wizard and two women who she had briefly seen the day she had barged into the club.

One of the women gave Doom's ass a sudden squeeze before breaking away from the group, which was taking the largest table in the club.

"Sorry I'm late. We were preoccupied, and time got away from me." The woman gave her a smile as she stepped behind the bar. "I'm Celeste, by the way."

Arden gave her a friendly smile back. "It's nice to meet you. I'm Arden."

Celeste looked around, giving an appreciative whistle. "Damn, I don't think I've ever seen this place so clean."

"It's a habit of mine."

"I need a habit like that. Unfortunately, I tend to make more of a mess than actually clean anything."

"I thought you were bringing us beers, Celeste?" Wizard spoke from the table just inches away.

The woman made a face at Wizard, but hurriedly grabbed three beers for the table.

Steadily, more members started arriving. A couple brought boxes of pizza. Arden was kept busy handing out beer. Luckily for her, Celeste saw she wasn't good at making the more complicated drinks and started filling those orders.

The whole time, Arden steadfastly tried to ignore Buck and Kat copulating just inches away, unable to mistake what was happening when Kat started bouncing up and down on Buck, nor the fact that it didn't bother them that they were having sex in full view of everyone. She was relieved when Kat unseated herself to go the restroom, and then horrified when Buck unashamedly stood with his jeans still open and headed to the back of the club.

She blushed when Celeste caught her embarrassment.

"You'll get used to it."

Arden highly doubted she would.

Feeling several pairs of eyes watching her reaction, she

started clearing the bar top where the empty pizza boxes were sitting. Neither Doom nor Wizard had looked her way. They had gone to the end of the room and were playing a game of pool.

Celeste grabbed the remote control and turned the television off before turning music on.

As the afternoon wore on, more members started coming more frequently. She was so busy that she didn't notice two new arrivals until they took stools at the far end of the bar.

She and Celeste had naturally divided the bar in half when Celeste had gravitated toward the side where Wizard and Doom were playing. The new arrivals were sitting in her area.

"Hi. What can I—"

"Burn, Hawk..." Arden was cut off when Celeste miraculously appeared. "I was beginning to think I wouldn't see you today."

Arden moved aside as Celeste started gushing over the men. Celeste leaned across the counter excitably, as if she wanted to snatch the two men up. Staring at her admiringly, Arden was frankly shocked the two men only gave her a brief glance, asking for beers.

When Celeste didn't move, preferring to remain standing with her large breasts planted on the counter so the pale-pink crop top would slip down her shoulders to expose the black bra underneath, as well as the cleft between her breasts, Arden reached into the cooler and took two out. When she placed the beers in front of them, the men thanked her.

"Arden, meet Burn—" Celeste nodded to the man with the dark chestnut hair, "and Hawk."

Arden didn't have to wonder how Hawk had gotten his

nickname. His penetrating gaze had the hairs at the back on her neck rising. He appeared to be in his early thirties, yet the look in his eyes gave the impression he had seen it all and life held no surprises for him anymore. Burn didn't put off the friendliest vibes, either. He just drank his beer, wanting to be left alone.

She glanced around the bar; everyone seemed to be good for now, so she gave the two men apologetic smiles and tapped Celeste on the shoulder. "If you don't mind, I'm going to take a twenty-minute break to eat my lunch."

Celeste and the two men stared at her.

"You don't have to ask for a break," Celeste told her. "Take however long you want. Just jump back in when it gets busy."

"Okay."

Embarrassed at the looks they gave her, she went to the kitchen to take out the food she had brought, but came to a standstill when she saw Lola bent over the kitchen table while Wizard pounded his cock into her. She started to back out, but hunger gnawing on her stomach had her rushing to the refrigerator. She grabbed her container and hurried out, wishing she could block out the sounds they were making. Eating in the kitchen like she had yesterday was out of the question.

When she returned the bar area, her eyes were caught by Doom's amused gaze. Never in her life had she ever wanted to flip someone off more.

She placed the container in the microwave then turned off the bar lights before starting it. As the food reheated, Arden grabbed herself a bottled water and a plastic fork. When it was finished, she turned the lights back on then turned around.

The whole bar was staring at her.

Seeing an empty stool next to Puck and Burn, Arden walked around the bar to take the stool. She self-consciously started eating while the talking in the bar returned to normal. She was aware others were still watching, though.

"What are you having?"

Arden finished the bite of food she had taken before answering Puck's question. "Meatball Napoli and garlic knots."

"Smells fantastic."

"Would you like one of the knots?"

"God, yes."

Arden laughed and gave him one. "If you tear it apart, I'll give you one of the meatballs."

Puck quickly tore the knot open, and she gave him a meatball before she resumed eating.

"How does it taste?"

Arden looked up from her food in surprise when Burn asked Puck about the food.

Puck's bliss-filled expression said it all. "Damn, this is one of the best things I've ever put in my mouth." Puck opened his eyes. "Where'd you get it?"

"Mama's Spaghetti. I work there. She gives me a tray of them every week on Sunday. I texted Doom last night, letting him know that I wanted to bring some today to share, but he told me no. He said Wizard didn't want me to make a habit of bringing food to share. Something about the members being spoiled in Kentucky and Wizard didn't want it to happen here."

From the expressions on the faces surrounding her, Arden thought she should have kept those texts to herself. However, she consoled herself that Doom had basically said the same thing when she first asked to become a Last Rider in front of everyone.

She noticed Celeste, Burn, and Hawk unashamedly watching her, so she tore the knots in half and added meatballs, then divided the food among them. Neither Celeste nor Burn refused the offering, leaving her only the same portion she had given them. Hawk, however, started to refuse the one she offered him. Arden didn't let him.

"It's okay. I still have almost a full tray at my place."

Puck looked like he was ready to snatch it out of Hawk's hand. "Give me your phone," he growled at her.

Arden didn't argue. She reached into her pocket and gave it to him.

"I'm giving you my number. Next time you want to bring food, call me. I'll be waiting at the door. I dare the motherfuckers to say anything to me."

Arden grinned. "I can do that."

"My brother is going to be pissed he missed out." Puck frowned at Burn and Hawk, who didn't seem concerned as they finished their portion.

"Your brother?" Arden asked, taking her last bite of food.

"Buck."

"Buck is your brother?"

"Yes." Puck nodded. "We're twins."

Thank God she had already swallowed her food. "*Twins*? You don't look anything alike."

"We're fraternal, not identical."

"That's why your nicknames are so similar."

"Yeah." Puck grinned. "Not because we're too lazy to come up with better names."

Arden moved the food container away then placed her head on the bar. "I'm never going to live down saying that, am I?" she mumbled.

Puck laughed. “Don’t worry; worse has been said about us.”

Arden raised her head. “How about next Sunday, I bring you and Buck your own tray of meatballs and garlic knots?”

He gave her a worshipping gaze. “Put it this way—and I speak for Buck, too—all is forgiven.”

CHAPTER 12

THE DISS

Doom shot the seven ball into the side pocket. Looking up, he noticed how several of the brothers were glaring at him angrily. Wizard was receiving his share of cutting gazes too.

"Why is everyone staring at us like they want to hit us with a pool cue?" Doom asked Wizard just as he was about to take his own shot.

Wizard glanced up from the table. Straightening, he returned their glare. The brothers didn't shift their eyes away from him like they normally would.

Wizard frowned. "Whatever it is, it's pissed them the hell off."

Deciding it might be better to ask someone who didn't look like they wanted to rip their heads off and shit down their throats, he called out for Celeste.

When she turned from the end of the bar and headed their way, he wished he had asked Margarita. Celeste's breasts were bouncing angrily as she walked toward them.

Doom moved to the other side of the pool table.

"I'm going to deal with this shit." Wizard might have put on a brave face, yet he did move to stand next to Doom.

"Damn, if she isn't careful, one of those implants are going to explode," he whispered to Wizard just as Celeste reached them.

Wizard didn't waste time. "What is everyone so—"

"Did you tell Arden not to bring a tray of meatballs today?" Celeste angrily thrust her hands on her hips, whipping her eyes to Doom.

Looking to where Arden sat with the brothers gathered around her, he clenched his jaw before looking back at Celeste. "I might have."

"There's no might about it; you either did or didn't," she snapped.

"I did."

Celeste's nostrils flared. "Do you smell that?"

He did. He had noticed the smell when Arden was using the microwave. "I noticed."

"She was nice enough to share what she did bring." Celeste's lips curled in anger. "You didn't have a fucking problem with Breaker bringing cheap-ass pizza, but you wouldn't let her bring meatballs my Italian grandmother could have made?" She started yelling. "That's bullshit! You're afraid we'll get spoiled?" Her eyes turned venomous. "You don't have a problem spoiling yourselves when you eat out, or bring takeout into the club to eat in the office or your rooms. Arden isn't even a member of the club yet, and she shared more food with us than either of you have. We put up with the cheap-ass beer you buy for us, but let me tell you something—" she pointed a finger at both of them, "next week, Arden is bringing Puck and Buck their own trays of meatballs and garlic knots. And unless Margarita and I get our own trays to share with the other women, the only pussy you'll be getting are the ones you see in fucking pictures!" She shot them another venomous glare, then turned on her heel to return to the bar.

Doom and Wizard stared at each other.

Wizard's eyes filled with rage. "Are you having any fun with her yet?"

Doom had to bite his tongue at Wizard mocking him about saying it could be fun when Wizard had asked what they should do about Arden.

"No."

"She's never talked to me that way before. I don't like it!"

"I can tell. I didn't enjoy it, either!" Doom snapped back.

"I'm not the one who told her not to bring the damn meatballs!"

"I did it because I remember what you said about coddling them."

"Since when do you listen to me when I say stupid shit? I was just trying to be an asshole in front of her."

"You're one all the time."

"Yeah... But I usually don't get called out for it!" Wizard gave threatening glares to the brothers who were still glaring at them until their gazes dropped.

"Get Arden over here."

"Arden!" Doom yelled.

Wizard gave him a withering look. "I could have done that myself. I wanted it done discreetly."

Doom gave one back, "Then you should have said that."

Usually, Sunday was his favorite day of the week. It was his day of rest and relaxation. It had gone to hell in a handbasket since he had woken up. He had tried to hold back so he didn't enter the bar at the same time as Celeste,

Margarita, and Wizard, but they had stubbornly waited for him to finish showering. He didn't know why he cared anyway. The woman wasn't anything to him, nor would she ever be. Hell, what had started out as payback to take the woman down a peg or two was turning into an attraction that was doomed for failure. He didn't do relationships, and Arden screamed to be a relationship kind of woman.

At his yell, Arden jumped from the stool. Doom didn't miss the way Burn's and Hawk's eyes trailed after her.

Becoming irritated for no reason, he leaned a hip against the pool table, interest in the game now gone.

"Yes?" She brought her eyes to his. "Do you need some more beer?"

"No!" Wizard snapped. "We don't need any beer. Does the restaurant you work at cater?"

"Yes."

"Text me a catering menu. Book us for tomorrow night."

Arden was already shaking her head. "Sorry. Mama's booked for the next two months. She's pretty popular for weddings and birthdays."

"Really?" he gritted out. "If she's so fucking busy, how are you going to bring Buck and Puck their own trays?"

Arden smiled at him. "Mama likes me."

"You couldn't use her affection for you to arrange for us to have some tomorrow night or another night this week?"

Arden's smile grew calculating. "That would be a huge favor for me to ask for, but I would—for a price."

Wizard glowered at her darkly. "What's the price?"

Arden's expression grew serious. "Just one vote. I'll even pay for the food."

Wizard's eyes filled with cold anger. "No. You want my vote, you'll earn it like the other women."

Arden shrugged. "That's fair. By the way, I might be

able to talk Mama out of a couple more trays of meatballs, if you ask me nicely. You sure neither of you want a beer?"

"Bring me a bourbon," Wizard ground out.

Arden left to get his drink.

"I have a couple of meatballs I'm going to give her..."

Doom had to smother his laugh.

Wizard angrily turned to him. "You're not pissed?"

"No. I expected her to try to trick or bargain us out of our votes. You didn't?"

"Yeah... But I didn't expect her to be so upfront about it, nor try it on me."

Doom couldn't hold back his laughter anymore at Wizard's affronted expression. He was kind of surprised at the woman's brazenness himself.

Wizard wasn't amused as he turned to hang the pool cue back on the wall. "You better not trade your vote away."

Doom shifted on his hip, turning toward Wizard. "Get real. Arden will never be able to earn my vote, even if she ditches the fuck-ugly clothes."

"Then I guess," Arden spoke from behind him, "I won't waste my time with you."

Doom turned to look over his shoulder at Arden, who set Wizard's drink down on the table next to the pool table.

Without glancing his way, she went back behind the bar.

He turned his head back to Wizard, and the two men stared at each other.

"I hope you didn't want her too badly."

Doom shrugged. "It's all cool. Like I said, she wasn't going to be earning my vote anyway."

Wizard grimaced. "We both know you don't mean it."

"Actually, I do." Doom straightened to hang the pool cue up.

"Brother... Fuck." Wizard crossed his arms over his chest. "Never mind. We'll deal with that screwup later. Have you ever eaten at the restaurant she works?"

Doom looked at Wizard as if he were crazy. "The closest I've ever come to a fine dining Italian restaurant is when I drive past to go to Little Caesars."

"Wonder if it's as good as Celeste says it is. There are Italian restaurants in the city."

Doom raised his hand. "How in the fuck would I know?"

"Burn!" Wizard yelled.

Doom gave him a mocking brow.

Wizard shrugged. "It's different when I yell."

"How so?"

"Because it's me." Wizard sprawled in a chair and reached for his drink.

Doom remained standing while Burn took a seat at the table, looking at Wizard.

"What you need?"

"How good was that fucking food?"

Burn looked up at him, as if Wizard had lost his mind for asking such an inane question.

"We're just curious."

Doom felt the heat of a blush rush to his cheeks when Burn looked at him the same way he had at Wizard. No wonder Puck wasn't upset at losing his rank. He could have been the one standing here, dealing with this.

Burn shrugged. "It's okay."

"Okay." Wizard straightened in his chair. "If it's just okay, then we can order from another restaurant. Hell, it'll probably be cheaper. I was going to splurge for the club—"

"You're thinking of ordering some food from there?"

Burn's expression had changed. "Let me know what night you're going to do it, so I can be here," he said eagerly.

Wizard's expression drooped. "I thought you said it was just okay?"

"That's when I thought you would ask us to kick in for it. I'm a broke-ass man."

"So, it's better than good?" Wizardly asked sadly.

"I'm not paying?" Burn asked.

"No," Wizard ground out.

"Then I'll put it this way: I only had half a meatball and half of a garlic knot, and I considered taking out Hawk before he could eat his."

In other words, Burn had thought about sacrificing his life for half of a meatball and garlic knot.

Wizard stared Burn down, checking if he was telling the truth, before he turned his head in his direction. "Doom."

"Yes?"

"I need me one of those fucking meatballs. Make it happen."

CHAPTER 13

THE BOSS

"Mama wants to talk to you. I'll take over until you come back."

Arden gave Andrea a quick nod of acknowledgement before escorting the party of six to their table. Maneuvering through the darkened restaurant with the ease of experience, she settled the customers in before she headed to kitchen.

She blinked at the sudden bright lights, so it took her a moment to spot Mama making dough. The woman was anything but a stereotypical Italian grandmother. Dodging one of the servers who was carrying a massive tray, Arden navigated herself through the bustling kitchen.

"You wanted to see me?"

Mama glanced up from the vat of dough that was the size of a linebacker to stare at her intently. "You look tired."

Arden pulled a wisp of hair back into her top knot. "Just a little. I'll get caught up on my sleep this week."

There was no need to lie to Mama; she would recognize it in a second. With Mama, it was always better to be honest than let her wear you down until you finally had to admit the truth. Arden was too exhausted to put up a token resistance to the barrage she would experience at any attempted lie.

"You said that last week. I can lower your hours. You're do for another raise, too, so you won't feel it in your paycheck."

Arden narrowed her eyes on Mama. "Don't you dare give me another raise. You just gave me one. I'm fine. Seriously. Leave the schedule alone. If I need a few hours off, I'll have Andrea lower my hours on the next schedule. You do too much for me already. Once I have enough to buy Luc a car, I'll cut back some."

Mama surveyed her critically. "How? I assume you'll be making the car payments for him, pay for the insurance, and provide gas money for him. You're just going to be increasing the need for more. Let me help you out. Please take the—"

"No," Arden firmly refused the loan Mama had been offering since her father had to stop working. "I'll make it work, like I always do."

Mama frowned at her. "You're making me unhappy. I don't like being unhappy. My bread won't rise the way I like when I'm unhappy."

"You can't be unhappy when I'm happy."

"How can you be happy when you're working yourself to death?"

Arden placed her arm around Mama's shoulder, giving her a hug. "How can I be unhappy when I have the best boss in the whole world?"

Mama shrugged out of her hug. "I don't need you to kiss my ass."

"I wasn't kissing your ass." Arden laughed. "I was trying to be affectionate."

"You want to show affection to me? Take my loan."

"Nope." Arden grinned at her. "Anything else? Andrea will mess up my seating chart if I'm gone too long."

Mama switched the mixer off, looked inside the steel bowl, and seemed satisfied with the dough before she turned back to her. "This morning, Andrea had a customer waiting outside for us to open. He wanted to place a large order for tonight."

Arden had a feeling who it was—one of The Last Riders. She hadn't mentioned to Mama that she was working part-time at their club, and she certainly hadn't told them about her becoming one of them.

"Really?" Pasting a fake smile on her lips, she tried not to look too perturbed.

Mama's gaze sharpened. "Yes. Of course, Andrea told them it was not possible. He was very insistent, so Andrea did some maneuvering. Friday, there is a birthday event scheduled, but the customer called and decreased the budget this weekend. They're not going to have the amount of guests they had anticipated. So, Andrea told the new client we can provide the food, but we wouldn't be able to deliver it nor provide any staff to set it up, as the van and staff have to go the birthday event already booked. The customer was buying for The Last Riders' club. Have you heard of them?"

There was no way she was going to lie to Mama, but she was going to be as evasive as she could be without telling her the full reason why she was working for them. Mama would have a fit, and no one came ahead when Mama was in a full-blown fit.

"Yes. I've—bartended for them a couple of times."

"Why? You have as much experience at bartending as Elio does."

Arden winced. Elio was the busboy.

"It's complicated."

"Then uncomplicate it and tell me why you're working there. If you want more hours, all you have to do is ask me."

"Luc was having trouble at school. The Last Riders are watching out for him. As a trade-off, I work as a bartender a couple days a week."

"Why did you not come to me if you're having difficulty with Luc? Rocco would—"

"I didn't want to involve Rocco."

"Why not?"

"Because Rocco would have gotten Luc thrown out of school. Your brother can be..."

Mama raised her eyebrows. "Yes?"

Arden tried to find the right word she was searching for. "Temperamental."

"Temperamental?"

"I love you, Mama, you know that, but you both can be a little—"

"Temperamental?"

"I was going to say over the top when you get angry."

Mama's face softened. "That is only because we're—"

"Crazy?" Arden teased.

Mama broke out in laughter. "I was going to say because we're Italian. We get as angry as passionately as we make love."

"Mama, the only part of you that is Italian is the DNA you get from your father, and you've never met him. You're passionate because you and Rocco are good people and care about others."

"My mother—God rest her soul—was a wonderful

woman, but her taste in men was not the best. Still, she managed to get me the recipes, which has made my business a success, so I forgive her for the poor judgment she showed when she was taken in by that cheater."

From the angry glitter in Mama's eyes whenever her father was mentioned, Arden tried to stave off another round of anger directed at her absent father.

"If that is all, I better get back—"

"That is not all. Going back to what we were discussing before. The customer suggested he could hire you for the night to deliver the food and set it up. Andrea could work as hostess Friday, if you are willing...? I had Andrea tell him he would have to be charged an extra fee for me to give you up on our busiest night of the week."

Arden tried not to laugh at the devilment on Mama's face.

"How much did you charge him?"

"One thousand dollars."

Arden gaped at her. "Are you serious?"

"I never, ever joke about money. The thousand is yours, of course, but only if you want to do it. If not, Andrea will call and tell him no."

The thousand would go a long way toward the deposit on the car she wanted to buy for Luc.

"I'll do it. Thank you, Mama."

Mama's face went stern. "I'm not happy you're working at a motorcycle club. Please be careful, and if you need my help—"

"You're the first person I'll ask," she promised.

"You won't." Mama gave a long, suffering sigh. "But I'm here if you need me."

"I'll keep that in mind." Arden gave her a cheeky smile

then reached to the side to swipe a cannoli Mama must have just made before she came to the kitchen.

"By the way..." Mama gave her another cannoli. "I better not see you riding on the back of one of those motorcycles. They are very unsafe."

"Mama—you'll never see me on the back of a motorcycle." Arden laughed. "There are prettier girls at the club than me, who they would prefer to ride with over me."

"You know I don't like it when you put yourself down." Mama frowned.

Arden bit her lip, her hurt feelings about what Doom had said the day before still stinging. She wasn't going to ask for any of their votes, anyway. Especially Doom, who was the biggest jerk in The Last Riders.

Avoiding Mama's probing stare, she hastily left, telling her she needed to get back to the hostess stand.

She was already dreading Friday...

Giving Andrea the extra cannoli, she went back to work, forcing a polite smile onto her lips.

At the end of the evening, she went back to the kitchen to clock out. Only Mama and she were left in the restaurant. Arden washed her hands then pulled a kitchen stool to the high-top metal table. She started to reach for a pair of disposable food gloves when Mama moved the box away.

"What are you doing?" Mama asked.

"I'm going to roll out some meatballs with you."

"No, you are not. Go home!"

Arden snatched the box of gloves away from her. Putting on a pair of the gloves, she started rolling out meatballs.

Mama gave her a frustrated sigh then continued making them with her. "I should fire you."

"You won't." Arden took a lump of seasoned meat,

rubbing it between her hands. "I wasn't going to leave you alone here, anyway, so it'll be quicker if I help."

"How long do you think you're going to be able to keep burning the candle on both ends?"

Arden raised frank eyes to meet Mama's. "As long as I have to."

CHAPTER 14
THE BET

Arden opened the trunk of her car, carefully stacking three trays together before lifting them out.

"Need some help?"

Turning, she gave Jesus a thankful smile. "You won't get in trouble leaving the door?"

"No. I texted Buck when I saw you pull in," he replied.

"Then yes, please. You can take these."

Placing the trays in Jesus's hands, she stacked three more. There were still eight left in the car.

"Be careful," she warned. "Mama put extra sauce in those."

Jesus lifted the trays to get a whiff of the appetizing aroma. "Dammit. There won't be anything left by the time I'm off duty."

"I'll make you a plate and bring it outside for you," she offered.

Giving her a grateful glance as they went inside, Arden nearly stumbled at noticing the amount of people. Correcting her step, she looked around.

Originally, she had planned to set the food up at the

largest table in the bar, but it was filled with Wizard, Doom, Puck, Burn, and Hawk. Wizard sitting with Lola on his lap wouldn't appreciate being asked to move.

She looked over at Jesus. "Where should we put them?"

"The bar?" Jesus suggested.

"I guess."

Left with no other option, she went behind the bar and started setting the trays out.

"I'll get Puck, and we'll carry in the rest for you," Jesus offered.

"Thank you. I appreciate your help."

Doom got up and made the people sitting at the bar move.

"I forgot we don't have paper plates and forks. When Puck comes back, I'll send him to the convenience store."

"No need. I brought them." She blithely opened the large bag she had hanging over her shoulder, pulling out two large bundles of paper plates. Then she removed a big container of plastic utensils. She opened everything and set them to the side before taking the metal lids off the food.

"Thanks," Doom said.

"No problem."

After he gave a cursory glance at her black slacks and black blouse that was buttoned to her throat with tiny pearl buttons, he went back to his seat.

Once Puck and Jesus returned and the food was laid out, Arden began swearing to herself. Taking out her cell phone, she called Mama.

"Hello?"

"Mama, I'm missing the garlic knots."

"I know. I was just about to call you. Gian accidently took them to the birthday party. He called when he realized what he had done. I've already picked them up and am driving them to you now. I should be there in about five minutes."

"All right, I'll tell them. Just text me when you're outside."

"Okay." Mama disconnected the call.

Arden went to Wizard's table. "There was a mistake with the garlic knots. They'll be here in five minutes. Do you want to let everyone start eating or do you want me to cover the food back up?"

Lola didn't let the interruption faze her as she caressed Wizard's bare chest under his parted blue jean vest.

"We'll wait."

Nodding, she went back to place the lids back on.

Moans and groans could be heard around the bar.

"It won't be long," she called out. "My boss is bringing the garlic knots."

She helped Celeste serve people at the bar as she waited for Mama to arrive. True to her word, Mama texted her when she was outside.

"I'll be right back," she told Celeste.

She moved around the bar and had made it to the door when it was opened and Mama walked in, carrying the four trays of garlic knots.

Arden started to take them from her, but Mama held on to them.

"Just show me where to set them," she ordered.

Arden self-consciously walked through the jam-packed tables to the end of the bar. "You can set them here." She motioned to an empty space.

Her and Mama's eyes met as she sat the trays down.

"Thank you for bringing them," she said nervously. "I guess I'll see you tomorrow."

From the gleam in Mama's eyes, Arden could tell she wasn't pleased.

"You're paid to stay until twelve. Call me when you get off." Mama's low voice meant business.

"I will," Arden promised.

As Mama went around the corner, Arden noticed Puck had left the table where he had been sitting with Wizard and was intercepting Mama, blocking her way. Arden had no idea Puck could move so fast.

Behind Mama, Arden moved to the side so Puck could see her mouthing a warning to him. Puck's eyes flicked back to Mama's, but he didn't heed her warning.

"You sure you don't want to stay and join the party? I can make a place for you at my table."

Arden squeezed her eyes tight, unable to bear the sight of Puck giving Mama a grin that he assumed was sexy.

"No, thanks. I don't sit on men's laps," Mama said sharply.

Arden glanced around the bar. She had been so busy that she hadn't noticed all the women sitting on the men's laps, other than her and Celeste, who were working the bar.

"And if I did, it wouldn't be on a man who could toss me off when another woman caught his eye."

Puck didn't have the grace to be embarrassed that Kat had been wrapped around him when Mama first walked inside the bar.

"I told Kat to move before you got here. She didn't listen, so I—"

"I did not ask for an explanation," she cut him off rudely and stared him down.

Puck tried again. "Baby girl, I'm just saying..."

Mama turned to Arden. "Make sure you call me," she snapped.

Arden nodded miserably.

Mama turned back to Puck. "Move."

"Or what?" He fixated his eyes on Mama.

"Puck—I wouldn't..." Arden tried to warn him again, looking over at the table where Wizard and Doom were sitting.

Wizard lifted his hand to shush everyone.

"Or nothing!" Mama snapped out, her hands going to the belt at her tight, black, mid-length black skirt. In one move, she slid a sharp knife out of the side of the buckle, exposing the shiny blade. "*Sei un cretino*," Mama spat out. "Arden may work here, but I do not. Enjoy this food. It will be the last time my restaurant will sell to this club."

The men around the club stood up hurriedly, except for Wizard and Doom.

Wizard raised his hand then put it down.

All the men sat at his command.

Wizard must have told Lola to get off his lap because Lola hastily disengaged her arms from around him and moved away.

"My bad." Puck took a step back. "You're a beautiful woman. I lost my brains for a minute."

Mama wasn't appeased. "The way I look is no excuse for your bad behavior."

"Agreed. I apologize."

"Arden, serve the food. I don't want it to get cold. I want them to know what they're going to be missing."

Arden immediately started taking the lids off again.

"You can leave. No one will bother you," Wizard assured Mama from his table.

Mama flashed him a belittling stare. "I do not need your assurance that I can leave. I'm not afraid of this *verme*, or anyone in this club," she sneered. "You're not prepared for the devastation I could bring down on your heads if anything happened to me or *Arden*."

Wizard's expression grew lethal in its intensity. "Puck apologized. I take any threats toward my club serious. Do you normally react so strongly to men hitting on you?"

"I do when I ask them to stop and they don't."

"Message received. You can put your knife away."

Mama didn't click her knife back in her buckle until Puck moved several feet away.

Hotly, Mama tossed her curly, black hair over her shoulder as she stormed out of the club in her four-inch heeled boots.

Arden dropped one of the lids when Mama slammed the door after her.

Puck looked at her curiously. "What did she call me?"

She started putting serving spoons into the trays without looking at him. "Which time?"

"She called me two names?"

"Mama called you a fool the first time, and then she called you a worm."

"She has everyone call her Mama?"

"It's a family restaurant; she considers all her employees family," Arden explained. "The food is ready."

No one moved to make the first plate.

"Eat," Wizard ordered, making no move to get up to make himself a plate while the others in the bar started swarming the food.

Arden managed to nab a plate from the grasping hands and started making Jesus one. After filling it to the brim, she grabbed a fork and bottled water. Then she made her way around Puck, who was standing in line as if he was starstruck.

"Tell me. How badly did I fuck up?"

Arden grimaced. "Well, you tossed Lola onto Doom's lap, but you lost any chance with Mama when you called her *baby girl*."

"Fuck," Puck swore.

"Yeah. Sorry."

Puck's lip curled in amusement. "No, you aren't."

Arden couldn't hide her humor. Leaving Puck regretting his life choices, she went to the door, opened it, and handed Jesus his plate. "Eat it while it's hot."

"Thanks." He grinned. "By the way, is the woman—"

"She's single, but uninterested."

Jesus frowned. "How do you know?"

"I can safely say anyone who belongs to this motorcycle club would receive a no as answer if they asked her out. Trust me."

Jesus's eyes went over her shoulder to the room beyond. "Someone fucked it up for the rest the rest of us?"

"Yes."

Jesus' shoulders slumped in disappointment. "Damn."

"You don't want to know who?"

"Puck. He's never been able to resist a great ass."

Arden angrily stepped back through the door, slamming it closed after her. Now she wished she hadn't given Jesus an extra garlic knot.

Stepping back around the bar, she started filling drink orders. Lucky for her, they mainly wanted beer. The ones who wanted mixed drinks, she told Celeste. Once everyone was settled and eating, she glanced over at Celeste, who was making a drink for Kat.

"I'll take it to her. You go ahead and make yourself a plate," Arden told her. "Take a break."

Celeste gave her a grateful smile. "Watching them eat was killing me. I'll hurry so you can eat, too."

"No need. I ate before I came," she lied. She couldn't eat if she wanted to. Mama was going to give her an earful when she called. She would be lucky if Rocco didn't show to make her leave.

Carrying Kat her drink, Arden tried to place it down and go back before anyone at the table could say anything.

Wizard had other plans.

"What's Mama's name?"

"Call and ask her." She started to head back to the bar, but Doom turned in his seat, blocking her path with a thigh.

"Wizard is the club president, and he asked you a direct question," he said coldly.

Arden crossed her arms over her chest. "A simple Google search would show who the owner of the restaurant is."

"If it's that simple, then you shouldn't have a problem telling Wizard, should you?" Doom mocked.

"Natalia Amato. Satisfied?" She pressed her lips together in a thin line.

Doom moved his leg.

She returned behind the bar and made a plate then placed another on top and went to put them in the refrigerator. Coming back, she started clearing the empty food trays and carried them into the kitchen to set them in the sink. She would wash them and carry them to the car when she left.

When she walked back into the bar area, she saw Doom staring at the empty containers she hadn't taken to the back yet.

"There isn't anything left? Wizard wanted a plate."

"I made him a plate. I set it in the fridge. Give me a minute." She stacked the remaining food trays. "I'll heat it and bring it to him."

"You might as well quit looking so angry. What does it matter if Wizard wanted to know her name?"

"Depends on why he wanted to know." Arden looked at Doom as if he was a toadstool.

Doom's brow began to pucker in anger. "The door is right there anytime you want to call it quits."

Biting her tongue, she carried the containers into the kitchen. She took the food she had prepared for Wizard to the microwave, even as angry as she was, and still unplugged the lights before she started it.

She took the food to Wizard when it was heated and set it down in front of him with the fork. The asshole didn't even bother to give her a thanks. She was going to have to warn Mama that Wizard had wanted to know her name.

When she made a mess of the drink orders that came her way without Celeste being behind the bar, she finally had to clear her mind of the guilt of bringing Mama into their world. Hell, she didn't want to be here herself, much less be responsible for Mama getting hit with bad reviews.

Men always made fools of themselves over Mama, which was why she never worked the front of the house. She preferred working out of sight in the kitchen, leaving the impression of a grandmotherly figure doing all the cooking. Any staff Mama hired soon learned she was all business where the restaurant was concerned. She was generous in her salaries and her affection for the restaurant employees, yet Mama would cut them off without a backward glance if they expressed any sexual interest in her.

Shooting a frigid glance at the table where Wizard and Doom was sitting, she saw Lola fawning over Doom since Wizard was plainly ignoring her.

Thankfully, Celeste finished eating and started helping out again.

“Tonight’s your third night.” Celest gave her a smile. “Congrats.”

Arden smiled back. “Thanks.”

Celeste handed over the drink she had just made. “Here you go. It tastes like a sugar cookie. Don’t worry; I didn’t put a lot of alcohol in it. I notice you’ve only been drinking water. Cheers.”

Arden took a small sip. “It’s good.”

“I’m glad you like it. You deserve it. You beat the odds. Well, as long as you don’t quit before the end of the night.”

“Odds?”

“Doom didn’t think you would last three days. You proved him wrong. Thank you. Now Doom has to pay up. I knew you would make it three days.”

Celeste looked like a cat whole stole the cream.

Arden downed the rest of her drink at hearing how confident Doom had been that she would quit.

“What did you win?”

“A whole night in Doom’s bed. He never lets anyone fuck or sleep in his bed. Tonight, I get to do the whole shebang. I get to get banged there, and then get to sleep there.”

CHAPTER 15

THE BLUFF

"I'm in fucking love."

Doom arched a brow in Wizard's direction. He didn't have to ask who with. The brother had been acting strange since Arden's boss had left.

"I think you're going to be shit out of luck there. Did you miss how she looked at you like you're a dog?"

Wizard's face filled with determination. "That woman was fucking fire."

"That woman looked at you like she wanted to kick you in the balls."

"She looked at all of us that way. I just need to change the way she looks at me, which is the only thing that counts."

"How do you plan to accomplish that? I have bad news for you. Puck is a hell of lot better looking than you, and he struck out."

"You can't drag a lioness to your den. You have to lure her there."

Doom's eyes went to the woman behind the bar as he listened to Wizard. The bar had become even busier as they reached the time when non-members were allowed inside. Celeste was overwhelmed making the drink orders while Arden tried to keep up and was failing miserably. If she had bartended before, he would kiss her ass. She couldn't make a screwdriver without fucking it up.

He signaled Kat to help out and stood up to move behind the bar.

"Take a break."

Arden whipped her head toward him. "It's too busy."

"Kat will take over until it slows down. I want to have a talk."

Arden gave him a harassed look, but she did follow him to a half-circle back booth.

He motioned her over and let her sit first. He wasn't going to try to talk over the loud music that was already cranked up. It would only get louder as the night progressed.

"Tell me again you bartended at Mama's?" Doom was curious if she would be truthful or try to bluff her way out the ineptitude he was witnessing.

"I'm still learning where everything is."

Bluffing it was, then.

"What goes into a screwdriver?"

"Orange juice and vodka."

Lucky guess.

"A seven and seven?"

"Fourteen?"

Doom narrowed his eyes on her.

"Are you ever in a good mood?" She sighed at his lack of response and grimaced at him.

"I just need a few more days to get more familiar with the drinks. I'm a quick learner. I'm watching Celeste and

Kat. In another week, I'll be much better at filling drink orders."

"Or you could quit," he cut her off. "We both know Puck, Buck, and Jesus will keep an eye on Blue. You're wasting both of our time. You're never going to fit in here."

A strange expression crossed her face that he couldn't interpret.

"I won't take that chance with Luc's happiness. I haven't seen him this happy since before my father got sick. My parents have noticed the change in him also, and it's a big relief for them. Would it hurt you to be a little understanding? If you don't think I'm competent enough to bartend, I'm willing to work at the factory. Surely, there is something I could do there?"

"If you were in Kentucky, you could work at the factory there. Here, you have to be able to lift fifty to sixty pounds."

"I coul—"

"No," he said tersely, "you can't."

She drew her shoulders back. "I'm not quitting."

Something just didn't make sense to him. Why was she so determined to become a Last Rider? He had offered her a way out. Maybe she was more into the club life than he had assumed? She was certainly going about it the wrong way.

"Arden." Placing an arm over the back of the booth, he leaned closer to her, watching as she started scooting over to put more distance between them. "It's not only your bartending skills that need improvement. You're making no attempt to get closer to us."

"I am," she protested.

Doom reached out to flick the tiny pearl buttons at her throat. "This outfit doesn't scream 'I want you to touch me.' It says 'Back off.' The gray sweatsuit you wore the other day said 'I would rather be working out than being here.'"

"I asked you what I should wear, and you told me to wear what I feel comfortable in. I feel comfortable in the other two outfits I wore here. Tonight, I'm representing Mama. This is how I dress there."

"The food is gone, so the rest of the night, I want you to spend having a good time. Relax, enjoy yourself." Doom turned his head to see who was nearby.

"Margarita."

The woman at the next table turned. Doom motioned her over. She got up to saunter over to their booth.

"Yes?"

"Arden is taking the rest of the night off. You have something she can change into?"

"That won't be necessary..." Arden looked as if she was a deer caught in the highlights of a semi. "If I can have the rest of the night off, I'd *rather* catch up on my sleep."

"Would you *rather* quit?" he said, giving her the ultimatum.

Arden gave him an angry glare before veering her gaze to Margarita. "I would appreciate some clothes, if it's not too much of a bother."

"No problem. We have a whole closetful of clothes that have been left here or I brought to keep in hand in case someone needs something."

Doom slid out of the booth. "No sweats or polyester," he warned her lowly.

Margarita gave him a sultry grin. "I got you."

Nodding, he went to sit back down next to Wizard.

"What were you doing?" Wizard asked sharply.

"Talking to Arden."

"What for?"

"I told her to take the rest of the night off and have a good time."

"Something tells me that isn't all you told her."

"I told her to either quit or join the party."

Wizard's expression became angry. "Did the brothers make you president, and no one told me? Don't be giving ultimatums out without my say-so. I want her in the club."

Doom stiffened at Wizard's rebuke. "Only because you want that ballbuster."

"That's not why. I admit I'll use her if I have to, but she's been working her ass off around here. You were right; the electrician told us it's a miracle the club hadn't burned down to the ground. I'm fucking curious why you're wanting her gone so bad before the electrician comes in next week to fix it and Arden finds out she did the club a solid or before Celeste makes you pay up for the bet?"

"You thought she was going to quit just as much as I did."

"Maybe so, but I didn't bet on it. If you don't want Celeste in your room all night, offer her another alternative. Personally, I like rolling over and having pussy next to me during the middle of the night, but to each his own."

"The problem is when they try to make it a nightly thing. I prefer not having a revolving door to my bedroom. Feelings get hurt, and that's when jealousy and arguments start. I can stay neutral while you and the rest of the brothers just make room in your bed for them. If I decide I want pussy in the middle of the night, all I have to do is go to one of the rooms with the open door." As he talked, his eyes went to the back hallway, watching as Arden and Margarita walked back in.

She had changed into a low-rise pair of jeans with a cream sweater that hung off her shoulders, exposing the creamy expanse of skin at her throat and chest. Her little brown boots added a couple of inches to her height, allowing her to slide onto a stool at the bar without having to use the bottom rail.

Seeing he was no longer focused on him, Wizard turned his gaze to where he was staring. "She looks pretty pissed. If she quits, I won't be happy," he warned.

"Arden won't quit," Doom told him without taking his eyes off her.

"How do you know?"

He gave Wizard a satisfied smile. "Because she's not a quitter."

CHAPTER 16
THE ORGY

Arden kept her gaze front and center on the front of the bar, focusing all her attention on the different brands of liquor lined across the wall. The partygoers were getting rowdier as the hours passed. From where she sat, the hallway could easily be seen. Many of the club members would leave the back of the bar to make their way to the bedrooms. Sometimes, as many as three or four would leave in a group and come back with flushed faces and misplaced clothing. Arden didn't have to guess what they were doing—the same thing they were doing at the tables, or the booths, except out of eyesight. The only ones she hadn't seen leave for the bedrooms were Wizard and Doom.

"You want another drink?" Celeste asked when she was able to take a breather.

"No." Arden gave her apologetic smile that she wasn't helping out.

"It's all good." Celeste smiled back. "How about a soda?"

"No, thanks."

If she drank anything else, she would have to go to the

restroom, and she really, *really* didn't want to have to pass a table where they were engaged in having sex.

"I'll take a whiskey."

Arden stiffened when she heard Doom's voice from behind her.

"Sure thing."

Arden wanted to gag at the soulful glance the woman gave Doom.

"The idea was for you to relax and have some fun, not sit here as if the world would come to an end if you caught someone actually having a good time."

At his snide comment, she turned around on her seat then instantly regretted it when she saw Buck getting a blowjob at the table behind Doom.

Giving Doom a dirty look because she had played right into his hand, she started to turn back around when, bracing a long arm along the bar counter, he effectually foiled the attempt.

"My idea of a good time differs from yours."

Doom arched a brow at her as he reached for his drink from Celeste. "What's your idea of a good time then?"

Her mind blanked. It had been so long since she'd had any free time to do anything she enjoyed that she couldn't remember when.

Frowning at Doom, she tried to come up with something to say that would impress him.

At her frown, he downed his drink then placed the glass on the bar. "Come play with me."

Her mouth went dry when he held out his hand. Not knowing why, she took it.

She slid off the bar stool and followed him to the back of the bar. When they reached the pool table, he handed her a pool cue.

"Have you ever played?"

"No," she admitted.

"Then let's teach you how."

As he gathered the balls from the pockets, Arden watched. Even though he didn't explain how to rack the balls, she took notice.

Showing her to use the pool cue, he corrected her hands by standing behind her. Concentrating on her hands, she tried not to notice how tall he was to have to bend down to lower to his head to her eye level.

The first game went exactly how she had expected—with her losing. The second game went much better with her managing to sink a couple of the balls. When he started racking the balls for a third game, she excused herself to go the restroom.

Inside the bathroom, she caught sight of her face in the mirror. She was smiling, and her cheeks were flushed.

After using the toilet, she went to the sink to wash her hands, noticing it was nearly twelve. Looking forward to another game, she opened the door only to come to a stop at seeing Celeste's arms wrapped around Doom's waist, their bodies pressed together intimately.

She changed directions and went into the kitchen to start washing the metal containers.

"What happened? I thought we were going to pay another game."

Arden turned at Doom's voice from the doorway.

"I didn't realize how late it had gotten. I need to finish these dishes so I can drop them back at Mama's for her to use tomorrow. You might get to sleep in tomorrow, but I have an early shift."

He gave her a frowning glance then started to leave.

"Doom."

When he glanced back at her, she smiled at him. "Thanks for teaching me pool. I enjoyed myself."

He gazed at her with a remote expression she couldn't read, then gave her a brief nod before leaving the doorway.

Arden stared at the empty doorway, relieved he was gone.

Returning to the dishes, she listened to the voices and laughter coming from the bar. She silently congratulated herself for managing to hide the hurt she felt at seeing Doom and Celeste wrapped together. However, it didn't ease the regret she felt at not going back to the pool table.

Just once, she wished she could be brave where men were concerned...

Shaking her head at herself, Arden told herself she had taken the wisest course.

She had witnessed The Last Riders going from one woman to another tonight. Forcing herself to be honest with herself, she had to admit to being attracted to Doom. He might not be the most handsome of The Last Riders, with Jesus and Puck taking that honor, but the attraction Doom held for her was more powerful than being based on looks. He had a raw sexual appeal that couldn't be missed by the way he moved and the way he would look at a woman. He was also the most lethal type of man known to womankind —he had a sexual arrogance that came from confidence gained from experience.

She worried her bottom lip as she dried the pans, her mind drifting off into Neverland, where Doom showed her firsthand just how amazing he would be in bed.

Shaking herself out her imaginings, she stacked the empty pans together, and then the lids.

Daydreams were meant for other people, not for women who were like her, who had to keep their feet planted firmly on the ground. Some lucky woman would bring Doom to his knees, but it wouldn't be her. To her, he would be a heartache she might never recover from.

She lifted the pans into her arms and left the kitchen to go back into the bar area. As she did, a woman climbed on top of the bar, dancing to the cheers of the crowd.

As the woman she had never seen in the bar strutted along the length of the bar, she took a sound horn off a shelf. Arden had seen it when she fixed the bar lights, thinking it was a decoration or to be used when they were watching games on the television. Curious as to what was happening, she watched as the woman squeezed the black bulb at the end. The sound had everyone in the club shouting.

"Choose! Choose!" they chanted.

The woman strutted back to the middle of the bar counter to peer through the crowd as she swung her hips side to side, slowly raising her short skirt upward to her waist, showing her pale blue thong.

"Choose!"

The area around the bar was so jampacked that there was no way she could get through. Forced to remain where she was, Arden set the pans and lids down on the bar. She couldn't retreat to the kitchen with the people at the back of the bar moving forward to get a better view.

The woman raised her hand to shush the crowd.

"I choose Doom!" she yelled.

Arden's eyes went from the gyrating body to see Doom shoulder his way through the crowd to stand in front of the woman.

His face didn't show if he was happy or unhappy at being chosen, his gaze intent on the woman. Arden's heart shuddered when he reached up to pull the thong down the woman's thighs.

Bending down to hold on to Doom's shoulders, the woman stepped out of the thong. Doom then tossed the thong to the cheering crowd, toward Wizard. Arden noticed Wizard shift slightly so a grinning Puck could catch the thong.

Moving her gaze back to Doom, she saw that he had lifted the woman to a sitting position on the bar. Leaning back on her elbows, the woman splayed her thighs wide open. Doom took a shot glass from Kat and poured the liquor onto her bare pussy. Then, taking a seat on the stool, Doom went down on her.

From where she was standing, she could see him lap at the spilled liquor as his hands went to her thighs to place them over his shoulders. Arden's stomach clenched when she could see his tongue dive between the lips of her pussy to rub over the woman's clit. The crowd surging behind her involuntary brought her toward the man and woman performing for the onlookers.

To her side, she saw Buck unzip his jeans to put a rubber on then raise Margarita's tight skirt to expose the nakedness underneath as she leaned closer to the bar to watch. Without hesitation, Buck thrust his cock inside of Margarita, who jerked her hips back to him to take more of his length.

Arden looked toward the booths and tables, seeing Buck and Margarita weren't the only ones participating in the burgeoning orgy.

Her gaze was drawn back to Doom. She watched the woman moan. From the position of Doom's mouth, he was tongue-fucking her into an orgasm.

Arden didn't move a muscle, and not because she was afraid someone would take it as a sign that she wanted to join in, but because watching them had brought out some dark need inside of her that had her wanting to clench her thighs at the desire burning out of control, which was dampening her panties.

She was about to jerk her eyes away when they were caught by Doom's. His eyes bore into hers as he tongue fucked the woman into a screaming orgasm. When the woman quit moaning, Doom raised his head with a final long swirl of his tongue on her clit, bringing another small scream from her. Removing the woman's thighs from around his shoulders, he lifted the woman back into a sitting position on the bar. He then stepped away from the bar and disappeared from sight.

With the show over, people around the bar started moving away.

Grabbing the pans and lids from the bar, Arden made a beeline for the door.

"You need some help with that?" Burn asked as she came outside.

"No, thanks. I have them."

The cool air allowed her to get her traitorous body back under control. How could she have felt anything but disgust at being a bystander to that sexual act taking place just inches away from her?

She opened the trunk and set the pans inside. Concern at her unexpected reaction had her slamming the trunk down angrily. She didn't judge anyone how they enjoyed sex, but nearly having her own orgasm by just watching, had her furious at herself.

When she walked to side of the car, she came to an abrupt stop.

As if the night hadn't been full enough with turmoil, the fates had decided to add more rubble to the heap in her life.

She couldn't catch a break if it was a mile long and was wearing a catcher's glove.

"Could be worse," she muttered out loud.

Her normal optimism went into an imaginary dumpster for her to set on fire. Tomorrow, she would return to her normal self. Until she made it home, it was time to let the bitch in her come out to play.

CHAPTER 17

THE KISS

"Dammit." Swearing, she went back to the trunk.

She had a flat tire. This morning, she had noticed it was low and had stopped to get air. Regretting not getting Rocco to take a look at it when she was the restaurant, she lifted the pans out and set them on the back seat before she took out her spare tire and leaned it against the side of the car before getting the jack. Then, sliding the two pieces of the jack together, she slid it under the car to jack it up.

"Need some help?"

"No," she told Doom curtly.

Pulling down on the metal lever, she started jacking the car up.

"Move. I'll do it."

Arden felt Doom's jeans brush against her arm.

"I told you I don't—"

Finding herself lifted off her knees and placed to the side had her glaring at Doom as he bent down to change the tire. As she imagined herself giving him a karate chop to the back of his neck, she glared at him.

"If I needed help, I could have asked Burn. What made you come outside, anyway? Shouldn't you be busy with Celeste?"

Doom clenched his jaw. "Burn texted me you had a flat."

Arden looked toward the club door to see Burn was watching.

"He could have changed it himself if it bothered him I was doing it," she said with snark.

Using the lug wrench next to the jack, Doom started taking off the nuts then pulled the tire off. "Whoever is guarding the door can't leave it unguarded without permission. He asked for permission, and I told him I would do it." He slid the spare tire on and started twisting the nuts back on.

"I didn't take you for a gentleman. Damn, I guess it's true you learn something new every day."

After cranking the car back down, Doom released the jack. He carried the tools and flat tire to the open trunk, where he set them inside before shutting the trunk.

"Thanks," she snapped, turning to open the driver's door.

She grasped air as she was jerked around until her back was against the door and Doom was towering over her.

"What's the matter, doll? I get your pussycat in an uproar?"

Her mouth dropped open. No man had ever talked to her that way before.

"Jerk!" Putting her hands out, she tried to shove him away. He didn't budge.

When he lowered his head and nuzzled her neck, Arden couldn't help the tingles that shot down her spine.

"Don't blame me you're hot and bothered. If you hadn't

been such a scaredy cat when you watched me with that woman, we would be in my room, and you would be the one my mouth would be on."

"It didn't make me hot!" she screeched at him.

"Let's find out," he growled into her ear.

Doom slid his hand under her sweater to the snap the button on her jeans. She grabbed his wrist to pry his hand away. Despite her effort, though, he managed to unzip her jeans and slide his hand under the band of her panties.

"You bastard!" Arden opened her mouth to scream more at him, but before she could, she saw the intention in his eyes. He was about to kiss her.

"Don't you dare put your mouth on mine after you—"

His lips silenced her as his hand found the dampness he was searching for. Embarrassed at him finding the truth about her lie, she tried to recoil from him. However, with his free hand, he grabbed the back of her head, holding her mouth in place as his tongue plundered her depths. Surprisingly, she tasted mint on his tongue and realized he must have brushed his teeth. All she could smell on his breath was the fresh scent of water and soap.

"Give me some more of that cream, doll," he growled into her mouth as he sank a finger into her opening. When his thumb started rubbing her clit, she clenched his T-shirt as her body did his bidding, making it easier for his finger to slide deeper inside of her. "Come back inside."

Jerking her mouth away from his, she used all her strength to shove him away from her.

He removed his hand and took a step away from her.

"Let me guess; you're going to run away again."

"Your night is already spoken for. I'll pass," she said shakily, reaching for the car door.

"Go ahead and run away."

"I'm not afraid of you," she snarled at him, jealousy eating her alive that he didn't deny he wouldn't be spending the rest of the night with Celeste.

"It's not me you're afraid of; it's yourself."

"Bull."

"It's true."

"I just don't see the need to spend the energy to get your vote after you told Wizard you wouldn't let me have it, anyway. There's a whole club full of men who can make me just as hot and who will give me their vote," she said cuttingly.

"Come back inside and let's find out," he taunted, the insult not bothering him.

She opened the car door and slid inside. Before she could close the door, however, Doom planted himself in its way.

"Go ahead and run away. I believe in giving fair warnings. The next time I touch your pussy, it won't be my finger—it'll be my dick. Me playing Mr. Nice Guy is over."

Arden rolled her eyes at him. "I haven't even seen you play Mr. Nice Guy."

"You saw him tonight when I didn't fuck you in the kitchen."

"I wouldn't have let you." She gave him the meanest glare she was capable of.

"Doll, you would have begged me."

She started the car. He had a right to sound so confident. She wasn't sure she would have been able to withstand an advance from him if Celeste hadn't shown up before she had come out of the restroom.

"Jerk face, I would have laughed. Move," she warned.

Doom moved, shutting the door for her. He was already heading back toward the club before she was done backing up. Putting the car in drive with shaky fingers, she headed back to Mama's to drop the pans off.

Blinking back tears at the jealousy gnawing on her insides, she wanted nothing more than to text Doom that she quit. The thought ended in the next second. Her dad had such little time left; she wouldn't upset the already burdened cart she was carrying. Doom was the least of her problems.

CHAPTER 18
THE HEADMASTER

She was so exhausted it was everything she could do to lift the trash bags into the dumpster. Calling Mama had been a big mistake. She had to listen to her beg her to quit The Last Riders, losing a good hour of sleep alleviating Mama's concern when she was basically running on energy drinks and what food she had eaten at Mama's during her thirty-minute break. It was beginning to take its toll.

Slinging another trash bag inside, she gritted her teeth, needing to get through the next ten oversized bags.

Finally closing the dumpster, she wearily went back inside the school. Doing a mental checklist, Arden checked off changing the lightbulb in the science lab, waxing the front lobby, and now all she had left to do was vacuum the front office and the headmaster's.

She headed to the janitorial closet and pulled out the vacuum, rolling it to the front office, where she plugged it in. Vacuuming, she saw the clock on the wall. She had a couple of hours before having to be at the club. Finishing earlier than she had expected. The headmaster's list had been much shorter than normal. Arden worried the list was so short because he was about to fire her dad, even though she had promised the work would be done the same way as if her dad were doing the work himself.

She had worked out the agreement with the headmaster when his sick time had run out. Her dad was just two weeks away from reaching retirement. When he did, she would no longer have to fulfill his duties. She could work extra hours at Mama's to pay for Luc's tuition, which wouldn't be due until the next school year. She only needed to make it two more weeks, she told herself as she dragged the heavy vacuum into the headmaster's office.

She hated the man with a passion and didn't trust him any further than she could throw him. When she was finished, she unplugged the vacuum and went back to the janitor's office. After closing and locking the door, she did a final walkthrough of the school, making sure everything was clean for the week ahead. Proud of herself at how professional it looked, she went out the front door, locking it behind her. She would catch a short nap in her car then drive to the club.

As she came up behind her car, her stomach sank. Not only did she have one flat tire, she had two. She didn't have another darn spare. She had planned on getting a new one when she got off work today.

Instead of breaking down in tears, she started to reach for her cell phone when a car pulled into the parking lot. Arden had to force a smile to her lips when the headmaster rolled down his window.

"Flat tire?"

"Two of them."

"I don't suppose you have two in your trunk?"

He might have meant it in a joking manner, but the stuck-up prick couldn't carry it off.

"No. The only one I have is unusable. I was getting ready to call a tow truck."

"I only came in to finish up some paperwork. I can you drive you to Walmart, get a couple of tires, and put them on for you," he offered.

Arden bit her lip. She hated to ask for any favors, but it would save her some money. The tow truck fee itself would be the cost of two tires that she could get at the discount store.

"Thank you. I'd appreciate it. Let me get my purse."

After grabbing her purse from her car, she went to the front of the headmaster's car. When she opened the door, she saw the seat was filled with folders.

"I wasn't expecting to give anyone a ride. Do you mind riding in the back seat?"

"Not at all." Closing the door, she went to back passenger door. Remembering the lesson her father had drilled into her head since she was a child, she looked at the child safety lock before getting inside. It was on. She went to unlock it, but it wouldn't budge. Getting a bad feeling, she looked to the front seat and saw the headmaster staring her in a way that sent a chill down her back.

"You know, this is silly to take up your time when you have work to do. I have a friend who I can call. Thanks, anyway." She closed the door and tried not to appear frightened as she moved in the direction of her car.

Terror hit her like a sledgehammer when the headmaster got out the car and grabbed her arm before she could reach her car.

"Let me go!" she shouted, reaching into the pocket of her sweatpants with her free hand.

"Fucking bitch! Get in my car!"

Trying to struggle free out of his hold, she started to

scream. A fist hit her in the mouth, knocking her backward into her car. Making herself remain calm, she pulled her keychain from her pocket, her fingers finding what she was searching for just as he hit her cheekbone. Ignoring the pain, she lifted the pepper spray and pushed the button down.

The headmaster released her arm and grabbed his face, giving a howl of pain.

"Slut! I'm going to make you pay for this," he threatened.

Arden gave another squirt in his direction before she ran to her car. Locking herself in, she called Mama. Thankfully, Mama answered, and she told her where she was and what was going on between blasts of the car horn she blared every time the headmaster banged on her window.

"Rocco and I are on our way. Stay on the line."

"I will." Showing the headmaster she had the phone to her ear, she was relieved to see him retreat to his car. Arden didn't take her eyes off the car until he pulled out of the parking lot with squealing tires.

"He's gone," Arden managed to get out through chattering teeth.

"Keep me on speakerphone until I get there. We're about ten minutes away. Rocco called 911. They should be there any minute."

"Thanks."

She heard the sound of an incoming call. It was the headmaster. "Hang on, Mama. I have a call."

"Don't," Mama protested.

"Just give me a minute." Pushing the button, she accepted the call.

"All I was doing was trying to help you, and you overreacted," he snarled.

"You grabbed me!"

"Because you were looking at me like I was trying to kidnap you. You didn't even give me a chance; you just assumed the worst. I have to be careful in my position."

"You had the child locks on."

"Because I have children. Are you really under the delusion I was going to rape you? Hanging out with trash has affected your judgment." His condescending tone switched to cajoling. "Are you really ready to put your father's retirement at risk for a misunderstanding? If I get arrested, do you think whoever takes over for me while this plays out in court will sign off on his retirement? Not a fucking chance. In fact, they'll ask for the money back he's been paid. Think about it before you do something you'll regret."

The line went dead.

Arden called the police dispatcher, telling them not to send a unit, that she was fine and it was just a misunderstanding. Hanging up, she laid her head on the steering wheel and cried.

A knock on the window had her lifting her head. She opened the door and found herself pulled out and into Mama's arms.

"Are you all right?"

Arden nodded.

"Your poor face!"

Arden's hand went to her throbbing lip.

Mama frowned at the action then glared at the empty parking lot. "Where are the police?"

"I called them off."

"Why?" Mama looked at her as if she had a concussion.

"Because he left. It's over."

"Hell no, it's not. The bastard needs to go to prison for what he tried to do!"

"I overreacted. He was trying to help, and I got spooked unnecessarily."

Mama didn't look any more convinced than her brother, who had been silently standing by.

"Arden, he planned this. You have two flat tires. He wanted to use them as a way to get you inside his car."

"It doesn't matter. I didn't."

Rocco took out his phone. "I'm calling the police back. You're going to press assault charges against him. Who did this?"

"Rocco, Mama, please drop this. I'm fine. If you want to help, can you take me to get some new tires?" she asked pleadingly. "Please, be my friend and let's forget about it."

Mama and Rocco shared a determined look. From their expressions, she was glad she had been so upset when she talked to Mama that she hadn't told her who had attacked her.

"I'm not happy, but we can go get your tires."

"Thank you."

"Don't thank me. I'm very unhappy with you. You would have done better to let the police handle this."

"Why?" she asked, locking the car to move toward Mama's.

"Because now Rocco and I will."

CHAPTER 19

THE LIE

Adjusting the over-framed glasses on her face in the rearview mirror, Arden grabbed the large Styrofoam cup before getting out of the car. Her attempt at getting out of working at the club had failed miserably when she had texted Doom and told him she wouldn't be able to work because of her two flat tires. He had texted back that one of the club members could come and fix them, that the other women had partied late last night because they knew she was scheduled to work today.

Groaning, she had accepted that she wouldn't be able to get out of working.

As she grew closer to Jesus at the door, she put the cup up to her lip, pretending to take a drink.

Jesus opened the door for her. "Running late, aren't you?"

"Yes." Arden hurried through the door so her back would be to him.

"Don't worry; everyone is still sleeping. I'll cover for you."

"Thanks."

Entering the bar, she was relieved to see Jesus had been right—it was completely empty.

Lowering the coffee cup, she went behind the bar. The whole place was a hot mess.

Grateful she had the place to herself, she didn't turn on the lights behind the bar like she usually did. Instead, she cleared the bar counter, then started clearing off the tables and booths.

She was washing a table off when Kat wandered out from the bedroom area, yawning. Arden didn't lift her head as she continued running a disinfected cloth over the table.

"Mind being on your own for a while longer?" Kat asked, going behind the bar to make herself a cup of coffee. "I need to go to the grocery store to do the club's shopping, as much as I hate to go," she complained.

"I could go for you if you want. I don't mind shopping. I do it for Mama all the time." Keeping her face positioned away so that Kat couldn't get a good look at her, Arden moved to another table.

"Girl, if you take over that chore for me, I'll teach you how to make drinks."

"Deal."

"Give me your number, and I'll text you the grocery list."

"When do you want me to go?"

"Now, before the men wake up and find I haven't gone. Usually, one of them goes with me to carry the heavy stuff."

Taking out her cell phone, Arden scanned the grocery list. "No need. This is pretty straight forward."

"I'll go get Wizard's card for you to use."

"I'm not comfortable using someone else's card. Would it be all right to use mine, and he can reimburse me?"

"I don't see why not. He'll love that I won't have to wake him up to get the card," Kat said cheerfully.

The more she worked with Kat, the more she liked her. Margarita had been unexpectedly nice yesterday when Doom had wanted her to change clothes. Even Celeste and Lola went out of their way to be friendly to her.

Taking the disinfectant water and towel to the kitchen, Arden managed to keep her face averted.

Tugging her baseball cap lower before heading out the door, she saw Jesus and Burn talking, neither man paying any attention to her as she passed them.

Thrilled she was able to switch jobs with Kat, Arden felt as if she had been given a brief break from the anxiety of this morning's attack.

When she had looked at her phone, she saw the headmaster had called her four times. She didn't know what to do about tomorrow morning. Usually, she would go into the school at five a.m. to take out the trash and make any repairs which had been ordered the day before. The school had many cameras, yet the video equipment was in the main office. Would it be safe? Would he be wary enough not to try anything else again?

She arrived at the grocery store, and it didn't take her long to do the shopping. The list was a bare minimum, which would only last for a couple of days, if that. Taking it upon herself, Arden picked up a several items she had heard members complaining they didn't have. As she moved through the aisles, she caught several sales which were too good to miss.

There weren't any hiccups at checkout, and with the assistance of a bag boy, it wasn't long before she was driving back to the club.

Making sure her cap and sunglasses were on before

stepping out of the car, she opened the trunk to grab two grocery bags, leaving the trunk open as she carried them to the door.

Jesus and Burn were outside, so she held the bags up high to cover her face as she thanked Jesus for opening the door.

"Would one of you grab the rest of the bags for me?"

"Sure," Burn said.

Kat was still the only one inside the bar.

"I'll put the groceries away," Arden told Kat as she went behind the bar.

"I can help."

"No need. I think I know where everything goes. If I have any questions, I'll yell out."

"Okay."

Arden started putting the frozen meals and hamburger patties into the freezer.

"You buy out the store?" Burn joked as he walked into the kitchen, setting the bags down on the back table.

"Nope. I left them a few things," Arden joked back. "I left the baby formula and the diet aisle alone."

Keeping her head in the freezer, she pretended to be organizing the meals until she heard Burn leave. Then, relaxing her guard, she went to the table to start unbagging the groceries.

She left the cap on but took the sunglasses off, tucking them into the neck of her sweatshirt so she could easily put them back on before leaving the kitchen.

Turning from the table with her hands full, she came face to face with Kat, whose mouth dropped open as she stared intently at her face.

"Burn forgot this one. Jesus and Burn said thanks for the deli sandwiches."

Arden walked around Kat to the refrigerator to put the milk and eggs inside. "There's more in the bag, if you want one."

Arden turned around to see Kat was gone.

Quickly putting the sunglasses back on, she left the kitchen to see Kat wasn't out there either. She returned to the kitchen and finished putting the groceries away, hoping Kat had just used the opportunity to go to the restroom.

Keeping the excuse she had come up with planted firmly in her mind, she left the kitchen, finding all the stools at the counter were filled with Last Riders. Neither Wizard nor Doom were sitting, though. They were standing at the end of the bar near the kitchen door. All of them seemed to be half-dressed and had just been woken up. None of the men had drinks in front of them, and Kat was still nowhere to be seen.

Kat must be in the restroom, she thought.

Ignoring Wizard and Doom, she started to where Burn sat with the unopened sandwich in front of him. "Let me get you a beer."

"Lose the hat and shades."

Arden froze in place at Doom's frostbitten tone. Then, taking off the hat, her fingers trembled with so many eyes on her. She took off the oversized sunglasses. Staring straight ahead, Arden didn't meet anyone's eyes.

"Puck, go to Margarita's room and ask her for some makeup wipes," Wizard ordered.

"That won't be necessary." Arden didn't want to remove the camouflaging makeup and expose the extent of the injury to her face. "It's just a small bruise. When I went to the coffeehouse this morning, I was going in and didn't see someone was opening the door. The door caught me in the face."

"Now, Puck."

Puck left the bar.

The unnatural silence in the room had Arden wishing she had just ignored Doom's order to come in today. *This is what I get for lying to Mama, telling her I was going home and was going to stay there*, she told herself.

Puck came back with the makeup wipes and handed them to Wizard. Doom took them out of his hand, moving behind the counter as he pulled out several wipes. Turning her in his direction, he gently started removing the makeup, revealing the dark purple-blue bruise under her eye and reaching her jawline. The whole time, Doom's eyes bore into hers. The rage inside his cyan eyes had her tensing under his touch.

When he was done, he moved aside so Wizard could see.

Wizard's expression was just as cold as Doom's.

Unable to look at them any longer, she looked toward the men sitting at the bar, only to find the same expression on their faces.

"I'm only going to ask this one time..." Wizard grated out between clenched teeth. "And you better not lie this time. Who in the fuck hit you?"

Arden pressed her lips together stubbornly, instantly regretting it. She lifted her hand to her hurt mouth.

Doom slammed his fist against the wall next to him, sending the sound horn tumbling down to the ground. "Who in the fuck hit you!" he shouted.

Becoming frightened at his anger, she took a step back. "I don't know who he was. He showed up when I came out and saw I had two flat tires. He pulled up and asked if I wanted a ride to get new tires." Arden told the men the partial truth, hoping it was believable enough to satisfy them. "I started to get in the car, but he had a bunch of stuff on the front seat and told me to get in the back. When I did, I noticed the child lock was on and decided I'd just call Mama to take me to get the tires. When I closed the door, he got out of the car and grabbed my arm. I started fighting him, but he hit me twice before I could spray him with my pepper spray. I should never have talked to him anyway. I called Mama."

"You call the police?" Wizard asked.

Arden couldn't tell if they believed her or not.

"No. He left."

"You didn't file a police report?"

"No. I just want to forget about it."

From Wizard's and Doom's expressions, they weren't about to forget about the bruises on her face.

"Where did this happen?" Doom took over the questioning.

"At my apartment building." she outright lied.

"Are there any security cameras there?"

"No."

"Why would you live in a place where there aren't cameras?"

"Because it's cheap," she told him honestly.

"What kind of car was it?"

"I don't remember. The whole thing is still kind of a blur. There is no need for your concern. I handled the situation. It's over. I learned a hard lesson to be more careful not to talk to strangers."

"How did you know to check the back door?"

"My dad drilled it into my head when I was younger."

"Yet he didn't tell you not to talk to strangers?" Doom asked sarcastically.

"I—had a lapse of judgment."

Wizard moved toward her, gently grabbing her chin to lift her face to the dim light. "You're having an even bigger lapse if you think we believe this bullshit."

"It's the truth."

"Wizard..."

Jesus's voice from the open door had all the men turning in his direction.

"We have a problem."

Wizard dropped his hand to give Jesus an irritated frown. "Deal with it. I'm busy."

"Okay, but I'm going to need some help. The whole parking lot is filled with Italians, and they're carrying bats."

CHAPTER 20

THE ITALIANS

Barefoot, Doom went to a front-facing window to look outside.

"Fucking hell," Wizard swore, standing next to him and peering out at the same chaos Doom was.

Without a word, Doom turned away from the cluster-fuck happening outside to stride toward the hallway.

"Where in the fuck are you going?"

Doom didn't glance back at Wizard as he snarled from over his shoulder, "Where in the fuck do you think I'm going? To get dressed!"

Doom made his way to his room and ignored the naked woman on his bed. He left on the pair of jeans he had hastily pulled on when Wizard had woken him after Kat told him about the bruises on Arden's face, and grabbed a pair of clean socks from his bureau before putting on the boots lying by the bed. He opened another drawer to take took out a clean T-shirt. He was still shrugging it on when he strode out of his room to go back to the bar area.

Nearly bumping into Wizard in the hallway as he came

out of his room, he saw his president had also taken the opportunity to get dressed.

"Let her in," Wizard mocked scornfully. "It'll be fun."

Doom grimaced at having his words thrown back at him for letting Arden into club.

"You still in love?" he mocked back.

The men outside weren't the only ones carrying bats; Mama was carrying a shiny metal one too.

Both Wizard and Doom came to a stop at the door of the club.

Wizard's hand went to the doorknob. "It died a quick death."

Doom wished he could say the same thing about his attraction to Arden. The woman was like a fucking splinter—the more he tried to fuck her out of his head with other women, the more entrenched she became.

He let Wizard go out the door first but was right on his heels with the rest of The Last Riders who had been waiting for Wizard to take the lead.

They had expected to be bombarded with swinging bats and fists, but the wind was taken out of their sails at seeing Arden had come outside and was arguing with Mama.

"I told you none of The Last Riders were responsible for attacking me."

"You're protecting them!" Mama argued back.

"No, I'm not!"

Arden gave him and Wizard flustered looks when she realized they had come out of the club, then gave them an apologetic grimace before turning back to Mama. "I wouldn't lie for them. If one of them had hit me, I would have told you."

"If it's not one of them, tell me who."

Arden's jaw set stubbornly.

"Then it is one of them. You're protecting one of them!" Mama's furious eyes moved from Arden to settle on The Last Riders. "Which one of these stonzetto touched my Arden?"

"What did she say?" Wizard asked from the corner of his mouth.

"How in the fuck am I supposed to know?" Doom looked at Hawk, who was looking amused as fuck. "What did she say?"

"She asked us which little shit tou—"

Wizard's expression grew harsh as he put a hand up to stop Hawk from finishing. "I got it."

Mama's anger focused on Wizard. "If you want to know what I said, ask me. I'll be more than happy to interpret for you."

"Or you could just insult us in English."

Mama disdainfully gave Wizard a withering look. "I doubt that would make a difference. Men like you understand only one language."

Doom saw the corded muscles in Wizard's neck clench.

"Which is?" Wizard asked in a deadly calm voice, which meant Doom was preparing to stop him if he made a move toward Mama.

"Prickless."

"Let me show you how big a prick I can be..." he said threateningly as he took an intimidating step toward Mama.

Doom reached out to grab his arm, but it came too late. One of Mama's men didn't like Wizard's move and used his bat to block him. In the next instant, Wizard grabbed the man's wrist, twisting it until the man dropped to his knees, and Wizard took the bat out of his hand.

"If you really want a fight," Wizard snarled, "we're not afraid to give it to you. And I can guarantee one thing—it won't be that fucking bat you're holding when I'm fucking done with you," he promised.

Arden stepped forward, bravely snatching the bat out of Wizard's hand with a frustrated glare. Then helping the man up, she returned the bat to him.

"Are you okay, Marco?"

Doom stiffened at the tender way Arden talked to the man.

"I'm good," Marco said with a bashful smile. "It didn't hurt."

Doom rolled his eyes at the fucker. It was apparent the young puppy had a massive crush on Arden.

Marco fed into her attention as Arden carefully inspected his wrist. When she was assured he wasn't hurt, she left his side to step between Wizard and Mama to face her friend.

"I ask you as a friend to drop this."

Arden had dropped her voice, so Doom could barely hear what she said. From Wizard's and the others' expressions, they hadn't been able to.

Mama pressed a hand to her heart. "I heard you screaming in terror when he was trying to get into your car. How can I, as a friend, ever forget what I heard? You promised to go home, yet you came here? One of them doesn't like that you're a good girl and is not taking no for an answer, are they?" Mama pointed the tip of her bat in Puck's direction. "It's him, isn't it? You can tell me."

Puck's complexion went pale as at least thirty bloodthirsty Italians shifted in his direction.

Arden hastily walked to stand in front of Puck. "I swear Puck has been a gentleman toward me."

Mama raised the bat to rest on her shoulder, eyeing

Wizard as if she was just waiting for an excuse to pummel him to smithereens. "Then which one?"

"None of them."

Doom watched Arden give Mama an exasperated look.

"I *swear* none of them were responsible about what happened this morning."

Mama's disappointment could be seen clearly on her face. "Are you sure?"

Wizard gave Mama an impatient glance at her not wanting to accept The Last Riders were blameless.

"Positive," Arden assured her.

"We were asking about what happened to her when you arrived," Wizard said, moving to the side instead of talking from behind Arden.

"I would stay right where you are," a huge man the size of a yeti warned Wizard.

Doom had noticed him taking the spot next to Mama when Wizard took the bat away from Marco.

Conflicting emotions crossed Mama's face as she asked Wizard, "What did she say?"

"I'm right here." Arden stepped forward to take Mama's arm. "I told him the same thing I told you. I appreciate your concern—all of you—" Arden gave the huge number of Italian men holding bats pleading glances, "but I have this handled. I'm fine, and I can assure you the person who hit me isn't here."

Arden started urging Mama to a van with her logo written on the side. Doom and the rest of the other Last Riders endured their threatening stares as they returned to their cars. All except for the yeti, who remained unmoving.

"Why don't you try to take *my* bat away?"

Only one word entered Doom's mind. *Fuck*. The yeti

hadn't meant it as a question; he was urging Wizard to try the same move on him as he did on his buddy.

Wizard was no one's fool.

"Would Natalia want you start a war with The Last Riders when her back is turned?"

The yeti's face became grim. "Which one of you is in charge?"

"I am," Wizard answered without hesitation.

"This place is a biker's hangout?"

"It is."

"Why is Arden working here?"

"I suggest you ask Arden that question yourself."

"We have."

Wizard crossed his arms over his chest. "Then it should be obvious as shit to you and everyone else it's none of your fucking business."

The yeti remained unfazed by Wizard's comeback. "Arden hates asking anyone for help. She's not la puttana like the other women who hang out here. From my understanding of what I've been told about biker clubs, Arden should have been under your protection regardless of whether she is here or not. Have I been told wrong?"

Doom felt the jab of the sarcasm directed at Wizard just the same as if it had been aimed at him.

Wizard's lips pressed into a thin line. "No, you're not wrong."

"Then you not only failed Arden but the club as their leader. I'm giving you time to correct your mistake. Do not fail Arden again. If I see another mark on the bambina, regardless of who put it there, my cousins and I will come back and beat the fuck out of each of your men, make meatballs out of what's left, and feed them to you one by one. Capisce?"

"I understand," Wizard gritted out between clenched teeth. "As long as you understand that the next time you step foot on our property, we're going to take those bats away from you and shove them up your asses."

Doom, who was more on eye level with the yeti than the three-inch-shorter Wizard, wanted to move closer to Wizard, but didn't. He could handle his own battles, and he was a skilled fighter, yet Doom thought the only Last Rider capable of taking the yeti down was in Treepoint.

Observing the large cross necklace hanging down from the yeti's thick neck, Doom kept his eyes trained on Arden's friend's hands.

The yeti gave Wizard an amused glance. "Why wait? Come on."

Doom braced himself. Wizard wasn't a brother who could be taunted without repercussions.

Pure mayhem erupted as the president of The Last Riders went for the yeti. Seeing Wizard was coming for him, the yeti swung out the bat. Instead of taking it away from him, he took a hit to the shoulder, then went for the thick chain holding the cross.

Reassured Wizard recognized it was a hidden weapon, like Mama's belt buckle, Doom grabbed another of Mama's goons, who was also going for Wizard. He caught the bat that had been heading for Wizard's back mid-swing, then jerked it out of the man's hands and threw it as far as he could before nailing the fucker in the nose. Doom ignored the howl of pain, picked him up, and tossed him toward the swell of Mama's men.

He prepared himself to be attacked by three who had managed to avoid being knocked to the ground by the one he had tossed, as he saw Puck going down under a barrage of men focused on getting payback for Mama.

Fighting his way through the barrage of Italian men, Doom was able to reach the spot where Puck had gone down. He tore two men who were kicking Puck away by the back of their necks, leaving him to deal with the more manageable of the three. He used their futile movements to get away to bang their heads together. They dropped like stones to the ground. He saw Puck had regained his footing and had one in a headlock, choking him out. Doom grabbed the other two, who were trying to release their friend, and used his steel-toed boot to send them flying to the side.

He checked on Wizard and saw he was still trying to strangle the yeti with the thick chain, while another Italian was punching him in the face to force him to let it go. Deciding Wizard was faring better than Jesus, Doom fought his way through the frenzied throng to reach the man who was taking hit after hit from several aimed bats.

Pulling one bat away when it was jerked backward to hit Jesus again, he used it to drill anyone stupid enough to come near him. Mama's men became baseballs to be hit out of his fucking ballpark.

"Motherfucker!" one of them screamed in pain.

"Get the fuck back, or I'm going to smash all of your fucking faces!" Doom roared at them. He was done doling out minimal damage to Arden's friends. The squad of Italians was out for blood. Unless The Last Riders stopped playing defense and started breaking bones, they were going to get their asses handed to them.

Realizing that he was done playing around, Wizard and the brothers started fighting back just as viciously.

A sharp command from Mama, which Doom couldn't understand, had the Italians breaking away from their fights to return to their vehicles.

Wizard wiped at his bloody lip as he gave the yeti a

promising glare when the hulking man stuffed himself into the front seat of a van.

"Another five minutes, and I would have had that fucker," Wizard said as he strode closer, wiping at his lip again. They were both observing Mama's fervent hand gestures as she and Arden continued to argue.

"Another five minutes, he would have used you as filling for his meatballs."

Wizard looked as if he wanted to deny the possibility, but then his shoulders slumped. "I should have chained Knox to the bar instead of letting him go to Kentucky with Viper."

That, Doom had to agree with. "Mistakes were made."

Wizard's expression grew calculating. The brother never stayed down for long. He could give Captain America a lesson. If he couldn't get a job done, he had no problem handing it over to someone who could.

"You think there's any chance we can bribe him to come back?"

"No. Especially not now. His old lady is still recovering from being nearly decapitated."

"Fuck."

"Buck might be able to take him," Doom reasoned.

"Not on his own," Wizard scoffed, nodding his head to the yeti; he had gotten out of the van and stood with Mama and Arden. "You think they're a couple?"

"The yeti and Mama?"

Wizard's lips twitched at his name for the man standing protectively next to Mama. "The yeti?"

"Can you think of another word to describe him?"

"Yeah. Cockblocker comes to mind."

"You in love again?"

"Brother, you only meet a woman like that once in a

lifetime. Not only does she have the perfect handles, but damn, her vase isn't nothing to sneeze at either. There's only one problem I can see keeping us from spending several months in coital bliss."

Doom rolled his eyes at Wizard. "Only one? I can name several," he scoffed. "She can't stand The Last Riders. As president, that means you. The yeti could be her lover."

"Those problems I can deal with."

"So, what do you consider your only problem?"

"Arden. She could seriously fuck my game up."

"I would already considered it fucked myself, but you're more of an optimist than I am where women are concerned."

"I would ask why, but I don't care." Wizard motioned the rest of The Last Riders back inside the club when all the cars began pulling out of the parking lot until it was only Wizard, Jesus, Hawk, Puck and himself who remained outside.

Wizard eyed the small group again. "Anyone else notice Arden shut Natalia up and moved her away before either of us could get more detail about what happened this morning?"

Doom nodded while Hawk and Jesus agreed.

"Doom, I want her tagged wherever she goes. Find out where Arden lives and put around-the-clock surveillance on her place. Check and see if she's telling the truth about the camera situation as well. She's lying about something, and I want to know what it is and who she's protecting. The fucker touched Last Rider property, and we need to make sure the repercussions are severe and long lasting."

"I get first dibs," Doom stated, drawing the other brothers' surprised reactions.

Wizard shook his head at him. "As president, I do. You

can't have first dibs unless you claim her as yours. You ready to do that?"

Arden had had his guts tied in knots since she had barged into the club. Still, he wasn't ready to claim her until he was good and ready to, not because he wanted to vent the rage he was feeling on the person who had struck her.

"Then no. You can have what's left."

Frustrated, Doom saw Mama and Yeti had gotten into the van and were driving away.

When Arden walked back to the clubhouse, his hands clenched at his sides. The full extent of the bruising was visible with the sun shining overhead. She had asked to stay home today, and he had told her no. His gut twisted into another knot. The woman was systemically wrecking the life he had worked so hard to build. Thanks to her, he no longer had free reign of his room. He hadn't even been able to enjoy fucking with the same satisfaction without picturing her instead. He had gotten more pleasure out of kissing and touching her last night briefly than he had tongue-fucking the woman on the bar, or spending the whole night with Celeste. He had never had a problem keeping his emotions under control where women were concerned, yet there was something about Arden that pushed every fucking button he had.

His survival instincts had clicked last night when he went back in the club and gave his own personal approval for two other women in the bar to become recruits after they sucked his aching dick dry before he grabbed Celeste to take her to his room to pay off his bet.

He'd had enough sex last night to do even him good for a week, yet, as she grew closer to where he and the brothers were standing, all Doom could think about was planting his cock so deep inside of her that she would be afraid he'd never come out.

Wizard might be fucked where Mama was concerned, but Doom was becoming more and more convinced he wasn't the only one. Arden could seriously upend the future he had devised for himself. When he came to a decision, he never deviated from it—until now.

When he had to run his hand through his hair instead of reaching out to touch her, Doom knew deep down all the future plans he had so meticulously made could be wrecked if he wasn't careful.

Last night, if she had come back inside the club and they had fucked, would he have been able to remain emotionally detached as he had with the other women, like he thought he could? Today, he wasn't so sure. He needed to get his head back on straight. No woman had ever been able to tempt him away from the future plans he had made. All he had to do was keep his dick in his jeans when she was near, and he'd be good. With the amount of pussy he had last night, how hard could that be?

CHAPTER 21

THE REVELATION

Watching Arden standing in front of Wizard, it struck Doom how exhausted she looked.

"I apologize. Mama was concerned someone from the club was responsible for what happened this morning. She didn't mean for anything to get out of hand."

"Bullshit. They came carrying fucking bats," Wizard snapped caustically. "What she didn't expect was us taking the bats away from them, despite being outnumbered so early this morning. I don't like the club being blamed for something some other motherfucker did. I want to know who in the fuck hit you."

Arden averted her face from Wizard's heated glare. "I prefer to handle this myself."

"You lost that right when you asked to join The Last Riders," Doom snarled at her. "An attack against you is an attack against us all."

From the stubborn set of Arden's lips, Doom could tell she was fighting back arguing with him. She had no intention of telling them who had struck her.

Sharing a glance with Wizard, he saw the same conclusion in his eyes.

"Go home. You're done for the weekend," Doom told Arden when she would have passed him to go back inside.

"My shift isn't over," she protested.

"It is now. I'll get one of the new recruits to come in to work instead."

"That's not necessary. I'm fully capable of working."

"Then why did you text me this morning asking for the day off?"

Arden didn't do any better meeting his gaze than she had Wizard's. "I'm feeling better."

"You look like hell," Doom told her bluntly. "Go home. You can come back on Monday. It'll give one of the new recruits the opportunity to be trained this weekend."

"Okay, then I guess I'll see you guys on Monday."

Catching the mix of hurt and relief on her face, Doom watched Arden walk to her car.

"Puck, take the club car and follow her," Wizard ordered when she pulled out onto the road.

Puck immediately strode away while him and the rest of the brothers went inside.

Upon noticing their set expressions, Kat started pouring them cups of coffee.

They drank their coffee as they made plans to set up surveillance on Arden.

"How are we going to keep her from spotting us?" Burn asked.

"By hiding in plain sight," Doom suggested. "I'll rent an apartment close to hers on a short-term lease. That way, we can watch her coming and going."

Wizard gave him an ironic glance. "Planning on killing two birds with one stone?"

Doom shrugged. “Hawk can have my room. He’s been staying with Puck and Jesus since he’s been back.”

Wizard’s lips twisted sardonically. “How did I know that was coming? You waited a long time to get that room; you sure you want to give it up for Hawk?”

“I’m sure. There’s no need for Hawk to be saddled with a long lease to rent a place when I’ll be leaving in a few months, anyway.”

Wizard cocked his head to the side. “Fuck, I was hoping you’d change your mind.”

“Why?” he denied. Picking up his cup, he got up off the stool. “I told you, as soon as Train has an opening on his team, I’m gone.”

Doom ignored the speculating gaze Wizard gave him. The brother might know him well enough to be aware of his attraction to Arden, but if Wizard had placed a bet on her changing his mind, he was going to lose his winning streak.

“I’m going to find something to eat then find the apartments where Arden lives.”

He walked into the kitchen and saw a fresh loaf of bread sitting on the table. Kat must have gone to the store, having taken his warning to heart.

He put a couple of slices in the toaster, then went to the fridge, hoping he could find some butter. He couldn’t remember the last time there had been jelly in the club, which would make the toast more palatable.

When he opened the fridge, he simply stared at it in amazement.

“What are you staring at?” Wizard asked, walking inside the room.

“Milk. There’s two gallons of it—in date.”

Wizard came to stand next to him. They both stared at the fully stocked fridge.

"Kat said Arden went to the store," Wizard told him. "She only noticed her face when she was putting the groceries away."

So much for Kat being afraid of her name going in the punishment bag, Doom thought.

"That's the biggest jar of grape jelly I've ever seen." Awestruck at the massive size, he picked it up. Fuck butter. He was going to have jelly on his toast.

As he turned toward the toaster, Wizard opened the freezer door.

"Damn. This shit must have cost me a fortune," Wizard complained.

Remembering seeing a receipt on the table beside the bread, Doom was curious himself after finding the bounty in the refrigerator. He picked it up, and his mouth dropped open at reading the huge total, and then coupons subtracted out, one after another. He handed the receipt to Wizard and found a plastic knife to douse his toast with jelly.

"Fuck. I hate eating my words," Wizard said, stealing the other piece of toast. "But this time, I don't mind. Arden can have my vote if she keeps buying groceries like this and saving me a butt load of cash."

Stealing the plastic knife away from him, Wizard dropped a big dollop of jelly onto his toast.

"Damn, if those steaks in the freezer taste as good as they look, I might be in fucking love."

Doom nearly choked on the toast. "She's not your type," he managed to get out.

Wizard reached for the loaf of bread. "She is now."

"You'll get over it when the groceries run out."

"That's the good part—she can go get more."

Doom lost his appetite.

"I don't see Mama and Arden being willing to share."

"I don't see why not? One likes to buy groceries, and the other likes to cook. It'll be a win-win. I can have the best of both worlds."

"I don't know what world you're living in, but it isn't the real one."

"Watch and learn." Placing the bread in the toaster, Wizard gave him a smug smile. "Oh, that's right; you'll be leaving when Train calls. You won't be around to watch."

Doom was aware Wizard was baiting him. It wouldn't work, though. Wizard had about as much of a chance of convincing the two women into a relationship with him as grass turning pink. Damn. The knots in his gut started tightening when he reminded himself of how Wizard had earned his nickname. He made the seemingly impossible, possible. How many women had ended up in Wizard's bed when the brothers would have bet their life savings they wouldn't?

Arden wouldn't, would she?

The pain turned excruciating. Was he willing to take that chance?

CHAPTER 22
THE ATTACKER

Doom turned his engine off after guiding his bike into the parking space next to L.C.'s truck. The dark parking lot had one lone light that was flickering on and off.

The apartment building where Arden lived was a fucking dump. It was so bad it made the one he had grown up in look like a luxury complex. It didn't take much imagination to guess most of the tenants had nowhere else to go. No one with any other alternative would choose to live here willingly.

He got off his motorcycle and headed in the direction L.C. had given him toward the apartment he had rented for him. Kicking a trash bag sitting in front of the stairs out of the way, he went up the steps and held his breath as the putrid smell of urine assailed his nostrils.

What in the fuck was Arden doing living here? Her family lived just ten miles away. No matter how bad her relationship with her family was, it had to be better than living in this dump that masqueraded as an apartment building.

At the top of the stairs, he read the apartment numbers.

Arden's door was the first one he passed as he walked down the walkway to the one at the end. He didn't knock, seeing Cyrus had installed a camera next to the door. They had chosen this apartment for the view it provided of Arden's door with the added benefit of seeing who was coming up the stairs.

L.C. opened the door for him.

"About time." The brother stepped aside to let him in. "I have to be at work in three hours."

Doom closed the door and shot L.C. an irritated glance as he removed the backpack he was carrying. "Next time, talk a little louder. The people living on the first floor might not have heard you bitching."

L.C. gave him an apologetic grimace. "Sorry, just want to get out of this shit hole. What in the fuck? If she's a recruit, why is Wizard letting her stay here?"

"We didn't know. She has two good jobs. When I checked her out, she gave the gated apartment complex next door as her address."

"She deliberately lied?" Cyrus rose from the couch he had been lounging on when Doom walked into the apartment. "Then why hasn't Wizard cut her loose?"

"Two reasons," Doom said, setting his backpack down on the new couch he had purchased hours before. "We want to know why she lied, and Wizard has a hard-on for one of Arden's bosses."

Doom watched Cyrus shrug into his jacket, preparing to leave.

"Whatever the reason, she needs to find another place to live. Neither L.C. nor I wanted to fall asleep with this excuse of a door. One hard kick would knock it in. This place is a shit hole. I can't believe you gave up your room at the club to move in here."

"It's just temporary." Doom shrugged. "I've slept in worse places. You get the cleaning supplies I asked for?"

L.C. gestured toward the small kitchenette. "On the counter. I bought some rat traps, too, which I already set out for you."

Seeing the two brothers were anxious to leave, he tossed Cyrus his motorcycle keys. "Take my bike. I'm going to need your car for the next few days."

Cyrus snagged the keys, looking toward the thin door. "She hasn't left her apartment this weekend. You going to catch some sleep?"

Doom glanced at his watch. "It's after three a.m.; I'm just going to clean until Arden leaves in the morning for her regular job."

Both Cyrus and L.C. gave him troubled expressions.

"If we didn't have to be at the construction site, one of us would stay to have your six." L.C. bent down to open a small drawer in the new end table to show the 9mm inside before sliding it closed.

"I brought mine, but thanks for the spare. I sleep light, so anyone who tries to break in won't get a foot in the door," Doom assured them, not taking offense. Cyrus and L.C. were always concerned about safety. It was what made them so damn good at their jobs, and why Wizard allowed them leeway about attending church meetings.

Doom shut the door behind them without bothering to lock the flimsy lock. Jesus, what in the fuck was Arden doing living here?

Rolling up the sleeves of his Henley, he went to the box that masqueraded as a kitchen. He took out the cleaning supplies and got to work washing down the counters and appliances. He pulled out the drawers to scrub down the worn, fake wood before moving on to the cabinet shelves.

He had learned to clean from watching his mother at an early age. Watching the delight on her face when she had come home from working and found a clean apartment made him feel as if he had lightened the load she carried by being their lone provider.

His mom had worked tirelessly to keep a roof over their heads after his father had left them for another woman when he was thirteen months old. He had watched his mom go through two more failed marriages before he was seven. His two stepfathers had started with showering his mom with gifts and promises, only to take their gifts back before leaving her with nothing but broken promises.

After her third failed marriage, she had quit bringing men home to meet him, yet he could tell from her attitude when she would meet someone she was interested in. Then the date nights would begin, when she would find a sitter to stay the night with him. For a few months, Doom would get his hopes up, along with his mother, that maybe this time, she had found the mysterious one whom she could find true happiness with... Until she would come home with tears running down her cheeks and knew another man had let her down.

By the time he was fourteen, going to school during the day and working at a grocery store, bagging groceries, in the evening to make enough money to pay the rent on their apartment to lessen the load his mom had been carrying his whole life, he had lost count of the number of times she had cried on his shoulder. That was when he was determined to never be the kind of man who couldn't keep his promises to a woman.

He had never made a commitment to a woman, nor did he promise anything more than the here and now. Hell, he was so stringent on the rules he held himself to, it was one of the reasons Doom refused to let the women members spend the night in his bed.

Pouring himself a cup of coffee from the pot that Cyrus had brought from his own place, Doom looked around the small kitchen, satisfied that it was as clean as it was going to be—unless the kitchen was completely gutted and a brand-new one installed.

He walked into the living room and was about to relax on the couch and decide what to clean next when he heard the notification on his phone that someone was within range of the camara.

Taking out his cell phone, he pulled up the camera footage and saw Arden leaving her apartment.

Fuck. Where was she going? His eyes went to the time on the corner of his screen. It was fucking four thirty in the morning. He hadn't expected Arden to leave her apartment until a little after six.

Setting his coffee cup down, he grabbed his jacket and Cyrus's car keys, watching his phone until he saw Arden go down the steps before walking out his door.

He pocketed his cell phone and hid behind a pillar to observe the parking lot, from where he sighted Arden walking to her car. Doom had to hold back until she was in her car and pulling away from the building before he rushed down the steps to hightail it to the vehicle he had borrowed. Arden had made a right onto the road, so he put the car in drive to take off after her.

Retaining a decent distance, so as not to spook Arden, he took out his cell phone and called Wizard.

"What in the fuck do you want?" a groggy Wizard answered.

"Arden just left her apartment."

Doom heard several feminine groans before a more alert

Wizard came back on the phone.

"I thought she didn't have to be at work until seven?"

"Me, too. She's heading in the opposite direction. I'll text you when I find out where in the fuck she's going."

"I'm going to get dressed and wake Jesus and Buck up in case you need us. I'm going to get Puck to go ahead to Arden's place. Maybe she wanted to leave early because she was afraid the person who hit her knows her schedule and she's trying to be precautious. Maybe Puck will spot someone hanging around."

Doom almost told him not to bother waking Jesus and Buck up, but his gut instinct warned him to wait.

Observing the blinker on Arden's car, Doom slowed down his speed. He was beginning to recognize the area Arden was driving through.

"She's heading for Blue's school," he told Wizard.

"What in the fuck is she doing there?"

"How in the fuck do I know? She's pulling into the school parking lot. I've got to find a place to park where she won't see me. I'll text you when I find something out." He disconnected the call.

He made a U-turn at the end of the street, doubled back, and saw Arden had gotten out of her car and was walking toward the main door.

He pulled into the apartment complex across the street. Luckily, there was a space facing the school. Turning off the engine and lights, he watched Arden take out a set of keys and go inside.

He was tempted to get out of the car and make a beeline for the school, to knock on the door and ask Arden what the hell she was doing there, but forced himself to wait for a couple of minutes, actually thinking she would come right back out.

His curiosity got the better of him.

He got out of the car and walked across the apartment complex lot until he could cross the street to a darkened corner of the school property. Skirting a partial brick wall with the school name on it, Doom ducked behind a large tree then moved to another where he had a better view of the front of the school. He had just moved to another tree close to one of the classroom windows when he was nearly caught in the headlight of a car turning into the school parking lot.

Freezing in place, Doom watched as the car parked in the headmaster's spot. A man got out and started walking quickly toward the main door.

Was Arden about to get caught breaking and entering?

He was about to distract the man from entering when Arden came rushing outside the door so fast, he could hear the smack of her hands hitting the metal of the door.

"What are you doing here?"

The fear in Arden's voice had Doom taking another look at the man he had sized up as an uptight prick. Then he brought his eyes back to Arden, noticing she was holding a small canister in her hands, pointed at the headmaster.

Doom clenched his hands at his sides, wanting to tear the fuckwad apart at the fear he had glimpsed on Arden's face.

Cleaning hadn't been the only hack he had learned from his mother. He could recognize the signs of a woman who was terrified and prepared to fight back against a looming threat.

Doom did a doubletake at the headmaster. The fucker might be an uptight prick, but he was also the person responsible for attacking Arden.

CHAPTER 23

THE PLAN

"What are you doing here?"

Arden's shrill voice stilled him from making his presence known to the two people facing each other down.

The headmaster gave Arden a scowl, backing up a step. "I wanted to clear the air between us. You've refused to answer my calls and texts."

"There's nothing to clear. It's hard not to understand you planned to kidnap me, and when I tried to get away, you hit me several times to force me into your car."

"I was trying to help you—"

"My tires didn't get flattened on their own. A friend of mine had them checked out. They had been knifed."

"I didn't—"

"You did... Just like you're responsible for me having to use my original spare."

"You live in a cesspool. Someone there could have—"

"They could have, but they didn't. *You* did."

Doom saw the headmaster's face become more infuriated each time Arden spoke.

"There's no proof, and that's what counts." The headmaster's disposition changed when he dropped the pretense of innocence. "No one would believe I tried to kidnap you. Look at you... You're ugly as fuck, live where known drug dealers live, and spend every night at a biker bar. You surround yourself with disgusting individuals who aren't fit to wipe my shoes."

"How do you know where I spend my time? Funny, you've made it your business to know everything about me, despite how unattractive you think I am."

"Of course, I had to check you out," the headmaster sneered. "I'm responsible for the welfare of every student who walks through the school's doors. I was chancing my job already by allowing you to take over your father's job before his retirement. I needed to make sure me feeling sorry for your father's circumstances didn't place any of my students in danger."

"Yet even after you found out I live in a *cesspool*," Arden mocked, "and I was going to a biker bar, you didn't back out of our arrangement."

"Only because of your father. He's been a valued employee for many years. I didn't want him to lose his retirement because he wasn't able to work due to his health. The retirement, don't forget, you begged me for my help, which you are now jeopardizing if you don't keep your mouth shut. I might lose my job by allowing you to work here, but your father will be the one who would have to repay the insurance money, which has been paid out fraudulently on his behalf."

Doom could tell the fucker's threats were getting to her when she started lowering the pepper spray.

"I'm not going to say anything as long as you stay away from me."

"I have every intention of doing just that—" the headmaster held out his hand, "as soon as you give me the school keys."

Arden jumped a step back at the movement. "How can I get inside the school in the mornings?"

"I have no intention of jeopardizing my career any longer. Your father will be officially terminated today unless he comes to work. It's the most I'm willing to do. My compassion has ended."

"My father isn't stable enough for him to work..." Arden words came out in a low whisper, as if she had the air knocked out of her.

"I would look into getting him on disability."

"If he applies for disability, he won't get his retirement... We were going to apply for disability after he retires."

"I guess he won't have the best of two worlds now, will he?"

Doom wanted to rip the fucker a new asshole at the cold-blooded comeback. The only thing holding him back was the security cameras mounted along the school.

"I want the keys."

Doom had to curb the instinct to interfere, remaining out of sight as Arden reached into her pocket to hand the keys over.

"Good." A satisfied smile crossed to the headmaster's face as he took the keys. "Would you prefer to tell your father about his employment, or should I?" The fuckwad just had to rub salt into the wound.

"I'll do it," Arden said, moving to the side as the headmaster moved toward the front door.

"Very well. Tell your father the school wishes him the best, and he will be missed."

Arden stood outside, staring at the door for several

minutes. Turned the way she was, Doom couldn't see her face until she turned, but then he could see her defeated expression. She had tears running down her cheeks.

A cold rage filled him at the way Arden had been treated. The fuckwad was already going to pay a price for hitting Arden. Now he had cemented his fate by putting the blame on Arden for not sticking to the agreement they must have come to, to work in her father's place until he could retire.

As Arden drove away, Doom carefully stuck to the shadows until he could cross the street back to Cyrus's car. He got inside and started in the direction Arden had taken. Trailing her until she made it to her day job, he waited until he saw her walk inside, carrying a change of clothes, before reaching for his cell phone.

"What'd you find out?" Wizard asked without preamble.

Doom told him everything he had overheard.

"Damn," Wizard swore. "That fucker is a piece of work. He tried to kidnap her—we both know what he intended to do—and then he put the blame on her when he didn't fucking succeed."

"How do you want to handle it?" Doom broke into the string of curses coming from the other end of his phone.

"We need to do something before he terminates Arden's father."

"No shit. Any suggestions?"

"Several, just none where we can do it in the school without having a SWAT team called out on us."

The line went silent for several seconds.

"Does Pepper still live in the apartments across from the school?" Wizard asked.

"Yeah."

"Text me her phone number."

"You want me to stay on Arden or head back to the school?"

"Head back to the school. The brothers and I will meet you at Pepper's apartment."

"You have a plan?" Doom did something he rarely did—he smiled.

"Yes. By time we're done with the fuckwad, he's going to be the one applying for disability."

CHAPTER 24

THE PEPPER

The brothers were already at Pepper's place when Doom arrived. He took the flyers he had made and got out of the car. That Wizard was as angry as him was evident by the amount of the brothers' cars in the parking lot.

He knocked on the door, and Puck answered to let him inside.

The apartment was full.

Spotting Wizard sitting on the couch, he made his way over.

"You got it?"

Doom handed him the flyers.

Wizard studied the flyers before raising his eyes. "Good job. Pepper!"

A door to the side opened at Wizard's yell. Pepper left her bedroom to the appreciative stares of the brothers. Her mid-length black hair fell to her shoulders, accenting the red crop top she was wearing. The sound of her metal link belt wrapped around her waist could be heard as she walked to where Wizard was sitting.

"You have them?" she asked.

Wizard handed her the sheaf of flyers. "You know what to do?"

Pepper gave Wizard a sultry wink. "Sure do. Piece of cake. Hand out the flyers to the kids going to school. Don't stop until Snotty Pants comes out, and then convince him to come back here for a quickie."

"Jesus and Puck will be watching from their car. He tries to take you anywhere else, give a signal, and they'll escort him the rest of the way."

Pepper gave him a thumbs-up before sashaying out the door.

Doom wanted to head to the window but didn't want to give their target a reason to raise any suspicions if he was sighted from outside. Wizard must have been as impatient as he was, taking out his cell phone.

"What's going on, Jesus?" Wizard put the call on speakerphone so they all could hear.

"Pepper just got to the parking lot and is handing out the flyers to the students."

He and the brothers listened along on the call without further updates.

"An old gargoyle is coming out. Pepper is ignoring her and keeps handing them out," Jesus informed them. "The gargoyle is giving up and going back inside."

Minutes passed before Jesus had all of them on edge.

"He's coming out. Pepper is doing her thing." Jesus gave a low, admiring whistle. "She's working those tits like a fly swatter. They're coming."

"Four minutes." Buck rose off the stool he was sitting on to pop his knuckles. "It's not her best record, but it's not bad considering she couldn't show him her tits with the kids around."

Buck rambled over to place himself behind the door, while Doom and the rest of the brothers moved to the other side of the room so when Pepper opened the door, the head-master wouldn't see them until the door was closed behind him.

Wizard remained seated with his legs sprawled out and his ankles crossed at the feet.

Doom's anticipation quickened when he heard the doorknob turn. Positioned next to Buck, he felt his body coil to strike if the headmaster bolted before the door was closed.

Pepper walked in the door first.

"This is my home sweet home. The sub-lease would only be for a year..." Pepper stepped further into the room.

"I can't continue to let you give out the flyers advertising the sub-lease, but I can post it on our online newsletter." The headmaster set one foot inside the door.

Doom didn't give him a chance to set the other one down, jerking him forward by using the necktie tucked neatly into his suit.

A feminine scream came from the fucker at being dragged off his feet and barreled into his chest. Doom glared down at the terror-stricken man.

"What—"

Without a word, Doom frog-marched the stunned man toward Wizard, where he released him, then stepped back.

The rest of the brothers made a circle, preventing any attempt of escape. Fear-filled eyes swept over them.

Disappointment filled him when the headmaster made no attempt to run.

"I don't have much cash on me." He reached into his pocket and pulled out his wallet. "You can have it." The headmaster held out his wallet toward Wizard.

When Wizard stood, Doom took another step back.

A swoosh of air escaped the man when Wizard's fist struck him forcefully in the solar plexus. He sunk to his knees, and the wallet dropped next to him.

"Stand up, you piece of shit."

The headmaster, still struggling to breathe, tried unsuccessfully to get to his feet.

"Help him," Wizard ordered.

Doom used the collar of his shirt to raise the man to his feet.

"Doom, is this the shithead who was stupid enough to call a member of our club ugly after he was unable to fucking rape her?"

"Yes," Doom answered.

"I didn't try to rape her," the headmaster wheezed out. "It was a misunderstanding."

"It didn't sound like a misunderstanding to me. Sounds more like you gaslighted her to cover your own ass. But maybe I'm wrong..." Wizard's cold smile had a chill running down Doom's back, and he wasn't the one on the receiving end.

"Repeat the conversation, Doom. Let the brothers decide."

The headmaster turned his head in surprise as Doom repeated the conversation, word for word.

"Did you record our conversation?"

Doom shook his head. "I didn't have to. I have an eidetic memory. I heard every fucking word you said to Arden."

"What do you think, brothers?" Wizard said, reclaiming everyone's attention.

"Yeah, he gaslit her." Buck was the first to speak up. The others followed suit in agreement.

"I didn't try to rape her—"

"How did you know Arden was going to our clubhouse unless you were trailing her?" Wizard blocked any further excuse the headmaster was going to lie about. "You aren't talking to someone afraid you'll drop an ax on one of my relatives."

"I've done nothing but help Arden out of a bad situation," he gasped out.

"Really? That isn't how I'm looking at it. You one of those sick fuckers who likes to kidnap and rape women you come in contact with, and they're too afraid to report your ass?"

The headmaster looked too afraid to answer.

"I think Arden isn't the first woman you've tried this bullshit on, not with a whole building full of women teachers you come in contact with every day. I think you've done it before. I don't think Arden is your first victim." Wizard's fist came out again, hitting the headmaster's jaw so hard two teeth flew out of his mouth as he crumbled to the ground. The uptight prick lay on the floor, sobbing, his face marked by Wizard's fist in the same area Arden's had been.

"But she will be your last. Doom, your turn."

Bending down, Doom jerked him by his hair to force his head up to stare into his face. "Have you fired Arden's father yet?"

"I was working on his paperwork when my secretary told me a woman was handing out flyers."

"Here's what you're going to do. The paperwork is going to be torn up and thrown away. Arden's father is going to get his retirement, isn't he?"

"Yes," he sobbed out.

"Where's your cell phone?"

The headmaster reached into his suit pocket for his phone, then held it out.

"Text Arden; tell her you've had a change of heart. Apologize to her for trying to kidnap her, that you have mental health issues, and after her father retires, you'll be resigning to work on your emotional well-being."

The prick tried to shake his hair loose from the hold Doom had on him. "I'm not going to resign—"

Keeping his hold on the motherfucker, Doom used his other hand to pull out the gun tucked into the back of his waistband, placing it against his temple.

"Oh… I think you will," Doom told him coldly. "You piece of shit. I can bury you where no one will ever find what is left of you. You should thank God I'm giving you this offer instead of putting a bullet in your motherfucking head. I still might if I find out you have hurt another woman, and you better believe I will be watching. I know people capable of finding out when you took your last shit."

He started crying harder. "Arden can come back—"

"Fuck no." Doom shook his head. "Arden isn't taking one step near you or that school."

"Who's going to clean the school? I won't be able to hire someone until her father's retirement goes through."

"Then I guess you're going to be taking out the trash yourself." Doom pressed the barrel of the gun harder against his skull. "I want you to remember how fucking scared you are at this moment because if you ever—and I fucking mean *ever*—come near Arden again, I'll put a fucking bullet in your head so fast you won't even be able to take a last shit." Doom gave a last jerk of his hand before removing his hand to rise.

"Start texting." Doom placed his gun back in his waistband.

He and the brothers watched as the frightened man texted Arden.

"Let me see before you send."

When he handed the phone to him, Doom read the text and pressed *send* then let it drop back to the floor next to the beaten man's knees. Wrinkling his nose, he took another step away.

"You might need to call your secretary and tell her you need to take the rest of the day off. You stink from where you shit yourself."

Managing to get to his feet, the headmaster warily looked at the men blocking his path to the door. "Can I leave now?"

Wizard motioned for the brothers to move aside. "Go."

As he stumbled forward, each of the brothers landed punches on his ribs, sending him back and forth down the line until Buck opened the door to toss him outside.

Wizard cast him a disappointed glance. "I wouldn't have taken it so easy on him if I hadn't expected you to fuck him up more."

"I couldn't." Doom shrugged. "The only thing that saved that motherfucker was I knew his secretary would find the paperwork on his desk, and I didn't want Pepper, Arden, or her father blamed if that sick fuck disappeared *today*."

Wizard cocked his head to the side questioningly, his lips quirking in amusement. "Today?"

Doom nodded, answering the silent question he could see in Wizard's eyes. "Tomorrow is another day."

CHAPTER 25

THE SPRAY

Arden had to reread the text several times, still not believing she had read it right. She didn't believe the headmaster had a change of heart any more than she believed there was a man in the moon. Had he been afraid the school cameras had caught him on tape hitting her? She doubted that. He was smart enough to have a well-thought out plan in place before attempting to kidnap her. He had probably erased the footage or made sure the camera wasn't working before slashing her tires.

Don't look a gift horse in a mouth. She tried to dispel the trepidation she was feeling at the text. Was he trying to lure her into another attempt?

Setting her phone down, she resumed her work, debating what to do next. She waited until her lunch hour before she looked at her phone again.

Thank you. Should I stop by the school after I get off work to pick up the keys? she texted.

Her sandwich lodged in her throat when her phone pinged with a text.

No. I will take care of the cleaning. There is no need to come to the school. I think it best if we keep our distance.

Arden was in total agreement. She hadn't been looking forward to having to see him again. The only reason she would have willingly put herself in his vicinity was for her father.

She finished her lunch and left the lunchroom, and as she passed a table where several women were sitting, the way Haven stared at her had her looking back curiously. If stares could kill, she would be fileted and fried.

Thankfully, they worked in different areas of the building, and the only interactions they had were when Haven would have to escort a patient down to her department.

With the relief of not having to go to her parents' house to tell her father he wouldn't be getting his retirement off her shoulders, the rest of the day passed uneventfully.

After work, she headed to her hostess job. Mondays were normally slow at the restaurant, but it was packed when she arrived.

Mama looked her over with an assessing look when she clocked in. "You're looking better."

Arden came up behind Mama as she rolled out the thick dough onto the counter to wrap her arms around her. "I am. Everything is good," she assured her. "There isn't anything for you to worry about anymore."

"If that is true, then you shouldn't have a problem telling me who hit you."

"We're going to forgive and forget."

Mama gave a sarcastic snort. "Italians never forget."

Arden gave her another hug. "I love you."

"Get to work. You're irritating me."

Laughing, Arden left Mama alone. Relieving Andrea, she soon had most of the waiting customers seated.

Unable to take a break until nine, she decided to forego her dinner break and end her shift early when the restaurant emptied out.

"You calling it a night?" Mama asked, placing a pan of knots in the commercial oven.

"If you don't mind. The tables are empty, and I finished rolling the silverware for tomorrow."

"Go. There's half a pan of lasagna left. Take it home."

Arden didn't argue, knowing it would be useless. She wrapped the lasagna to go and placed it in a bag. Mama shoved several more containers inside before she could close the bag.

"I'm going to have to buy a new wardrobe if you don't quit giving me so much food."

"I'm doing you a favor. Men want women with meat on their bones."

"In what century? In this one, they want you to be a size zero and have boobs the size of cantaloupes."

"Then you're halfway there," Mama joked.

"Kill me," Arden joked back. "See you tomorrow. Make sure you leave with Rocco. I don't want you staying by yourself."

"I'm having an early night myself. I have a date."

That stopped her in her tracks. Her friend hadn't had a date in six months, when she had broken it off with a man she had dated for several months.

"Who with?"

"Someone you don't know."

"Who with?" Arden repeated.

"Okay, I met him on Tumbler."

"Natalia... I told you no more dating sites. The last one you went out with stole your wallet."

Mama took off her apron. "I'm taking precautions this time."

"What precautions?" she asked suspiciously.

"Rocco is going to follow us and come inside the bar we're meeting at."

"Then I suppose that's okay."

Mama gave her a big hug, nearly lifting her off her feet. "You are like a little sister to me." Putting her back on her feet, she gave her a kiss on both cheeks.

"Little?" Arden laughed. "Have you sampled the wine?"

Mama's eyes narrowed on her. "I don't like it when you put yourself down."

"Yes, Mama." Pretending to be chastised, Arden blew her a kiss as she headed out the door. "Have fun."

As she drove home, the smell of the food in the car had her stomach growling. She regretted not eating earlier but forced herself to imagine getting in the dress she had purchased online. It had been meant as an incentive to get herself on a diet, which she swore every day she would stick to until she went into the restaurant only to have her willpower smashed into smithereens.

Once in her apartment, she put the food in the refrigerator and took out the salad she had prepared the day before.

Still hungry and clinging to minuscule willpower, struggling to survive, she decided to wash a load of clothes instead of tearing into the food she had brought home.

She went into her bedroom to pick up the basket of dirty clothes, placing the detergent on top before she headed toward the door.

Locking the door behind her, she carried the basket downstairs, waving at a couple who were sitting outside their apartment door, smoking a cigarette.

"How's it going?" she called out to them.

"Not bad," the woman replied. "Andy and I were thinking about going to the convenient store. You need anything?"

"No, I'm good. Thanks for asking, Lizzy."

"Can you spare a couple of quarters?"

At the question, Arden took out the roll of quarters she kept at the bottom of the laundry basket. Balancing the basket, she peeled several quarters from the pack to hand to the woman who had quickly gotten up to walk over to her.

"This enough to get what you want?"

Lizzy gave her grateful smile. "I only needed a couple."

Arden smiled back. "That way, you can buy you both a beer."

Lizzy and her boyfriend took off to get their beers while she made her way to the laundry room, which was next to the front office.

The room being empty didn't bother her. She was used to washing her clothes this time of night. She knew it wasn't safe, which was why she kept her pepper spray within easy reach as she loaded the washing machine. She started the cycle then picked the basket up to leave the room. She had lost several baskets before, so she'd lost the trust to leave them until she returned.

Bounding up the steps, she unlocked her door and went inside.

She took a shower and dressed in loose sweatpants and an oversized pajama top that used to belong to her father. He had lost so much weight after his heart surgery, her mother had been about to throw it away when she had asked for it. She didn't bother to put her bra back on when all she was going to do was finish her laundry and go to bed.

After brushing out her damp hair, she went into her

bedroom check the time. Then, gathering her basket and pepper spray, she went outside to retrieve her clothes. She had a foldable laundry rack the clothes would dry on placed under the heating vent, so the clothes would be dry before morning.

She removed the clothes and placed them in the basket before heading back out the door, but when she turned to the left, she rammed into a body that was rushing toward the door at the same time.

Startled, her survival instincts kicked in at the same time as a flashback of being attacked by her brother's headmaster had her raising the pepper spray to press the button. Closing her eyes to prevent the spray from burning them, she began madly swinging the basket of clothes toward her assailant.

"What the fuck!" a familiar voice roared. "Arden, stop! It's me, Doom!" A furious move ripped the spray out of her hand.

Her eyes sprang open, and she saw Doom's face was filled with a mixture of agonizing pain and fury.

"What are you doing here?"

CHAPTER 26

THE RETALIATION

"I live here."

Arden dropped the basket she had been swinging at Doom. "I'm so sorry," she gasped out at his reddened eyes. Then she grabbed one of his arms and started urging him along the small walkway to the steps. "Don't you know not to startle a woman in the middle of the night?"

His furious face turned toward her, making her cringe at seeing the pain she had inflicted on him.

"How was I supposed to know you were coming out at the same time I was coming in to check on you?" he snarled.

She led Doom up the steps and managed to take her keys out of her sweatpants. Opening her apartment door, she ushered him toward the kitchen sink. She turned the faucet on and maneuvered him closer.

"Bend down," she instructed.

"So you can drown me?" he snapped snidely, but did as told.

"Don't be ridiculous. It's not like I meant to hurt you. You just scared me because it's so late at night."

"What in the fuck are you doing washing your clothes at this time of night, anyway?"

Arden started splashing cold water on his eyes. "It's the only time the machines aren't full."

"Yeah... Because they don't want their bodies found in the morning."

"No one would hurt me here."

"*No one would hurt me,*" he mimicked her. "Be fucking real. There isn't a fucker here who wouldn't cut off your body parts to make a fucking dime."

"That's not true." She continued to splash water on his face, then opened a drawer to take out a clean dish cloth. Soaking the cloth, she placed it in his hands. "Here, press this to your face but don't rub. Take off your shirt. I'll be right back. I'm going to find you something to wear."

She rushed to her bedroom and opened a drawer in her bureau, taking out a large T-shirt that her father used to wear, then carried it back to the kitchen. Her hands went to the towel pressed to Doom's face.

"Let me see."

Doom resisted her effort, asking, "Where's the pepper spray?"

She wanted to bop him with the shirt but resisted the urge.

"I must have dropped it when I realized it was you."

Doom lowered the hand towel.

Arden tried controlling her expression at the sight of his swollen eyes.

"How bad is it?"

"Perhaps I should drive you to the emergency room."

Doom turned the water back on and lowered his head back under the stream.

"It'll wear off. I'm not going to the emergency room. The brothers would never let me live it down."

"That's ridiculo—"

"Arden—calling me ridiculous while my eyes feel as if they've had a hot poker stuck in them might not be in your best interest."

"Okay... You don't have to be so snippy. Jesus... I said I'm sorry. When did you move in, anyway?"

"Yesterday."

"I thought you have a room at the club?"

"I gave it up. Looking for a place anyway, I thought I'd check out where you told me you lived. Imagine my surprise when I pulled in across the street only to find out you live in this dump. Since I'm such a good guy I decided to sacrifice my own comfort to play bodyguard to you."

"How are your eyes?" she returned sarcastically. "They look like they hurt."

A small shriek escaped her when Doom wrapped his hand around her neck, jerking her into his chest.

"Little girl—be very careful. I'm about one centimeter away from me showing you just what I fucking mean. Did you even fucking think before you barged into The Last Riders' clubhouse? If you had come barging into any other biker hangout the way you did ours, you wouldn't be standing here; you'd still be at the other club, being used by anyone with a hard-on." He gave a sarcastic laugh, which had her recoiling from his touch. Doom turned sideways and pressed her body into the kitchen counter, preventing her escape.

"They would have laughed in your face when you threatened to call the cops. You were naïve as fuck when you thought I wasn't going to rape you because it was an office and not a bedroom. If you've learned nothing else since you've started coming to the club, you should know we don't need a bedroom to fuck.

"But coming to The Last Riders' club is the least of your screwups," he growled disdainfully. "You moved into what can only be classified as a shithole, filled with sketchy motherfuckers. I could break your door down with a shove of my shoulder, much less an addict needing money for his next fix. You think because you're nice to them, they'll leave you alone? They'll slit your throat and party next to your fucking body. The only reason I'm willing to bet they haven't is because Mama sent the Yeti over here to threaten the motherfucking hell out of them."

Arden became confused. "Who? I don't know any Yeti."

"It's just a name I made up for him. The fucker who came to the club Saturday with a bat, the one the size of a yeti."

"You mean Rocco?"

Doom's face became even more caustic. "Of course, that's the fucker's name. I should have known. He's the size of a boulder. What's he to Mama?"

"They've been in a relationship ever since I've known them." Being protective, Arden kept their true relationship to herself. Wizard seemed too interested in her friend for it to just be curiosity. Mama was a beautiful woman; it wouldn't be the first time someone tried to pry information out of her to get an advantage.

"She ever hook up with any other men?"

Maybe Wizard wasn't the only one interested.

"Never," she said truthfully. "She's a one-man woman. Of course, you can try your luck. Good luck with that."

"I would if I were interested. I'm not."

"You seem interested." Arden could have kicked herself for not dropping it.

Doom's red eyes bore down into hers. "Women like Mama don't attract me. I prefer women I don't have to worry will pull out a knife if we get in an argument. I like to keep everything casual, without the expectation of us being in an exclusive relationship. I don't want to be hooked into a relationship. I'm thirty-six; I won't get serious about a woman for at least ten more years. By then, I'll be ready to settle down in a long-term relationship and have a couple of kids."

Arden couldn't believe the gall of the man to stand there, basically revealing all he wanted from a woman was sex. Why was she even shocked? It should be The Last Riders' motto.

"Then I can definitely say Mama isn't your type of woman. Cheating is a hard no for her."

Doom's fingers started caressing the nape of her neck. "Forget Mama." His voice lowered seductively. "How about you, Arden? What's your hard no?"

CHAPTER 27
THE GUESS

"Does it matter?" Arden tried to sidle to the left to escape from the heat of his body. Doom had removed his shirt while she'd been in the bedroom. With his jeans hanging low on his hips, she found it hard to keep her eyes on his face instead of letting them roam free.

"Just curious."

The smile Doom gave her heated her feminine coil like tinder. She nearly reached to the side to turn the faucet on and splash some cold water on her face. Squashing down the raging hormones threatening to make a fool out of her, she mulishly jutted out her chin, which had his head going back. *Guess he's still skittish after getting pepper sprayed*, she thought antagonistically.

"All right, then. I'll tell you. A hard no for me is not getting involved with men like you."

Arden felt Doom tense against her.

"You think, by stating the obvious, you'll get a quickie without any woman expecting anything more from you, other than having the pleasure of having sex with you? Am I supposed to feel challenged to get you to break your ten-year plan? Or was that the same sewage you tell all women before you have sex with them, so when you get bored and it gets too messy for you, you can say, *Hey, remember when I told you not to take me seriously*? Please..." Arden drawled out sarcastically. "You think I haven't heard that crap before? Look at me. I'm not exactly Miss America. I'm used to men not seeing me, or if they do, I'm supposed to be an easy lay for them to get their rocks off instead of them using their hands."

Arden glared up at him. "I didn't need you to reiterate that you, or *any* of The Last Riders, are emotionally unavailable. Hell, the rules about how to become a member for the women says it for you guys.

"What's the matter, Doom? Since you no longer live at the club and don't have the women there at your beck and call, you want me to make myself available to you outside of the club? Worried it might bite you in the ass because you said I wouldn't get your vote, and you'd be able to keep the members from finding it out you're hitting it on the side?"

She lifted her hands to push at his chest. "So help me God, if you don't let me go, I'm going to show you how well I protect myself. And by the time I'm done, your eyes won't be the only thing hurting!"

Amusement filling his face, Doom held his hands up and met her fiery gaze. "I believe you."

Realizing she had dropped the shirt, she bent down to pick it up and handed it to him.

He took the shirt and started to put it on then paused, his eyes dropping to the pajama top she was wearing. "Whose shirt is this and the one you're wearing?"

She stared at him in confusion. "They're mine."

"These are men's clothes."

Sure she was mistaken at the jealous tone in his voice,

Arden couldn't figure out why it mattered. "They were my father's."

He slid on the shirt and crossed his arms over his chest. "You have any food? I haven't had the chance to go to the grocery store yet."

She moved toward the refrigerator, took out the to-go containers she had brought home, and handed them to Doom. "Knock yourself out."

When he set the containers on the counter, she assumed he wanted to check to see if he wanted to eat the food in the containers or ask for something else. Frowning, she started to tell him beggars can't be choosers when he started putting the foil containers in the oven. He turned the oven on, then went to the fridge to take out a soda, making himself at home.

"Doesn't your apartment have an oven?" she asked with raised brows, hoping he would take the hint and leave.

"Yes, but I haven't had time to clean it yet."

Any protest she was about to make about his rude behavior withered and died at remembering the disgusting mess she had found when she had moved in.

She could excuse his bad manners since his eyes were still red and probably still stinging for him not to want to go out to drive to the nearby convenient store.

Doom opened the soda can while moving to take a chair at the small table, which she had bought at a thrift store.

"Bad?" she sympathized.

"They're stinging, but at least they don't feel as if you took a fucking blowtorch to them."

Arden grimaced at the graphic description.

"How this whole apartment building hasn't been condemned blows my fucking mind."

She had to agree with him. When she had moved in, it

had taken her three days to clean her apartment, gagging most of the time. The previous renter had lived there ten years and had been a hoarder.

"Probably because no one complains."

"Did you?"

"No."

"Why not?"

Arden pulled the food out of the oven and set it down on the table. Then she went to a cabinet to get him a plate and fork.

"You don't want any?" he asked when she set the lone plate down.

"No, it's all yours. I ate before I washed my cloth—" Arden broke off, realizing her laundry basket and wet clothes were still outside the laundry room.

"Where are you going?"

Arden stopped to explain her rush to the door. "I left my—"

A knock at her door had her opening it without looking through the peephole.

"What in the fuck are you doing?" Doom yelled, jumping up.

"Answering the door, obviously." She felt bad as the snide remark left her lips. Maybe he was having trouble seeing.

Lizzy was on the other side of the door, her eyes darting to the side when Doom came stalking up behind her. "I found these outside on the walkway." She took the basket from Andy, who was standing out of sight next to her door. Lizzy gave Doom a provocative smile as she handed her the basket of clothes.

"Thanks, Lizzy."

Rudely nudging his body in front of hers, Doom maneuvered her back enough to shut the door in the couples' faces.

"They were being nice." Arden angrily carried the basket of clothes to the bathroom to lay the damp clothes on the drying rack. Fuming, she returned to the kitchen to see Doom unaffected by her anger, eating the heated food.

His steady gaze lifted to hers when she sat down at the table across at him. Fuming, she was tempted to take the food away from him.

"He was going to rush through the door if I hadn't been here." Doom casually reached out for another garlic knot.

"No, he wasn't," she argued back sharply.

"Then why was he standing to the side where he couldn't be seen?"

"I don't know, and neither do you."

"Have they come to your apartment before?"

"Not when I'm here. Other than for sleeping, I'm not here much," she admitted.

"Which I'm willing to bet is the only reason you are still alive to tell the tale."

His sarcasm was grating on her nerves.

"You feel this place is such a dump, why don't you move out?"

Doom derisively put his fork down to steeple his fingers, as if he were trying to keep from strangling her. "Three guesses. And the first two don't count."

As she stared at him blankly, it took her a full minute to comprehend what he was telling her.

"You seriously moved in here because of *me*?"

CHAPTER 28

THE HEARTBREAKER

The mixture of feelings crossing Arden's face had Doom hiding his amusement. Unaware he knew the real truth about what had happened to her, it was plain the full realization of the lies she had told The Last Riders were the reason he was there.

Doom couldn't resist letting her dig the hole she had dug herself even deeper.

"No one fucks with a Last Rider and gets away scot-free."

"You moved in here to protect me." She wasn't questioning him this time. Arden said the words as if she needed to reinforce just how badly she had screwed up. "I just thought you were trying to scare me for washing my clothes so late."

"I moved in here so The Last Riders could find out who attacked you and return the favor."

"You should have told me. I would have told you it was unnecessary. It was a simple misunderstanding, which I have taken care of on my own."

He resumed eating. "Exactly how have you done that?"

Arden's lips parted like a fish searching for water. Doom supposed she was having a problem coming up with a believable lie. Being the nice guy he was, he decided to save her the effort.

"Did you bust Blue's headmaster's lip and give him a black eye?"

Her shoulders slumped in defeat. "No."

"I didn't think so. When I saw him this morning, he didn't have a mark on him. Of course, the last time I saw him, I can't say the same."

Arden's face went pale. "You hurt him?"

"I didn't lay a hand on him. Wizard, on the other hand, had a field day."

A shaky hand went to her face. "You don't know what you have done."

Doom leaned back his chair. "Chill. Your father's retirement is safe. Didn't he text you that it was?"

"Yes, but—"

"There aren't any buts. Your father's retirement will go through as planned. Blue will even have a new headmaster."

"He's going to quit?"

"It was better for his physical health to come to that decision."

"How badly was he hurt?"

"Does it matter?" he asked curiously.

"What if he presses charges? I don't want any of The Last Riders going to jail for taking up for me when what we were doing was illegal."

"You were doing it for your family, while that shitbag used it as an opportunity to attack you and keep you under his control."

Shamed filled her expression. "He was only able to

because I gave him the opportunity by asking him to commit fraud."

"Whose idea was it for you to take over your father's job?"

"His, when I went by the school after he called to tell Dad he had used all his sick leave."

"I bet you jumped at his solution."

Nodding, she bit her lip. "I'm ashamed to say I did. I could have swung financially supporting my parents without my dad's salary and the pension he had coming to him, but there was no way I would have been able to pay their medical bills. Dad's are astronomical, and Mom's are almost as high."

The more Arden revealed, the angrier he became. She was damn lucky to have escaped what the headmaster had planned for her. Doom would bet his last dollar, if he had succeeded in his attack, Arden wouldn't have pressed charges, and it was a big *if* the fucker had let her live.

There was no way it was the first time the headmaster had pulled that stunt. He had put his ducks in a row to carefully keep from being caught. That attention to detail only came with experience.

Burn was using his contacts to find more personal information on the headmaster. Any hint there was a victim, and The Last Riders would make damn sure atonement would be taken for them as well.

"You don't have to worry about it any longer. Your dad's retirement will go through without any hiccups."

"You don't know how much of a relief that will be, not having to talk to him again. He creeps me out, but I thought I was imagining it. I had no clue he could act that way."

She sighed. "How long of a lease did you sign?"

"Monthly."

"You should ask Wizard for your room back at the club. There isn't any need for you to stay here."

"Wizard's already given it to Hawk."

"I feel terrible that you gave up your room."

From her expression, Doom could tell she meant it.

"I can find you a better place to live," she offered.

"There is no need—" Doom started to tell her he wouldn't be staying in Ohio much longer.

"You don't need to be worried about me living here much longer. It was nice of you to be concerned about me. I'll finish this month out and move back into my parents' home. There's no need for me to live here any longer."

Keeping the fact to himself it was a club decision to protect her by moving here, Doom looked at her questioningly. "Then you do think they were going to rob you."

Arden looked at him in confusion. "You mean Lizzy and Andy?"

Doom nodded.

"They weren't going to rob me. You're mistaken."

"Okay..." he drawled out. It didn't matter, anyway. She would be moving out. "Then what changed your mind about living here?"

"I only moved here so my parents wouldn't notice what time of the morning I had to leave to clean the school."

"They didn't know you had taken over your dad's job?"

"No, my father would never have let me. It would have hurt his pride too much."

"Your mother?"

"Yes, but I didn't want to put her in the position of lying to my father. She would have understood about me protecting Dad."

Fuck. Doom stared across the table at her. He didn't want

to admire the lengths Arden had gone to for her parents. He'd already been fighting the losing battle because she came to the club when she had been concerned for Blue. Pinning his hopes she was just a thorn in his side until he could work it out or when Train called him up for duty, he was beginning to become concerned nothing other than fucking her out of his system would work to drive her out of his mind.

Imagining her on her knees in his bed, with him fucking her until she was screaming in pleasure, had his dick going rock hard.

He got to his feet and carried the empty food containers to the trash can, putting the fork and plate in the sink. "Thanks for the food. I need to hit the road. Make sure you lock up after me," he snapped, coming out from behind the counter.

"Okay. I guess I'll see you tomorrow at the club when I work." Rising from the table at the abrupt way he was moving, Arden followed him to the door.

It took all his willpower not to slam her against the door and kiss her until she begged him to fuck her.

Doom stopped in his tracks. His willpower could only hold out so long, and every instinct in his gut was telling him to stay the fuck away from her. Viper, Razer, Knox... All the brothers had bit the dust when they had fucked the wrong type of woman, and Arden was the wrong type of woman for him. Everything about her screamed commitment, wedding rings, kids, and a picket fence. The only commitment he wanted at this point of life was to get the position he had busted his ass to qualify for.

"We don't need you tomorrow night."

"Then when—"

"Look, Arden, I'm just going to be straight up with you.

The Last Riders don't want you. Save yourself the drive and stay home."

Arden looked as if he had struck her in the face. She should be jumping up and down at getting off the hook. Instead, she looked just as upset as she had that morning when the headmaster had told her he wasn't going to get her dad his retirement.

"See you around." Without glancing back, Doom rushed through the door, snapping it closed behind him. Instead of going to his apartment, he went down the steps to the parking lot. He had switched the car for his bike when they had returned to the club earlier that day.

Starting the bike, he took off, needing to clear his mind. The wind hitting his face calmed the arousal racking his body. He got a firmer grip on the handlebars now that his hands had quit shaking.

He had come so close—so close to breaking... To becoming the one thing he had sworn never to do—to be a woman's heartbreaker.

CHAPTER 29

THE WRATH

"You told her what?"

Doom braced himself.

Wizard, who had been working on paperwork while sitting at the bar, turned sideways on the stool to look at him as if he'd misheard what Doom just said.

"I told Arden not to come into work, that The Last Riders didn't want her."

Wizard's face went artic. "Why?"

"She's wasting our time." He shrugged.

"Why do you give a fuck?" Wizard folded the papers he was working on.

"She hasn't gotten one vote since she's been coming here, has she?" He dodged telling the truth.

"As a matter of fact, I was going to give her mine. I was going to tell her when she came in."

Doom just had the wind knocked out of his carefully thought-out way of getting rid of Arden.

"How did she earn your vote?" he snapped.

He relaxed his hands when he realized Wizard had noticed him unconsciously clenching his fists.

When Wizard flipped the folded papers toward him, Doom picked them up to scan them. "Not only did Arden catch the wiring was bad behind the bar, she caught a vender shorting us on the beers on tap. It's untold how long that shit has been going on."

"Celeste didn't catch it?"

"No, and neither did Margarita nor Kat."

"Fuck."

"Yeah." Wizard raised two fingers at Kat, which had her reaching under the bar for the pack of cigarettes he kept there. She set the pack and lighter down before she hurried to the other end of the counter.

Doom guessed Kat had been catching hell for not counting the kegs as they were brought in when she was on duty before he came to the club.

It was not a good sign Wizard had asked for the cigarettes. At one time, Wizard was a two-packs-a-day smoker; now he only lit up when he was trying to prevent himself from breaking necks.

He lighted a cigarette, then his eyes narrowed on him through the smoke he blew out through pursed lips. "Arden —" Wizard took another hit of his cigarette, "has done more to benefit this club in the short time she's been here than any other motherfucker in this fucking bar." Wizard pointed the fingers holding his smoke at him. "You going to clean the urinal in the restroom the next time someone clogs it up when they throw up in it?"

Disgusted, Doom shook his head. "No."

"Arden did!" Wizard snapped. "That fucking urinal hasn't worked in a fucking year."

Doom's jaw firmed. "You always say we don't need anyone cleaning up after us," he reminded Wizard.

"Obviously, I was fucking wrong," Wizard snarled back.

"I like standing at the urinal to take a piss instead of having to go the bathroom in my room. Do you know how much a fucking plumber costs?" Wizard waved his fingers holding the cigarette at him again. "Which makes more sense economically? Paying for a fucking plumber or keeping Arden, who can fix shit around here for free, plus go grocery shopping for your fucking milk, and still be fucking willing to pour our fucking beer? But what fucking flips my chain is you took it upon yourself to cut her loose without my permission."

By the end of Wizard's tirade, many of the brothers started leaving to head to their rooms to avoid raising his wrath.

"Wizard..."

Wizard stood up from the stool and stabbed the cigarette out. "Office."

Already regretting telling Wizard what he had done before he was drunk off his ass, Doom followed him under the sympathetic gazes of the remaining brothers.

Wizard waited until he walked through the doorway before he slammed the door after them and angrily confronted him. "What in the fuck!?" he railed at him. "Since when do you pull shit like this?"

Doom moved farther into the room. "I didn't think it was a big deal. Usually, when one of us wants someone out before they become a full member, you say, 'Okay, I don't care.'"

"I fucking care this time. Arden was the only *in* I have with Natalia."

Ah... Now he understood why Wizard was blowing a gasket.

He started to tell Wizard he stood as much of a chance of hooking up with Natalia as shitting flowers out of his ass, but then decided against it when Wizard must have read his face.

"You got something to say?"

"No."

If Wizard wanted to chase after a woman who was more likely to slit his throat than fuck him, who was he to tell the brother not to go for it?

Blowing out a heavy, irritated sigh, Wizard threw himself down in the office chair. "Why'd you really blow her off?" he asked calmly.

"If she keeps coming around, I'm going to fuck her," he bluntly admitted.

"Then fuck her. What's the problem?"

"That's probably the same thing Razer, Viper, Knox—"

Wizard raised his hand to stop him. "Brother, I get it. None of us wants to follow them down that road."

"Not only that," Doom steamed ahead, "but we both know she isn't the type of woman who is going to have sex without expecting a relationship. I don't want to be the bastard who breaks her fucking heart when she realizes all I want to do is fuck her before I leave. Hell, you didn't give a rat's fart when I pulled the plug on Heaven coming around."

"Because Heaven flat-out said she didn't want to be a member. She only came on the weekends to be with you; it wasn't the club's decision to make. The same can't be said about Arden. Hell, is she even into you? From what little I've been around you and her, I didn't see her give you any special treatment, other than buy your fuckin' milk. I think you're worried about nothing."

Refraining from punching Wizard's snide face inside out, he curbed his own escalating temper.

"I don't want to chance it."

"I don't see why not," Wizard said blithely, unconcerned about Doom's desire to keep distance between him and Arden. "Could be wishful thinking on your part."

Doom wasn't about to confess he and Arden had shared a kiss that had set his dick on fire like they were in high school.

"Maybe." He shrugged. "Does it matter anymore? There's no way she will come back now."

Wizard gave him a steely look. "She will when you fix it."

Resolutely, Doom stared down at Wizard. "Nope. Count me out. You want her in the club, you convince her."

Wizard gave him a questioning glance. "You wouldn't have a problem if I or one of the other brothers took a run on persuading her back?"

Hell yes, he would; he just wasn't prepared to make Wizard aware of the fact. He could talk the other brothers out of going along with Wizard, but once Wizard set his mind on something he wanted, he never changed it. Wizard had set his sights on Natalia, and he needed Arden to make it happen. Doom tried to turn the table on him.

"What's the matter, Wizard? Seems to me you're the one who can't accept a woman isn't interested in you. I think we should both chalk up Arden and Natalia as losses and move the fuck on."

"Brother, remind me, have I ever asked your advice on whether or not it was worth to chase after a woman? It might be your forte to play the nice guy, but, brother, that ain't me." Wizard's voice had turned withering. "Now, are we going to be stepping on your balls if we ask Arden or not?"

He was trying to come up with a plausible reason, other

than jealousy, after Wizard had ground his nuts into dust, when a knock sound at the door.

"Come in," Wizard barked at the interruption.

Burn poked his head in the door. "Wanted to give you a heads-up that Arden came in about five minutes ago."

Wizard perked up. "Get her for me. Tell her I want to talk to her."

Doom was a second away from planting his fist in Wizard's gloating face when Burn opened the door wider.

"I will, as soon as she comes out of Buck's room. It might be a while."

CHAPTER 30
THE VOTES

Would they even let her in? Arden questioned herself as she walked toward the club door. It took every ounce of her determination to approach, expecting Jesus to deny her entry. Relief nearly had her knees buckling when he opened the door for her.

She went inside and waited to be greeted like she had the first time she came by, being told to leave. Instead, the members sitting around gave her welcoming smiles, which eased the anxiety that had almost kept her away.

Pretending a blasé attitude, she confidently strode toward the side of the bar where the bedrooms were. Coming to a stop at the door she remembered Buck had opened when Doom carried her to the office, Arden knocked.

"Yeah?"

Taking that as an invitation to come in, Arden opened the door.

Buck was lying on his bed, propped on a pillow, watching television. Surprise filled his face when he saw it was her.

She maneuvered herself in the tight space as she closed the door, asking, "Can I talk to you and Puck privately?"

Buck scooted off the side of his bed, took two steps, and banged on the wall before sitting back down to mute the television.

When she heard the doorknob turning, Arden had to sidle to the side of the bed to make room for Puck to enter.

Puck was just as surprised to see her as his brother had been, raising a questioning brow at Buck, who just shrugged. Puck shut the door and leaned back against it, waiting for Buck to tell him why he had been summoned.

The room was so small it was making her feel claustrophobic. It was nothing more than the size of a large closet, and the large bed Buck was reclining on took up most of the space.

Getting to the point before she lost her nerve, she glanced at both men. "I want your vote."

Puck leaned away from the door to take off his T-shirt, while Buck patted the space next to him.

Arden quickly shook her head as she reached into her purse to take out an envelope, handing it to Buck.

He took it, opened it, then pulled out what was inside. He lifted his head, staring at her, dumbfounded. "These are Super Bowl tickets."

"Yes. There's only one condition. You have to let Luc go with you."

Puck nearly knocked her onto the bed to take the tickets away from his brother. "Where did you get these?"

"My dad is a big football fan." Her eyes went to the tickets Puck was holding. "When the tickets went on sale, he bought them when Arizona was picked as host. He's originally from Arizona. He bought them for Luc, me, and himself."

"You're giving us your dad's and your tickets for our vote?" Puck started shaking his head. "We can't..." He tried to hand the tickets back to her.

Arden didn't take them and said, "Dad's too sick to go." She had to clear her husky voice before continuing. "We both know Luc would prefer going with you two than me. Besides, I can't leave my parents right now. So, you see, this works out for all three of us. That is... If you want to go. If you'd rather, I could ask Wizard and—"

"You have my vote." Puck tucked the tickets into his back pocket.

"Mine too."

"There is just one other small catch."

The two brothers stared at her dubiously.

"Who we gotta kill?" Buck asked matter-of-factly.

Arden couldn't help but laugh. "Nothing that extreme. I want you both to say I earned your votes by us having sex, like the rest of the women did. I want this to be our little secret." Her cheeks felt like they were on fire at the way they were looking at her.

"Are you asking us to lie to the brothers?" Buck asked.

"Yes."

Buck and Puck shared a silent glance before Buck grinned.

"We have no problem with that." His expression then turned grim. "But if we do, I better not hear you let it slip to anyone in the club it's a lie."

"I won't," she promised easily.

Keeping that promise will be a cake walk, she thought happily.

Puck was just as intent on making sure of the repercussions she would face if she didn't live up to her end of the bargain. "You rat us out—"

"I know you'll take your vote back," she finished, nodding understandingly.

"No." The normally goofy Puck she was used to disappeared, his visage changing into one that was almost unrecognizable. Sheer ruthlessness shone out of his eyes to the extent she shivered in the warm room. "There's no getting a vote back once it has been given," Puck told her. "Are you willing to make the lie a reality if you tell? We're ready to keep the lie if that's what you really want, but we won't have our faces rubbed into it that we lied to the brothers if you suddenly come clean. So, make sure you want to play it this way."

Her mind played back how callously Doom had told her none of The Last Riders wanted her, like a vicious recording.

"I won't. I swear."

Puck grinned and again became the man she was more comfortable with.

Arden caught sight of the speculative gaze Buck was giving her. "What?"

He leaned back on his pillow with the air of a big cat who just ate a deer for dinner. "Nothing."

Arden narrowed her eyes on him. She didn't trust the look he was giving her.

"Tell me what you're thinking." Was he going to back out?

"Nothing... Other than I've never known any woman able to keep a secret."

"Well, you do now." She raised her nose up haughtily.

"All right. Then—" Buck's gaze switched to Puck, "we need to make this believable."

Arden jumped when Buck unmuted the television and the sound blared out in the small room. Turning her head to the television, she saw he had switched the channel from wrestling to porn, and a woman was screaming as a man was driving his cock inside of her.

Having always assumed Victorian women had pretended to faint during embarrassing moments, Arden learned from firsthand experience the fainting might not have been as feigned as she supposed.

When Puck sat down on the foot of the bed and started jumping up and down while Buck raised his hand to shake the headboard, she wished she had smelling salts.

Arden raised a hand to cover her face when Buck raised the volume even more. Obviously, they took her for a screamer.

After ten minutes, she tried to take the remote control away from Buck. "Give me that."

He moved it to his other hand, out of her reach, unless she wanted to climb on the bed to take it away from him. Not about to get in a wrestling match with him, she shot him a killing glare.

"We want this to be believable," she hissed.

"We are." Buck grinned unrepentantly. "Give it another twenty minutes."

Arden rolled her eyes at him. "Egotistical much?"

Puck reached forward to pull her toward him. "We're more than willing to demonstrate our stamina."

Slapping his hand away, she tried to move out of his reach. "I'll take your word for it."

Before she could stop him, Puck pulled her shirt off.

"Wait... This is just pretend."

He turned her shirt inside out and gave it back. "Have to make it believable."

She put the shirt back on and felt them taking in her appearance. "What now?"

"Bite your lips."

Feeling like an idiot, she bit her lips until she felt blood rushing into them.

"Better." Buck nodded approvingly. "Mess up your hair. The women know I like to grab their hair when I fuck them."

She could have spent the rest of her life unaware of that fact.

Arden ran her fingers through her short hair, thinking she was doing a good enough job until Puck got up and tousled it even more.

"There, that should be good."

"Just one thing," Buck said, giving a loud moan, which set off Puck making the same sound.

When it dawned on her what they were doing, she lightly slapped her cheek since she didn't have high hopes Buck had smelling salts in his room.

"Now you got the idea," Buck encouraged her.

When the brothers finally stopped groaning and jumping on the bed, she grabbed for the doorknob before they told her they needed to give a repeat performance.

Biting her lip, she paused and turned back to them. "Uh... Do you guys mind doing me a teeny favor?"

At her question, the brothers, who were staring down at the Super Bowl tickets Puck had pulled out again, glanced toward her cautiously.

"If any of the brothers..." Arden embarrassedly cleared her throat. "I don't think they will, but if they do—especially Doom. If any of them ask if I was any good, will you tell them I was?"

Buck took the tickets away from Puck. "For these seats, you're the best either of us have ever had."

CHAPTER 31

THE WRATH PT. 2

When Arden opened Buck's bedroom door, she managed to suck back the gasp of surprise at seeing Doom leaning against the opposite wall.

"Wizard wants to talk to you. He's in his office."

"Okay."

Shifting her feet, she turned in the other direction. She walked the short distance to Wizard's office under Doom's scrutinizing gaze. Since the door was wide open, she walked in, aware Doom was still behind her.

Wizard's searching gaze was almost as disconcerting as Doom's. The only difference was Wizard seemed to be amused by something, while she felt the heat of Doom's anger drilling a hole into her back. She must have infuriated Doom by returning to the club, despite him telling her she wasn't wanted.

Too freaking bad then. He can take a flying leap off the nearest high-rise as far as I am concerned, she thought vindictively.

"You continually surprise me, Arden." Wizard rested his intertwined hands on his flat abdomen. "Doom was just in here talking about how he doesn't think you're cut out to be a Last Rider, then the next thing I hear is you're in Buck's room, and Puck's in there, and all three of you are going at it."

Was she expected to give a postmortem? Nope, that wasn't going to happen. She might have learned to become a proficient liar since her father had become sick, but making up details involving having sex with two men was definitely out of the realm of her capabilities with her limited experience.

"I guess he was wrong."

Her cool demeanor nearly cracked when she nearly jumped out of her skin at Doom's abrupt move to stand where he was able to see her face.

"Apparently." Wizard leaned forward in his chair. "The thing is... He usually isn't."

"He is this time."

"Puck and Buck give you their votes?"

Doom's doubting gaze had her determined to convince him. He was acting like she was freaking chopped liver, and there was no way possible any man would want her, much less two. The anger filling her at his behavior steamrolled past any reticence she had about lying.

"Yes, they were ecstatic when I left them." She was looking at Wizard for his reaction when she told him the bald-faced lie. What she hadn't expected was for him to suddenly jump up.

"We should get a drink to celebrate."

Before she could tell him she didn't want a drink, he started pushing her out of the room.

"Burn!" Wizard's sudden yell had her arching away from him, but he kept moving her determinedly forward.

Not understanding why he was practically throwing

her out the office, she started to turn her head to see what was going on behind her but became distracted when the door across the hall opened and Burn came barreling out.

"Office," Wizard barked, moving them out of Burn's way.

"Is something wrong?"

"Nothing Burn can't handle," Wizard told her, propelling her down the hallway. "How about that drink?"

"I better not. I need to drive home."

"A small one won't put you over the limit." He guided her to a barstool, then practically shoved her down.

"Kat, give us a couple of beers," he ordered. "We're celebrating!"

Wizard's strange behavior was making her wonder if he was already under the influence.

Kat brought them their beers with a wide smile. "What are we celebrating?"

"Arden has three votes!" Wizard enthused.

Arden turned her head to gape at him. "I only have two," she corrected.

Wizard popped the tops of their beers before handing her one. "I'm giving you mine for catching the vendors stealing me blind."

Arden didn't miss the heated glare Wizard shot Kat, who started to argue but changed her mind.

Who was she to look a gift horse in the mouth? It wasn't like she had any more Super Bowl tickets to bargain with.

"Thank you," she said hesitantly.

"No, thank *you*."

Arden stiffened when two arms came around her to hug her against a bare chest as a bearded jaw came into her field of vision. Buck rubbed his jaw along hers. Then, releasing his tight hug, he took a seat on the stool next to her.

Giving Buck a wary glance as he asked for a beer, she hastily took a sip of her own, belatedly wishing she had asked for something stronger.

"Did I hear you say you gave Arden a vote?" Buck talked over her, as if she wasn't seated between him and Wizard.

"I did."

Buck raised his beer. "You're halfway there to getting your tattoo."

Her head jerked in his direction. "What tattoo?"

"When you get your final vote, you get a tattoo of the date and whatever else you want. Didn't any of the women tell you?"

"I must have forgotten." Hell, she had been overwhelmed her first day here; she only remembered half of the rules she had been told.

"You should start thinking about ideas." Buck reached out to trail a finger below her collar bone. "Several of the women have gotten hockey pucks, but my personal favorite is the antlers with the brothers' name tattooed inside."

There was no way in freaking hell she was getting antlers tattooed on any part of her body.

She was trying to come up with a polite way to tell him that when she suddenly felt herself lifted off the barstool.

"What the—"

"The only way she's getting antlers or a fucking hockey puck is over my fucking dead body," Doom snarled next to her ear as he carried her to the front door.

Finding herself being inexplicably carried out of the club like a sack of flour took a full minute for her to comprehend.

Struggling against his hold, she tried to pull herself away. "What are you doing? I'm not ready to leave."

Doom set her down next to the passenger door of her car. "Give me your car keys."

"Are you insane?" she screeched at him.

He bent down low enough his eyes were directly in front of hers. "Give me your car keys. I won't ask again."

Huffily, Arden turned in the direction of the club.

"We can go back inside then. You're already on a roll today. Let's add my vote to your tally."

The anticipatory way Doom waited for her next move had her rushing to the driver's door of the car.

"I'm afraid I'll have to take a raincheck, as amazing as that sounds. I told Mama I could work tonight when you told me I didn't need to." She got inside her car and locked the door. Looking at him through her rearview mirror, she backed out and put the pedal to metal, speeding out of the parking lot. She didn't slow down until the club was out of sight.

Releasing a nervous laugh that she had escaped so easily, Arden decided to make good on her lie and drove to the restaurant.

She got her hostess clothes out of her trunk and went inside to surprise Mama, who didn't ask any questions, just rearranged the hostess on duty to another area of the restaurant.

The rest of the night passed by slowly, and she clocked out at nine, ready to go home and put her misgivings about what she had done behind her.

It's spilt milk. Nothing you can do about it now, she kept telling herself over and over.

How was she was supposed to know Doom would become so angry when she went behind his back to collect the votes he thought she would never get? What skin was it off his nose, anyway? She was baffled as to why he had seemed so upset.

Saying hello to the couple sitting outside their apartment door, she asked if they wanted the leftovers from the restaurant. Delighted, Lizzy took the bag from her, promising to repay her the next time she made her carrot cake.

"I'm going to hold you to that," Arden told her, walking up the steps.

When she reached the landing, she came to a stop at seeing Doom standing outside her door.

"I need some sugar."

Arden debated telling him she was out. Everyone had sugar.

She didn't know what to do. Dammit, she was going to have to give him the sugar.

As she walked toward her door, she searched his face for any sign he was still angry. Seeing none, she opened the door.

"Give me a second, and I'll get it for you."

"Cool."

"What are you making?"

Expecting him to stay by the door, she tried to appear unruffled when he walked inside and shut the door.

She opened the cabinet and reached for the bag of sugar.

"Nothing." His voice sounded from behind her.

She stiffly turned around, setting the bag of sugar down on the counter.

Doom braced his hands on each side of the counter next to her, effectively trapping her inside his arms.

"The sugar I want isn't in a bag."

Involuntarily, her eyes were drawn to his lips. "Unfortunately, the only sugar you're going to get from me comes in a bag."

His hand went to the side of her neck to slide caressingly to her nape. "How did you earn Puck's and Buck's votes?"

The sensual way he was stroking her neck had her nervously backing up against the counter. She only was able to suck in a nervous breath before his body closed the small distance separating them.

"The normal way," she said hoarsely.

When he lowered his head to rub his lips along her jawline, she reacted like a scalded cat by jumping up on the counter. She might have just made a fool of herself, but at least their hips weren't still plastered together, she consoled herself.

Doom didn't allow her to congratulate herself for long.

He pressed himself between the vee of her thighs, his hands at her hips to hold her in place.

"I seriously underestimated you if you think having sex with two men is normal."

Arden shuddered when she felt him lick the lobe of her ear.

"I know I have far to go in your estimation." Arching her neck back, she tried to avoid his mouth wreaking havoc on her senses. "According to you, no one would want me. You didn't think I would get one vote, much less three."

"To be fair, I didn't count on you being such a handy person to have around the club." Doom's hands splayed across her ribcages as he buried his face in her neck. "I thought you talked a good game, to get what you want out of the club, but had no intention of actually getting down and dirty with any of us to actually fuck any of us."

"You were wrong." Her hands went to his wrists when

his thumbs began circling the sides of her breasts, stilling them. "I'm exhausted, Doom. Maybe some other time."

He ignored her attempt to get him to leave, still focusing on the first thing she'd said. "So I found out. You want to know what I find really interesting?"

"Not really..."

Disregarding her again, he started massaging her ribs. "Buck rubbed against you like you were the fucking cat's meow when you were sitting at the bar. I've known the brother a lot of years and have not ever seen him react that way." His body and hands were clinging to her like monster tape.

Maintaining a cool expression was nearly impossible when all she wanted to do was grab him by the neck and pull his mouth to hers. From the look in his eyes, she could tell he knew how he was affecting her.

Anger overrode the lust he was working so hard to achieve. He wanted her like putty in his hands. Hell would freeze over before she would let him achieve his aim after he had told her The Last Riders didn't want her.

"What can I say...?" Condescendingly giving him the most frigid bitch glare she was capable of pulling off, she said, "I'm just that good."

"I'll be the judge of that."

CHAPTER 32
THE TASTE

Doom was the worst type of man, which was like catnip for women. He was a double *I*: irritating and irresistible. She wondered how many women he'd had sex with to reach the degree of self-confidence he wore as easily as Iron Man wore his. This time, however, he'd met his match. She swore to herself that her willpower wouldn't break.

"Perhaps another time."

His mouth swooped down, destroying what was left of her willpower. The bastard was just too damn close, smelled too damn good, and was too damn sexy to deny herself another taste of the passion he could raise in her at the snap of his fingers.

Letting her arms wrap around his corded neck, she kissed him back with all the pent-up desire she had been hiding.

Men never gave her second glances, which was why what he had said had stung so bad. To have a man like Doom want her soothed a part of her pride she would have sworn on her life hadn't been hurt. It had hurt. People could be intentionally or unintentionally cruel when seeing someone who wasn't attractive.

She could have experimented more with makeup and wore more flattering clothing. Mama had offered on a million different occasions to show her how. The reason she had refused was because she was the spitting image of her mother. Her father had fallen in love with her mother in high school, convincing her to get married the day after their graduation. She had been blessed to witness their love firsthand. She wanted the same love her parents shared. To her father, her mother was the most beautiful woman on earth. Was it bad she had been searching for the same type of love?

Winding her legs around his hips, she opened her mouth to his demanding tongue. Sleekly, he dove inside, conquering with his taste alone.

Arden knew why Eve had taken the first tempting bite of the forbidden fruit. Despite knowing it would lead to consequences she would ultimately regret, the promise of bliss was too hard to resist.

Lifting her off the counter, Doom cupped her bottom in his hands as he carried her through the open bedroom door. No second thoughts went through her head when she felt herself lowered to the mattress. Under no illusion about Doom's feelings for her, she had challenged his authority within the club by returning. He wanted to exert his dominance over her in the most basic way possible.

She should be showing him the door instead of letting him remove her clothes and lie down on top of her to resume their kiss. He would only win their battle of wills if she let him, and she had no intention of doing so. She might not be the most popular woman in Ohio, but she damn sure wasn't a pushover either.

Kissing Doom back as passionately as he was her, she shoved his tongue out of the way to enter his mouth. Her hands slid under his gray Henley to tug it up, breaking the kiss long enough to remove the garment and toss it over their heads.

She smoothed her hands down his sleek back, shuddering at how good he felt. It was the most wonderful sensation she had ever experienced. Placing teasing kissing on his mouth, she would twist away when he tried to snare her into another deep kiss, preferring to let her mouth wander downward to the base of his neck. She let the tip of her tongue investigate the small hollow before trailing to his shoulder.

Doom's body was a work of art, with broad shoulders and a muscular chest that tapered down to lean hips. It was masculine enough to make a nun reconsider her vows.

Letting her lips transverse his male flesh, searching to trace the tattoos scattered across his chest, she heard a low groan escape his mouth.

Arden's eyelids flew open when she felt him jerk out of her clinging arms. Was he changing his mind?

Catching her gaze, Doom unzipped his jeans and pulled them down to step out of them. She licked her suddenly dry lips and wanted to pinch herself to make sure she wasn't dreaming.

Going to his knees on the mattress, he bent over her to cover a nipple with his mouth. Sucking it teasingly. She arched under him, pushing her breast further into his mouth.

"Do you want me?" he muttered against her skin.

"You know I do," she admitted.

His hand circled her neck. "Then why go to Buck and Puck first?"

Arden wasn't so far gone enough not to know she was walking a tightrope.

"I thought you didn't want me."

"You knew I did when I kissed you outside the club."

His mouth started sliding lower down her body, his hands going to the sides of her dress pants to tug them down.

"Doom, your attention span concerning women lasts about as long as it takes frozen butter to melt." Arden willingly squirmed her hips so he would find it easier to remove her pants. "Why does it matter to you if I was with Puck and Buck? You don't hear me asking you to play kiss and tell about the woman ringing the bell at the bar, or how, right after kissing me, you spent the night with Celeste."

His mouth hovered over her pussy, creating a heightened anticipation about what he was going to do next. Then two fingers parted her cleft to make room for his thumb to rub the nub of her clitoris. She sucked in a hiss of breath, her fingers clutching his hair.

"I don't mind playing kiss and tell. You want me to go first, or do you want to?"

"I don't want to play," she replied, wiggling her hips to show him she wanted more action than talk. "You're the one making a big deal out of it."

"I'm not making a big deal." He finally lowered his mouth, then his tongue brushed against her clitoris, almost giving her the orgasm her body was clamoring for. "Amy is the woman who rang the bell. She wants to become a Last Rider. She prefers having sex in front of a group more than going into the bedrooms. Do you want to know what she tastes like?"

"No..." she moaned as his mouth went to her thigh to take a small bite of the flesh there.

"I'll tell you, anyway. Her pussy tastes like strawberry-flavored water. She brags about drinking a liter of it a day just for that reason."

Arden lifted her eyes from his mouth to his eyes. "I've never heard of that before. Does it really work?"

A salacious smile curled his lips. "Her pussy does taste like it, but maybe it could be because she planted the thought in my head. I told her to start drinking peach-flavored water so I could see if I could taste the difference."

That he was discussing what another woman tasted like so matter-of-factly while he was going down on her should have been a big turnoff. Instead, it ratchetted her desire to another carnal level.

A burning question filtered through her mind, but the urge to ask how she tasted was pushed aside. *I don't want to know*, one part of her mind shouted, while the other part wanted the answer.

His mouth roved back to her pussy. "You taste like morning dew."

"Is that good or bad?" her naughty side asked.

"Clean, fresh." Rubbing his mouth back and forth on her pussy, he raised his head to lick his wet lips. The erotic way he seemed to be savoring the moisture clinging to his lips fueled a lust she had meant to keep reined.

Losing control, she tore his hair. "Quit teasing me."

"Do you want my mouth or my dick?"

She let her yearning gaze give her answer.

Raising up, Doom got off the bed to reach for his jeans, pulling a condom out of the back pocket. "Come here." He opened the packet and started stroking his penis as she crawled over to him. "Wet my cock for me."

He stared at her as if it were dare, as if he didn't really

expect her to. Arden was no fool. She knew he was testing her.

Making sure Doom wouldn't have to ask twice, she lowered her head to take his cock into her mouth. Covering the tip, she circled the rim before opening her mouth wider, taking as much as she could manage without showing her inexperience. Faking a competence she didn't possess, she laved at his stalk until a rough hand went to her hair to tug her away.

He smoothed down the condom, then used his shoulders to press her back to the mattress.

"How did I taste?" he asked as he thrust inside of her.

Arden would have sworn she saw stars at the penetration. Telling herself not to give in to the beckoning ecstasy, she managed to keep her voice in the normal range.

"Like cotton candy."

CHAPTER 33

THE VIRGIN

"Cotton candy?"

Doom's low sultry growl sent shockwaves through her groin. His warm breath on her lips made Arden twine her arms around his neck to pull his tempting mouth down to hers. As his mouth plundered hers, she felt the silky glide of his cock entering her slowly. His shoulders tensed under her hands as he exerted more pressure to fill her. When she wiggled her hips to make it easier for him, Doom tore his mouth away from hers to search her eyes.

"You're going too slow," she complained, wiggling her hips again. The movement finally nudged him higher inside of her.

"Slow down," Doom rasped out, his mouth closing over her nipple. "You're not ready..."

She clasped her thighs around his waist. "I am."

Fervidly, she arched under him, driving his cock deeper. She could feel her tight sheath protesting then giving away, allowing his cock easier access to the depths which had been resisting his efforts.

"Jesus—Arden, you're going to hurt yourself," he groaned against her breast.

"It doesn't hurt," she moaned. "It feels *so* good. Guess what?"

Doom lifted his head. "What?"

"I don't break."

His expression told her he wasn't amused. "I think something did."

She felt his muscles bunch as if he was preparing to move away. Hastily, she tightened her arms around him, refusing to let him withdraw.

"Nothing broke I want back."

She grew discontent that Doom had stopped moving and started to move away from her, so she used his momentum to shove him until he was on his back with her on top of him.

"I like this much better." She bent down and caught his bottom lip between her teeth. "Much better," she crooned, sliding herself down on his cock.

A loud groan from Doom expressed his own enjoyment at her taking control.

The sensations assailing her had Arden lifting herself then sliding back down on his cock. Slowly at first, then faster as it became easier until she felt her sheath slickly gliding up and down Doom's cock. When his fingers started tugging and plucking at her protruding nipples, her movements intensified.

As she moved on him, she stared down into his eyes, wanting to remember every detail of his expression. She wasn't holding out any hope that he would want to have sex with her again, so she wanted to remember every detail she could.

He was so darned sexy it almost hurt to watch him without giving her emotions away.

She clenched her muscles around his cock and saw his eyes widen with lust. Increasing her movements, she rode him hard, blowing past boundaries she had never imagined herself surpassing.

His hands left her breast to grab her hips to grind her down harder on him as he rose up into a sitting position. Sucking a nipple into his mouth, he started rocking them back and forth, changing the trajectory of his cock. He cupped her breast as his teeth tormented her sensitive nipple.

Wanting to savor every moment, she fought back the orgasm fighting to be released. Biting her lip, she tried to put off the inevitable and was failing miserably when she felt her muscles starting to contract.

To hold back the scream filling her throat, she bit down on his shoulder as shudders overtook her body when she felt his own throbbing release.

Limply, she could only give a low moan when Doom shifted her so his cock could slide out and he could move to lie next to her on the mattress. She expected him to lie down so was startled when Doom jumped up to stalk into the bathroom.

Self-conscious, she righted herself enough to slide under the covers, where she lifted her knees and rested her cheek on them as she waited for him to return.

She raised her head when she heard him walk out of the bathroom to see him irritably jerk his jeans on.

"Is something wrong?" she cautiously asked.

He reached for his shirt on the bed when he glared at her. "You were a virgin."

Arden licked lips, which were as dry as cardboard. "So? What does it matter?"

His glare intensified. "You being a virgin never entered my mind," he snapped. "Especially after you supposedly fucked Buck and Puck this afternoon."

She straightened her shoulders, angered at his behavior. He was ruining her first time.

"There's more than one way to have sex. I wasn't aware the only way to get votes was having intercourse."

"It isn't!"

Giving him a shrug, she glowered back at him. "Then what's the problem?"

He picked up his socks and boots then sat down on the bed to put them on. "The problem is I don't fuck virgins. Taking a woman's cherry comes with complications I don't want."

"You're the one making it complicated. I don't expect or want anything from you."

"Yeah. Right. If it wasn't a big deal, why were you still a virgin? Why didn't you give it to Buck or Puck or another Last Rider?"

"I don't know." She did, but she would be damned if she told the big ass.

He didn't believe her. "Bullshit. You had to have a reason."

"I wanted you," she gave him a partial truth. "I didn't see why not."

"I can tell you why not." He snapped to his feet. "You should have given your first time to anyone but me. Someone who could appreciate it."

His words stung, one after the other, shooting holes through her fragile pride.

"Can I ask you a question?"

Almost to her bedroom door, he stopped. “What?”

“Why are you always so mean to me? I think you get more pleasure at being a jerk to me than having sex with me. Why?”

Doom’s body went rigid. “I don’t intend to be mean. Look, let’s just pretend this didn’t happen and move on.”

Keeping the hurt at bay until he left, she gave him what he wanted. “I can do that. You can even keep your vote; I don’t want it from you. You can go. I think you answered my question,” she dismissed him as if he were a guest who had overstayed his welcome.

She rose unconcernedly under his scrutiny and moved to her dresser to pull out a sleeping top to wear.

Breezing past him as if he were invisible, she left her bedroom and headed to the front door, opened it, then held on to the doorknob for dear life, promising herself a good cry once he’d left.

Staring at her set face, Doom appeared to have misgivings about the way he had acted.

“Listen, I’m—”

“I need to get some sleep. Having sex with three men has exhausted me.” She ignored what he had been about to say.

“I’ll kiss your ass if you had sex with Puck and Buck,” he said, moving to the door.

“I’ve got a news bulletin for you,” she said, giving him a smile that didn’t reach her eyes. “Your lips are never coming near my ass again, but feel free to make the offer to them. Just wait until I’m there; I want to see your face when they tell you to pucker up.”

Before Doom could respond, she slammed the door in his face, locking it for good measure.

“Hargh...” She stormed through her living room back

into her bedroom. All desire to cry gone, she peeled the sheets and blanket off her bed, then remade it before she carried them to the hamper in the bathroom, not wanting any of his scent left behind. With the same thought in mind, she showered and washed her hair. It was over an hour later before she was able to turn the light off and go to bed.

Still furious, she vented by calling him every derogatory name she could think of and might have invented a few new ones. It was only when she found herself unconsciously punching her innocent pillow that she was able to regain control of herself.

"I promise you one thing," Arden promised Doom as if he were there, pulling the pillow over her face to soak up the tears she could no longer hold back. "I'll never let you make me cry again."

She had given her virginity to a man who didn't hold the least liking for her. Whose desire for her was as unsubstantial as the cotton candy she had likened him to. Hell, hindsight was foresight. The next time she was with a man, unless he showed signs of being a Jolly Rancher, her one and only excursion onto the wild side would be her last.

CHAPTER 34

THE MUG

Doom headed to his apartment. Inside, he made a beeline to the refrigerator to grab a beer.

"Nice job, dumbass," he blasted himself. "What in the fucking hell were you thinking?"

He opened the ice-cold beer and gulped it down, hoping to cool the raging lust he hadn't fully spent on Arden.

Running the glass of the bottle over his forehead instead of bashing his numbskull against the closest wall, he replayed the sexual encounter, realizing belatedly more than one mistake had been made.

He should never have touched her. Thinking Arden would cave into admitting she hadn't had sex with Puck and Buck this afternoon, he had lost sight of the goal once he had touched her. Their attraction was a powder keg waiting for a stray spark.

Deciding to head back to the club, he finished his beer and took a shower. As he dried off, however, he couldn't work up enough enthusiasm to get dressed. He couldn't remember the last time he had gone to bed before three or four in the morning. Closing his eyes, he planned to rest for a few minutes before he got dressed.

When a bright light began irritating his eyelids, he regretted not turning his light off. He opened his eyes and was startled to see the bright sun shining into the room.

Rolling over, he saw it was nine in the morning. What the fuck? He had slept through the night.

He dressed and left his apartment, then walked down the steps, where he saw Andy smoking a cigarette. As he passed the man, Doom realized he wasn't as old as he had thought him to be.

Releasing a puff of smokey air, Andy took a step back to give him enough room to pass. "What's up, dude?"

"Not much." Doom gave him a curt nod as he walked past him. He wasn't buying the laidback attitude Andy was putting off.

"How is it going living here?"

"Okay," Doom answered shortly without bothering to turn his head, not seeking to prolong the conversation.

"Arden is a sweet kid."

He stopped in his tracks at Andy's derisive tone.

"It'd be a shame if someone hurt her. Lizzie and I watch out for her. Had the old fart running the place move us to this side of the building so we can make sure no one fucks with her when she comes and goes. The other night, we heard you go in her apartment, and again last night." Andy threw the cigarette out to crunch it under his worn boot.

"That's why you were standing off to the side when Arden opened the door?"

"Like I said. she's a sweet kid. Not too many people give us the fucking time of day. Arden always makes it a point to makes sure Lizzie has enough food to eat. She even paid our rent when the old fart wanted to throw us out after we refused to pay because the fucking rats were taking up more space than we were. She even paid an exterminator, so we didn't have to put up with it any more. People usually look down on my Lizzie, but Arden makes her feel like a friend."

Andy nodded his head at the jacket Doom was wearing. "You're a Last Rider?"

"You don't get the jacket unless you are."

"I don't want any trouble with them."

Doom raised an eyebrow at him, seeing the man underneath, who had been beaten down by whatever happened to him in life. "But…?"

"I will fuck you over until the only thing you're capable of riding is a wheelchair if you hurt her."

"I don't want her hurt either."

"Glad we're on the same page then."

Guessing Andy was done saying what he wanted to get off his chest, considering he went back into his apartment, Doom got on his bike. Something gnawed at him about Andy. He didn't know what it was. Unable to put a name to what was bothering him, he was still racking his brain when he pulled up to the club.

"Bro, you look like shit," Doom told Burn insultingly.

The brother looked like death warmed over.

Doom didn't immediately go inside, even though Burn was holding the door open for him.

"Feels like it," Burn said, letting the door spring closed.

"You stay up all night partying?"

"I wish. No, I spent the whole fucking night trying to reason with Taylor. She's moving to Kentucky in two weeks. My lawyer is for shit, and now she's said if I don't quit arguing with her, she's going to stop talking to me and let our lawyers be our go-between."

Doom grimaced. "Sorry, brother. You know, if you need some cash to get a better lawyer, I can—"

"No. Wizard's already offered. He's helping me find one."

"Good luck, then. If there's anything I can do to help, let me know," Doom offered.

"Nothing you can do. I stepped in this shit all by myself."

He left Burn cursing ever hooking up with Taylor. There wasn't anything he could say to make him feel better. Taylor had grinded her heels in Burn's balls since she decided to get a divorce.

At first, he'd thought Taylor and Burn's breakup was amicable. It had only gone down the toilet when Taylor went to Kentucky to attempt reconciliation with Reaper. When Taylor came back, she took the gloves off and made Burn pay for Reaper not wanting her, and for his own refusal to give their marriage another chance.

Doom couldn't blame Burn; it would be hard to take a woman back when she had left him to pursue another man.

He spent the rest of the day on chores Wizard had told him to do. It was eight o'clock before he had time to make himself a sandwich and eat at one of the back booths, ignoring the fact that Arden had come while he was out running Wizard's errands.

When she didn't seem miffed at being pointedly ignored by him, he found himself sulking into his beer.

Wizard shot him a wry glance from across the table. "Who pissed in your cornflakes?"

"No one."

"Could have fooled me," Wizard scoffed, turning so he could stretch his legs on the booth's cushioned seat.

"Nothing's wrong."

"Fine. You don't want to talk, don't. Want to shoot some pool?"

"Sure."

They slid out of the booth and went to the empty pool table. Doom let Wizard go first since he had won their last game.

"Were you able to find Burn another lawyer?"

"Arden, bring me a beer!" Wizard shouted. "Not yet." Wizard hit the 1 ball into the corner pocket. "None of the fuckers I called want to take Burn's case."

Doom kept his gaze leveled on the pool table as Arden brought Wizard his beer.

Sinking the 2 ball, Wizard took aim on the 3 ball. "We both know why no one wants to stick out their neck to take the case."

"The mayor," Doom voiced the person who had been seeking The Last Riders since his daughter became fixated on Moon.

"Yep. The fucker gets more pleasure out of making our lives miserable than getting a hefty donation."

Walking to the other side of the table so Arden would be out of sight with his back turned as she cleaned the booths and tables nearby, Doom said, "What are you going to do?" He was still waiting to take his first shot. Wizard was on a roll, sinking all his shots.

"It's irritating as fuck. I should never have promised to help Burn. Hell, I can't even get the building permit approved so we can expand the back of the club. The brothers want more bedrooms, and if I hear one more time why Margarita is the only woman who has a room, I'm going to shoot myself in the dick."

When it was finally his turn, Doom had to walk around the pool table. At the same time, Arden picked up the loaded tray with beer mugs to carry it back behind the bar. Wizard didn't miss the haughty way Arden shifted her gaze away from him.

"What's going on with you two?"

"Nothing."

Wizard made a face at him. "Bullshit. You still butt hurt she did Buck and Puck before you?"

Doom straightened from the pool table after he missed his shot. "I wasn't mad."

Wizard made another face. "If you don't want to talk about it, I'll shut the fuck up. But..."

"Then shut the fuck up."

Wizard laughed. "Okay, I can take a hint."

"Since when?" Doom sarcastically looked across the bar to see Arden was talking to Buck and Puck.

Wizard caught him staring.

"Why don't you make it even more obvious?" He nodded his chin toward the trio.

Doom wanted to ram his pool cue down Wizard's sarcastic throat but caught sight of two new recruits sitting close to Puck, starting to argue with Jesus, their loud voices drawing everyone's attention. Another recruit sitting at a table behind them joined in the disagreement, voicing his opinion. Wizard had already nicknamed him Roid because of the recruit's huge mass of upper muscles on his body. In the week Wizard gave him the opportunity to join the club, Roid had been severely argumentative and confrontational.

"He's going to have to be given the boot."

Doom nearly laughed at Wizard's downcast expression.

Wizard really wanted someone to be able to even the playing field with the Yeti in case The Last Riders went up against Mama's minions again.

"No shit." Wizard looked like a dog who was about to lose his favorite chew toy.

Doom set his pool cue down on the pool table as the argument escalated. He was already moving toward the side of the table when Roid picked up his heavy beer mug and threw it at Jesus, who was smart enough to duck, unwittingly giving the mug a clear shot at Arden.

Doom ran at full speed when he realized Arden was about to be struck, and he wasn't going to make it in time.

"Duck, Arden!" he yelled, rushing behind the bar. The fucker had thrown one of the thickest mugs the club owned. If it struck Arden, it was going to do some damage.

He had lost count of how many life-and-death situations he had been involved in in the military, and since joining The Last Riders, none of them had brought home the sense of terror that watching the mug sail through the air straight toward Arden did.

Instead of ducking, Arden froze, turning her head to look toward him.

His legs pushed harder to reach her when he saw it was going to hit her in the temple with the way her head was turned.

It seemed as if everything moved in slow motion as his eyes clung to the mug. His heart nearly stopped when Buck leaned forward on his stool to catch it in his hand.

Coming to a complete stop at seeing the threat to Arden neutralized, he had to grab the side of the bar to catch his breath. In the second it took him to regain his equilibrium, he turned his focus on Roid.

Red-hot fury encased him. Then, releasing the rage

boiling inside of him, he gave a yell that had the brothers freezing in place. Without conscious thought, Doom used his hand that was clinging to the bar to lift himself up and over the bar to land on the other side.

"Holy fuck!" Wizard shouted out. "Doom, wait! Let me handle this!"

Doom didn't stop. The moment he reached Roid, he started beating him without mercy.

"Motherfucker, I'm going to kill you!" he snarled, landing several punches on the stunned man before Roid had the wherewithal to start fighting back. Doom didn't even feel the punches Roid managed to land.

Using his shoulder, he barreled into Roid, knocking both of them down and taking a table and a chair with them. Unaware the brothers were trying to break up the fight until he felt Buck and Wizard jerk him up and back, Doom took a heavy breath as he watched Puck and Jesus get Roid to his feet.

"You're fucking done here!" Doom yelled at him.

"Says who?" Roid lifted a hand to swipe at his bloody nose.

"Me," Wizard stated calmly, still holding Doom back. "You could have seriously hurt Arden if that mug had hit her."

Roid looked shocked. "You're throwing me out because of a stupid cunt?"

"Dude, you've got about two seconds to get your ass out of here, or I'm going to let Doom go. Take my advice and run."

Roid didn't stick around to argue.

Doom still tried to shake Wizard and Buck off even after the door had closed after Roid.

"Jesus!" Wizard called the brother to his side.

"Yeah?"

"You know what I want?"

Jesus nodded, then hurried out the door and after Roid.

"Where's Jesus going?" Doom heard Arden ask someone from behind the bar. He heard Puck answer her.

"To deliver some divine intervention on Roid."

CHAPTER 35

THE TICKETS

Shrugging out of Wizard's and Buck's hold, Doom turned back to the bar.

"Why in the fuck didn't you duck?"

Arden's raised her hands up quizzically. "I didn't know you meant me."

"Christ Almighty!" he snarled, practically leaning over the bar. "I was running right toward you. If Buck hadn't caught that fucking mug, you could have been fucking hurt! The next time I fucking yell out to do something, do it! I don't give a fuck who you think I'm yelling at, *just fucking do it*!"

"I can hear you fine; there's no need to yell."

"Really? So help me..." Doom reached out to snatch her ass up and drag her into his arms, forgetting the whole club was watching them.

Wizard grabbed his arm and moved him to the side. "She got the message. Don't you, Arden?"

"Yes." Arden nodded.

"Give him a beer."

Doom shot Wizard a killing glare as he was shoved down onto a stool.

"It takes Doom a while to calm down when he gets pissed."

Taking steadying breaths, he reached for the beer Arden placed in front of him before she hurried to the other end of the bar.

"You cool?" Wizard asked, taking the seat next to him.

"No." The heavy weight of the mug in his hand was a stark reminder of how close Arden had come to getting hurt. "These mugs are going to be thrown away."

"They keep the beer colder longer."

"I don't give a fuck. This isn't the first time some stupid-ass recruit has thrown them or used them to bash someone in the head with."

Wizard cocked an eyebrow at him. "Brother, you didn't give a flying fuck when Margarita smashed Celeste with one during the Halloween party."

Doom shifted on his stool. "Wizard, shut the fuck up."

Wizard shrugged. "Just saying."

"Well, don't." Having enough of Wizard, he turned his head to look at Buck and Puck, who had returned to their seats.

"What in the fuck were you two arguing with Roid over?"

"Who was going to win the Super Bowl," Buck answered. "Roid thinks the Chiefs will; we told him the Eagles."

"You couldn't have saved that argument for Sunday?"

Doom was lifting his mug to his lips when he saw the brothers share a glance he didn't understand.

"We won't be here." Puck grinned. "We're going to the game."

Doom frowned. "What game?"

"The Super Bowl." Buck's pearly whites showed through his bushy beard.

"Since when?" Doom asked doubtfully.

"Last night." Puck provided the information with a side look at his brother.

Doom smelled shit, and it wasn't on his shoes. "How you score tickets?"

"Blue offered us the tickets."

Doom's eyes went to Arden, who was chatting with Kat.

"Blue, Arden's brother?" Doom asked to make sure they were talking about the same person.

"Yep. Isn't it great?" Puck beamed.

"Sure is." Doom narrowed his eyes on the two brothers, whose expression remained unchanged under his scrutiny. "How Blue score tickets?"

"They were his father's tickets. He's too sick to go."

"Lucky you."

"We think so." Puck's grin grew wider.

Doom turned his head to stare at Wizard, who was listening. He noticed the same doubt in Wizard's eyes as he was experiencing.

Doom pivoted back to the brothers. "Who was the third ticket for?"

The telltale sign was when they stared at each other, as if they were trying to come up with a believable lie.

Buck, who had always the better liar of the two, shrugged. "Didn't ask."

"Arden!" Doom called out. "Come here a second."

Arden broke off her conservation with Kat to make her way down to where they were sitting. "Yes? You need something?"

"No, I'm good." Doom pinned his steely gaze on hers.

"Buck and Puck were just telling us they are going to the Super Bowl."

"My brother gave them the tickets," she hastily explained. "My dad is too sick to go."

"That's what they said. I'm curious... Your dad bought three tickets?"

"I don't have any more, if that's what you're asking."

"No, I was just wondering who the third ticket was for?"

"Me. My mom hates football."

"Then why didn't your dad just give Blue two tickets and give you the third one, as he intended to do?"

Doom could see the wheels turning behind her eyes.

"Oh... Because with Luc gone, I need to stay at home to be on hand in case of an emergency."

"I hate for you to miss out," Doom told her magnanimously. "You should go. I'll foot the bill for a licensed nurse to stay with them."

Arden visibly paled. "Thank you for the offer, but I would feel uncomfortable leaving my parents with someone I don't know. Besides, I was only going to make my dad happy. I'm not really into football."

Doom almost rolled his eyes. Arden had the loudest mouth in the club when a game was on. She was practically as bad as Buck at commentary about players' mistakes.

Doom winkled his nose. "You smell that, Wizard?"

"I do." The brother wriggled his nose too.

Confusion filled Arden's face while Buck and Puck started shifting on their stools.

"Smell what?"

"Pure bullshit," Doom ended her confusion quickly. "You gave them Super Bowl tickets for their votes, didn't you?"

"Of course not."

"You did."

Arden shook her head. "Nope."

"Liar."

Her shoulders arched up stubbornly. "Prove it. Since you weren't in the room with us, you can't."

"Or we could all go back to Buck's room, and you could give a repeat performance."

When she glared at him, Doom didn't have to imagine the names she was calling him in her mind.

"I'm not in the mood."

"Buck and Puck are pretty good at putting women in the mood."

Steam was practically coming out of Arden's ears. "There are some performances too magical to repeat, and you don't want anything to spoil the memory." Her voice turned insulting. "Then there are others you just plain try to forget."

Doom had to take a drink at her disparaging tone.

"I'll take a cold one," Wizard told Arden.

After Arden handed him the beer, Wizard stopped her before she could move away. "I left some dishes in the office. Mind getting them for me?"

It was written all over her face that she wanted to tell him to go get them himself. Doom admired her restraint when she did actually leave to go get them.

Doom waited for her to reach the hallway before he slid off the stool.

"Thanks," he muttered aside to Wizard.

"Have fun..." Wizard raised his hand to meet Doom's fist halfway for a fist-bump, "getting the truth out of her."

"Oh... I will. Count on it."

CHAPTER 36
THE TRUTH

Arden glanced around Wizard's office but didn't see any dirty dishes.

"What the heck?" Spinning around in irritation, she was faced with Doom standing in front of the closed office door. She hadn't heard him enter, much less the door being closed.

"Someone else must have already taken the dishes." Breaking eye contact to double-check in case she had missed any, Arden was determined to remain aloof and pretend last night had never happened.

"There weren't any." Crossing his arms, Doom made it plain she wouldn't be leaving the room until he allowed her out.

Pretending an indifference she didn't feel, she mimicked him by crossing her arms over her chest. "Say what you want to say; I have things to do."

"You gave Puck and Buck the tickets for their votes."

"Like I said—*prove it*." Arden was sick and tired of Doom trying to intimidate her. "What does it matter to you how I got their votes? It's no skin off your nose. What reason would I have to lie about it? I could have just come out and said I gave them the tickets for their votes, and no one would care."

"Exactly," Doom agreed. "That's what I'm interested in —why lie about it?"

"Because I didn't."

"You did," he stated, unperturbed. "I have to say this, Arden, you are the most complicated woman I have ever met in my life. And that says a fucking lot."

"Did you just insult me?"

"Take it for what it's worth."

"Which isn't worth a lot where you're concerned," she replied insultingly. "I've got a revelation for you too... You're a goon."

"A goon?"

"A goon." She nodded her head at him. "You should ask Buck and Puck how to treat a woman after sex. At least they acted like gentlemen."

"I would have, too, if you had given me Super Bowl tickets."

She gave him a haughty sniff. "Your performance wasn't Super Bowl worthy. It was flag ball all the way."

Arden saw Doom's anger building, but she couldn't stop herself. Not only had the big goon ruined her first time, but he was also determined to find out the truth. If that happened, she would have to come through on the promise she had made to Buck and Puck. She liked the two men, just not enough to have sex with them.

Doom pushed away from the door and strode toward her. "I was the one who pushed for you to enter the club. I thought you might last a couple of nights then take off running so fast the door wouldn't be able to hit your ass on the way out. We're not idiots; we knew you had no intention of having sex with any of us, but I admit I was bored. I thought it would give us a good laugh."

Each word he said was a slash to her pride.

Curling her nails into her palms, she managed to keep her indifferent façade from breaking into a thousand pieces.

Doom gripped her by her upper arms and gave her a small shake. "I told Wizard it would be fun." He gave her another small shake. "Ask me how much fun I've had."

She had to admit the flag football barb might have been too much for a man like Doom to weather.

"I'd rather not."

"That's the first smart move you've made," he growled, jerking her to his chest. "I want the fucking truth!"

Having taken about as much of him as she was going to take, she started pummeling his chest with her fists.

"Go fuck yourself!" she screamed.

Doom grabbed her wrists to pin them behind her back. "Why should I fuck myself when I have you?"

Arden stomped her foot in frustration. Despite her hands being incapacitated behind her, she wasn't afraid of him. Hell, he should be the one scared.

"I wouldn't have sex with you again if my life depended on it!"

"No?"

Arden gave a small yelp when her feet left the floor as he brought her to eye level with him.

"Like you said, *prove it*."

She angrily narrowed her eyes on his lips, which were moving closer to hers.

"I wouldn't," she snarled.

Doom laughed in her face. "You don't have the stomach to bite me."

"Kiss me and find out."

"As intriguing as that sounds, I'll pass. I wasn't going to kiss you." Doom's lips didn't touch her mouth; they went to her neck. His tongue laved at the pulse she could feel quickening to warp speed. Damn.

He angled his head to the side, and his mouth went to the curve of her breast. "Did it feel this good when Buck put his mouth on you?"

Tightening her lips to keep from sabotaging herself, Arden didn't put up a token resistance. How could she? It felt so good.

"Aren't you going to hit me?"

"I'm debating it," she lied.

She could feel his laughter against her breast.

"When are you going to decide?"

"When you do something I don't like."

"What happened to you wouldn't have sex with me again if your life depended on it?"

"I don't consider this sex."

"What do you consider this?" he asked, releasing her hands.

Her hands went to his muscled shoulders. "A science experiment."

"How is this a science experiment?"

"To see how far you will go to make me admit I gave them the tickets for their votes."

"Did you?"

Tangling her hands into his hair, she lifted to his mouth. "Why do you have to be such a jerk about it? Why can't you just let it go?"

"It's the point of it."

She frowned at him in confusion. "What point?"

"It means I was completely wrong about you, and I know I wasn't."

"You want the truth?"

"Yes."

"Even if it means I have to go back on a promise and the penalty would be to make the lie a reality?"

He placed her back on her feet to rake his hand through his hair. He opened his mouth to say something then snapped it closed as he stared at her in exasperation.

"I didn't come close when I said you were complicated. Have you ever in your life thought of the consequences before you plowed headfirst into situations you have no business putting yourself in?"

"My dad and mom used to tell me that all the time when I was growing up."

Doom shook his head at her. "Seems to me you haven't stopped; you've just gotten sneakier with age."

Arden had to admit he was right.

Angrily walking to the desk, Doom leaned a hip on the side. "I'll let it go if you tell me why. Why didn't you three tell the truth in the first place?"

She stared down at her feet, embarrassed. "Because you said not to come here anymore. I want to be a Last Rider."

"Why are you so determined to be a Last Rider?" he asked, putting his hands up questioningly. "Christ, I've told you the brothers would stay friends with Blue. You don't make any sense... You're not like the women who want to belong. You were a fucking virgin, for fuck's sake!"

Arden glanced up from her shoes. "I've never been very close to Luc. I suppose we're just too different." She had adored Luc from the moment her parents brought him home from the hospital. He had been premature and four months old before he was stable enough to leave. Her parents were too terrified she would get the fragile baby sick, so they'd constantly told her not touch or get near him until he was well over two years old.

"What does that have to do—"

"My parents are dying, Doom." Arden blinked back tears. It was the first time she had admitted out loud she didn't have long left with them.

Doom gave her a sympathetic look.

"I need The Last Riders to be for Luc what I can't."

"What's that?"

"Brothers."

CHAPTER 37

THE SACRIFICE

"Brothers?" Uncertain, Doom frowned. "You mean having Blue's back?"

Giving him a self-depreciating shrug, she kept her voice steady, not wanting Doom to see the heartache that her parents' approaching deaths were causing her. "I mean the whole nine yards. I've watched how The Last Riders treat each other. You're more family than friends. That's what I want for Luc. When we lose Mom and Dad, he's going to feel all alone."

"He won't be alone. Blue has you."

"He resents me." Dismally, she concluded that the only way Doom would get a better understanding of her relationship with Luc was if she opened to him. After the way he'd behaved last night, it was hard to open herself, but she loved Luc more than holding on to her pride.

"I had the childhood he wanted with my parents, when they were young and healthy. There are pictures all around our house of me growing up, playing softball with Mom as the coach, with Dad teaching me how to fix things, the vacations we took. Luc's childhood was much different. He was premature and had several health issues. Because they had come so close to losing him, they were overprotective. They didn't give him the same experiences I was fortunate to have.

"As he grew older, while Luc's health improved, my parents' deteriorated. My dad had a heart attack, and Mom was diagnosed with ovarian cancer, which had her undergoing several treatments and surgeries. I was given the perfect childhood, while Luc got the short end of the stick."

Doom eyed her doubtfully. "You really think Blue would resent you for something beyond your control?"

"Maybe not consciously, but deep down, I think it has placed a wedge between us." Arden linked her fingers together, pressing down to crack her knuckles on both hands. It was a habit she had developed when she played softball to release the tension she was feeling.

Dropping his eyes, Doom noticed the movement. "Have you tried talking to Blue about his feelings?"

Arden rolled her eyes. "Too many to count."

"It didn't go well?"

"With Mom and Dad being so sick, I had to take on more of a parenting role, which only added to Luc's resentment."

"I don't see you coming off as being hardcore disciplinary."

"I wasn't, but Luc wanted a sister with whom he could share his feelings instead of making sure he gets his homework finished, goes to bed on time, and doesn't do anything to upset our parents."

"I can have Puck and Buck talk with him," Doom offered.

"Please don't. Luc's feelings are his own. Maybe someday, he'll understand. Luc really likes Buck, Puck, and

Jesus. He doesn't have to share them with me, and they give him someone to complain to about me. I don't want them to have to convince my brother to love me. I love him and would do anything for him, and Luc knows that, which is all that counts."

She quit pressing down on her knuckles when Doom remained silent.

"Are you going to tell Puck and Buck you know the truth?"

"No," he said. "I think you would be better off taking me up on my offer and letting me hire someone to take care of your parents so that you and Blue could go together."

"Luc would be miserable."

"How can you be so certain?" Doom argued. "You could have at least asked him. Maybe you're the one putting up the roadblocks keeping you from growing closer. Perhaps where you're going wrong with Blue is, you're making decisions for him he's more than capable of making himself. You're right—The Last Riders do look at each other as brothers, but that doesn't mean we don't have good relationships with our families. It's a mix, actually. The only difference is, we don't try to interfere in their lives."

Feeling guilty, Arden looked away. She was well aware of her propensity to meddle, especially with Doom's constant reminder.

"After this, with Buck and Puck, I plan to take a backseat approach with Luc."

By his doubting look, Doom didn't seem to believe her.

"So, you're willing to give up becoming a Last Rider?"

"I mean..." she hastened to explain, "once I'm a Last Rider. I'll take a backseat. I just want to make sure Luc—"

"Woman, all your tinkering is going to blow up in your face. You should have learned that lesson with the asshole who tried to kidnap you. Especially—" Doom's expression grew increasingly angry, "after this fiasco with Buck and Puck. I'm not going to stop you from becoming a Last Rider. I think you're underestimating how Blue is going to feel when he finds out you're trying to become one."

Arden paled. "Are you going tell him how women become a Last Rider?"

"Me? Fuck no. But I can guarantee one of the other brothers will. What will you do then? I don't think he'll be pleased if someone tells him that's why Buck and Puck took him to the Super Bowl."

"If that happened, I'd tell him the truth, obviously."

Arden took a step back when Doom appeared as if he wanted to shake some sense into her.

"You think Blue is going to come running to you if he finds outs?" he yelled at her.

"Of course."

"Are you fucking nuts?"

Arden took another step back.

"The first thing he's going to do is try to rip off Buck's and Puck's heads," Doom snarled at her.

Arden was sure Doom was wrong. "Luc doesn't have a violent bone in his body."

"You're looking at it from a woman's perspective."

"How should I be looking at it? From a man's?" she scoffed.

"No, from a brother's."

"Where I'm concerned, Luc's brotherly instincts are non-existent."

"You don't know jack shit about how a man's brain works!"

"Luc is a teenager."

"Which makes it even worse. He's going to go off. If

your true objective is to make the brothers grow closer to Blue, and he finds out, it'll have the opposite effect." Doom's eyes narrowed on her. "Or is this your game plan all along?"

"Doom, I swear it's not," she said sincerely. "I admit, at first, that was my plan, but that was before I got to know everyone. Just because I don't want to participate in the sex with the club doesn't mean I can't appreciate the friendship the club offers. How the members have everyone's back. I want that for Luc. You say okay, Puck and Buck will continue taking Luc under their wing, but what about in a year or two—three? If I'm a member,

.... you'll still have mine and my family's. Am I wrong?"

From Doom's expression, she wasn't.

"The Last Riders aren't your only choice, if that's the case." Frustrated, Doom ran a hand through his hair. "You have Mama, and don't tell me you don't. Hell, that fucking mob she brought here would scare the shit out of anyone who gives you or Blue trouble."

Grimacing, Arden had to agree Doom was right on that observation.

"I love Mama—don't get me wrong—but she can be somewhat volatile."

"*Somewhat*?" Doom snorted, his shoulders slumped in defeat. "Dammit."

Doom looked away from her then turned his gaze back to her. "Fine," he snapped. "Just don't say I didn't warn you."

Arden breathed a sigh of relief. "I won't," she eagerly agreed. "And we're good where Buck and Puck are concerned?"

Doom held his hands up in surrender. "I won't say another word."

Arden thought that would be a miracle, but okay.

She happily started for the door, but Doom caught her by the wrist.

"Where are you going?"

"Back to work."

"I thought we could continue with your science experiment?"

"No, you were right. I want to be able to tell Luc about the votes, that I never really had sex to get any."

"That's a little late, don't you think? Did you forget about last night?"

"That doesn't count," she said unperturbedly. "It was in my apartment, and I told you I didn't want your vote. If we had sex here, I would get your vote."

She could see Doom didn't like the point she was driving home.

"If I enjoy myself."

"I guess we'll never know. I'd rather be able to look my brother in his eyes than have sex with you. I might not enjoy myself." Arden couldn't help the small snicker as she jerked her wrist free to walk past him. Getting one comeuppance by him felt glorious. Her body was back under her control, and ultimately, Doom was right—she didn't want to endanger Luc's relationship with The Last Riders.

"If I have to give up the chance to have sex with you for Luc, then it's a sacrifice I'm willing to make. Thanks for setting me straight. I appreciate all your help. I could have made a terrible mistake."

She walked out the door and shut it behind her, almost giving herself a high-five when she heard something breaking against it. The satisfying sound did a hell of a lot to ease the raw pain he had inflicted on her pride after they had sex. Checking herself when she remembered how weak-willed she had become when he had touched her, she assured herself it was a momentary lapse. Every woman had them, she told herself. As long as she didn't repeat her same mistake, she was good and could forgive herself. But—if it happened again, she was going to buy herself a female chastity belt and hide the key where she had to drive twenty minutes to retrieve it. By then, she would have come to her senses. Nope... After giving it further thought, she decided it would be much easier not to be left alone with Doom. The belt might chafe areas she didn't want chaffed. She was a smart, independent woman; she hadn't kept her virginity as long as she had by being stupid.

Hearing the office door open before she could get down the hall put a sprint in her step.

There was no need chancing her resolve if she didn't have to. You should never start a diet when you're still hungry.

CHAPTER 38

THE NICKNAME

"Is there something going on between you and Doom?"

Arden pulled her head out from under the bar to see Kat leaning against the counter, watching what she was doing.

"Nothing. Why?"

"He's done nothing all night but watch you, and it's pretty obvious you're ignoring him."

"I'm not ignoring him," she lied, going back to what she had been doing so she wouldn't have to look into the woman's eyes.

"Mmhmm. I would prefer you tell me to mind my business than lie to me."

Arden pulled her head out again. "Sorry. Mind your business." Her head went back under the bar top.

"What are you doing?" Kat bent down curiously. "Unless that's too personal for you?"

"The men have been complaining about the beer being warm. I'm adjusting the coils to make it colder."

"We can do that?"

Arden scooted out from under the bar to stand. "We

shall see. Let's give it a couple of minutes, and then we can check if I was able to fix the problem."

Taking a glass, Arden waited uncomfortably under Kat's scrutinizing stare.

"Nothing is going on." Putting the glass under the spigot, she poured a small amount of beer. She drank it and was satisfied the beer was colder than it had been. "The men should be happier with the temperature now."

Kat gave her an ironic smile. "You should know by now that The Last Riders are never satisfied."

Jesus was walking up to the bar with an empty mug and heard the tail end of what Kat was saying. "You're not talking about me, are you?" Placing a hand over his heart, he gave Kat a seductive glance. "It takes very little to satisfy me."

Kat took his empty mug away from him to fill it. "Since when? I want more... Kat, just a little more—come on, woman, I want some more."

From Jesus's pained expression, Kat must have nailed her impersonation of him.

Arden burst out laughing at Jesus, and Jesus smiled good-naturedly, taking the laughter at his expense.

"Uh-oh," Kat muttered under her breath. "Careful."

Arden looked at her quizzically. "What's wrong?" She glanced around the bar, but didn't see anything that would have caused Kat to issue the warning.

"Doom is watching." Kat shifted so her back was to Doom, who was sitting at the far end of the bar next to the pool table.

"So?" Arden was mystified as to why it mattered. Looking at Jesus, she expected him to seem just as perplexed. Instead, he appeared just as worried. "Is there something I don't know about?"

"That's what I was asking you a few minutes ago," Kat hissed. "Has Doom told you you're his property and you guys haven't told us yet?"

"God, no. I'm not his property. Property? Are you kidding me? If a man ever told me I was his property, I'd—"

Kat shook her head at her. "Property means he claims you as his girlfriend. No one can fuck with you, or they'll have to answer to Doom. It's not a bad thing. It's a good thing."

"A good thing?" Arden snorted. "I'll take your word for it. Besides, it doesn't matter, anyway. Doom doesn't consider me his property."

"Are you sure about that?" Jesus picked up his mug and took a drink of beer. Then he pulled the mug away from his lips to stare at it intently before taking another drink.

Arden looked at him curiously when Jesus set the beer down and seemed about to cry.

"Are you okay?" Arden worriedly reached out to touch his hand sitting on the bar.

"The beer is cold."

Frowning, Arden nodded. "I fixed the kegs and redid the coils. Shouldn't I have?"

"Are all the beers cold?" Jesus rasped out.

"Yes. Look, I can change it back. I didn't mean to upset you."

"Will you marry me?" Jesus turned his hand under hers to grip it tightly.

Arden breathed a sigh of relief. "No, I'll pass, but I'm glad you're happy with the beer."

"You two better chill." Kat reached out to separate their hands.

"You're being ridiculous, Kat." Picking up Jesus's mug, she refilled it for him.

"I like you, Arden, so I'm going to give you a heads-up. Doom wasn't given his nickname because of his winning personality. He's normally a mean motherfucker. Except, when you make him angry, he makes it his personal mission to annihilate the cause."

About to make light of what Kat was telling her, Arden stopped when she saw from Jesus's expression he was agreeing with Kat.

"I know Doom comes across as heavy-handed, and he certainly doesn't give the impression of being Mr. Rogers, but me being friendly with Jesus isn't going to bring down his hellfire on me. We had a small disagreement when we were in Wizard's office, which wasn't a big deal. He'll get over it before the night's over. You'll see," she assured them.

"I sure hope you're right." Kat gave her a sympathetic pat on her shoulder. "If not, it was nice knowing you."

Rolling her eyes at Kat, she looked at Jesus for help. "Can you help me out? Kat's making a mountain out of a molehill. She's blowing a small argument out of proportion."

Jesus took another sip of his ice-cold beer. "Are you going to marry me?"

Margarita, who was coming from the back, gave Jesus and her inquiring stares before moving away toward the pool table.

"Of course not."

"Then I'm staying out of it. I've already risked my neck enough tonight to last me for a lifetime." Jesus leaned forward until he was practically lying across the bar top to whisper, "In case you haven't figured it out yet, I'm more of a lover than a figh—"

About to laugh at Jesus's overdramatic tone, her eyes widened in shock when Doom's hand descended on his head, plastering his face to the bar.

"Why are you whispering, Jesus? We're all dying to know what's so fucking funny!" Doom snarled.

"Doom!" Arden reached out to remove his hand from Jesus.

Kat jerked her back. "Stay out of it. I warned you," she hissed.

Jesus tried to struggle out from under Doom's hand unsuccessfully. "I was just playing—"

Feeling sorry for Jesus, who looked like a smushed fish, she tried again to make Doom stop, but Kat pushed her farther away.

"Did I give you permission to play with Tink?" Doom snarled.

"*Tink*?" Jesus questioned, trying to lift his head, only to have it smacked down again with Doom pressing his full weight down on his skull.

"Arden."

Doom had nicknamed her Tink? She didn't know how she felt about it. Then she decided she did. She hated it.

"I didn't know I needed to," Jesus mumbled out.

"Now you do." Doom pressed down harder. "Any questions?"

"Not any I can think of at this moment."

Struggling against Kat's hold, Arden caught sight of Wizard rounding the counter.

"Let Jesus go, Doom."

Doom did, but not before banging his head on the counter one final time.

Wizard glared at Doom. "Was that necessary?"

"No, but it was satisfying as fuck."

Finding herself released from Kat's hold, Arden started forward to check on Jesus.

All three men stared at her with various expressions.

Jesus was frantically shaking his head at her, while Wizard warned her to stay where she was. Yet, it was Doom's that held her in place. He was practically daring her to take another step. Arden decided it was in her best interest to remove herself from a situation she had no idea how she had gotten herself into in the first place.

"You know, it's late. Too late to have to deal with this. Kat, you mind if I take off?"

Kat gave her an approving nod. "I think that would be an excellent idea."

"Then I'll see you tomorrow. Good night, everyone."

Hurrying around the bar, she felt eyes boring into her back as she made her escape.

"Whew!" Arden breathed a relieved sigh once she was outside then flushed at seeing Burn's puzzled look.

"Rough night?"

She had to bite back what she really wanted to say. "You have no idea."

"One of the brothers giving you a hard time? If they are, just let me know, and I'll tell them to lay off."

"You'd do that for me?" Her exasperation with The Last Riders made the offer tempting. Burn had been really nice and polite toward her since she met him. He was one of the few Last Riders who wasn't constantly having sex within her field of vision.

"Sure. Who is it?"

She answered without hesitation, "Doom."

Burn's face underwent a drastic change. "Oh, maybe you misunderstood him."

Arden arched an eyebrow at him. "He just face-planted Jesus on the bar because he was talking to me. Wizard made him stop."

"That's good." Burn gave his own relieved sigh. "Wizard's handled it then."

Her jaw dropped. Were all The Last Riders afraid of Doom?

Snapping her mouth shut, she gave him a killing look before making for her car.

"Unbelievable." Grinding her teeth together, she got in the car. "Those people have some serious problems," she ranted in the confines of her car while mentally envisioning strangling Doom, Jesus, and Burn.

The only one who got off scot-free from her imaginary hit list was Wizard. She didn't have high hopes he would remain on her no-hit list for long. You didn't become president of Neanderthal men without being the biggest douchebag of them all.

CHAPTER 39

THE DECISION

"Bro, what's your problem?"

Doom refrained from answering Jesus's question, too intent on wanting to ask his own. "Why in the fuck are you asking Tink to marry you?"

"Tink?" Wizard interjected.

Kat quit chewing on her fingernails to provide the information. "Tink is the nickname Doom gave Arden."

"Oh. Carry on." Wizard waved at them magnanimously. "I want to hear this myself."

He glared at Wizard as he took a glass and filled it with beer; Doom wouldn't be surprised if the fucker pulled out a pack of M&Ms to enjoy while watching the fight he had initiated with Jesus.

"Why in the fuck did you ask Tink—"

"Goddamn, what in the fuck happened to the beer?" Wizard gasped.

"Ar—Tink," Kat hastily corrected, "fixed it so it's cold."

"I wanted to cry too," Jesus interjected. "That's why I asked Tink to marry me."

"What she say?" Wizard took another drink.

"She told me no."

"Good. I'm going to put my jacket on her. I've been thinking of settling down lately."

Doom started to come over the counter.

Wizard put his hand out to stop him. "Hold it right there, Hoss. A woman who can keep this fucking old contraction working is worth fighting you for."

"You wouldn't stand a chance in hell of convincing Tink to marry you. Stick to your lane and stay out of mine."

Wizard eyed him over the rim of his glass as he finished his beer. Wiping his mouth with the back of his hand, he refilled his beer. "And exactly why wouldn't I stand a chance with her?"

"Stick with Mama; she's more your speed."

"I don't disagree with you. Mama's more like a Harley. Tink, on the other hand, is more of a scooter, but when I fine tune her—"

Red fury nearly blinded him for an instant. An instant Wizard used to duck for cover.

"I'm just fucking with you," Wizard laughed, hunkered down behind the counter.

Leaning over the counter to stare down at Wizard, who was sitting on his ass, drinking his beer, Doom warned, "I'm going to fuck you up when you stand up."

"I'm pretty damn comfortable. Don't see that happening anytime soon. I can sit here all night."

"I'm not in a hurry," Doom threatened. "Or maybe I should go check and see what Mama is doing tonight? I could give her something big to put in her oven," he taunted.

Doom braced himself before he got the last dig out. If he was jealous over Tink when he didn't have a fucking jealous bone in his body, Wizard would go ballistic at the thought that someone else would take something he wanted before he got his first taste.

"Bro, that's fighting dirty," Jesus muttered under his breath. "I like it."

Having forgotten about Jesus, because Wizard had gotten under his skin, Doom's fist went to the side, punching Jesus in the jaw. The brother fell of his stool backward.

Kat gave a screech and started to rush around the counter, but Wizard grabbed her thigh, forcing her to stay still.

"What did Doom do?" he asked her.

Doom, who hadn't taken his eyes off Wizard, answered for her, "I punched Jesus. His whispering pisses me the fuck off."

"Everything pisses you off these days. You need to get your anger under control," Wizard advised him. "Instead of using us as punching bags to release your frustrations, why don't you go pound it out on *Tink*?"

Doom started to tell Wizard he'd rather pound him into next week when what Wizard said finally connected. Wizard was right.

"Give me a beer," Doom snapped.

Kat filled him a big mug. He took the mug from her he swallowed a big gulp, then another.

"Fuck."

Wizard poked his head up. "Right? Slides right down your throat, doesn't it?" Eyeing him as he rose to his feet, Wizard refilled his glass.

"Damn." As he swallowed the contents of the mug, Doom heard the sounds of chairs scraping the floor.

Wizard frowned. "What's wrong?"

"I can't get rid of the mugs now."

The brothers began gathering around the bar with bated breath.

Wizard eyed the mug. "Good?"

"Better than good. Might be the best beer I've ever had."

Wizard reached under the counter for one of the mugs to fill one for himself. The brothers pressed so close to the bar that Doom had to elbow Buck and Puck away as everyone watched Wizard try the beer.

"Damn." He appreciatively licked his lips. "Brother, you know what I've got to do."

Doom nodded. He knew what was coming as soon as Wizard's mouth touched the mug.

"You want to tell her, or you want me to?"

"I'll tell her." Doom shouldered his way through the crowd behind him.

"By the way," Wizard called out, "you sure you want to call her Tink? I think we should call her Frosty."

"She's not a Frosty."

Tink might be able to make the beer taste as if it had come from the Ice Age, but she had managed to blast away every reserve he'd had about becoming involved with her. Bit by bit, she'd removed each reason to withstand her until all he was filled with was raw, aching need. A need that he was willing to admit no other woman was going to fulfill, at least until he was satisfied.

It only took for him to get on his bike before his conscience started in on him. *What about when you leave?*

He would be upfront and honest, Doom assuaged his conscience as he started the bike. It wasn't like he wouldn't keep in touch. He could come back to Ohio every so often until she was ready to move on... Yeah, it was going to work.

Speeding out of the parking lot, he couldn't wait to see her. He hoped she wasn't in bed yet... Hell, what was he thinking? He hoped she was. The first thing he was going to tell her was that Wizard was going to make her a full member. Then he was going to rip whatever T-shirt of her father's she was wearing off. Making a mental note of which T-shirt he was going to give her, he debated over a couple he no longer wore.

He swung his bike into the parking lot of their apartment complex, then around the corner to where their building was located. He had to brake hard to keep from hitting several people.

As he gathered himself from nearly taking out three people who were fighting, he realized it was Andy taking on two other men.

He stopped the bike and saw Andy's girlfriend lying on the walkway and Tink fighting off another man who was still beating Lizzy.

Taking out his cell phone, he pressed a button. In the same movement, he got off his bike while keeping his cool to assess the situation, determining which neck he was going to break first. When he found his target, he moved with lethal intent. It didn't bother him that he was about to take a life—the fucker who had been beating the unconscious woman with a metal pipe deserved to die. The wrath heading his way wasn't about the unconscious woman but because he was aiming it at Tink now. He had sealed his fate when he struck a Last Rider's woman.

CHAPTER 40

THE KILLS

Doom caught the sawed-off steel pipe an inch from Tink's face.

Caught by surprise, the man turned his head toward him. Doom didn't give him time to react; he rocked the fucker's world with a strike so hard he crumpled to the ground.

Without pity, Doom struck him again to make sure he was down for the count. Then, seeing Tink had run to Lizzie before the man had landed on the ground, he jerked his phone out of his pocket. "Call 911."

Tink raised frightened eyes to his. "Help Andy."

"Baby, you don't have to ask." He tightened his hand on the pipe and started toward the two men fighting Andy.

One caught sight of him and broke off from punching Andy preparing to take him on, shouting toward the man on the ground.

"Micah, what in the fuck are you doing? Get up!"

Doom coldly laughed. "Save your breath. He won't be getting up."

"What did you do to my brother?" the man screeched, taking a swing at him as he drew closer.

Doom dropped the pipe and took the hit, using the opening to grab the man by the neck and jerk him closer. Closing his hands around the scumbag's throat, he started squeezing.

He heard strangled gasps coming from the man and ignored his ineffective struggle while checking on Andy, who was struggling to get away, his frantic gaze on Lizzie.

Lifting the man he was strangling off his feet until they were eye level, Doom head butted him. "Lights out, motherfucker."

He released the shitwad and only had to take one step forward to kick the man fighting Andy. "Go. I've got this."

Andy took off at a run.

Watching the man who had fallen to his knees trying to get back up, Doom heard the sounds of motorcycles coming near.

When he saw who had dropkicked him, the young man held up his hands in surrender. "Sorry. We'll go."

Doom stared at him without pity. "What in the fuck started this shitshow? You better tell me the truth. The girl in the T-shirt is mine, and she'll tell me if you're lying."

"We were stealing a car's carburetor when the alarm went off. The old man and woman came out of their apartment and tried to stop us. Micah and Cory started fighting them."

"Don't tell me you're a fucking innocent bystander."

"I couldn't leave my friends behind."

The Last Riders speeding around the corner had both of them looking as sirens sounded in the distance. Doom didn't know which one freaked the man out more, but he jumped up and started running. As he did, a car came speeding up behind him then stopped with a squeal of brakes. The fleeing man jerked the door open. He was able to get one foot inside before Doom tore him away and sent him flying. Before he could get up and start running again, Wizard was there, a foot on his chest.

Wizard opened his jacket and showed him the gun tucked into his waistband. "I wouldn't move," he warned.

Whoever was driving the car must have decided it was time to ditch his cohorts shifting the car into reverse to drive instead of plowing ahead with The Last Riders blocking the front of the car.

Quickly, Doom picked up the pipe he had discarded and rushed forward, then slammed it down on the windshield. The window being smashed must have frightened the driver, causing him to brake.

Using the opportunity, Puck slung the passenger door open to get inside. Doom opened the driver's door and saw Puck had removed the key.

"Put the car in *Park*," Doom snarled.

The driver behind the wheel looked to be around Blue's age and scared enough to piss himself.

"I didn't do anything!" the kid belligerently shouted at him, but did put the car in *Park*.

Using the kid's T-shirt, Doom ripped the little shit from the seat and threw him on the pavement.

"Jesus, deal with this shithead," Doom ordered the brother as he made his way to where Tink was standing with Andy, an arm around his shoulders.

They stayed out of the way as the paramedics treated Lizzie. From the looks of it, the woman was in pretty bad shape. When the cops arrived with more paramedics, Doom talked to them, explaining the scene he had driven into as other paramedics worked on the two men in the parking lots. One of the paramedics approached to interrupt the questioning between the police officer and him.

"One's dead. We're going to transport the other. Don't know if he's going to make it, either."

Doom's gaze didn't waiver from the cop's when he turned away from the paramedic's.

"You're going to need to come to the police station with us for questioning."

"I told you what happened. I'm finished talking to you until I have my lawyer present. Andy and Arden will confirm everything I told you. These punks beat a woman, from what I can see, to within an inch of her life, and he would have done so to the other one if I hadn't stepped in. The rest of them are damn lucky they'll be leaving in your back seat instead of you having to call for another ambulance."

Seeing the paramedics had loaded Lizzy onto the gurney, Doom strode toward a shivering Tink, taking off his jacket as he stepped up onto the walkway. Another cop was questioning her.

As he drew closer, Tink's eyes met his. Unable to get to her with the cop standing in front of her, he held his arms out. "Come here, honey."

She gave a sob and brushed past the cop to throw herself into his waiting his arms. Placing his jacket over her trembling shoulders, he closed his arms around her.

"Lizzy's hurt badly," she wept against his chest.

"I know."

"Can you take me to the hospital? I don't want them to be there alone."

"Of course. I was going to take you anyway." He reached out to gingerly move the hair away from the wound on her forehead. "You're going to need a few stitches."

With the hair moved out of the way, the wound became visible, blood running from the gash.

"You really should go in an ambulance. You'll have to get a CAT scan for the hit you took."

"I need to get dressed first." She put a hand to her forehead.

"They're just going to put you in a gown when you get there." Moving her hand away, he used the bottom of his shirt to wipe the blood off. He did, however, see how upset she was, so he didn't argue further. "Come on. I'll help you get changed."

"I don't need any help. I'll be right back."

"Nope. I'm not leaving you alone until we get your head checked out."

He turned her around then helped her up the steps. At the top, Doom noticed Tink must have hurried out so fast she had left her door open.

He shut the door behind them and followed her into the bedroom. While watching her as she slipped into a pair of sweats and a sweatshirt, he made sure no one had taken advantage of the open door.

She tugged on her tennis shoes before she stood up from the bed. Then she picked up his jacket and handed it back. "Thanks."

Doom didn't reach out to take it from her. "Wear it. The air is cold."

"I can grab one of my own."

Taking it from her, he held it out for her to put on. "There's no need getting blood on that one too."

"Oh." Tink turned around to slide her arms through the holes. "I'll get it cleaned before I give it back."

"Don't worry about it. You ready?"

"Yes, thanks." She shivered even though she was wearing his jacket. "I don't know what would have happened if you hadn't come when you did."

Unfortunately, Doom did. Andy wouldn't have been able to hold off the two men he was fighting much longer, and Tink would have probably ended up in the same shape as Lizzie, or worse.

Deciding not to disclose how much worse it could have been, he ushered her out of the apartment. More cops had shown up since they had gone upstairs. The cop who had talked to him now wanted to talk to Tink.

"You can talk to her while you give us a ride to the hospital." Doom showed the cop the wound.

"She can ride with me. You'll have to ride separately." Doom started to argue. "Give me a break," the cop told him. "I shouldn't have let you go upstairs with her until I had her statement."

"We'll follow behind," Doom acquiesced to save time, knowing Tink wanted to get to the hospital to be with her friends.

The brothers were waiting on their bikes next to his.

"Thanks," Doom said to all The Last Riders who had come as he got on his motorcycle.

Wizard leaned an arm on his handlebar. "Anytime. Not like we were doing anything." He nodded toward Tink as she got inside the patrol car. "You let her wear your jacket?"

"Yeah."

"You claiming her?"

"Yes."

"Cool. We going to the hospital?"

"I am. You can all go back to the club."

Wizard started his bike. As he did, the rest of The Last Riders did the same.

"I think we'll tag along. Save us from having to get back out if they arrest your ass."

"They aren't going to arrest me."

"I wouldn't sound so sure. I sent Puck to trail after the ambulance to give updates. The dude you headbutted was DOA. This go-around tied you with Shade."

Doom hit the gas when the patrol car started moving. He didn't have any feelings about tying with Shade's kill tally. There was no way it was accurate. The tally was more an estimate where Shade was concerned, anyway.

Shade was the most lethal Last Rider to wear a jacket. Anyone who ever fucked with him ended up finding out the true meaning of 'fuck around and fuck out.' The brother could bring out a cold sweat in other men just as proficient at killing as Shade was.

No remorse filled Doom for the lives he had taken tonight. The men had the option to run after being caught by Andy and Lizzy. Instead, they had chosen violence. A choice that had a fifty percent chance of succeeding and a fifty percent chance your luck just ran out. Tonight, two men's luck hadn't been in their favor. The other three, *if* they hadn't touched Tink, would hopefully make better choices in the future. *If* one of them had, Shade's and his tie wouldn't last long.

CHAPTER 41

THE TINK

Arden walked back into her apartment feeling as if she had left a lifetime ago and not the mere two hours that had passed.

"Can I get you anything?" Doom asked, shutting the door behind them.

"No, thank you." She sank down onto the couch and lowered her head to her hands. "He's not going to make it without Lizzie. She's Andy's whole world."

"I saw."

Arden felt Doom sit down next to her.

"I still can't believe she's dead." She choked back the hurt-filled scream at the thought of never seeing her friend again for such an incomprehensible reason. "I would have given them the whole car to leave them alone. Lizzy's dead because of me," she moaned, rocking back and forth.

"Your friend's dead because those punks wanted to make a quick buck."

"They wouldn't have come out of their apartment if it wasn't for my car alarm going off. You were right; I mess everything up. Lizzie and Andy would have been better off if I had never spoken to them. I tried to make their life easier. Instead, I destroyed it." As she cried into her hands, images of the couple sitting outside their apartment filled her with heartbreaking sadness.

Arden felt herself lifted onto Doom's lap. She lay her head on his shoulder and gave full vent to her tears.

"Don't piss me off by blaming yourself again. You treated them like you treat everyone—with kindness. Which is more than I can say about myself. That's why Andy warned me not to hurt you, why he was standing outside your apartment that night to make sure you were cool with me being there. They were both brave enough to be willing to take me on if you needed them to. Just like you took up for them when they would have been evicted after complaining about the rats, why you were paying their rent for the last six months."

Arden lifted her head. "How do you know? The office manager promised she wouldn't tell anyone."

"She wanted something I had for the information."

"What? Money?" She had started paying the couple's rent when she saw the eviction notice taped to the couple's door after they had gone out. She took the notice, went to the office, took care of their back rent, and had been paying it ever since without their knowledge. She had asked the manager to tell them the rent had been paid with government assistance for renters with low income.

"My dick."

"You had sex with..." Arden angrily started to throw herself off his lap, but his arm wrapped around her waist, holding her in place.

"Chill. I didn't give it to her."

The assurance had her calming down.

"Why not? Josie isn't unattractive."

"I don't fuck around with married women."

So, if Josie hadn't been married, he would have had sex with her? Why was she not surprised?

Arden tried to get off his lap again. "I'm tired. I need to get some sleep," she said stiltedly. "I called in today at the office, but I want to catch some sleep before I go to work at Mama's. Thank Wizard again from me for convincing Andy to go to the club with him. I'll call and check in with him before I go to work."

Doom stared at her as if dumbstruck. "You want me to leave?"

"Yes."

His face became etched in stone. "I'm not leaving. We don't know shit about those punks. I can guarantee the two I left breathing are already out on bail. If not, it won't be long. They could be part of a theft ring. If they are, their first order of business will be to take out witnesses. In case you have trouble figuring out who that is, it's you, Andy, and me. You're not staying here alone, and I'll be taking you back and forth between jobs."

"I don't need you to stay here."

"I'm not arguing. I'll sleep on the fucking couch, but I'm not leaving," he told her stubbornly. "Besides, how are you planning to get back and forth from work? Your car is out of commission until you can have it fixed."

"Fine," she snapped. "I'm too tired to argue." Being reminded of her car being out of commission poured cold water over the jealousy she had felt over Doom. How could she have given in to the petty emotion when Lizzie had been killed before her eyes?

Pinching the bridge of her nose, she stopped herself from breaking into tears again. All she had to do was make it to her bedroom and shut her door, and then she could cry to her heart's content.

She moved toward her bedroom closet to retrieve a blanket and a pillow, then returned to the living room and laid them on the couch. "Help yourself to what drinks and food I have in the refrigerator." Arden reached out to touch his arm when he would have swept past her to go the kitchen. "I'm sorry. I should be thanking you for saving Andy and me. Instead, I'm being a witch." Giving a disgusted sigh at herself, she tried to shed some light on her behavior to herself and Doom.

"I make a mess of everything. It's no wonder my brother doesn't like me. I shouldn't have given the tickets to Puck and Buck for their votes. I'm never going to be able to keep my mouth shut. I shouldn't have tried to join The Last Riders. Luc would really hate me if he found out The Last Riders only befriended him because I interfered." She gave a bitter laugh at herself. "I can't do anything right. It takes a woman being killed for you to want to stay with me, yet when we had sex, you couldn't take off fast enough."

When Doom opened his mouth to say something, she shook her head at him.

"Don't bother; it's okay. You plainly have a different viewpoint on sex than I do. You actually did me a favor. I let my attraction to you overrule my better judgment."

Doom's eyes narrowed on her angrily. "What in the fuck does that mean? You're no longer attracted to me?"

"I am," she admitted, embarrassed. "But I have to quit letting my heart overrule my head. A woman died because of me, and despite what you say, I am responsible. If I hadn't been working at the school for my father, I would have never moved in here, and Lizzie would still be alive."

"More likely, both could be dead." Doom looked at her,

his exasperation showing. "Without you here, they would have been thrown out months ago. These apartments have the lowest rent in town, which is why you probably chose to live here. If they had been evicted, where would they have ended up? Let me answer that for you. Nowhere with a roof over their heads. Lizzie looked as if a hard wind would blow her away, and Andy doesn't seem much better. I don't know what led to them living here, but I know for damn sure it wasn't you.

"Even putting that shit aside, you can't say if you hadn't been here, they wouldn't have come out if the thieves chose another car. But I can say without a doubt I wouldn't have been here to save Andy.

"I learned a hard truth when I was in the military. Shit happens. You can't bear responsibility for what evil people do; you can only clean up the mess and hope none of the blood gets on you."

Arden lowered her eyes to the jacket she was still wearing before glancing back at him. "Like you killing those two men?"

"Exactly," he confirmed. "Those men were given the choice to run away when Andy confronted them and again when I showed up. They didn't. They chose to take a life. Andy chose to confront them instead of calling the cops. All of them chose wrong. Each of them will have to live with their decisions for their rest of their lives. The only one who couldn't choose how to react was you. When you saw Andy and Lizzie were being attacked, there was no way on God's green earth you would have been able to stand back and watch from the safety of your apartment. Shit happens, honey." Doom lifted his hand to show her the bloodstains on the arms of his jacket.

Arden began gasping for air, not wanting to cry in front

of him. Then, unable to hold it in any longer, she burst into sobs. "I couldn't bring myself to talk to Andy. He must hate me."

"Tink, no one could hate you."

"Don't call me that nickname." Arden arched away, using the sleeve of his jacket to wipe her tears away.

"Why not?"

"The other women are given nicknames, like Kat, Margarita, Siren. They're sexy." She crinkled her nose at the thought of the nickname Doom had given her. "I can deal with Honey."

Doom shook his head. "Sorry, Honey has been taken. She's in Treepoint currently, but she goes back and forth every couple of months."

Figures. She should have known all the good nicknames were taken.

"Then why have you been calling me Honey?"

Doom started removing his jacket from her. "Tink might not sound sexy to you, but men find it very erotic."

Not believing him, she aided him in taking the jacket off. "Yeah, right."

"Let me clear up some confusion you seem to be having. I nicknamed you Tink because your tinkering around with the wiring saved The Last Riders from having a fire, which Wizard had already decided to give his vote for, but when you fixed the temperature of the beer, you had some of the brothers wanting to marry you. Any woman can act sexy, but damn... A woman who can fix anything she sets her mind to—whew; those are the ones who will get us killing each other over." Doom tossed the jacket onto the couch to draw her tighter against him. "By the way, when I called you honey, it wasn't as a nickname. I used it as an endearment."

"Oh..." She was flabbergasted at what he was telling her. "You did?"

"I did." His hand went to the nape of her neck to tilt it back.

She felt a blush rushing to her cheeks at his revelation.

Tearing herself out of his arms, she took a backward step. "I'm going to listen to my head and go to bed."

Turning on her heel, she made for the bedroom, hearing his low laughter trying to lure her back. She shut the door and went into her bathroom to take a shower. Drained of energy, when she was finished, Arden grabbed the first T-shirt she touched in the drawer. The moment she managed to pull it on her still damp body, she threw herself down on the bed.

The chastity belt would have been a waste of money, she groggily told herself. She was fully capable of curbing the attraction she had for the hunk of masculinity outside her bedroom door... As long as he didn't call her honey. Some torture would be too hard to endure.

CHAPTER 42
THE QUESTION

"Arden, wake up! Come on, honey, wake up."

Startled awake, Arden sat up, clawing at her throat, feeling as if she was being strangled. The bedroom was so dark she could only make out a shadowy face in front of hers.

Screaming, she tried to throw herself out of the bed.

"It's me—Doom. You were having a nightmare."

Doom's voice managed to cut through the nightmare battle scene she had been fighting in.

With her legs dangling off the bed, she let him pull her back to the middle of the bed.

"I'll turn the light on."

She shivered as she felt his weight leave the bed and pulled the covers back over her.

The light filling the room had her eyes adjusting to the change. She opened them and saw Doom returning to the bed, wearing a pair of gray sweatpants barely hanging on to his hips. Her hands went to her throat, still feeling as if she were unable to get a deep breath.

"Stop." His hands pried hers away from her throat. "You've scratched the fuck out of yourself."

"I did?"

"Yes. Must have been a hell of a nightmare."

Arden nodded, staring down at the hands still holding hers. "I was having a nightmare about Lizzie being hit with that pipe."

Doom grimaced. "I had a feeling you would. Hell, it was pretty fucked up what they did for a hunk of metal. I'm sorry I wasn't there sooner."

Arden wrapped the blanket around her tighter, feeling as if she would never be warm again.

"I'm just grateful you showed when you did. Usually, you're still at the club at that time of night. Luckily, you left when you did."

"I don't know about luck. I only left the club to see you."

Arden frowned. "Were you going to throw me out of the club again because of the argument we had?"

"No, I was coming to tell you Wizard was going to give you the rest of the votes you needed to become a Last Rider."

Her jaw dropped. "Why?"

"For fixing the beer."

"Are you serious?"

"Yes."

She started laughing. "Beer is considered more important than sex?"

Doom rolled his eyes. "Apparently." His expression grew more serious. "Wizard let you have the votes because you were the one who made the effort to fix what was wrong with the beer. Just like the wiring, which needed fixing before the whole club caught fire. We've become so used to Viper coming to handle anything messed up, and his absence caught up with us. He kept telling Wizard the club was his responsibility, but Wizard is easily sidetracked."

"Then why do you all keep him as president if he isn't taking care of the club?"

"Because he might not be taking care of the maintenance of the club, but Wizard is busting his ass doing the rest of the shit that goes along with being president. He's helping Burn getting custody of his kid. No lawyer in town wants to represent him because Moon, one of the brothers you haven't met yet, had the mayor's daughter chasing after him. The mayor blames Moon for his daughter trying to commit suicide after Moon didn't want to become serious and wouldn't let her hang out at the club anymore. Moon finally had to leave for Treepoint when charges were manufactured against him. Celine pressed charges saying Moon raped her and she was pregnant. We don't know how, but the charges against him were finally dropped. Which was great for Moon, but the mayor still uses his power to browbeat anyone from doing business with us locally. The warehouse is always short-staffed because no one wants to work for us. Wizard can't get permits to expand the club by adding more bedrooms and enlarging the kitchen, the mayor is trying to have it classified as a historical building. So, until the council decides, he can't do shit. Every council meeting, one the mayor's flunkies pushes the discussion back to another date."

Placing her pillow behind her back, Arden relaxed into a more comfortable position. Listening to Doom helped take her mind off Lizzie's death.

"Has Wizard thought about getting a lawyer?"

Doom lay down sideways on the bed, putting him at her feet.

"They take his money and do jack shit." He casually

started massaging her foot that was peeking out of the blanket. "Just like Burn's lawyer."

"I can see how Wizard has his hands full."

"I wasn't even counting the number of shifts he pulls at the warehouse when we're short-staffed."

Arden started to feel ashamed of herself for assuming Wizard always appeared so exhausted when she saw him at the club because of his partying lifestyle.

"I thought he spent all his time partying," she confessed, watching as her toes curled under Doom's machinations.

He gave her a wry smile. "He likes to burn the candle at both ends, for sure."

Arden laughed. "I think most of The Last Riders could say the same."

"We do like to party," he admitted.

"Don't you get tired of it?" Glancing away as if the answer didn't matter, she tried to move her foot away.

"No." His hand slid under the blanket to find her other foot.

"At least you're honest."

"I am. People might not like what I have to say or do, but I'm not going to lie to make someone else happy."

Arden quit trying to hide her foot and let him have it.

Glancing back at him, she swallowed hard. "Tell me something I don't know."

"Cool. I don't want any misunderstandings between us."

Arden stared at him quizzically. "Like how?"

He arched his brows at her as his palm cupped the bottom of her heel and his fingers slid between her toes. "You're not getting what I'm referring to?"

She could only stare at him in confusion. "I must not be."

"I claimed you as mine before I left the club last night."

"You did?"

Doom nodded. "That's why I left the club—to tell you." Doom left her foot to slide toward her ankle, his hand caressing it before moving higher to her knee.

Each movement he made felt as if he was opening a bent-up dam of need begging to be acknowledged. Fighting it back, she gripped the blanket so hard her knuckles turned pale.

"Doom..." She breathlessly tried to find her voice to stop him. She would definitely stop him if his hand reached any higher.

"I was going to take you to my apartment and get you to try on some of my T-shirts."

"Why would you want—" her breath hitched, "me to do that?"

His hand left her knee to glide to her sensitive thigh. "I don't want you in any other man's shirt, regardless of whom it belongs to."

The possessive way he looked at her got past her guard enough to let his hand skim higher. When Doom's fingers brushed against the soft material of her panties, it was too late to close her thighs to stop him.

You have a mouth, she told herself. *All you have to do is say stop*.

She regretted not buying the chastity belt as the material was pushed aside by probing fingers starting to explore the wet flesh underneath.

Curling an arm under her knee, Doom lowered her from a sitting position to a supine one with his dominating body over hers.

"I'm not your property, Doom."

"You sure?"

She clutched his shoulders when a finger started strumming her clitoris. "I'm not yours." Her head tossed and turned on the pillow as he plunged a finger inside of her.

Back and forth, Doom played with her until she felt his hand withdraw, leaving an aching, raw, unfilled need behind.

When he straightened away from her, she felt the loss of his body heat.

"You're not?" Nudging the blanket aside, Doom's hand went to her breast, his thumb circling the protruding nipple under her shirt. "I think you are."

Her lips tightened into a thin line, irritated at her body's failure to give credence to her lie.

"Okay, I'll play along." Rising into a sitting position, she smacked his hand away, deciding to even the playing field. She had played enough softball to know Doom thought he was going to win with little effort. Just because she hated confrontations didn't mean she was a pushover. Doom was about to find out why the team she had played on in high school had won championships four years in a row. The dude was about to strike out.

"If I'm yours, does that mean you're mine?"

CHAPTER 43

THE RULES

Arden could tell Doom was debating what to say next.

"From your hesitation, I'll take that as an no." Flipping the blanket back over her, she waved at the door. "Please close the door on your way out."

"Damn, honey, let's—"

"Nuh-uh... None of the honey stuff."

Doom's jaw clenched. The big boy wasn't used to striking out.

"I claimed you in front of all The Last Riders. I suppose it means the same."

"*Suppose*?" she scoffed. "How about if we do it this way, I take it means I'm no longer expected to keep the rest of The Last Riders company?"

"No, not unless you want to, but you have to ask for my permission, and I have to be there."

Arden could tell he liked the idea of him being able to veto who she would be with. *Jerk.*

"Then I will be able to veto who you're with, and I have to be there?"

"Not all the time, but I would tell you if I did, and I would make sure to wear a condom."

"From what Kat told me, wearing a condom is a hard rule regardless."

"Not when I claim you."

"Isn't that convenient?"

"I would be one hundred percent safe with other women."

Doom had mistaken her sarcasm. The big, randy fool didn't realize it was more of a jeer than her doubting he would stick to the rule.

"That's good. Then you can make one of them your property."

He raked his hand through his tumbled hair. "Fine," he snapped. "I'd tell you first and get your approval. Are you sure you want to be there?"

"If I give permission, I'm there, or it's a no-go. Why would it bother me to see you with other women? It's not like I haven't seen you lick a woman like she was your favorite flavor of snow cone."

"She wasn't my favorite flavor."

Arden wasn't fazed by the seductive smile he was giving her.

His hand moved back toward her breast. Arden smacked it away again.

"We play by the same rules, or we don't play," she stated firmly.

His jaw clenched, but he nodded. "As long as you understand I won't be dealing with any hurt feelings or recriminations afterward."

Why am I even considering this? Arden asked herself. She should say to hell with him, yet when she started to say exactly that, the look in his eyes stopped her. Doom wanted her as much as she wanted him. Would she just be a new toy to play with until he grew bored?

Don't do this to yourself. Going along with this was like running full force into a semi and praying for it not to hit her.

Instead of putting on the brakes, she continued on her run. She could always swerve at the last minute, couldn't she?

"Same."

Doom eyed her critically. "You're not as blasé as you're pretending to be, Tink. I'm going to be upfront with you. Claiming you isn't in the same category as getting engaged. There's not going to be a wedding ring in the future, at least not with me. In a month or two, I'll be leaving Ohio. The only reason I'm still here is because I'm waiting for the man I'll be replacing to retire. I think we could have some good times until then, but I want you to keep in mind, regardless of how good this turns out to be between us, I'll still be leaving... Alone."

Arden shrugged. "Then if you don't want me to grow attached, I won't. I appreciate your honesty. This actually works for me. With my parents in such bad health, I don't know how long I have before I'll have to turn my main focus on them."

"I'm still not buying it. I really don't want to see you hurt."

"Sounds like you're changing your mind."

"When I'm with a woman, I don't want to leave any damage behind when it's over."

"You want a clean conscience when it's over, then stick to the conditions we agreed to. I'll wave you off when you're ready to leave town," she promised.

Doom didn't seem convinced, but his hand moved

toward her again, and as he leaned forward, her breast met him halfway.

"I'm cold, Doom, inside and out. I feel as if every part of my life is death. Lizzie..." she choked out. "My parents..." Her head fell to his shoulder. "I need to be warm again before I forget what it feels like."

Doom stood up from the bed. Thinking he was going to remove his sweatpants, she was surprised when he picked her up in his arms. Holding her steady, he bent to pick up her cell phone from the nightstand then carried her out of the bedroom. Curious, Arden remained silent until he reached the apartment door and went out.

"Wherever we're going, I need to lock my door."

She heard Doom shut the door behind them, and then he carried her to his apartment.

"Like that would make a difference. My camera will pick it up if someone gets near your door."

"I should get one."

"Don't bother; I'll be there before any cops would be anyway."

She felt the prick of tears at the reminder of him coming in time to keep her from suffering the same fate as Lizzie.

The sound of beeps had her glancing at the door as Doom pressed buttons on a computerized doorknob.

"I'm not going to ask how you got approval for that," she said as Doom strode through the doorway.

He grinned at her as he shut the door. "I let Puck ask her for permission."

The apartment was shrouded in darkness as he walked through his living room. She could only make out shadows of where she assumed he had placed his furniture.

Doom didn't turn the lights on until they were in his bedroom.

Stunned speechless at what the light revealed had her taking it all in as Doom carried her to the masculine, tobacco-colored bed. A tufted leather headboard looked as if it were six inches thick and reached nearly to the ceiling. The nightstand was white on the bottom with wood the same color as the headboard it sat next to.

She was still craning her neck to take everything in when he laid her down on the soft sage-green comforter. Embarrassed at how cheap and mismatched her furnishings were compared to his, she began to feel self-conscious. Not only did this room scream taste, it was shouting money, money, money! The headboard alone probably cost more than what she had spent on her apartment furnishings in total.

Wrapping her arms across her chest, she wanted to make an excuse to leave.

As if sensing her hesitation, Doom placed a hand on the bed next to her hip to give her a kiss that had her reconsidering that option. *So what if he has money? He can be my sugar daddy anytime,* she thought mischievously as she appreciatively watched him walk to a dresser and open a drawer. When he came back, he removed her T-shirt, replacing it with the one he had taken from the drawer. Then his hands went to his hips to pull his sweatpants off.

He climbed onto the bed, his mouth pausing a centimeter away from hers. "I wish I could take the pain you're feeling away, but I can't. All I can do is share your grief with you. I can't make your parents better, either, but if you need a shoulder to lean on, use mine. You want to feel warm enough, so you'll never have to worry about forgetting? Honey, I can do that too."

Covering her mouth with his, Doom drove the chill out

of her bones with the warm glide of his tongue. The man kissed as if he had a PhD in the art of what to do with his tongue. She tried not to think about the numerous women Doom had gained his experience from. Damn, she wanted to hate them, but being the one benefiting from their instruction drove the emotion out of her mind. How could she hate the ones who had gambled their heart on Doom before her?

Twining his tongue with hers, at the same time as his legs, Doom rocked their bodies until he was on the bottom and she lay on top of him. His hands went to her waist to scrunch the T-shirt over her breasts, leaving them dangling. Detaching his tongue from hers with a slow glide to the roof of her mouth, he lifted her higher over him, latching his mouth onto a nipple.

"Do you know how long I've wanted to see you in my shirt?"

"No."

"Too fucking long," he moaned against her breast. He lowered her body onto his to plump her breast. "Your breasts are the perfect size."

"They aren't very big," she lamented one of her pet peeves about her body.

"Woman, anything bigger would just be a waste for me." Licking the crevice between her breasts, his mouth turned to the other one eagerly waiting, tugging at the nipple with his teeth. Arden felt a searing heat hit her groin like a nuclear blast.

Startled, she froze.

Doom released her nipple to lift questioning eyes to hers. "Did I hurt you?"

Embarrassed, she shook her head, unable to meet his eyes. "No."

At his confident smirk, she tried to throw herself off his supine body. "I hate you."

He placed a restraining hand on her belly so she couldn't get off the bed.

"There's nothing to be embarrassed about. These little beauties are—" he squished the offending nipple between his finger and thumb, "very sensitive."

Shrugging her shoulder, she managed to free her nipple.

His smug look brought the competitor out in her. It was time to bring some heat his way.

Exploring kisses traveled down his chest as she moved her body over his. Darkly tanned skin felt smooth as satin. Arden showed her appreciation of his body with each kiss and caress as she searched for, to her, unchartered territory. For tonight, and until Doom called it quits, she was his. He was her property as much she was his.

Doom is mine. The heady thought emboldened her. He had to *like* her to have claimed her in front of The Last Riders, didn't he? She could deal with like. It was more than any man had felt for her before. What she saw as imperfections, he made her feel as if she should be walking on a Victoria Secret runway.

From the moment she had seen him at The Last Riders' clubhouse, she had felt a burgeoning awareness. Masking that she had developed a crush on him had been difficult when she was working at the bar. She knew the exact moment when Doom had become aware she was hiding her feelings. The first kiss they shared had done her in. He had read her feelings like a blind man read braille.

Committing each sensation of touching him to her memory so she could remember it in the long years ahead after he left Ohio, she boldly slid between his thighs, her hand reaching for his protruding cock, her tongue going for the glistening tip, until Doom's hand went to her hair to pull her head back.

"You don't have to."

"You're not the only one who likes snow cones," she purred, jerking her hair from his clasp.

Arden licked the glistening tip before surrounding the head with her mouth. Inexpertly, she sucked on him, her confidence soaring when his hips rose off the mattress. Taking it as a sign he wanted her to take more, she did, stopping when she had reached her limit. She slid her mouth back up, licked his shaft all the way, then swirled around the tip before going back down.

At first, she went slow, afraid she would choke and humiliate herself, but then she lost the fear when she heard the groans coming from Doom. Working on her speed until she was bobbing her head over his cock, she realized the side effect of giving him a blowjob heightened her own arousal, which had her grinding her panty-covered pussy on his thigh that had maneuvered itself between hers. Having his cock in her mouth, under her control, made her feel sexy. The newness of feeling that way emboldening her further until she was going down on him further than she had believed possible.

Not even the sucking sound she made, when with a grunt, Doom lifted her up to stand on the bed, embarrassed her. She was too afraid of falling, but Doom's corded muscles held her firm.

"Pull off your panties. I want to see your pussy," he demanded.

She carefully removed the panties, letting them drop to the bed.

"Bring that sweet thing here, honey..." His low voice hit

her like a lightning bolt where he was staring at her. "I want my pussy where it belongs—on my dick."

Luckily, her knees didn't need any help; they were already giving out beneath her, sliding her onto his cock, her insides melting as Doom's cock surged inside.

Her head dropped to his chest. "This feels so good..." she moaned.

"You haven't felt anything yet," he promised with a guttural voice.

Doom made good on his promise. His hands on her waist set a rhythm that had her biting her lips to keep from screaming each time he jerked her down.

"Raise my shirt over your breasts. I want to see your titties while you ride me."

"You don't want me to take it off?"

"Fuck no!" he hissed through pursed lips.

Scrunching her shirt up, she held the bottom under her chin as she rode him.

As Doom's expression grew fiercer, Arden could tell he was about to climax.

"Honey, as much as I'm enjoying this playing around, playtime is over."

Playtime?

A startled yelp escaped her when, in one movement, Doom raised his upper body off the mattress to push her backward on the bed. Untangling their legs, he didn't miss a stroke as, pulling her legs up to her shoulders, he started pounding inside of her.

"If I get too rough, tell me to slow down."

"Okay..." she moaned, her hands gripping his hair to pull his mouth down to hers.

His body powerfully moved over hers as his thrusts grew stronger and faster. At his first stroke, she found out

Doom had been reticent about giving her his full length. Nothing was held back now as he surged inside of her, making the whole bed shake. With her legs clasped over his arms and hands hooked her over her shoulders, she was a willing captive to his demands.

"You doing okay?" His raspy voice had her nails digging into his back.

"Better than okay."

"Your pussy is as slick as honey."

"That isn't much of a compliment," she complained. "Honey is sticky."

"Not when it's hot."

She was unable to argue or form a coherent thought as his cock took possession of what was left of her mind and body.

"We're going to come together. I don't want you too sore for me to fuck in the morning,"

"I'm not ready... Just a few more..."

Doom's mouth went to her breast, covering the whole nipple.

"No..." she pleaded, aware of what he was about to do.

Ignoring her plea, he bit down, sending her into a climax that had her twisting to get away, afraid she would splinter into a million pieces.

Gently releasing her nipple, his mouth went to the curve of her breast to administer a harder bite.

"Fuck..." he groaned as he stopped moving and his full weight dropped, bearing down on her. It took several minutes before either of them could move, mainly because of Doom's prone body being on top.

When he rolled off, Arden managed to lift her head to look at him, seeing his arm over his eyes.

"Fuck..."

Hesitantly, she rolled over to lay her chest on his chest. Using her hands to prop her head up, she eyed him consideringly. "The way you're saying that, I can't tell if it's good or bad."

Doom didn't remove his arm from his eyes. "Honey—don't talk."

Hurt, she started to roll away, but Doom forestalled her by using her movement to roll over with her.

"I'm trying like hell not to keep going at you until you can't walk into work tomorrow morning."

"Oh..." Sighing, she quit struggling to get out from under him.

"Yeah... *Oh,*" he mimicked.

"There is another option..." Wrapping her legs around him, she gave him a teasing glance. "I can call in sick."

CHAPTER 44
THE HAVEN

Arden clicked on her mouse while giving the patient on the other side of her desk a warm smile. "You're all set. Your appointment is scheduled for March 17th at 9 a.m. Is there anything else I can help you with?"

"Not unless you can give me another shoulder so I don't have to undergo this surgery."

The young man might have been joking, but Arden could see the fear in his eyes. Sympathizing with him, she gave him a reassuring glance. It was one thing to be told you need to have surgery, but when a date for the operation was scheduled, the reality of it really happening, the fear factor began a countdown. Arden could sympathize as she was waiting for her own countdown to begin.

The day Doom told her he was no longer interested, or he was leaving Ohio, her fear factor, which had her constantly on edge, was that she didn't know which would come first.

Handing the paperwork to the patient, she tried to reassure him as much as she was able. "Don't worry," she said as she saw Haven and another patient stop before reaching her workstation, waiting for their turn. "Dr. Dickerson is an excellent surgeon. You'll be back on the basketball court next season." She opened the drawer to her side, took out a certificate, and handed it to the young man. "Here's a gift certificate for a free custard at Fran's Frozen Custard." Arden gave him a conspiratorial wink. "The strawberry with Captain Crunch is my favorite."

The smile she received from the patient as he left with the certificate and paperwork was worth the reproving frown she received from Haven as she directed the older woman forward.

"Good afternoon..." Arden greeted the woman, taking the paperwork from Haven and glancing down at the name. "Mrs. Stevens. Thank you, Haven."

Haven gave a curt nod then left the patient for her to complete the necessary paperwork.

Arden watched the nurse walk away, wondering why Haven had given her such a cold glare as she turned to leave.

She put the curious encounter to the back of her mind so she could concentrate on the patient and spent the next ten minutes scheduling her for a knee replacement surgery.

The woman took the paperwork when she finished, but didn't immediately get up.

"Is Dr. Barr as good as the reviews say he is?" Mrs. Stevens asked worriedly.

Arden gave her a confident smile. "Better. If I had to replace my knee, Dr. Barr would be who I would get to perform my surgery."

"Whew, that's a relief."

Reaching in her drawer, she took out another gift certificate to hand to the woman. "Stop at Ralph's when you leave. He makes a mocha latte that is out of this world. Tell him not to skimp on the drizzle."

"Thank you."

"No problem. You have a great day."

When the woman was out of eyesight, she turned in her computer chair to talk to her coworker.

"Celia, I'm leaving for break. You want me to bring you back anything?"

"No," she replied frostily. Her coworker didn't even to bother to look away from her computer screen.

Taking her purse, Arden stood to leave, noticing Celia give her a once-over.

The odd behavior started to grate on her nerves as she made her way to the breakroom. What was going on? She was used to being ignored by her coworkers, but this cold behavior they weren't making an attempt to hide felt bizarre to her. Had she messed up some paperwork she was unaware of? It couldn't have been because she had called in yesterday.

She had called in to HR, but instead of telling them she was sick, she had taken another personal day, as she had the day Lizzie had been killed. They couldn't be angry she had taken two personal days. It made no sense to her.

In the breakroom, she bought herself a soda before choosing a small, empty table in the corner. Taking out an apple and a book from her purse, she started reading as she ate.

Tingles of awareness had her lowering her book. Several people were talking but would glance intermittently toward where she was sitting. It was a no-brainer she was the focus of their conversation.

She was about to look back down at the book when Haven got up from the table and made a beeline toward her.

"Can I help you?" Arden asked when Haven came to a stop.

"Does Dr. Dickerson know you're giving out coupons to his patients?"

Arden laid her book on the table at the aggressive tone. "I'm not sure if he is or isn't. I asked Dr. Barr, and he said it would be fine. I assumed Dr. Barr would have told the other doctors in the practice during their staff meetings, but I can't say for sure if he did or not."

"I asked Dr. Dickerson, and he said no. He's checking out where the money is coming from accounting for the gift certificates."

"Then it will be a futile search. I used my own money to pay for the certificates," Arden informed her. "I asked Dr. Barr if it would be okay to give them to certain patients who were afraid of their surgeries. I don't do if often; usually only two or three patients a day."

Haven didn't seem any happier she had used her own money. "Some of our patients have dietary restrictions."

Arden nodded. "Which I can see on their paperwork before I give them a certificate."

Weirdly, Haven became even more upset. "I'll inform Dr. Dickerson that you make a habit of going behind his back to give coupons out to promote other businesses."

"Certainly, I don't consider it going behind Dr. Dickerson's back as I discussed it beforehand with Dr. Barr, but you should do whatever you feel is right."

Arden didn't go into the difference between gift certificates and coupons. Haven knew the difference. She was just twisting it to suit her own agenda.

During her years at working at the practice, she had never had an issue with Haven before.

"I will," Haven snapped.

Expecting her to leave, Arden stared at her expectantly.

"He's going to dump you just as quickly as he dumped me," Haven spat out suddenly.

"Dr. Dickerson fired you?"

"You stupid bitch. I'm talking about Doom."

A sick revelation came to her as Haven appeared ready to scratch her eyes out. Arden felt the color wash out of her skin when she realized everyone in the room was no longer making any attempt not to watch the confrontation taking place between Haven and her.

"I don't find this an appropriate conversation for us to be having during working hours."

"Why not? We're on break," Haven snapped. "I can say anything I want to you."

"Within reason," Arden agreed. "If you have something to say, we can discuss it after work." Arden gathered her things and started to rise. Shockingly, Haven pushed her back down, and not one person in the room said anything about the overt aggression she showed her.

Taking a napkin from the holder, Arden started cleaning the spilled soda. "Say what whatever you want to get it off your chest."

"Don't come off as little Miss High and Mighty. We both know you're spreading your legs to any of The Last Riders who give you a second glance. You must have really showed Doom a good time for him to claim you."

Each word coming from Haven's lips felt like a smack to her cheek.

"At least I didn't give it out to any other Last Riders, which is why they wouldn't let me join the club. Doom dropped me after a couple of weeks. Let's see how long before he quits stopping by your place for a midnight ride."

"How did you find out Doom claimed me?"

"You figure it out, you stupid bitch! Congratulations," she added snidely, "on becoming a Last Rider. You can get your tattoo. I recommend getting '*Slut*' as a tramp stamp. Doom prefers giving it from behind."

Shaking, she watched Haven storm out of the room.

As she cleaned up the soda, Arden felt the censure of her coworkers' eyes. She wrapped her book in napkins, then threw the soda and apple away before returning to her desk.

When Cecil put her phone down, Arden knew someone had already gossiped what had happened in the breakroom.

Three hours remained before she could leave. Pretending she was unfazed by the encounter brought on a headache, which only grew worse as the day progressed.

When the last patient left, she shut down her computer, scooted back her chair, and left, telling the other workers goodbye as she usually did. They never acknowledged it, anyway.

She proudly walked out of the building as if she didn't have a care in the world while, inside, her soul felt as if it had been shattered beyond recognition.

As she drove toward Mama's restaurant in the loaner car her insurance had rented for her, she sniffed back tears, determined not to give in to the hurt feelings. She wasn't angry with Haven. The woman was hurting and had taken it out on her instead of the person who had initiated the hurt. Doom.

In a few weeks, I'll be her.

The day before had been the best day she had ever had. She and Doom had spent the morning in his bed before spending the rest of the day lounging around his apartment then returning to his bedroom to spend the rest of night having sex. Doom had ordered pizza, and they ate on the bed as they watched a movie. He had allowed several sides of his personality she hadn't seen before come out. Unbelievably, he could be carefree, humorous, and fun, which had only made her fall in love with him further. She had hated waking up this morning to leave him sleeping in bed to go to work.

Lamenting to herself that she should have taken another personal day, she nearly wrecked when the car in front of her suddenly braked. Getting herself in check, she forced her mind to focus on driving instead of Doom and Haven.

When she arrived at the restaurant, she changed clothes then checked in with Mama.

Mama took off her food gloves to hug her, then pulled back and eyed her critically.

"Let me see," Mama said sternly.

Pulling back the swatch of hair, Arden showed the stitches, which she had used her hair to hide.

"Do they hurt?" Mama asked with concern.

"No, I'm good," Arden assured her.

"If you're sure... Let me know if you start feeling unwell or need a break."

"I will."

Mama went to the sink to wash her hands. "We have a special guest coming in tonight at nine. He asked if you would be here before he booked. I'll call if you decide to leave early."

Arden didn't have to ask who the guest was. Only one guest would call ahead to ask if she was working.

"I'll make sure the private dining room is ready."

"I appreciate you." Mama grinned, starting her mixing bowl.

"Same."

Going to the hostess stand, she wasn't given time to

brood over the ugliness Haven had sprouted off at her. The evening rush was usually busy, but tonight, one of the runners had called out sick, so Arden pitched in to help whenever she had a chance. At eight, she went to the private room and set a table for three, making sure it was perfect before heading to the kitchen to put in an order she wanted them to begin preparing at nine. Going to the wine cooler, she then chose a wine from Mama's private stock and placed it in an ice bucket she had brought with her. She glanced at her watch as she carried it to the back room. After giving the room a final appraising glance, she went to the side door.

Three minutes later, she heard a knock. She opened the door and stepped aside to let the small party enter.

"Good evening, Governor Benning, Mrs. Benning, Larisa."

"Good evening, Arden."

Arden took the hand the governor extended to her to find herself pulled into a warm hug.

"I told Merryn I was tired of eating out. I needed some homecooked food."

"I'm glad. I've missed seeing you all." She gave him a warm hug in return, then turned to the waiting arms of his wife.

"How are you, Arden? You look pale. The next time Larisa and I have a girls' day out, you're coming with us. And this time, I won't take no for an answer."

"I won't," she promised as she turned to their daughter, who gave her a friendly smile.

"I think you look good. Don't listen to Mom. She thinks I've lost weight." Larisa rolled her eyes toward her mother. "I've gained six pounds just from the Valentine candy Mom and Dad bombarded me with. With Bryony going to college, they deluged me with her share."

"I can't get used to my baby being gone." The governor's wife sniffed back tears.

"I miss her too." Arden grimaced. "We used to hang out once a week. It's been a couple of months since I've seen her."

Arden began ushering them to the private room she had prepared for them. She seated them, then poured each of them a glass of their favorite wine.

"Excuse me, I'll be right back. I've put in your appetizer order. It should be done."

"Take your time. We're in no rush." Merryn gracefully placed the linen napkin on her lap.

"Speak for yourself, woman. I've been thinking of those fried zucchini blossoms all day."

Arden hurried toward the kitchen, hearing what the governor said. Luckily, the appetizer was ready. Nabbing a fresh loaf of bread, she carried both back to the private room and placed the dishes on the table, then took their orders.

"I'll put your orders in. Can I get you anything else?" she offered.

The governor, who had eaten three of the six blossoms, looked up from his plate. "You can bring another order of the blossoms and bring another plate. You haven't eaten yet, have you?"

"No, but I don't want to impose myself on you."

The governor gave her a mockingly stern look. "We go through this every time we come here. You're family. How many times do we have to tell you this? You practically lived with us when Luc was in the hospital, and Merryn coached you all through grade school and high school, and you spent more weekends with Bryony than I have. So, unless you want to break this old man's heart and my wife's, bring another plate back with you."

Merryn lifted the napkin to the corner of her eye. "I couldn't have said it better myself."

Arden and Larisa shared an amused look at her parents.

"I think you did, Mom, the last time we were here." Larisa snatched the last blossom off the platter before her father could. "Hurry back, Arden. I'll show you the pictures of my new apartment."

Excusing herself, she returned to the kitchen to place the order and grabbed another plate and setting. Going to the wall, she clocked herself out.

"I'm just going to clock you back in."

Dodging the dish towel Mama snapped at her when she was walking by, Arden laughed, feeling the first bit of hurt Haven had inflicted on her right itself.

"Fine." Arden warned, "Then I'll buy gift certificates for The Last Riders. You wouldn't be able to turn them away then."

Glaring at her, Mama started winding her dish towel again. Arden knew when it was wiser to run.

Taking a seat at the table, she eagerly flipped through Larisa's pictures as she and Merryn talked about the vacation she wanted to take to visit Bryony.

Arden didn't talk throughout the meal, mainly listening as they talked.

"You're very quiet tonight, Arden," the governor said intuitively.

It's now or never.

"I'm sorry. I have something on my mind, and I could use your help, but I hate to ask. All I need is some advice—like you gave when I was growing up. But I hate to ask now that you're governor." Arden talked in a rush, embarrassed to ask for anything from the people she considered a second family. "I don't want to impose on our friendship, so if I'm out of line, I'll drop the subject, and we'll forget I ever mentioned anything."

Immediately, the governor put his fork down. "In all the years I've known you, you've never asked any of us for a damn thing. Tell me your problem, and I'll see what I can do to help." The governor gave her gentle smile. "Ask away."

TIRED, Arden let herself into her parents' house. She flicked on the living room lights as she made her way to the den, which they had converted into her parents' bedroom. Quietly opening the door, she saw her mother sitting up in bed, reading a book. Softly tapping, so as not to startle her, Arden waited until her mother noticed her before walking further into the room.

Her mother lay the book down and gave her a searching look. "You should be in bed."

"I just wanted to check in with you since I didn't come by yesterday." She bent to place a kiss on her mother's cheek.

"Arden—you worry too much. I would have called if we needed anything."

"I know. I just wanted to double-check."

Her mother sighed, aware it was futile to keep arguing.

"How's Dad doing?" Arden asked, looking to where her father was lying on the other side of the bed. His face looked tired and worn, even in sleep.

"Had a little bit of an upset stomach earlier. He says nothing tastes as good as it used to."

"I'll make him some potato soup and a loaf of bread for dinner tomorrow. That always makes him happy."

She moved to the other side of the bed to check on the machines that were keeping her father alive while he slept.

"I remember when he first got this oxygen and sleep apnea machine. I wondered how you both could sleep with all the noise. I don't pay attention anymore," she said more to herself than her mother.

"Is something wrong?"

Arden shook her head. "No." Moving back to her mother's side, she carefully crawled onto the bed to lie down between her parents. Laying her head on the pillow next to her mother's shoulder, she reached for her hand.

Her mother clasped her hand back. "Rough day?"

"No." Arden had stopped confiding in her mother since her father's heart attack. "I actually had a good day. The Bennings stopped by the restaurant for a visit."

"Merryn said they might when I talked to her earlier today."

Her mother and Merryn Benning had been friends since birth, becoming friends like their own mothers had been. Merryn and her mother had each chosen each other as their labor coaches to be with them during their children's births.

"Do you ever regret that Landen stood you up for the date you had with him?" Arden asked her mother curiously.

"God, no." Her mother gave a panting laugh as she fought to catch her breath. "Landen and Merryn were meant for each other; everyone could see it but them. They were too busy trying to outdo each other by being the most popular. Landen standing me up was the best thing that ever happened to me, and to them. If Merryn hadn't gone to give him a piece of her mind for standing me up, they might never have gotten together."

"It did work out. They are very happy." Arden couldn't help but imagine if her mother would have been the healthy, vibrant woman Merryn had been tonight if that date had taken place.

"I'm just as happy." Her mother clasped her hand tighter. "Very happy. I had the life I wanted with the only man I ever loved. I have two children I adore. Can you imagine me having Bryony or Larisa as my daughters?" Her mother gave another panting laugh. "Bryony doesn't have a thought that lasts longer than a minute, and Larisa, bless her, nearly smothers me with blankets any time she comes to visit me. I had to switch doctors when she called to cuss his nurse out because my medicine hadn't been called in to the pharmacy."

"Larisa even scares Mama." Arden giggled.

"She scares me too." Her mom reached for a tissue when she started coughing as she tried to laugh again.

Arden straightened off the pillow to raise her mother higher to pat her back.

"You okay?" she asked when the coughing spasm ended.

"Yes."

After she helped her lie back down, Arden resumed her position on the pillow.

"Go to sleep," she told her. "I'll leave when I see you're asleep."

"I don't want you to drive home tired."

"I won't, I promise," she assured gently.

Arden moved herself into a more comfortable position on the bed, listening to the sound of her mother's breathing as the machine poured more oxygen into her lungs.

She was about to doze off when she heard her father turn onto his side.

"Your mother would have been miserable with Landen. He doesn't know the difference between a can opener and a wrench."

"You ever tell Mom you beat Landen up for asking her out?" Arden reached out her other hand to take her father's.

"Baby girl, some things a woman doesn't need to know."

CHAPTER 45
THE VISITORS

"What's up, bro?" Jesus greeted him as he strode into the club. Tilted backward in the chair with his legs propped on the table, Jesus was holding a mug of beer and using his stomach as a table. The motherfucker looked as if he didn't have a care in the fucking world.

Brothers sitting at the bar and the surrounding table eyed him warily. He gave Puck a disgusted look when the brother moved to sit at the other side of the bar, and asked Kat for a beer.

Waiting for it, Doom glanced at the only two brothers unbothered by his glowering stare.

"When did you two arrive?"

"Shade and I got here about thirty minutes ago," Moon answered. "We were having a good time until you walked through the door." Moon nodded toward Jesus, who had moved to sprawl out in a booth. "I see you aren't getting any mellower in your old age."

"I'm younger than you," Doom replied snidely, taking the beer from Kat.

He was lifting it to his lips when Wizard came in from

the hallway, only wearing jeans. Scratching his stomach, Wizard gave him an irritated glower as he passed to head behind the bar.

As he poured himself a cup of coffee, the bar went quiet; even Margarita and Kat cautiously stayed out of Wizard's way.

Wizard moved to face him with his coffee cup in hand. "Can you tell me why Jesus texted me you're looking for a fight?"

Doom shrugged. "I have no idea."

"I'm too tired for this shit, Doom. When you left last night, you were in the best mood I've seen you in since..." Wizard broke off to drink a sip of his coffee before setting it back down to scratch his stomach again. "Okay, since fucking never... This afternoon, I get woken up after I worked nine hours to load a fucking truck—to some bullshit about you picking a fight with Jesus. What's the problem?"

Doom wasn't fazed by Wizard's irritation. "Why don't we ask the motherfucker who texted you?"

"That would be me." Shade met his gaze head-on. "I was trying to give you a break. Acted like you a few times, and it always came back to the same reason—a woman. And since I'm not in the loop anymore of who has your nuts in a twist, I gave Wizard a heads-up. So, if you start the same shit with me that you tried to start with Jesus, I'm going to stuff that glass up your left nostril and yank it out the right. Now, are you going to let me finish my beer in peace, or are we going to have a problem?"

As he considered his answer, Doom heard a cell phone ring. He glanced around and saw Margarita answer it then say something into the phone before heading to the kitchen. Curious, Kat walked to the doorway, unashamedly listening to Margarita's conversation.

Next time he talked on a cell phone, he would make sure Kat wasn't within listening range. In fact, Doom was surprised at how nosy Kat was being. It was unlike the woman.

Turning his mind back to the men waiting for his answer, Doom made himself deescalate the situation with Shade. He had been brewing for a fight, and since he couldn't find the real source of his annoyance, he had settled on Jesus.

"No problem."

"You're good?" Wizard confirmed.

"Yes." Doom went back to drinking his beer as Wizard reached across the bar top to fist-bump Shade's and Moon's hands.

"What are you motherfuckers doing here?" he asked amiably. "Viper didn't say anything about you coming when I talked to him this morning."

"Moon and I are only here for a few days," Shade told Wizard.

Doom tuned out Shade and Wizard's conversation, his thoughts back on the true cause of his discontent. Arden.

The day after they had spent the night and the whole day together, he had expected her to blow his phone up with texts and phone calls like every woman he had allowed to spend the night. He had prepared himself to make nice but make it plain that texts, calls, actually any communication other when they hooked up, fell into a relationship category he wasn't interested in. After Arden left his apartment to go to work, he had waited for the first text to come in, but nothing. Zip, zilch, nada. As the day progressed, he had come to the club, still in a pretty good mood. He'd even worked several hours at the warehouse. After work, he'd returned to the club to play several hours of pool with Puck and Buck. At eleven, he knew her shift had ended at the restaurant, so, giving her an hour to get home and shower, he'd left the club.

Not seeing Arden's rental car, he had still gone to her apartment to knock. When it remained unanswered, he had gone to his apartment to sit on his couch and wait for her to come home. Instead, he had fallen asleep waiting for her.

Determined not to text her, he had showered and dressed before heading out. Could something have happened to her parents? Growing concerned, he had driven by her work to see the rental car in the parking lot.

Was she ghosting him? Was that why she wasn't texting him? He completely forgot that had been his intention for her.

The whole way to the club, all he could think was his eagerness to get to her apartment and fuck her only to feel like a fool when she wasn't there.

He wasn't demented. He knew it was crazy to feel the way he was feeling, but he did despite trying to reason with himself.

He emptied his glass and was going to motion for Kat that he wanted a refill when he noticed she must have gone into the kitchen with Margarita.

As he turned the corner of the bar, he heard a commotion coming from inside the kitchen. Hurrying, Doom entered the kitchen to see Kat and Margarita fighting.

"You bitch!" Kat yelled at Margarita. "You should have kept your mouth shut. You shouldn't be running your mouth about shit to—"

Doom nearly took a header into the refrigerator when he went sliding on the slick floor.

"What in the fuck did you spill?" Doom yelled, catching himself.

Kat shoved Margarita away from her, making her stumble against the kitchen table.

"Nothing," Margarita muttered, smoothing down her hair.

Kat gave the other woman a death glare. "She told her cousin you claimed Tink as your property. From what I heard Margarita saying on the phone, Haven must have humiliated Tink at work yesterday."

Doom's stomach clenched in a sickening rush. He should have given Tink a heads-up there was bad blood between Haven and him.

Switching his gaze to Margarita, he was about to ask her himself what Haven had said to Tink when Wizard beat him to it.

"Why did you tell Haven Doom claimed Tink?" Wizard gingerly walked into the room.

Turning his head, Doom saw Shade, Moon, and several other of the brothers had come to find out what the disturbance was about.

"I didn't think it was a big deal." Margarita pulled out one of the chairs to sit down. "I didn't think about her embarrassing Tink in the breakroom. She loves her job. She's worked there for seven years. I didn't think she would jeopardize her job—"

"What did Haven say she said to Tink?" Doom cut her off.

His jaw clenched when Margarita repeated some of the things Haven had said to Tink. The more Margarita talked, the more furious he became.

As much as he wanted to yell at the woman who was staring fearfully at him, Doom remained silent. Wizard had first dibs as president to speak first.

"Kat, you can have Margarita's room." Wizard reached

out to grab Margarita out of the chair. "Get your shit out of that room. I don't give a fuck where you find to sleep, but it won't be here as soon I can get everyone here to call a church meeting. We keep club business to ourselves. Haven doesn't belong to The Last Riders, and you are aware of why fucking not."

"She's my cousin—"

"I don't give a fuck if Haven's your fucking sister. Did you not learn anything from Racy?" Wizard snarled down at her. "She picked family over The Last Riders when she was in Treepoint and, as punishment, was sent back here. Do you see her here anymore?"

"No," Margarita said in a low whisper that could barely be heard.

"That's right; she fucking isn't." Wizard picked up the chair just to slam it back down, smashing it into five pieces. "Let me fill you in on something. This morning, I got a text from Tink. She's hooked me up with a lawyer to help me expand the club. Now, I don't know if she is sincerely trying to help the club or if this is some type of payback because you fucking had Haven humiliate her."

"She texted me this morning too. Tink gave me a lawyer's number to help me fight custody for Kaden." Burn looked at Wizard worriedly. "I went to his office, and he's going to file an emergency hearing. You think I'm walking into a trap?"

Wizard raked his hand through his long hair. "I have no fucking clue. She's not scheduled to work until this weekend. It wouldn't do any good to call or text her. If it's a trap, she won't tell the truth anyway."

"Let me see if I have this right," Shade said from the doorway. "Tink is Doom's woman?"

Doom nodded.

"You going to see her tonight?"

"I had planned to see her last night, but she didn't come home to her apartment. I think she stayed at her parents'," Doom revealed.

"Shiiiit..." Wizard hissed angrily. "It's a fucking trap. I knew it was too fucking good to be true. Hell, I'll probably be served with papers that Daniel Boone pissed here, and this place is going to become a historical site."

"Let's not get carried away," Shade said reasonably. "What do you think, Doom? Is your woman trying to be helpful, or is she a vindictive bitch like Margarita?"

"I'm not vindictive!" Margarita cried out. "Haven was the one being vindictive. How was I supposed to guess she would go trash Tink at work?"

Shade stared at her piercingly with his blue eyes. "You might not have expected your cousin to go off on Tink at work, but what about somewhere else? If they work together, it would be a fair guess Haven would confront her somewhere else or in front of their co-workers."

Margarita shook her head. "No, because Haven says no one has anything to do with Tink at work. Tink thinks she's too good to be friends with any of them."

Doom watched his footing as he stepped closer to Margarita. "Bullshit. That doesn't sound like Tink at all."

"How would you know?" Margarita argued back heatedly. "How do you know she hasn't been making fools out of all of you?" Antagonistically, she jutted her chin out at Wizard. "The other night, Jesus and you wanted to marry her for fixing a fucking cooling coil. I haven't heard you offering to marry me despite how many fucking blowjobs I've given you. Shade, Wizard's giving her votes as if they're confetti while the rest of us take months to earn them."

Margarita's venomous rant had the brothers' expressions growing cold.

"I was unaware you felt that way."

Doom could practically see ice particles dripping with each word Wizard spoke.

Margarita, who seemed about to snap back at Wizard's comment, must have belatedly realized she had gone too far. Her expression turned pleading.

"I didn't mean it the way it sounded, Wizard", she tried to backtrack hastily, glancing around at the faces in the room, trying to find someone to support her. Not even Kat stepped up to take her back.

"You didn't seem to have a problem with Tink when she brought that eyeshadow palette you searched high and low for and asked all of us to buy if we found it before it was sold out, and she didn't say jack shit when you didn't pay her back."

Doom placed a calming hand on Kat's back. The woman was shaking, she was so angry at Margarita.

Margarita flushed at being called out by the other woman. Then, finding no support, she tried again to turn the tide her way. "Why are you all taking up for her? She's turning us all against each other. We all know she lied about how she earned Puck and Buck's votes. They went along with the lie for Super Bowl tickets."

"Were you in the room?" Wizard asked. "It was no skin off our ass. We were all happy to see some of us get to go. If it bothered you so fucking bad, why didn't you ask for a church meeting?"

"I thought she would be found out as a fake. Doom didn't believe it was a coincidence, either. He's sergeant-of-arms; it never crossed my mind he would sweep her lies under the rug and make her his property."

This spitefulness was what he had been afraid of. Under the scrutiny of Shade and Wizard, Doom knew he didn't have a leg to stand on. Tink had practically confessed to the tradeoff and the repercussions if she failed to live up to the agreement the three had made.

"We'll still have the church meeting tonight concerning your punishment, Margarita. Friday before the party, we'll have another meeting regarding Tink, Puck, and Buck." Wizard didn't seem any more thrilled about the upcoming meeting than he was.

Fuck it to hell and back, Doom was well aware none of them would get in trouble for the tradeoff for the votes. It was the lying about how it occurred that would draw the punishment. It was the punishment Doom had tried to save Tink from.

Margarita couldn't hide the satisfied smirk on her lips at getting Tink in trouble with the club.

"Should I call the emergency hearing off?" Burn's devasted appearance at having his hopes raised by the lawyer Tink had sent him to, only to have the hope dashed by the drama Haven and Margarita had created, sickened him.

"Don't be hasty," Shade advised. "Doom, try to hook up with your woman tonight. It won't be a good sign if she's dodging you two days in a row. If you do bring up the encounter with Haven, see how she reacts. You're good at reading people, or you wouldn't have claimed her. If you sense something is off, you can give Burn the time to get another lawyer and give Wizard a heads-up to watch for trouble."

Doom nodded in agreement. Fuck, he didn't believe Tink had planned this elaborate scheme to get back at them because Haven had humiliated her at work. Still, she hadn't bothered texting him, yet she had no problem texting Burn or Wizard today after ghosting him.

"I'm gonna wait for Tink outside the restaurant. She gets off at eleven. She won't be expecting me. It shouldn't take me long to figure out her mindset. I'll text both of them when I see how the wind's blowing. Will that do?"

"I guess it will have to."

Wizard kicked the busted chair out of his way as he walked to the door. "Margarita, you can clean this shit up before you clean out your room."

Doom stayed where he was as Wizard and the others returned to the front room.

Margarita reached out to touch his arm placatingly. "I was just trying to watch out for you and the brothers."

Doom jerked his arm away in disgust. "Don't ever touch me again. From now on, you're dead to me. If you need something, you can ask Puck, and he can relay the info to me."

"Doom, don't be this way. We've been friends for years. I've proved my loyalty to this club for years, and you're automatically picking her over me? Do you even know how deeply this cuts me?"

"The cut goes both ways." Doom let Margarita's entreaty slide off his shoulders. "I've always remained impartial where the women were concerned. For you to say I haven't and not to ask to talk privately to me before coming out with your grievances in front of the brothers is like a smack in the face. Tink has done nothing to earn my distrust, while you tried to cause friction between the brothers and me to save yourself. When I give a person my trust, it's theirs to lose. You lost mine. Deal with it like you should have dealt with your jealousy over Tink before you lose the other brothers. They aren't any better at giving second chances than I am."

Turning, Doom saw Shade and Moon had remained behind to listen.

"Damn, Shade, I need to meet this woman." Moon might have been talking to Shade, but his eyes were focused on him. Doom could see the competitive glint; Moon made sure of it. "What restaurant she work at? Shade and I were planning on going out to eat."

The motherfucker was the most competitive bastard he knew when it came to women. Moon took it as a national duty to fuck as many women as he could before he settled down and got married, swearing he planned to be faithful once he met the right one. The problem was he hadn't met the woman yet, and his second mission was to make all the brothers miserable until he did.

Doom barged forward, grabbing Moon by his shirt, both men barreling backward until the bar stopped them.

"You go anywhere near my woman, you'll be sucking your food through a straw," he threatened.

Unrepentant, Moon grinned at him. "Brother... I'm just joki—"

"Deacon? Is that you? Are you passing through Ohio, or come for a visit...?"

Shade's voice had both their heads turning to see who he was talking to.

Shade came around the counter to where Andy was coming out the back part of the club. Releasing Moon, Doom watched as Shade went to where Andy had stopped when he'd heard his name called.

"Shade?" Andy's sorrow-filled face broke as Shade reached him.

"Brother, Lucky and I were just saying the other day we

wished we hadn't lost contact." Shade, who had extended his hand toward Andy, found himself catching the man as his legs seemed to give out. Shade's expression grew concerned. "Deacon, what's wrong?"

"They..."

Doom could hear the anguish in Andy's voice.

"The coroner's office wants me to cremate Lizzie instead of burying her. She's afraid of fire. I can't cremate her. I don't have the money to bury her..."

As Shade helped Andy to a chair, Doom strode over, curious as to how the brother knew Andy. Once Shade had Andy seated, he pulled another chair closer.

"I'm sorry about Lizzie," Shade commiserated.

"I don't know what I'm going to do without her... I should have been the one who died." Grief-stricken, Andy looked wildly around, as if searching for something to end his torment.

"Deacon." Shade's sharp tone had Andy focusing back on him. "I'll tell you what you're going to do. We're going to call Lucky and get him here. Then you're going to make any arrangements you want to make for Lizzie. Don't worry about the cost. I'll—"

The club door opened, spilling fresh sunlight and air into the room. Everyone blinked to adjust their eyes. Refocusing, they saw it was Tink.

Seeing everyone standing so close to the door, she abruptly stopped. "Excuse me. I didn't mean to interrupt." Seeing where Andy was sitting, Tink walked hesitantly forward. "I just wanted to drop this off for Andy."

Burn and Wizard moved to the side to give her more space to talk to Andy.

"I know I'm the last person you want to see, but I hope you will accept this for Lizzie." Tink's face was etched with pain, as if it took everything within her willpower not to cry. "Lizzie loved pink." Tink carefully laid the garment bag on the table next to Andy. "I bought a dress and undergarments for Lizzie. There's also a matching sweater; I didn't want her to be cold." Her lips trembled as she handed an envelope out for Andy to take. "There's a cashier's check inside for fifteen thousand for Lizzie's burial expenses. If you need any more, I can borrow it from Mama."

"I can't accept—"

Tink's hand dropped to her side. "I understand you hate me, but please..." Her lip trembling increased. Doom expected her to break down into tears at any second.

"You think I blame you? Lizzie and I considered you the daughter we were never able to have. I could never hate you. The only one to blame is me. I wasn't able to protect her."

Tink reached down to hug Andy, giving him the feminine touch he needed to release the grief he had been holding back.

"Then, as your daughter, I want you to take this money and give Lizzie the memorial service she deserves. Afterward, Mama wants you to invite anyone you want to the restaurant for a funeral reception. In the envelope is also a card for a flower shop. My mother wants you to pick out any arrangement and flowers you think Lizzie would like and said she would consider it an honor if you would allow her to take care of the cost."

Doom felt a lump in his throat when Tink wiped the tears away so they wouldn't land on Andy's hair.

"My father wanted to take you out to get a suit, but because of his ill health, Dad asked if his best friend could take you and help you make arrangements for Lizzie's funeral. He should be here in about thirty minutes."

Straightening away from Andy, she moved his hands away from his face to give him a stern look. "Have you eaten?"

"I'm not hungry—"

"I'll text him that you haven't eaten. You have to eat, Andy, for Lizzie. You know she wouldn't want you to be hungry. Okay?"

"Okay," Andy replied meekly.

Giving him a hug, Tink stepped away. "I have to get back to work. My lunchbreak is nearly over. Oh... I almost forgot." Tink reached into her pocket to take out a cell phone. "I got you this so I can check in with you. I keyed in my number, and your phone number is in the envelope. Can I get you anything before I leave?"

Andy's lips moved, but it took a couple of seconds before he could get any words out. "No... Thank you."

"You don't owe me one thanks... I loved her too." Tink's stern façade broke into the mirror image of the same grief which was on Andy's. "Lizzie would be sitting by her door or inside by her window to make sure I got upstairs safely before she went to bed. I couldn't bring myself to go to my apartment last night because I knew she wouldn't be there. When I said Lizzie was my second mother, I truly meant it. I loved her, and I love you too. I used to joke with her you were my papa bear."

Andy's mouth cracked into an affectionate smile. "An old, broken-down one."

"No way. Doom was scared of you."

Disbelieving, Andy looked to where Doom was standing. "No, he wasn't."

"He was," Tink affirmed. "Doom thought you were going to try a home invasion with him in my apartment. So, you might feel old and broken down, but Doom recognized a grizzly when he saw one."

She gave Andy another hug when he broke into laughter. "Now I'm going to be really late. I'll call later to find out what arrangements you've made."

Doom and all the brothers watched Tink leave in stunned silence.

Shade looked away from the door to give Doom a wry glance. "She's your woman?"

"Yes." Doom said proudly.

Shade's gaze shifted to Wizard and Burn, who appeared as stupefied as he felt. "I wouldn't worry about her motives. You're good."

CHAPTER 46

THE CLAIM

"I agree." Doom was able to swallow the lump in his throat once Tink had left. "Tink doesn't have a vindictive bone in her body."

"Arden?" Andy asked.

"I call her Tink," Doom confirmed who he was talking about.

"No, she doesn't. Who said she did?"

"It doesn't matter. It's going to be dealt with." Doom looked at him. "How do you know Lucky and Shade?"

"I met Lucky when I worked undercover for the ATF. Lucky introduced me to Shade. Every now and then, Lucky and I would be in the city working, and we'd share a beer or two. Shade came with Lucky a couple of times."

"He was Lucky's commander at one time." Shade's normally expressionless face held a look Doom couldn't decipher. "Deacon risked a high-priority case to save Lily's life."

Doom wanted to smack his forehead as the memory returned. When Lily had gone missing, Viper had sent for the brothers here to get to Treepoint. Once Lily had been recovered, he had stopped by the sheriff's office before leaving to say goodbye to Knox. While he was at the receptionist desk, he had seen Lucky and a man leave Knox's office. The man had left without glancing in his direction. At the time, Doom hadn't paid any attention to the stranger when Lucky noticed him coming to greet him. The stranger had been Andy.

Doom tried not to blame himself for not recognizing him; Andy was a shadow of the man he had only gotten a fleeting glance of years ago.

"I never could tell Lucky no when he asked for a favor," Andy said ruefully.

The explanation allowed Doom to realize it was gratitude Shade felt toward Andy.

"When I asked Lucky what you were up to, he said you hadn't been responding to his texts or messages." Shade said reproachfully.

"I was too embarrassed to talk to him. Might as well tell you before Doom does. I haven't been living in the best of circumstances. The last case I worked, I fell in love with my informant. I jeopardized the case and lost my job. I didn't care. I'd do it different if I could, but I didn't realize I loved her until it was too late. My gut was telling me she had been made as snitch when a meet was rescheduled. When I tried to pull her out of the meet, I was overruled, and she was sent in. I knew it was going bad when they started questioning her instead of talking about business. I saw one of them pull a gun. I never let him get the shot off. I went in and got her ass out. All the work in trying to get the arrest couldn't be used because of my involvement with her. I should have retired, but if I had, I would have never met Lizzie.

"I never regretted losing everything I had. She was a

drug addict who promised every single fucking day she would kick it. Then, by noon, she would be begging me to help her. I put her through three stints in rehab. I spent my last dime to get her to a rehab center in Ohio. The day before she was supposed to go, I caught her taking a bottle of pills. I stopped pressuring her after that. You want to know something funny?"

Doom had a feeling it wasn't going to be funny, so he didn't speak up. No one else did either. Andy told them anyway, despite their lack of response.

Concentrating on Margarita and Kat, who had maneuvered themselves through the brothers so they could listen, helped him keep the emotions assailing through him in check. Unlike the brothers, he didn't have to imagine the connection between Andy and Lizzie; he had witnessed it himself.

"Lizzie asked me the week before she died to see if I could get her back on the list for the rehab center. Arden had told her about her mother dying. She wanted to get better for Arden so she could be there for her when the time came."

Doom was never good at comforting other men, yet he couldn't stand there and not say anything.

"Lizzie might not be there when Arden loses her mom, but I was there and saw what was happening when you were fighting the other two. The punk hitting Lizzie thought she was dead and swung for Arden. Lizzie reached out and caught him by the foot, and he turned back to her. Lizzie protected Arden with her dying breath."

"Hey," Hawk broke the profound silence when he cracked the front door from the outside to poke his head in. "Does anyone know why a limo just parked in our parking lot?"

Fifteen startled gazes looked at Hawk in surprise. Then Doom and the other brothers started for the windows facing the lot.

"Who is it?" Shade asked from his chair.

Wizard and he stared at each other in disbelief, sure they were imagining the elegantly-dressed man who got out of the limo to button his suit jacket.

"Is that...?" Wizard began.

Doom couldn't believe it either, but nodded his head, confirming who they were all seeing. "The fucking governor."

STRIDING INTO THE OFFICE BUILDING, Doom saw the bank of elevators just as Margarita had described. He stepped inside the elevator and pressed the button for the fourth floor. When the elevator reopened, he confidently walked past the workstations to make a right. Doom headed for the fourth door in the corridor and keyed in several numbers. This was where his plan could go wrong if Margarita had given him the wrong code. A green light shined by the doorknob. Turning the handle, he found himself in a tiled corridor leading to a room with a door being held open by a trash can. He made his way down the tight corridor and didn't pause before he entered the room.

Taking his sunglass off, Doom spotted the woman he was there to see.

As he drew closer to where she was sitting, Haven sent him a frightened smile.

"Doom, you shouldn't be here. This is for employees only."

"I won't be staying long. Since you wanted to air our

dirty laundry in front of your coworkers to humiliate Arden, I thought I would return the favor of telling them the truth. I didn't fuck you over after two weeks. Never, at any time, did we have a relationship to break off. You were an easy lay, which I grew tired of when you texted me about twenty times to hook up again. I took what you offered until I didn't want it anymore.

"You had the fucking nerve to tell Arden to have *slut* tattooed on her, while you don't need it tattooed on you. It was obvious from the way you sucked my dick in front of all The Last Riders and had your cousin record it. That's why you weren't allowed to become a member. Not to mention you becoming a fucking stalker anytime I left the club."

"Doom, please..." Haven put a hand up to cover her red face.

"Look at me when I'm talking to you," he snarled. "I don't want to hear Arden's name coming out of your mouth again. I don't care if you're at work or shitting in your bathroom. We both know your beef with Arden isn't about me. Margarita said you've been running your mouth about her since she started working here. That you managed to get these shitheads turned against her is their fucking loss, not hers. Not one of you fuckers, from what I heard, said jack shit to this bitch for pushing Arden or tried to take up for her."

One of the weenies sitting at another table stood up aggressively. "You should go before I call security."

"Sit the fuck down." Doom stomped his foot in the weenie's direction.

The fucker sat.

"Thought so." Doom gave a mirthless laugh, daring anyone else in the room to open their mouths.

When he saw the embarrassed man pull out his cell

phone, Doom rolled his eyes on him. "Save yourself the trouble. I'm almost done."

Doom turned back to Haven. "You couldn't stand that Arden is kind, sweet, and loyal, everything you pretend to be. Don't blame her for me being able to see beneath that pretty package you hide behind. I saw the ugliness inside and decided to return it to sender."

Pivoting on his booted heel, he casually turned his back on Haven and strode between the tables. Stopping at Arden's table, he placed a hand on her trembling shoulder. "Honey..." Doom drawled out in the most seductive tone he could manage, spearing a hand into her hair to tilt her head back. "I'll see you tonight." He kissed her passionately until he could feel her lips stop trembling, then raised his mouth and gave her a wink before he left.

Whistling as he let himself out of the employee's entrance, passing the employee's workstations, Doom gave a wave of his hand when he saw their craning necks trying to get a look at him. He pressed the elevator button and wasn't surprised to see security guards inside.

"Don't worry; I'm leaving." Doom stepped inside to push the first-floor button.

The two guards stared at each other before the older one had the courage to speak. "We're supposed to detain you until the police arrive."

"You feel like going to the ER instead of going home in an hour?" Doom started removing the thick rings he had on his fingers, placing them in his jacket pocket.

"No, sir."

"Then you two should stay on the elevator when I get off and ride it back to the fourth floor. By the time you do that, I'll be off the premises."

The younger guard started to reach for the taser on his belt, but the older one placed a hand over it.

"Works for us. You have a nice day, sir."

"Back at you." Placing his sunglasses back on when the door slid open, Doom put out a hand to prevent the door from closing. "Stop by the club sometime. I'll buy you two a beer. Tell whoever's at the door Doom invited you."

"We'll do that." The older guard nodded. "Thanks."

When he left the building, he saw Wizard's, Shade's, and Moon's bikes parked next to his. They had been at the club when he left.

Doom swung a leg over his bike. "What are you three doing here?"

Wizard took a drag off his cigarette. "Wanted to make sure you didn't get your ass arrested."

"How'd you know I was coming here?" Taking his rings out of his pocket, he slid them back onto his fingers.

"Shade figured it out when you went to Margarita's room to make sure she packed all her shit." Wizard held his hand out to Moon. "Pay up."

Doom looked at them questionably as Moon took a wad of cash out of his vest pocket to smack it down on Wizard's palm.

"What was the bet?" He wasn't surprised about the bet. Moon couldn't go a day without betting on something.

"We bet where you would give Haven blowback for Tink. I bet you'd get her at work; Moon bet after work in the parking lot."

Doom looked at Shade. "You didn't bet?"

"No."

"Why not?" he asked curiously.

Shade shrugged. "No reason. We ready?"

"Just a second." Doom got off his bike to take off his jacket, spreading it across the hood of Tink's rental car.

He then got back on his bike and started his engine. "Now we can go."

"Sure you don't want to take a piss on her tire before we leave?"

"Nope. That should give everyone in there my message."

Doom was ready to put his bike in gear when he saw Shade holding his hand out. Both Moon and Wizard forked their cash over.

"What in the fuck did you bet on this time?"

Shade put the cash in the upper front pocket of his vest. "I bet you would do something to warn everybody she worked with not to fuck with your woman. Laying your jacket on her car shows not only your protection but that she has The Last Riders'."

"How'd you know I was going to do something? Hell, I didn't plan on doing it until it occurred to me just now. I wanted the fuckers who weren't in the breakroom to get my message."

Shade flicked his kickstand up, preparing to ride. "Because it's what I would have done."

CHAPTER 47
THE SOUP

Arden's hands went to her hips when she saw Doom's jacket spread over the hood of her car. She was going to kill him, she promised herself, hurriedly snatching the garment off to bundle it in her arms.

She gritted her teeth behind the smile she gave her coworkers who were walking past, looking at her curiously.

"Have a great evening," she called out, getting inside her car and shutting the door. "I'm going to kill him," she promised herself again.

She started the car and fumed all the way to her parents' home.

Arriving home, she left the jacket in the car to go inside. Using her key, she found Luc sitting at the dining room table, doing his homework.

"What's up?" she asked her brother. Usually, her mother was sitting in her chair at this time of day.

"Nothing. Just finished an assignment." Luc closed his Chromebook to pick up the dishes he must have used for a snack.

Self-conscious, Arden remained standing at the table

while he took the dishes into the kitchen. When Luc came back to pick up his laptop, she made another attempt at a conversation.

"How was the game and the trip?"

"It was okay."

Arden had expected Luc to tell her how much fun it was.

"You didn't have a good time?"

"It wasn't the same without Dad." Luc started for the stairs.

Arden followed him.

"I'm sorry. I thought you would have a good time with your friends since Dad couldn't go."

Luc paused with his foot on the first step to stare at her angrily. "It wasn't only because Dad didn't go; you didn't go. All three of us used to go together. It wasn't the same."

Arden placed her hand over his. "I didn't go because I thought you'd rather go with Puck and Buck instead."

Luc jerked his hand away. "You could have asked me. I would have told you to give my ticket away too."

"You're right; I should have asked you. I'm sorry." Contritely, she tried to touch his arm to prevent him from going upstairs, but he wrenched away from her touch as if stung.

"It's the same ole, same ole with you, Arden. I wish you would quit treating me like a twelve-year-old. What do I have to do for you to stop treating me as a kid?" Disregarding her, he started climbing the steps.

"Luc... I treat you the way I do not because I think of you as a kid but because I love you. You've had to miss out on so many things I was able to do with Dad. I didn't want the Super Bowl to be another one. I've been told I meddle too much. I guess he was right."

Luc turned to face her. "I didn't share the Super Bowl with just Dad; you were there too. You could have come, and we could have both picked who we wanted to invite with us."

"I didn't think of it that way," she conceded. "I just assumed you would prefer someone else. Next time, I'll ask."

Luc's expression grew morose. "There probably won't be a next time. Dad's good days are getting further in between. They've both been sleeping since I came home."

"I know. That's why I'm moving back home next week."

"At least you didn't sugarcoat it like you usually do."

"The time has gone past sugarcoating anything concerning them. There's no way to prepare for what's coming, but anything I can do to help, all you have to do is ask."

"Okay." Glumly, Luc stared down at her.

"I need to be at work at the restaurant in thirty minutes. You want me to send some dinner over?"

"That sounds good."

"I'll check in with Mom and Dad before I go. Text me when they wake, so I can talk to them."

"I will."

Saying goodbye, Arden returned to her car. She made it to work with three minutes to spare and checked in with Mama to order dinner for her family.

"What time do you want me to send it over?"

"Six. Mom and Dad should be awake by then, but if you have a lot of orders, they can wait."

Mama narrowed her eyes at her, swinging a mallet down on a head of garlic. "Other customers can wait. I'll make your parents my special soup."

Wincing for the poor garlic, she moved to the side. "Uh... Is something wrong?"

Mama halted the mallet mid-air. "What makes you think something is wrong?" The mallet came down with such force that Arden felt a piece of garlic hit her lip.

"Other than the garlic being pulverized rather than being minced." Arden eyed the trash can. "It looks like you burnt four trays of knots too."

Mama gave a heavy sigh. "I'm done with men." Scraping the garlic into a pan, she picked another victim from the basket of garlic. "I caught Calvin texting another woman."

"I'm sorry he didn't work out."

"He really was no loss." The mallet slammed, squishing the garlic. "His dick was the size of a cocktail shrimp."

Arden flicked off another spray of garlic that had hit her arm.

"Yes—well..." She started edging away. "Try, try, try —again."

Mama scraped the garlic into her pan. "Do you think women cheat as much as men?"

"I think it depends on the person whether they cheat, regardless of their sex."

"So, I'm picking the wrong men to date." She slammed the mallet down on the counter. "How can I own and run the most popular business in Ohio but suck so bad at choosing men?"

Arden bit her lip. She wasn't going to mettle... She wasn't going—

"It might have something to do with you picking men to date who are..." She couldn't think of the right word to use.

"Are...?" Mama prompted.

"Aren't as..." Finally, it came to her. "Confident as you."

"Confident?" Mama slowly nodded, making a face. "In other words, I pick weak men."

"No! I wasn't—"

Mama rolled her eyes. "You're right. You don't have to worry about hurting my feelings. I like weak men. That way, I can mold them into what I want them to be."

Arden laughed. "I love how honest you are. Most women pretend they don't want to change men then start changing them. At least you're upfront from the get-go."

"Unfortunately, I'm also getting nowhere."

She shooed her off so she could remake her garlic knots, so Arden left to go to the hostess stand. The restaurant was fairly slow. At nine thirty, Mama told her she could leave.

On the way to her apartment, she called and talked to her parents. Ending the call when she reached the turnoff to her apartment, Arden felt a clutch of sadness in her throat that Lizzie and Andy wouldn't be sitting outside their door.

She headed up the walkway, turned to go up the stairs, and nearly dropped the plastic container she was carrying when she saw Doom sitting on the steps.

"Why are you sitting out here?"

"Waiting for you."

"Because of what I said earlier to Andy?"

"No, I thought if you got inside, then when I knocked, you might still be too mad to answer."

Arden met Doom's searching eyes. "I wished you hadn't come to my office. What Haven said didn't bother me."

"I don't believe you."

"Then don't. Regardless, I don't need your protection. They aren't going to treat me any better or worse despite you playing avenger or frightening them with The Last Riders. They are just normal, everyday people finding a way to relieve the boredom of having to relive the same, boring day five times a week."

"That's no excuse for the way they treat you."

"What makes you think they treat me badly?"

"Margarita told me."

"Ah... She's the person who told Haven you claimed me."

"She's Haven's cousin."

"You could have given me a heads-up that I work with one of your exes."

"Haven was never my girlfriend. I took what she was putting out on a few occasions. When Haven started texting and calling me, I never answered and started avoiding her when she would come to the club on Fridays. One time, she caught me shit-faced, and I let her give me a blowjob. Jesus caught Margarita recording it on Haven's phone. I busted her phone. Hell, I really didn't give a fuck she recorded it; what pissed me off was she didn't ask. We had a church meeting, and she was barred from the club. Margarita had to work a couple of months at the warehouse and hasn't been allowed to invite anyone to the parties for two years. For running her mouth about me claiming you, she lost her room. She's on thin ice with the club. One more strike, and she's out."

"I like Margarita. Don't punish her for me. If Haven had asked if I had been claimed, I would have told her. I didn't think it was a state secret. Was I wrong?"

"No, but it was your information to give, not Margarita's. She had to know Haven would be angry and would go after you. Intent counts as much as the deed."

It would be useless to argue with him. Doom's mind had been made up.

She had learned several surprising facts about The Last

Riders since being around them. They had each other's back, which was what she wanted for Luc. What had taken her longer to figure out was their intrinsic principles of the men they held themselves to. Honor was first and foremost the most important. Loyalty came next. Margarita had stepped out of bounds when she discussed Doom and her with Haven.

"The head of HR was in the breakroom today. Haven was called to come to the HR office before we left for the day. She was given a written notice of a meeting scheduled between HR and the doctors in the practice."

Doom was unrepentant. "Good. She deserves to lose her job."

"I was called down too. My meeting is before hers."

"They won't fire you."

"You can't be sure."

"You haven't done anything to be fired over."

"They could say I gave you the code to access the breakroom."

"I used Haven's code."

"If I get fired, I won't be happy. Haven is a nurse. She won't be easy to replace. They're short two nursing positions as it is now. I will be much easier to replace," she said worriedly. She really liked her job.

Doom reached out to catch her hand in his. "Honey, you aren't going to lose your job."

"You can't know that. Haven works closely with the doctors. I say hi and bye to them as they leave."

"That's what I'm counting on. If they work closely with Haven, they know she's a conniving bitch."

She scowled at Doom, but he missed the intended mark, too intent on the plastic bag she was holding.

"What's for dinner?"

"Nothing for you."

"Come on; give me a break... I'm starved."

"Fine." She handed him the bag, then went up the steps.

Opening the door, she turned to close it, only for Doom to maneuver himself through before she could.

"You do have a microwave at your place." Exasperated, she removed her coat.

"I hate eating alone." Striding through her apartment, he set the bag on the counter and started unpacking the soup container.

"You'll still be eating alone. I already ate. I wasn't in the mood for Italian, so I grabbed a burger on the ride home."

Doom's head jerked back when he opened the carton.

Arden giggled at his reaction. "The soup is a special creation. Mama says it boosts immunity."

Doom braved another whiff. "What she protecting them from? Count Dracula?"

"Probably. She only makes it when she's in a bad mood."

Putting the soup in the microwave, he leaned nonchalantly against the counter. "Why was she in a bad mood?"

"I didn't ask." Sitting down on the couch, she slipped her shoes off.

"You're lying."

"It's none of your business." She shrugged. She went to the kitchen, took a bowl from the cabinet, and gave a him a spoon. "Here you go. I need to take a shower. Some of that garlic splattered on me. I've been smelling it all night."

"Might as well wait then."

"Why?"

"Because I'm hungry. I'm going to eat this vampire soup, and then we can shower after we have sex."

Her hands went to her hips. "Who says we're going to have sex? I'm still angry at you."

"If you were that angry, you would have poured the soup over me, not given it to me to eat."

"I don't believe in wasting food." She gave him a sniff of disdain.

Doom broke into laughter. "What's the longest you've ever been mad at someone? Five minutes?"

Her shoulders slumped. "Ten minutes. I've never been able hold in anger for long, but with you, it's getting easier."

"I've been told that before." He poured the soup into the bowl, then went to the cabinet and took out another bowl. "Come on; have some with me."

"No way. You're welcome to all of it."

Doom timidly dunked the spoon into the soup. Taking a cautious taste, he looked at her amused expression before he started taking larger spoonsful.

"You had me worried. You can barely taste the garlic." Arden propped her chin on her hand as she leaned into the counter. "The soup is like Mama," Arden warned, not saying anything else.

When he seemed confused, Arden laughed again. He would figure it out for himself. Mama came across as attractive and normal, but the more you got to know her, the more you realized how lethal she could be.

When Doom refilled his bowl, she couldn't help but to give him another warning. "I would go easy—"

"My stomach is made of iron." Doom wiggled his eyebrows at her. "Some of the meals I had to eat when I was in the service would turn your stomach. Mama deserves a culinary award for this soup."

Her lips trembled with laughter. "I didn't say it wasn't delicious." Should she warn him again?

Nah—he should find out on his own.

Pouring them a glass of wine, she watched him finish the soup and rolls, preventing herself from rolling her eyes at him when he patted his stomach like a well-fed tiger. The burgeoning idea that had come to her mind when he had bragged about his iron stomach fell to the wayside when his gaze turned seductive. The dangerous tiger had been fed, and now he wanted to play.

"I want to fuck."

Arden raised an inquiring brow at him. "Are you sure you're going to be able to after eating that much food?"

Taking her wine glass from her, Doom lifted her into his arms. "Let's fuck around and find out."

CHAPTER 48

THE GARLIC

Arden slid a mug of beer across the counter toward Jesus. Then, as she took a breather while no one was yelling for a drink, she surveyed the bar. The place was always packed on a Friday night, but this weekend, so many were still trying to get inside that Wizard had to go outside to tell them to leave.

Kat took the same opportunity to rest, grabbed a bottled water, and ran it over her forehead. "It's hot as blazes in here," she complained.

"I should have worn a tank top, like you." Arden grabbed another bottle of water to rub it against the back of her neck while watching Wizard coming back inside with a couple of women.

"I thought Wizard wasn't letting any more people in?"

Kat looked to where she was staring then gave her a rueful glance. "Their breast size guaranteed their admission." She gave her a curious lift of her eyebrows. "Does it bother you when the newbies hit on Doom?"

Arden shook her head. "Not when they have boobs that size. I think Doom is scared of big-breasted women."

Kat looked at her like she was crazy.

"Watch." Arden nodded her head at the women.

Both of them watched as the new arrivals maneuvered themselves in Doom's direction. Kat had told her, with Doom being Sergeant-of-Arms, anyone who wanted to join The Last Riders had to get past him first.

The two arrivals slid up to Doom, wrapping their arms around his waist, their breasts nudging the sides of his chest. Arden had to stifle her laughter when Doom pushed himself from between them.

"I think he's afraid of being smothered."

Kat turned her head to the side so none of the brothers sitting at the bar could hear her. "You should tell Doom he needs to take a shower."

"He showers a couple times a day."

Kat made another disgusted grimace. "Then what's that odor? There's no way that's cologne."

Arden lowered her voice so it was whisper thin, "You promise you won't tell?"

Kat raised two fingers in the air. "Girl, I got you. Tell me."

"Doom has been eating dinner with me every night, and on the weekends, we eat most meals together."

"So?" Kat stared at her blankly.

"Since I moved home, we ended up at his apartment after working at the restaurant. He's been eating a lot of food lately."

"So…?"

"Garlic," Arden supplied the answer.

Kat's mouth dropped open. "Then why don't you smell like…?"

"Because I don't eat it two days in a row. I tell Doom I've worked at Mama's long enough I need breaks, and I go through a drive-thru before I go to Doom's. He's been eating all the leftovers himself, and Mama loves her garlic." Arden put a hand over her mouth. "I might even have told Mama how much I love extra garlic on the garlic knots."

Kat looked appreciatively at her. "He smells so bad that I saw the skunk who lives under the building pack his bags and move away."

They broke into tearful giggles.

Kat wiped her tears away and shook her head. "What shocks me is none of the brothers have said anything to him."

"They don't come close enough to talk to him anymore." Arden snickered behind her hand. "Neither do the women once they get a good whiff of him."

"Girl, I have to give you credit." Kat pressed her lips together and still couldn't hold back her giggles. "Doesn't the smell bother you? Especially when you're having sex?"

"Nope. I just hold my breath or put the pillow over my face. He thinks I don't want the neighbors hearing me screaming."

She glanced at her man to check what he was doing and was satisfied to see the women had moved on to greener pastures. Giving Doom a small wave of her fingers when she was caught staring at him, Arden then turned her head back toward Kat to see her scrunched-up, out of sight, laughing her head off into a dish towel.

"You're lucky Shade, Moon, and Lucky left," Kat rasped out from the dish cloth. "They would have told him."

She was actually shocked her plan had worked out so well. Each day, she expected Doom to say something or stop eating the food, yet he would chow down each time she offered what Mama had sent. Arden believed he was saving himself from buying groceries.

Kat was right; she had only met Shade, Moon, and Lucky briefly after Lizzie's funeral when they had come to Mama's restaurant afterward. During the meal, Andy had told her that Lucky and Shade had talked him into going to Treepoint with them. Not only was she losing Lizzie, but now she was losing Andy too. Forcing herself to be positive, she had choked down the food past the lump in her throat.

"I won't be gone long."

Arden forced herself to give him a reassuring smile while hiding her feelings. "You should take as much time as you need. A new town and job will keep you occupied."

"I'm going to miss you."

"I'll miss you. We can Facetime until you're ready to come back."

Andy slid an envelope she recognized next to her plate. "I won't be taking your money. Shade has given me a loan to pay for Lizzie's services. I'll be able to pay him back from the job he's giving me."

Aware that the conversation at the table had paused, as the others listened in, Arden tried to slide it back. "Then use the money for a fresh start. I saved this money for a car for Luc, but he doesn't want one; he wants a motorcycle. I can't bring myself to buy him one. If something happened to him while he was riding, I'd never forgive myself."

Andy placed his hand over hers, stopping the envelope. "I'm not going to take your money. It never sat right with me, taking money from you. I only did it for Lizzie. I'm going to be okay, Arden. Shade and Lucky will take good care of me."

Arden felt tears well up in her eyes. "But I won't be there to check."

"Like you said, we'll Facetime every day. I also didn't take your dad's money. Lucky wanted to pay for it. I did let you pay for the flowers, though. I know you loved Lizzie."

Arden looked across the table at Shade and Lucky. Their expressions comforted her that they would watch out for her friend.

Nodding, she took the envelope and placed it back in her purse.

"Arden, you should buy your brother the motorcycle. You have a habit of wrapping people you care about in bubble wrap. I've watched you work yourself into the ground providing for everyone, including Lizzie and me. You can't protect against the unforeseen. Your bother could just as easily get hurt in a car accident or get sick. Don't instill your fears into him. A flower won't bloom if you don't give it enough sunlight or space to grow."

"I'll think it over."

"You won't buy the motorcycle." Tolerantly, Andy pointed his finger at her. "Shade, Lucky... Let me tell you something about my friend here. She comes across as the sweetest and most imperturbable person I've ever met, but in reality, Arden is hard-headed, finagling, and patient, which drove me nuts more than a time or two."

Arden felt a blush of embarrassment fill her cheeks. "I don't think I'm hard-headed."

Everyone sitting at the table laughed except Shade. Arden wasn't surprised. Shade didn't come across as a person who smiled often.

Conversations resumed. Listening in, she saw the connection between Lucky and Andy, which made her feel better about his leaving.

Deep down, Arden knew Andy wouldn't be returning.

The three weeks he had been gone had compounded the grief she felt at losing Lizzie. Each time she visited Doom at his apartment, her eyes would go to the place where the couple would sit outside.

How much worse was it going to be when her parents passed? She had grown up in the same home until she moved out. Would she and Luc be comforted by their memories, or would the home just become a source of pain-filled reminders of their passing? She was determined to cross that bridge when she had to, not before.

"Moon's back from Treepoint. Something must be going on for him to come back so soon."

Jerked away from her grim thoughts, she looked at Kat's worried frown.

Moon hadn't entered the door alone. A woman was with him. Her heart sank. Whoever she was, she was Doom's type.

"Who did Moon bring with him?"

"No clue." Kat avoided her inquiring gaze.

Arden didn't buy that for a second. "Then guess."

"I might be wrong... But if I have to, then I guess she would be a probate from Treepoint."

Whoever she was, the woman was gorgeous. She was wearing a white asymmetrical dress, which lovingly skimmed her body. The V-neck design pertly showed off the firm thrust of her breasts while the color of the material revealed she wasn't wearing a bra. Unable to help herself, Arden dropped her eyes to the lower portion of the dress. While it ended at just below the top of her thighs, the way the material was cut asymmetrically upward barely covered her crotch if she didn't move.

As the woman followed Moon through the crowded room on red high heels, Arden saw the small patch covering her privates. Her stomach twisted nervously. They were heading in the direction where she had last seen Doom and Wizard.

"She's come for votes." Arden kept her expression deadpanned as she switched her gaze from them to Doom's. He had spotted Moon and the woman. Her abdominal walls shuddered as if she had been sucker-punched when she saw what he was focused on.

"Probably," Kat agreed. "Hell, she could get votes by just walking."

If the distance between the woman and Doom were farther away, the probate darn sure would get Doom's that way, Arden sickly surmised.

Doom and she had agreed they would ask before having sex with someone else. So far, she had dodged that bullet. Tonight, she wasn't going to be that lucky.

CHAPTER 49

THE OASIS

"Well, well..." Wizard drawled out appreciatively. "Who did Moon bring?"

Doom shot a searching glance for Moon around the room and wished he hadn't. The new probate, whom Moon had texted he would be bringing along for the ride, might as well have printed *Fuck Me* on her dress. Every male's eye in the bar was on the probate, and most of the women's. It wasn't because her clothes were more revealing than any of the other women's; it was the air of sexuality that clung to her like a second skin.

Moon's grin showed he was pleased about their reaction.

Turning, Moon placed a hand on the small of the woman's back to bring her forward. "This is Oasis."

Doom gave her a nod when Moon introduced him then Wizard.

Wizard reached out to take Oasis's arm and pulled her to his side. "Moon says you need two votes, baby." Wizard's hand went to her ass. "I'm ready to give you mine as soon as you rest up from the ride."

Oasis's hand went to Wizard's bulge, stroking the cock behind the faded denim of his jeans. "I don't need a rest." The tip of her tongue came out to lick her highly glossed lips. "Moon made several pit stops. I'm all rested and raring to go."

"Isn't that a coincidence? I am too. You want to party out here or my room?"

"Your room first so I can give you my undivided attention. then we can bring the party to us, if you want."

Wizard sent Doom a wink. "Give me an hour then come knocking." With his hand still on Oasis's ass, Wizard scrunched his hand on the back of her dress, giving Doom a bird's-eye view of the tiny red thong she was wearing. What little material covered her pussy was the size of a postage stamp.

Doom expected to experience the same sign of arousal Wizard was sporting, but his cock felt a remarkable lack of interest. Had he fucking lost his mind? Oasis was a fucking thirst trap. There wasn't a man in the club who wouldn't give their eye teeth to be picked when Wizard would open his door, ready to share her.

"Surprised you're not getting in line. Brother, she's as good as she looks. Wizard's expecting you to come knocking before he can get his boots off."

"There's no rush." Doom's eyes strayed to the side to catch Arden watching him. She looked away and responded to something Puck said before going into the kitchen.

"Afraid of the old lady?" Moon took a step forward to a chair next to him then recoiled back as if he had been electrocuted. "Brother..." Moon made a gagging noise, his hand going to his stomach. "You fucking reek. What in the fuck? You been dining on skunk?" Moon made more gagging noises. "No wonder Oasis wanted to go to Wizard's room. She loves to put on a show..."

Doom looked around and saw everyone within listening distance was avoiding his gaze. "It's that bad?"

More gagging came from Moon. "Brother, I've got a strong stomach, but this is beyond me to deal with." He went to the window to open it.

"Why didn't any of you fuckers tell me I stink?" Doom bellowed.

While he was yelling, Doom saw Arden come out of the kitchen then go back in.

"We didn't want to hurt your feelings," Jesus spoke up, eyeing him with pity. "We didn't know if you had developed a medical condition."

Doom ground his teeth together, making for the kitchen. As he walked through the door, he saw Arden making a sandwich.

She innocently gave him a welcoming smile. "Puck wanted a peanut butter sandwich, so I made him a couple. You want me to make one for you?"

His chest puffed up in outrage. "Why didn't you tell me I stink?"

Her eyes widened in sham innocence.

Doom had never been this disconcerted by anyone before. The woman was better at lying than he had imagined she could be.

"You don't stink—to me." Wiping her hands on a paper towel, she came closer to put her hands on his chest. "To be honest, though, I've worked for Mama since I was sixteen. I lost my sense of smell where garlic was concerned by the time I was eighteen. Don't forget; I warned you."

"I thought you were warning me against eating so much

of it because I'd take a case of the shits, not have BO bad enough to incinerate the whole club."

"They're just giving you a hard time. You don't smell that bad."

He crossed his hands over his chest as Arden finished the sandwich. "Bad enough to keep women sitting on the other side of the bar from me."

As she reached for a paper towel, Doom was taken aback that she didn't exhibit one ounce of guilt. He expected her to be embarrassed or regretful at not telling him to lay off the garlic, yet she unsparingly met his gaze head-on.

"You want to know why you don't notice the smell?" With pursed lips, she came toward him to poke a finger into his chest. "You might come in the club smelling like a vat of garlic, but within an hour or two, you smell like a perfume counter." She gave him another hard poke before she leaned her head closer to him to take a hard sniff.

"What the fu—"

"Tonight, you smell like Channel. I can also smell some Dior and a faint whiff of Givenchy. You smell more like a flower garden than garlic." Angrily, she puffed her chest out. "Smell me. What do I smell like? I guarantee you won't get any whiff of men's cologne."

"Uh... That's okay." Doom dropped his arms to his side, falling off his high horse. "I'll take your word for it."

Turning back toward the counter, she reached for another paper towel to wrap the sandwiches. She held them in one hand as she picked up an apple from the fruit basket and threw it at him, Doom managed to catch it before it struck him.

"Eat a couple of these. They'll kill most of the stink of

the garlic. Unfortunately, you'll have to take a shower and wash your clothes to get rid of the perfume."

Brushing past him, Arden left him alone in the kitchen, feeling guilty as he ate the apple. He was on his second when his anger kicked back in. How had he not been aware his woman was diabolical? Arden, cunning? Who would have thought?

Tossing the second apple core into the trash can, whistling as he left the kitchen, Doom got himself a bottled beer. As he twisted the cap, he saw Moon was chatting with Tink.

"Can I get you something?" Kat asked.

"No, I'm good."

It didn't take him long to notice that every time Tink moved away to wait on someone, Moon would pull her back into a conversation. The brother was on the prowl, and he had set his sights on Tink.

Waiting until she was waiting on Buck, he angled behind Kat and moved to stand in front of Moon.

"How was the ride down?"

Moon grinned. "Not bad. It didn't hurt I had company."

"I was surprised you were the one to bring Oasis. I figured one of the other brothers would have volunteered."

"I didn't mind."

I bet he didn't, Doom thought snidely. Moon was notorious about trying to steal the other brothers' women away. He got off on the fucking chase, but once he achieved his goal, he quickly lost interest. Everyone in Kentucky and Ohio wanted to be in a relationship, have a couple of kids, and start a family. The problem was boredom would kick in, and then he would catch the scent of another woman.

Doom tipped his beer to his lips. "When you headed back?"

"In a few days. I'm not in a big rush." He shrugged, his eyes flicking to where Tink was cleaning a table.

Gritting his teeth, Doom forced himself to retain his composure as he finished his beer off. "I'm going to burst your bubble. Tink isn't going to fuck you."

Moon wasn't perturbed at being called out for his intentions. "My time to waste. Besides," he scrunched his nose at him, "she might want to be with someone who doesn't smell like a..."

Doom waited for another comment about the garlic, preparing to give a cutting comeback.

"Flower garden."

"You were listening?"

"Brother... All's fair in love and war."

One second, he was standing there, taking in Moon's smug face, and the next, he was jerking Moon over the counter and punching the smug bastard wherever he could land a blow.

Chaos ensued with Kat giving a loud screech and several of the brothers rounding the bar to try to break up the fight.

He dunked Moon's head in the ice cooler and knocked Buck back when he tried to pry his hands off Moon's neck. Buck, never the easiest-going of the brothers, took exception at being pushed and launched his own attack on Doom.

Keeping one hand on Moon, Doom reached for a bottle of tequila and smashed it over Buck's head when he came barreling toward him.

Puck furiously took exception to his brother being whacked and decided to take Buck's back. Still on the other side of the bar, he leaned across to grab Doom around the neck, trying to pull him over the counter like Doom had done Moon.

Burn got out of his booth, trying to stop Puck, as he was the closest to him. When he jerked Puck back, his elbow accidently struck a new recruit on the jaw, setting off another fight between them.

"What the fuck?" Wizard's outraged voice yelled out over the sounds of female screams and bottles breaking. "Puck, I'm going to fuck you up if you don't let go of Doom!"

Puck, who was leaning over the bar, trying to shove Doom's head into the cooler next to Moon's, didn't waver at Wizard's order.

"Doom started it!" he yelled back.

Wizard shouted, "Doom, let Moon go!"

"Mama!" Tink's shrill voice rang out over Wizard's. "What are you doing here?"

Doom gave Moon's head another push down into the ice before letting him go.

Standing back, he saw Wizard standing in the front of the bar, stark naked, with Oasis just as naked as him. Grimacing when he saw Mama standing there with her mouth hanging wide open, Doom knew he was dead meat. If Wizard didn't kill him, Tink was going to by their furious glares directed at him.

Everyone in the club froze, too afraid to move.

Tink rushed toward Mama. "What are you doing here?"

"Luc was under the impression you were working at the restaurant tonight. He called looking for you, said you weren't answering your phone. Your parents' nurse had an emergency and had to leave. Another nurse came, but she can't find your parents' medication sheet to see if they were given their bedtime medications. I tried calling you as well but couldn't get an answer, so I drove here."

Mama's contemptuous expression fixed on Wizard,

whose thick dick had shrunk to the size of a pencil nub, before she glanced toward Oasis, who, noticing Mama's expression turn pitying, moved to stand behind Wizard to hide her nudity. They weren't the only ones who felt the blast of Mama's withering condemnation. The party atmosphere was doused with many of the women straightening their clothes to a more modest level, which wasn't easy to do considering their erotic clothing. He also heard more than two or three grunts from the brothers at their hard cocks being shoved back inside of their jeans.

"I'm sorry. I must have accidently put my phone on silent," Tink hastened to explain.

Mama nodded, but Doom didn't miss the intentional way she looked at Tink. He had heard a tremble in Tink's voice, as Mama must have. Tink was lying about why her phone was off.

"I'll call Luc right now."

"I'll see you tomorrow then."

"Thanks, Mama."

"No problem. I'm always here for you and Luc."

Doom stayed still, like everyone else in the club except Tink, who had run behind the counter to grab her cell phone then darted into the kitchen. The only other one brave enough to move was Moon.

Doom didn't even flinch when Moon shook his head and slung water toward him. "I don't want her to leave with a bad impression of us. I'll make sure she gets safely to her car," he offered, hurrying from around the bar.

As Moon passed, Wizard didn't even move to block his path.

"Save yourself the trouble."

Wizard's cutting tone stopped Moon faster than his fist would have done.

"You see how she looked at my dick? If she can shrivel my dick, then, brother, you don't have a shot of her not freezing yours off."

Moon was unfazed and went for the door. "It doesn't hurt to try."

"Wanna bet?"

Moon turned. "I'm always up for a bet."

Wizard looked Moon dead in the eyes. "Then bet me what I'm going to do if you try to go out that door."

CHAPTER 50

THE SEXCAPADES

"You know I'm going to crush you to a pulp right after I finish with Oasis?" Wizard fumed.

Doom nodded, grimacing. "Brother, I'm sorry. I shouldn't have let Moon get to me."

Wizard's eyes narrowed into slits. He didn't give a rat's ass what Moon had done to start the brawl. "You better pray, and I mean pray hard, that I still stand a chance with Natalia."

Doom looked up at the ceiling, away from Wizard's flaccid cock. "To be fair, you didn't have much of one anyway."

"I did before she saw me!" he ranted. "Women always want to know what I'm packing. Now the mystery is gone."

That's for fucking sure, Doom thought, trying to keep his lips steady. "You should have turned. Your ass is your best feature."

"Are you trying to be funny? I don't want her sucking my ass. I want her to suck my dick!"

Doom dodged the chair Wizard threw at him.

"I'm just trying to lighten the situation. Hold up." He raised his hand to prevent Wizard from throwing another chair. "Do you really want to hurt the only person who can save your ass?"

Wizard's gaze grew more intent. "Yes, I do."

"I'll fix this, I swear. By the time I'm done, Natalia will think you're God's gift to women."

Dropping the chair, Wizard strode toward the bar. "Kat, give me my cigarettes."

Doom noticed Wizard's hand was shaking when he lit his cigarette. He let him take a couple of puffs before saying anything else. Then he let him take a couple more. The brother was the angriest he had ever seen him.

When Wizard finally turned his face in his direction, he knew his life had been spared.

"Brother, I hope you know how close you came to dying."

"I'm aware."

Wizard blew out another jet of smoke. "That woman makes me ballistic."

"I'm aware of that too. I'll fix it; don't worry." Doom slid his foot to the side then moved the other one, trying to stealthily make his way to the kitchen.

Wizard's eyes dropped to his feet. "I'm not the one who should be worried." He used his cigarette to point at him. "Don't think I don't know why you let the stink on you get so bad. I don't care if you smell like an outhouse. Next Saturday, we're having church about Puck's and Buck's votes. It would be in your woman's best interest if I'm in a much better mood before then. Capeesh?"

"Understood. I should go check on Tink. We good?"

"For now." Wizard stubbed out his cigarette.

When he finally made it around the counter, Doom saw Oasis come up behind Wizard to twine her arms around his neck.

"May I make a suggestion?"

Maybe he should have waited until Wizard cooled down a little more, but his work was going to be hard enough as it was.

Wizard lit another cigarette. "No."

"Fair enough. I'll keep my opinion to myself then."

"Do that."

"I will."

With the kitchen door next to him, he darted inside, feeling a huge relief that he had dodged a bullet. His relief was short-lived, however, when he saw Tink staring down at her cell phone with a frightened look on her face.

"Is something wrong with your parents?"

Guiltily, Tink shoved her phone into her dress's pocket. "No, the nurse found the chart and gave them their medicines."

"Something else going on then?"

"No. I'm just mad at myself that Luc wasn't able to get a hold of me."

"Accidents happen."

Tink's eyes skirted away from his. "I should go home and check in with him." She moved toward the door, but Doom caught her lightly by the waist.

"If everything is cool, what's the rush to leave?"

"Aren't you still mad at me?"

"No, I'm over it. I'm going to let you off the hook this time. Even though..." He couldn't help but bring up the most disturbing part of her plan. "I find it interesting we have so many apples here, and as far as I can recollect, buying fruits wasn't on our grocery must-haves."

"I really should go home—"

"Soon. You have your phone back on ring now?" he asked solicitously.

"Yes, thank you. It must have happened when I put in my pocket."

"Hmm..." He tugged Tink closer to him. "You just put it back in your pocket. Do you need to check it again?"

"No... I was careful this time."

He tried to remember where the paddle was that Shade had left behind from his bachelor days. His woman might have a diabolical mind, but she couldn't lie worth shit.

"Before you leave, we need to have a discussion."

"About what?" Looking suspicious, she tried to pull away. "If this is about Mama coming inside the club, I'm not going to say anything to her. She was doing me a favor. You really should tell Wizard he needs to make a club rule about people being naked outside of their room."

"I tried to make that suggestion before coming in here."

Tink's interest piqued, and she stopped trying to escape. "What did he say?"

"Currently, he isn't receptive to any suggestions I want to make."

Tink frowned. "He's that upset at being interrupted?"

"He's upset Mama saw his dick."

Despite the pain-filled grimace on her face, Doom didn't miss the laughter dancing in her eyes.

When she bobbed her head to the side, Doom realized Tink was making sure no one was listening nearby.

"To tell you the truth, it wasn't the spectacular sight I thought it would be." She giggled.

He winced for the brother. "To be fair, most men have cocks his size."

Tink gave him a pat on his chest. "Don't worry; I won't tell him yours is bigger."

Doom stared at her, not knowing how to respond. Was she that naïve after knowing how The Last Riders liked to party that Wizard wouldn't know what his dick looked like?

"Size doesn't matter where women are concerned. What counts is girth."

"I wouldn't know." Tink mischievously linked her hands behind his neck to rest against him. "I get the best of both worlds."

The walls of his chest constricted as a dart of loving warmth struck his heart unexpectantly.

His hands went to her ass to lift her higher in his arms. The movement rubbed his cock against the butter-soft material of his jeans, bringing his mind back to a question he was determined to find the answer to.

"As great as it is knowing how much you appreciate my dick, we need to get back to what I wanted to talk to you about."

"Oh... I thought it was Wizard you wanted to discuss. What do you want to talk about?"

"I want your approval for me to give my vote to Oasis."

Hardening his heart, Doom watched the light in Tink's eyes die. To give her credit, she didn't attempt to get out of his arms, actually acting so cool about it that he almost believed she didn't care.

Until he felt the sting of her nails biting into the back of his neck.

"Go ahead. Have fun."

He put her back on her feet at her quick acceptance, and as soon as her feet hit the floor, Tink took off for the kitchen doorway.

He followed her out of the kitchen and saw her reach for her purse under the bar.

Placing a hand on each side of her on the counter, he effectively caged her in his arms with her back turned toward him. "Where are you going?"

"Home."

Doom lowered his head to talk softly next to her ear. "You can't go home yet. Remember how you wanted to be there?"

"I don't have time right now."

He removed one of his hands from the bar and circled her wrist to put her hand back under the counter. "This won't take long. You won't need your purse."

Doom heard the sound of her purse dropping from her fingers.

Straightening off Tink, he released her wrist to circle her waist. He maneuvered her from behind the bar and through the crowded space, tightening his grip on her waist as he felt her tensing. Out of the corner of his eye, he saw her head turn toward the door and knew she was seriously thinking of bolting. He moved her to his other side, then propelled her toward the hallway.

"I don't know how I got so lucky to find a woman as understanding as you are."

"Why should I care—"

Doom almost laughed at her stilted movements as they walked down the hall. He practically had to lift her to make her feet move.

"—if you want to have sex with another woman? It's not like we're in a normal relationship."

Quizzically, he stared down at her. "You don't consider our relationship normal?"

"I meant it isn't a committed relationship."

"I get your meaning. That is what we agreed on. Just never had another woman who didn't have a scream-fest for us to go back on our agreement."

"Yes... Well—I wouldn't do that." Her reply was so strangled he could barely make it out.

"I appreciate it," he said, bringing her to a stop outside of Wizard's door.

Holding her snugly, he knocked on the door.

On hearing, "Come in," Doom opened the door.

A gasp coming from Tink didn't deter Doom from his plan.

"Mind if we—"

Even with him holding Tink tightly, she managed to squirm in his hold until she was able to turn around, which was what he had expected from her scandalized expression. He allowed her enough room, so she was able to slide to the side, where she could no longer see Oasis sitting on Wizard's face while she sucked on his cock.

"—watch?" Doom moved his body to hold her against the wall. From where he was standing, he could easily tilt his head to see into the bedroom while keeping Tink contained where he wanted her.

Wizard lifted Oasis's hips so he could see what they were doing in the doorway. "You can come in. You don't have to stand out there."

"We're good here—for now."

"Whatever." Wizard lowered Oasis back to his face.

Turning his head back toward Tink, he started nuzzling her neck as his hands went to her waist to lift her higher up the wall.

"See anything you want?"

"No." In an attempt to crane her neck away from his

lips, Tink had to lift her legs to his hips to get more traction. Doom let her wiggle as much she wanted, feeling his cock thickening behind his jeans.

"Your breasts are better."

"They're bigger."

"Bigger isn't always better."

Her eyes narrowed angrily on him, and then her expression grew thoughtful. "I see what you mean about girth."

Amusement curled his lips. Gliding them away from her neck, he started kissing her while he nimbly unbuttoned her blouse.

"I thought you might," he murmured against her lips.

"How does he fit it—never mind."

"He comes several times before he fucks. The hornier he gets, the bigger it gets."

"Ouch... There's no way..." She shook her head.

Doom took it to say no way in hell was Wizard's dick ever coming near her, which was cool with him.

"Wizard is still doing a deep dive into Oasis's pussy—in case you're wondering."

"I wasn't," she said, blowing out a shaky gasp.

"I was." Nudging the cup of her bra aside with his mouth, Doom found her pert, little nipple. He sucked it into his mouth, then flicked it with his tongue before sucking it hard. He released it when Tink whimpered, her hands clasping his neck tighter to hold him in place.

"Tell me: why did you silence your phone?"

Desire-filled eyes turned frightened. "I didn't."

Doom gave her a hard kiss. "Don't lie to me. I won't be with a woman who lies to me about important shit."

"It isn—"

"Careful... You're getting ready to lie again. I wouldn't," he warned. So far, he had played fair with Tink. Someone unethical would have taken advantage of her inexperience, which he had tried not to do by going slow and letting her set the pace of how adventurous she wanted to be. The fear in her eyes showed she was hiding something even from Mama.

"Wizard and Oasis are both coming. Do you want to watch?"

Loud moans and groans came from inside the room as Doom continued with the byplay.

"Nooo."

"Your loss. Wizard had her switch positions, so her ass is facing the door, giving me a bird's-eye view of her pussy. You want to see?" He slid his hand under her dress, his fingers sliding inside her silky panties.

"No..." she whimpered.

He grinned when Tink's mouth went to his shoulder. The pain in his cock was worse than in the shoulder she bit. Holding her against the wall, he had to loosen his jeans to lessen the pain that threatened to burst the zipper.

"I can see how wet she is for him." He freed his cock and gave a sigh of relief. "Can you hear her begging him to fuck her?"

"They can hear her in the parking lot," she muttered against his shoulder.

With his cock free of the constricting pain, he started playing with Tink's clit. Usually when they had sex, he was gentle with her, giving her the care she needed to build her desire. Tonight, he played with her like an opponent used to the game. He was done letting her win because of her inexperience.

"Your pussy feels just as wet as Oasis's looks."

Hearing footsteps, Doom turned his head to see Hawk,

Jesus, and the two women Wizard had picked out of the crowd outside before turning others away.

Hawk opened the bedroom across to the right of where he and Tink were standing. The three of them would be able to see what they were doing in the hallway, while Tink and he would have to turn their heads to watch them.

Doom turned his gaze back to Tink, who was staring at him with wide eyes.

"Hawk, can you help a brother out for a second?"

While Jesus and the other two women went inside Hawk's room, Hawk moved to stand next to them.

"What you need?"

Doom scrunched Tink's dress to her waist.

"Take her panties off. If I set her down, she'll take off."

"Glad to help." Hawk's hand went to the waistband of her panties,

Loosening one of Tink's legs, Doom watched as Hawk maneuvered her leg enough so he could slip the panties free. Tink bit his shoulder harder as she hid her face.

Doom mouthed, "*Thanks, bro.*"

Hawk moved to the other side and slid the panties off Tink's other hip when Doom switched the leg he was holding.

Dangling the panties from his fingertip, Hawk gave him a sympathetic glance at the plain undergarment. "What you want me to do with them?"

"Trash them."

Hawk laughed as he moved away to his room.

Tink stopped biting him long enough to threaten, "I'm never going to forgive you for that."

"You will in—" adjusting her back against the wall, he started rubbing her clit again, "about ten seconds." He used his chin to nudge her head out of his shoulder then to turn her head in the direction of the open doorway.

"They can't see anything we're doing. Your dress is covering anything important. All Hawk could see was the sides of your hips. I protected your modesty," he assured her. "He was a gentleman and didn't try to sneak a peek."

"He didn't?"

"No, and I watched him to make sure he didn't." Doom craned his neck. "You want to know what Wizard and Oasis are doing?"

"I'll pass."

"You don't know what you're missing. Wizard is—"

"I can hear what he's doing."

Lowering his eyes, he saw she was watching the room across the hall. Hawk had left the door open.

The two women had removed their clothes. The blonde was bouncing on Jesus's cock as he lay on the bed. The brunette was on her knees, unfastening Hawk's jeans.

"We can join them if you want. Hawk left his door open," Doom offered.

"No, I'll pass."

Unsurprised, Doom slid a finger inside her wet pussy. "Works for me. I get the best of both worlds." Repeating what she had said in the kitchen, he slowly stroked his finger in and out of her. "I get my favorite brand of snow cone while I get to watch the brothers have to settle for generic."

Tink's eyes flew to his. "You don't want to be in there with them? Not even Oasis?"

"Why would I want to? Oasis might be a thirst trap, but, honey, there isn't anything there to quench the thirst. Women like her use their bodies and sexuality to lure men to them. Once you fuck them, you get some relief, but it doesn't last long. I've had more women like Oasis than I care to admit. The front of the club is filled with them. They aren't hard to find. What is hard to find is a woman who can satisfy every single craving your body desires, so no mirage, no matter how attractive, has the power to lure you away from what's within your grasp."

CHAPTER 51

THE SHOW

Arden was confused about why she hadn't thrown herself out of Doom's arms when the sounds of uninhibited sex were taking placing not only within earshot but eyesight. Peeking toward the door Hawk had left open, she could clearly see a woman giving Hawk a blowjob while the other one was riding Jesus as if he was a bull at a rodeo. She was so fascinated at the erotic sight that she was unaware of the sigh of delight she made when Doom removed his finger to thrust his cock inside of her. The dark hallway gave her a sense of guilty pleasure that no one would be able to clearly discern what they were doing.

When Hawk grabbed the woman's hair to pull her closer to his pelvis, she obediently opened her mouth wider to take more of his cock.

She was embarrassed when she caught Doom's attention on her and not Wizard's room, as Arden had supposed. Her arousal had blinded her to the fact Doom wasn't as lost in what they were doing as her. His intense scrutiny sent off warning signals to her brain that just wanted to remain in the pleasure-induced haze Doom could create with little effort.

Arden began squirming to get away, and Doom noticed in the next instant, thrusting harder and higher inside of her while his mouth covered an areola, sensually sinking her back into the haze there was no escape from.

"Oasis is coming. Watch."

Unable to help herself, she peeked around the corner to see the ecstatic expression on the woman's face.

Doom's mouth left her breast to slide to her ear. "Wizard isn't ready to give her his vote. By the time he's done with her, she'll be lucky to crawl out of his room, much less walk."

Oasis wouldn't be the only one unable to walk if Doom lifted her thighs any higher.

Grabbing his shoulders, she held on as the first tingling of her orgasm started, her vaginal muscles quivering.

Suddenly, Doom paused with his cock buried to the hilt, leaving her building orgasm stymied.

"Why did you silence your phone?"

Comprehension dawned too late. He hadn't forgotten she hadn't answered him before. Instead, he had lulled her into a false of security.

"Doom!"

He didn't budge.

"This isn't fair," she hissed, lowering her voice when she saw Jesus and Hawk looking in their direction. "It's none of your business."

"At least you didn't tell another lie."

Glaring at him, she tried to wiggle to bring herself to the peak he had carried her to, only to discover Doom had manipulated her body. He was in total control.

"I'm waiting. I can pull out and, in less than one minute, have my dick in a pussy who won't give me the hassle yours does."

"Go ahead! I don't want it anymore," she lied. "I knew that Oasis stuff was bullshit, anyway."

"Honey—" Doom nuzzled her neck, sucking a tiny piece of flesh into his mouth, "I'm not the one who has the penchant for lying. I'm not stupid. I know you're hiding something on your phone, that there is a reason you silenced it, despite how ill your parents are." As Doom talked, he started moving slowly within her, turning her mind back to mush.

"Tell me," he encouraged in a tone she had never heard from him before. He was asking her to trust him. Even before her parents had become ill, she had fought most of her battles alone rather than ask for help. She hadn't wanted to bother her parents when they had to deal with Luc's premature birth, nor had she turned to the Bennings when she'd stayed with them because she didn't want to trouble them enough to call her parents. Even with Mama, she had turned to The Last Riders rather than ask for her help because of her hot temper and didn't want her to jeopardize her business. She had turned to The Last Riders for the simple reason they could provide the male influence she was unable to give him to fight his own battles.

If she trusted Doom to lower her inhibitions enough to have sex in a hallway, then she should be confident in him that he wouldn't act rashly when she told him what she was hiding.

"Can I come first?" she bargained. Arden didn't have enough trust he wouldn't be so angry he would leave her hanging again.

"You'll tell the truth?"

She nodded.

"Then yes, you can come."

The wicked smile on his lips had her thighs clasping tighter around his hips. Her heart was pounding in excitement, as if she was going up a steep hill on a roller coaster. As he gradually increased the speed of his strokes, his thrusts went from gentle to ramming his cock so hard inside of her she could hear the smack of her bottom hitting the wall.

"Please... Doom—please." Lost in pleasure, her voice rose to a pleading wail.

Doom accelerated his thrusts as his mouth went to her ear. "You want to know what Wizard, Hawk, and Jesus are doing?"

Arden shook her head, past the point of rational speech.

"They're watching you."

At the height Doom had taken her to, it was too late to get off the roller coaster. There was only one way down, and that was Doom.

"Oh, Doom..."

"Give me your sweet," Doom groaned, "sweet honey..."

With one thrust after another, Arden felt the walls of her vagina contracting around Doom's cock, the contractions growing stronger and stronger, making her whole body shake in an orgasm so strong she couldn't prevent the scream that slipped out when she felt Doom tense and his cock started throbbing inside of her.

Gasping for breath, she let her head fall limply onto his shoulder as he slid his cock free and gently disentangled her legs, which felt like rubber when her feet found the floor.

He braced his hands on the wall next to her, so Arden remained ensnared withing the confines of his arms.

Cupping the back of her head with his left hand, Doom

gently rubbed his fingers over her scalp. "Did you bump your head?"

"I think you gave me a concussion. I might need to go to the ER for a CAT scan." Her attempt at humor failed miserably.

"Be serious."

"Okay."

"Are you ready to live up to your end of the bargain?"

Arden nodded. "It really isn't a big deal," she tried to preface.

Doom's expectant expression showed it would be a wasted effort to gloss over what she had been hiding.

"I've been getting texts from Haven and Margarita, advising me to stay away from the club—and you."

Doom frowned. "How do you know the texts are from Margarita and Haven?"

"They told me. I got the first text from Haven the day after she was fired. I asked who it was when I received the text."

"What did the text say?"

"Haven said The Last Riders caused her to lose her job, and she was going to make sure I lost mine too. The texts really don't threaten anything much. I just don't want my parents to become involved. Their health is very fragile, and I don't want them to worry. They don't even know I've been coming here or that we've been..." She swallowed hard, having a hard time coming up with a word to describe their relationship. She couldn't bring herself to say *booty call.* Miserably, she looked down as it hit her that was what it was.

Doom didn't have the same problem. "Fuck buddies?"

Arden felt the color drain from her face. "I didn't even think of that term."

"So, which term were you hesitant to say to your parents?"

"Booty call."

Doom rolled his eyes at her. "Neither applies. How often has Haven been texting you?"

"Several times a day and night."

"When did Margarita start?"

"The same day as Haven."

"How do you know it was Margarita?"

"The text came from a different number."

"Let me guess, you asked who it was?"

Confused, she frowned at him. "Shouldn't I have?"

"Yes, you just have to keep in mind that, just because they tell you who they are, doesn't necessarily mean that's who they really are."

"Ah..." Her frown cleared. "I'm sure it's Haven and Margarita."

"Can I see the texts?"

Not having anything to hide from him anymore, she searched for the phone in her pocket.

"It's on the floor," Doom told her helpfully.

She looked down then back up to glare at him.

Doom arched his brows, remaining still.

"Aren't you going to...?" Arden waved her hand in the direction of his cock.

"I was hoping we weren't done for the night."

"Trust me; we're done."

Zipping himself back into his jeans, he reached for her phone.

Arden took it from him with a glare then keyed in the code to her phone.

"Can't blame a guy for trying." He shrugged.

She pulled up her text messages and showed him the ones she had received from Haven and Margarita.

Doom took the phone to scroll through them before giving it back. "Don't respond to any more of the texts. I'll contact Margarita and Haven. Take a snapshot of the texts if they do and send it to me."

"Okay. I should be getting home. The nurse leaves at twelve."

Doom gave her enough space to leave.

"I guess I'll see you later," she said.

"Later."

Angry he didn't offer to walk her to the parking lot, she moved away from the wall. Seeing Wizard's bare ass standing at the foot of his bed, with Oasis's upper body on the bed with her legs over his shoulders, had her eyes jerking away from the erotic sight, only to turn in the other direction and see the orgy of flesh entangled together on Hawk's bed.

She barely was able to stop herself from asking for God's divine intervention to spare her more embarrassment. She would have died if she had distracted Jesus's attention as she gaped at them.

As she stomped down the hallway, she went over several life choices she had made since her mother had called to complain about Luc. *That was phone a call I would have been better off not answering,* Arden thought snidely.

The big goon had laughed at her reaction to the two rooms.

Arden came to an abrupt stop at realizing Doom wasn't following her to go back to the front of the bar. Turning about, she went back down the hallway, seeing him watch Wizard and Oasis.

On hearing her approach, Doom turned his head.

She reached his side and placed a hand over his eyes.

"You forget something?" he teased.

"Yes, your ass is still here."

CHAPTER 52
THE CALL

Doom grinned below her hand. "Would you like me to walk you to your car?"

"Yes, please."

Tink didn't remove her hand until he rotated and could no longer look into Wizard's bedroom.

He slung an arm over her shoulders and walked with her down the hallway then through the bar.

Outside, several of the brothers were sitting on their bikes, drinking beer with the dozen or so women who couldn't get inside the club.

When they reached her car, he opened the driver's door. "There you go. Happy?"

Tink didn't get in. "Are you—"

He wrapped his hand around the nape of her neck and gave her a passionate kiss. "I'm going to have a beer and then go my apartment. I won't be giving out any more votes tonight."

Giving him a relieved smile, Tink got into her car.

A troubled frown marred his forehead as he went back inside the club to take a seat at the bar.

"Kat, give me a beer and Wizard's cigarettes."

Kat gave him the beer then reached for the cigarettes.

"They're old as dust. He's almost out," she said, giving him the cigarettes.

"I'll buy him a fresh one when I come in tomorrow." Opening the pack, Doom took one of the two cigarettes and lit it, then placed the lighter back inside the pack. He couldn't remember the last time he smoked.

Sucking in the smoke, he rubbed his hand over his forehead. Never before had he taken the effort to reassure someone he wouldn't party with other women. When Tink had made her approval part of their hooking up, he hadn't really thought they would still be together. Instead of growing bored of her, she had become more addictive. After three puffs, he came to the conclusion he was going to give it a couple more days before he would break it off. Three at the max.

"He's probably gone to bikers' heaven."

As he smoked the cigarette, Doom listened to the two probates sitting next to him.

"What in the fuck is bikers' heaven?" the younger of the probates asked.

"It's where bikers go when they die. Goody two-shoes goes straight to the heaven in the sky, sinners go to hell, and bikers go to a place in between. We ride the roads unseen by the living. During the day, we go up and pretend to be good, and at night, we go down below to party."

The probate cracked up. "Do we get to party down below like we do here?"

The older probate laughed back before answering the question seriously. "Better. We get a brand-new Harley waiting for us when we die, which we ride for eternity. All the beer is ice cold, and we get blowjobs every ninety minutes."

"That's bullshit."

Doom butted in to support the older probate, "It's true."

The probates, seeing Doom was listening, changed the subject. Doom wasn't ready to let it drop though.

"Who died?"

"Scorpion," the older one replied.

Doom cocked his head to the side. "What makes you think he's dead? He's been on the run from the law. No one has heard from him or seen him in years."

"Yeah. That's how we know he's dead."

Doom took a drag of the cigarette. "He's not in biker heaven," he said doubtfully. "But he is probably getting a blowjob every ninety minutes."

Still smoking the cigarette, Doom felt someone taking the seat next to him.

"I should charge you for that." Picking up the pack, Wizard took the last cigarette. "These fuckers are expensive."

"I'll buy you a pack."

"Don't bother. I'm quitting after this one." Wizard stared at the glowing tip. "You think Margarita and Haven are the ones texting Tink?"

"You heard?"

Wizard gave a sarcastic laugh. "No way I couldn't. Fuck, you had me feeling bad for her. I was about to offer her my services when she gave in. Sad she'll never know what she missed."

Doom turned his head, leaving the cigarette dangling from his lips.

Shaking his head, Wizard twisted his lips at him. "Chill.

I'm joking." Wizard stared at him through the smoky haze. "You get the numbers?"

Doom nodded. "I texted them to Hawk. He'll get on it when he comes up for air. You think it's Margarita or Haven?"

"No. They're in the Bahamas until next week. Margarita isn't happy about being barred from the club for the month, but I don't see her jeopardizing getting thrown out of the club altogether. Besides, if Margarita did want to get back at Tink, she would be smart enough not to identify herself."

"I think so too." Doom stubbed the cigarette out. Then, finishing off his beer, he stood.

"Where you going?"

"Home. Going to have an early night."

"Since when do you go home this early on a Friday night?"

Using his foot, Doom pushed the stool under the counter. "I'm exhausted. Watching you fuck Oasis to prove to Tink the size of your dick doesn't matter wore me out. I couldn't let you outdo me."

Doom went on the alert at the sardonic expression that crossed Wizard's face.

"You sure it's not because you don't want to be distracted by a mirage when you have the real thing in your arms?" he said sarcastically.

Doom winced. "You're never going to let me live that down, are you?"

Wizard smacked him on his shoulder. "Fuck no, but I'm going to memorize what you said. Hell, it even tugged on my heartstrings." He gave a feigned sniffle, his hand resting over his nonexistent heart. "When I use it on Natalia, I'll remember to thank you for the inspiration."

Doom released a puff of air. "You're going to need more than inspiration to lay that woman. What you need is a fucking miracle—and two more inches."

Doom cut and ran out the bar when Wizard stood up. He was still laughing as he got on his bike. Starting the motorcycle, he expected to see a threatening text from Wizard when he opened his phone.

He cut his motor and called the number of the man who had sent the text.

"What's up?" Doom asked when Train answered.

"You ready to join the unit?"

"Hell yes!"

As the words came out, the first flush of excitement passed to be replaced with a sinking feeling of dread.

"Cool," Train said. "I'm looking forward to having you on the team."

"You want me to ride to Treepoint or—"

"No. Rider and I will be flying in on Thursday. We'll leave Friday."

"Rider's coming?" Doom asked curiously.

"Yes, 'cause it's such a short trip, he wanted to hitch a ride to see everyone."

"Oh... The brothers will be excited to see him."

Within a span of a month, three original members had come to Ohio. That was more than the last two years. Moon was still here, which already had Doom suspicious something was going on, which neither Wizard nor Shade had given him any hints about.

"Does a week give you enough time to settle any loose ends? Your first assignment will be going undercover. We're anticipating from six to eight months, if not longer."

Once he left, it would be at least six months before he would return to Ohio.

"It'll only take a couple days to get my apartment cleaned out. I had already decided to sell my furniture. Anything I want to keep, I can get organized in storage by the time you get here."

"Sounds like you're better prepared than me," Train grumbled. "I'm only going to be gone from Treepoint for a couple of weeks to make sure you're settled in the assignment before I hand it over to Asher."

Asher Hayth had been born in the military, with his father serving overseas and his mother serving as a United States ambassador to Cyprus. Asher was a stickler for his team members' safety and had a nearly one hundred percent success rate of catching the perp he was sent in to bring down.

He had met Asher when he tried out for the special ops unit that consisted of several branches of the military. To even be asked to try out was an honor in itself. The few who did make it through were placed on a list to wait for an opening to become available. Even with each member of the unit having to pass annual physical and performance tests, openings only became available every three to four years, and that was when a member decided to retire or was KIA.

Doom might not know the details of the operation he'd be working on, but if Asher was involved, it was dangerous, and the government wanted results.

"Killyama hid my helicopter keys until I finished the two pages of chores she wants done before I leave."

"Could be she doesn't want you to leave."

Train laughed. "Bro, you don't know my wife. If Killyama didn't want me to go, she wouldn't use odd chores to get me to stay; she'd knock my ass out."

"I wish I'd met her when I was in Treepoint."

"Say that to Jesus or Puck and see what they have to say. Killy takes a little time to get used to."

"Puck and Jesus have spent quite a bit of time there."

"It takes *years* to get to know her. Take it from me, it takes years—"

"Then I take it you're going to finish those chores before you leave?"

Train sighed. "Yes, I will. I'll let you go. I'll email the paperwork over for you to fill out. Send it back as soon as possible. I don't want any hiccups with incomplete paperwork preventing the start of the mission."

"I'll get on it as soon as it comes," Doom promised. "I'll see you on Thursday."

Disconnecting the call, he put his phone back in his pocket. Making no effort to restart his motorcycle, he stared at the club, committing it to memory. When he came back after his assignment was over, the club would be different. With the help of the lawyer Tink had put Wizard in contact with, it seemed they might actually be able to start the renovations.

Burn had asked to buy his furniture when he was ready to sell. Doom would talk to him tomorrow and get everything moved out before Train arrived. What was left to do would be easily organized. He was prepared—except for Tink.

He sat on him motorcycle so long the brothers keep shooting him curious glances.

"You good?" Buck called out.

"I'm good."

Doom started his motorcycle and rode out of the lot. All his plans for leaving hadn't included Tink, assuming she would no longer be in the picture. When Wizard had jabbed at him about what he'd had said about Oasis, Doom played it off. Truthfully, he had forgotten about the others being able to hear.

The chilly night air brought cold reason back, cutting through the wayward emotions he felt for Tink. Emotions he didn't want to put a name to.

Doom reasoned with himself. It was only because he hadn't yet instigated breaking it off with her. Instead, Train's phone call had initiated what he would have done eventually anyway.

Tink had provided a break from riding a merry-go-round he used to with other women. After the assignment was over, he would hop back on until he was ready to jump back off again, this time when he was ready to settle down and start a family.

Doom sped up, trying to out-race the last part of what his cold reason was telling him but couldn't. It kept catching up to him.

When you do jump back off—Tink won't be waiting.

CHAPTER 53
THE BREAK

Juggling the two coffee cups and a bag of fresh bagels, Arden knocked on Doom's apartment door.

She heard the doorknob turn and smiled as the door opened. Her smile slipped, however, when Celeste opened the door.

"Hi." Celeste smiled at her.

"Uh..." Flustered, it took a second for her to find her words. "I brought Doom some breakfast."

Celeste opened the door wider. "Come on in. He's in the bedroom. He should be out in a minute."

Stepping into the apartment, Arden didn't notice Celeste shutting the door, too taken aback with the boxes sitting on the counter and the coffee table. Doom hadn't told her he was moving when she was at his apartment Thursday, nor had he said anything last night.

Forcing her feet to move, she walked toward the kitchen counter. She found an empty spot to place the bag of bagels and was setting them down when Doom and Burn walked out of the bedroom.

Her heart plunged as if she had been thrown off a

skyscraper at the guilty expression on his face when he saw her.

Before he could say anything, Arden hurried to extract herself from the pain-filled encounter of finding Doom had gone back on his word about having sex without her approval.

"I bought some bagels to take to the club. I thought you might like some, too." Moving toward the door, she managed to pin a smile on her lips. "I hope you enjoy them. I better be going."

Doom didn't let her make it to the door. Catching her by the waist, he brought her up short.

"Hold on." He turned them both to face Celeste and Burn. "We can settle up later."

"Cool. I promised Celeste pancakes, so we'll be heading out."

Reluctantly, Arden let Doom move her aside so Celeste and Burn could leave.

Doom released her to close the door but kept his body between her and the doorway.

She was sick to her stomach that she wouldn't be able to escape Doom putting a fait accompli on the short time they had been together.

Nervously going back to the counter, she picked up one of the coffees. She took a sip and motioned toward the other. "I brought you a coffee." Stating the obvious, she pasted a benign expression on her face, attempting to get through the next few minutes.

"Thanks." Doom ran his hand through his hair. "I know what you're thinking. Nothing happened. Burn came to look at some furniture I'm selling. Celeste tagged along because they are going out to breakfast—"

"For pancakes." Arden nodded. "Yes, that's what he

said."

Uncomfortably, Doom stared at her, as if deciding what to say.

Arden decided to make it easier for him so she could get away to lick the wound she knew was coming. "Are you moving?" The husky tenor of her voice had her taking another sip of the hot coffee.

"Train called after you left last night. I'll be leaving Friday."

"I bet you're thrilled. We'll all be sad to see you go."

"We'll?"

"The Last Riders and me, of course."

"I was going to tell you when I came to the club this afternoon."

Arden clutched at the first excuse she could. "Well—it looks like you have some packing to do. I should be getting to the club." She moved to go around him.

Doom frowned as he let her pass. "That's it?"

Her shoulders stiffened, but she didn't falter in her steps to the door. Fixated on controlling her emotions, she didn't answer.

"Hell, at least Celeste begged me not to go."

Tersely, Arden swung back in her sneakers. "Aw," she spat out angrily. "Was that before or after she kissed you?" She stormed forward, and her hand came out to swipe over his mouth. Pulling back, she turned it so Doom could see the bright red lipstick on her hand. "Or—" she waved her hand under her nose, "after she hugged you? Celeste is pretty heavy on her perfume. You should buy her a quart before you leave. It smells as if at least that much rubbed off on you."

Doom grimaced. "I don't want this to get ugly between us."

"Then you should have let me leave when I wanted to." Arden raised her hands up in defeat. "What do you want from me? If I show no reaction, you're not happy. When I do, it's too much. I just can't seem to please you." Sarcastically, her hands went to her hips. "Maybe it would be simpler if you just told me what would make you happy?"

Doom's mouth tightened into a tight line. "I thought we could spend the morning together."

Her mouth dropped open. "Doing what? Having sex?" Arden winced at the shrill sound of her own voice.

At least he had the grace to turn red when she must have said what he was thinking.

Her mouth opened and closed. If the coffee weren't hot, she would have thrown it at him.

"You're something else. No, I won't be staying to let you get your rocks off in me one more time. You have my permission to do anyone you want!" She rushed toward the door, and her hand went to the doorknob, but instead of turning the knob, she laid her head on the wood of the door when he didn't stop her.

"Why couldn't you let me leave when I had some pride left?" Shakily, she turned around to lean back to brace her weight before her knees gave out on her. "You're not an idiot. You know I'm in love with you. That's why I had sex with you. That's why you ran out of my apartment as if it were on fire. You may have claimed me to ease your conscience when you wanted to have sex with me again, but we both knew deep down how I feel about you."

"Honey..."

Arden raised her hand. "Stop! Please, just stop with the honey, and Tink... I'm no more special to you than any other woman you've been with at the club. We're just a way to pass the time until the job you were waiting for came through. It has, so you couldn't wait to get your life all boxed up and disposed of before giving me the courtesy of telling me."

Doom shifted on his feet. "I didn't expect you to come by this morning."

"You couldn't wait to pack, but you could wait to tell me? The first was a priority, the second an afterthought." Arden sucked in a deep breath, hoping to dispel the aching pain that had settled in her heart. "It's okay, Doom. I get it. You made it perfectly plain to me there was no emotional attachment on your part, so I only have myself to blame that I feel this way. I think it would be best if I stay away from the club until after you're gone. I don't want to leave Kat in a lurch today, so do you mind not coming in today until I leave?"

Doom took a footstep toward her.

"Don't. Please don't. I'm not going to beg you to stay, nor am I going to break and give you a going-away hookup. It will be better for me if we just end it here with our goodbyes." Leaving the doorway, Arden walked toward him and hugged him, giving him a quick kiss on his cheek before stepping back. "Goodbye, Doom."

"Bye, Arden."

Keeping her face averted, she turned. Making sure not to look back as she closed the door behind her, she went to her car. She wanted to break down into tears; only the thought of who was standing guard, seeing her red-rimmed eyes, kept her strong.

She hadn't broken down into tears when her mother told her she didn't have long left.

She hadn't broken down when her dad told he wouldn't see another birthday.

She hadn't broken down when Haven humiliated her in the breakroom.

She hadn't broken down when Doom told her he was leaving on Friday.

No, she was saving all her tears for the day he left.

CHAPTER 54

THE NECKLACE

"Can I get you another refill?" Kat asked, pausing beside the table.

Doom slid his empty mug across the table that Train, Deacon, and he were sitting at. "Thanks."

"Train?" she asked the man sitting next to him.

"No, thanks. I'm going to catch a few hours' sleep." Standing, Train stretched and yawned.

"Deacon, Wizard said he'd give you a ride to see Arden whenever you're ready. Just let him know."

"I will."

"You look good," Doom complimented Deacon once Train had left.

Making a wry face, Deacon took a drink of his beer. "Considering how I used to look?"

"Yes." Doom didn't mince words.

"Gained twelve pounds and bought some clothes that fit instead of wearing someone else's second-hand ones."

"Good food doesn't take long to pack the weight on."

Deacon's weary gaze leveled on him. "Having food wasn't the problem. Arden made sure Lizzie and I had plenty of good food. The problem was I couldn't stomach it. Train said you're going to be doing the type of job I used to do," Deacon said, glancing down at his beer thoughtfully.

"The undercover part, yes."

"There is something I want to give you."

Doom watched as he withdrew something from his shirt pocket. Not able to see what it was, he held out his hand when Deacon handed it to him. He stared down at it and saw it was a woven leather necklace with a thin circle brass disk. Drawing his hand closer, he read the writing. "*Today, I will remember Rule #1.*"

"Lucky gave it to me a lifetime ago. I wore it every day until, my last assignment."

Flipping the necklace over, Doom saw there was more engraving on the other side.

"*#1: To Thine Own Self Be True.*"

Doom started to hand it back. "I can't take this. It was Lucky's gift to you."

Deacon didn't take it back. "When Lucky gave it to me, he said he wore it every day until he didn't deserve to wear it anymore. Then I wore it until I didn't deserve to wear it anymore. I offered it back to Lucky a few days ago. He said he couldn't take it back, just like the person who gave it to him refused to take it back. Lucky never told me why he quit wearing it, only that he had broken the rules. I stopped wearing it because I lost myself when I fell in love with Lizzie.

"Don't get me wrong; I don't regret loving her. I never will. What I regret was not admitting I was love with Lizzie before I almost got her killed and destroyed my career. Neither of those are why I quit wearing the necklace.

"I didn't ask Lucky why he quit wearing it when I tried to return it to him, but I can tell you why I did. I stopped wearing it when I first bought drugs for Lizzie. It went against everything I stood for, what I had spent years working against. I tarnished a part of myself that can't be restored.

"I'm going to tell you what Lucky told me when he gave it to me. 'I'm giving you this necklace. Wear it every day, conscious of the integrity it takes to be true to yourself. If you do, the weight of necklace will be easy to carry. When it becomes a choker, you're not the same man who was given the necklace to wear.'"

Using his thumb, Doom smoothed the cord lying on his palm. The woven cord had a knot, which allowed the necklace to be adjusted. Gauging it was looped around three times, Doom estimated the necklace could extend to at least twenty-four inches.

He raised his eyes from the necklace to Deacon's. "Why are you giving it to me?"

"The night I met you, Lizzie said she liked you. I told her you were a fucking prick. She said you reminded her of me. I took her stash away from her, told her she was high enough. The night Lizzie died..." Deacon's voice choked up, "If you hadn't reacted so fast, Lizzie would have seen the woman she considered a daughter killed right in front of her eyes. I will be forever grateful she didn't, *that I didn't*. It's bad enough I lost Lizzie. If Arden had died..." Deacon broke off.

Doom could see from his shattered expression the warrior Deacon used to be couldn't have taken two losses.

Using his forefinger, Deacon slid the necklace closer to Doom. "Six men have worn this necklace before me. I'm hoping by giving this necklace to you, I'm giving it to the wearer who it was meant for all along—a Last Rider."

"Lucky is a Last Rider," Doom told him.

"He wasn't when he wore the necklace. I've known Lucky since when he was and wasn't a pastor. He always put his faith in God first. I'm not sure since I wasn't the one who gave it to him, but I'd say his faith in God was why the person gave it to him. I'm giving it to the man who I have *faith* in to always do what is right, despite the cost."

Deacon folded his arms onto the table. "Go ahead and put it on. Wear it." He shrugged. "The worst that could happen is it could end up around another person's neck. The man I saw when I was fighting for everything I held dear wasn't afraid of shit."

Doom picked up the necklace and put it over his head. He adjusted the cord until the pendant rested just below the collar of his T-shirt.

"Looks better on you than it did on me."

He took the beer Kat set down; the coldness of the glass reminded him of Tink. Respecting her wishes, he hadn't gone to the club until the next day. He had texted her to make sure she hadn't received any more texts from Haven or Margarita, but she hadn't responded. Tink had left his life just as abruptly as she had entered it.

"When are you going to go see Arden?"

"We're having lunch in an hour at Mama's restaurant. You want to join us?"

"I don't think she'd appreciate me showing up. We're no longer together." Doom pushed the beer toward Deacon, no longer wanting it.

Deacon nodded in understanding. "I had a few breakups in my life. They're never easy."

"You don't want to give me a hard time about breaking it off with her?"

"No, I love Arden, but I can understand why it didn't

work out. There are two types of women: the forever kind that you can never get over and—"

"What's the other type?"

"Catastrophes."

Doom laughed. "Had several of those."

Deacon gave him a twisted grin. "I had too many to count also. When I met Lizzie, if anyone had warned me I would lose my heart to an informer and I would throw my career away, I would have laughed in their face. Then she did one thing that stole my heart, and I was a fucking goner."

"What did she do?"

"We had to meet at out-of-the-way places. Usually, our interactions would only last a couple of minutes. She would drop off the information in the front seat of my unlocked car while I would go inside a store. One day, I came back, and she had left an insulated cup."

"You fell in love with her because she gave you a cup?"

"Yes..." Deacon shook his head as if he was still bemused. "It was just a fucking cup. I started using it when I was waiting for her to show, or when on a stake-out... Then I brought it inside my house and started using it there. I wanted to get to know the woman who was so worried about me drinking cold coffee that she bought me a fucking cup. Then I realized the cold, hard truth—the cup was just an *excuse* to do something I already wanted to do."

Unconsciously, Doom's hand went to the necklace. Their eyes met in silent communication. He was about to start a future that Deacon had already lived. Doom felt as if the engraved words were burning into his flesh.

TO THINE OWN SELF BE TRUE.

"I better be going if I'm going to meet Arden. I guess I'll see you tomorrow when we leave. Train said they're giving you a going away party tonight. Arden and I are going to visit Lizzie's grave then catch a movie."

"Have a good time."

"I will, thanks." Deacon gave him a smile. "You too."

Sitting in the empty booth, Doom took out his phone, checking to see if the information he was waiting for had come through. Irritated when he saw it hadn't, he was about to put it back in his pocket when a notification flashed across the screen. He pulled the text message up and read it carefully. Then, rising from the booth, he made his way for the door.

"Doom!" Celeste called out to him. "Don't forget the party. I have a going away present to give you."

"Don't worry; I'll be back. I just have something I need to take care of."

"I have something for you to care of too," she quipped back.

Doom walked out the door and headed for his bike, taking deep breaths. He had one piece of unfinished business to do before he left Ohio, and it wasn't fucking Celeste.

CHAPTER 55
THE PARENTS

Doom knocked on the door, staring around the two-story home. The older house was modest compared to the rest of the neighboring homes. While the house was old, everything about it showed it was carefully maintained, from the short grass to the plants underneath the windows and along the walkway. There was even a plastic duck sitting on the lawn, wearing a raincoat and holding an umbrella. Who needed to watch the weather forecast when all you had to do was look out the window and see what the duck was wearing?

The door opening had Doom turning back toward it.

"Doom?"

"Blue."

Tink's brother held the door as if afraid he would barge inside without an invitation. He would if he had to, but Doom preferred to play nice at first.

"Mind if I come inside?" Doom stared the boy down.

"Sure." Blue reluctantly opened the door wider.

Striding inside the entryway, Doom looked around while Blue stood there uncomfortably. The entryway allowed him to see that the living room was to the right and a formal dining room on the left. To his right was where Doom discovered why Blue was so nervous.

A frail woman was sitting on a chair in the living room. Even from where he was standing, Doom could see the gray color of her skin. Her mouth was open, as if she wasn't getting enough air, even with the oxygen bubbling next to her.

"What can I do for you?" Blue asked nervously, glancing toward his mother.

"I'd like to have a quick chat with your dad."

"Dad is sleeping..." Blue started making faces that his mother couldn't see. Doom got the unspoken entreaty not to upset his mother.

"Who is it, Luc?"

Pushing past Blue, Doom strode into the living room. "Hi, I'm a friend of Andy's. I just wanted to stop by and thank your family for all you did."

"No thanks are needed." Tink's mother's pain-filled face broke into a smile. "It was our pleasure for what he did for our family. I wish he had allowed us to do more."

"You did more than enough. I'm sorry, I should have introduced myself first." Doom held out his hand. "Karson Foster."

"It's nice to meet you, Mr. Foster. My name is Mary."

"Nice to meet you as well. I was hoping to thank your husband as well, if it wouldn't be too much trouble?"

"Not at all. He just woke up from a nap. I'm afraid he isn't able to leave his bedroom, but Luc can show you to his room."

"I would appreciate it. I promise I won't take up too much of his time."

"Take as much time as you'd like. I'm sure my husband would appreciate the company," she assured him warmly.

Doom looked over Tink's mother's shoulder to where Blue was standing behind her.

"Lead the way." He pasted a polite smile on his lips while making sure Blue could see he wouldn't allow any interference from speaking to his father.

Satisfied from the slump of Blue's shoulders that he had received his message, Doom moved around the chair to follow him.

The living room led to a small hallway that had a closed door. Blue's hand shook as it went to the doorknob.

"My dad's in bad health. What did you want to talk to him about?" Blue stared at him pleadingly. "I haven't told him about me hanging out with Puck, Jesus, and Buck."

"I'm not here about you," Doom told him shortly.

He frowned. "You're not? Then why—"

"Blue, open the door."

He did and went inside. Doom went in after him, seeing a slender man resting on the bed, breathing through an oxygen tube. As he drew closer, he could see the blue tint on his lips.

"Dad, this is—"

"I know who he is, Luc."

The thin, whispery voice might have surprised Luc, but it didn't him.

"You can leave, and shut the door behind you."

"Are you sure?" Luc didn't want to leave.

"I'm sure, son. Go on."

Standing with his feet apart, Doom crossed his arms over his chest, uncompromisingly showing the strength and the formidable power his body was capable of.

"If you're trying to scare me, save yourself the effort.

Anything you could do to me would just be a favor at this point."

"You must be scared of something I could do, or you wouldn't be sending text messages to frighten your daughter away from me."

"How'd you find out it was me?" Tink's father didn't bother to deny the accusation.

"I read the text messages the women you tried to frame supposedly sent." Doom gave him a twisted smile. "I claimed Tink as my woman. They aren't brave enough to cross me."

"It could've been several other people."

"It could," Doom agreed. "At first, I thought it could be Mama, but Mama is more the type to tell me to my face to stay away from Tink. For a while, I thought it could be your wife since the messages claiming to be from Margarita came from her phone. The messages from Haven, however, came from yours. Most of the messages came during the day when Luc was in school or when he was with some of The Last Riders."

"You're not stupid. At least that's a plus." Tink's father snorted sarcastically.

"No, stupidity has never been a fault of mine," Doom concurred. Glancing around the bedroom, he noticed several pictures scattered around the front of the bookcases lining two walls. Wandering across the room, he studied several of them.

"The Navy SEALs don't admit dumbasses."

"No, they don't." Doom stared at one picture. "You were a Marine."

"For a few years. After Arden was born, when my time was up, I didn't reenlist."

"You miss it?"

"No. I enjoyed being with my wife and Arden more. I missed being at Arden's birth. She was six months old before I could make it home. She cried every time I picked her up. I knew I wasn't going to reenlist when she let me hold her. I could handle not being a Marine, but I couldn't deal with my daughter being afraid of me."

As Doom listened, he reached for a picture frame. Tink's father was in the prime of his life in the picture, his body similar to his own. He was a sitting on a motorcycle, wearing a leather jacket and jeans, with Tink as a toddler sitting in front, holding the handlebars. The gaping smile as she stared up at her father spoke volumes of her adoration for the man holding her.

Swallowing down the unexpected lump in his throat, Doom placed the picture back.

"There was no need for you to go to the trouble of frightening Tink away from me. I'm leaving Ohio."

"I know."

Tink's father reply surprised him.

"Then why put yourself through the trouble?"

"Kept her away from you this week, didn't I?"

He walked to the foot of the bed. "Her not seeing me has nothing do with the texts you sent. She stopped seeing me when I told her I was leaving in the morning."

"I bet you didn't like that."

"I understood."

"Bullshit." Tink's father narrowed his eyes on him. "It pissed you off. You think I haven't been where you are? I married right out of high school. I still thought I could have Mary and have my cake on the side. I was overseas; how was she going to know? I didn't get it when I left, but the first time I went to a motel room with a hookup, I found out the truth. Jesus... As soon as it was over, I hated myself. I called

Mary, somehow thinking it would make it better. I was going to tell her; I just thought I wouldn't feel so shitty about myself if I could pretend to be a good husband over the phone. It just made me feel worse. That was when I found out I was going to be a father. I was so sick I cheated on my pregnant wife that I didn't even look at any women because I was afraid I would be tempted to cheat again.

"When I made it back stateside and came home, my kid cried anytime I walked into the room, and my wife somehow knew I had cheated. She never said a fucking word about it, but I could see the hurt in her eyes. I would rather have taken a bullet to the gut than see how badly I hurt her. When I left her, I told her when I came back, I wouldn't leave again."

"And how does this pertain to me? Like I said, I'm leaving. I've made no commitment to Tink. I won't be coming back to start over with her. When I leave, I'm gone for good."

Tink's father gave him a pitying look. "Then why are you here? You knew the texts were from me, you knew she was in no danger, so what purpose could you have to come here?"

Doom's hands clenched into fists. He had walked into a trap.

Her father gave a satisfied nod. "You care more than you think you do."

"I'm leaving," Doom asserted.

"I hope you do. You're not the man I would have picked for my daughter. I'm hoping, with you gone, she'll find a better man than either of us. Arden has a heart of gold. She deserves a man who will put her above everything else. A man who will be there to wipe her tears away, to sleep next to her at the end of the day, and spend years with her rather than a few hours here and there. Time goes so fast, and I don't want her wasting another minute with you."

"Tink must take after her mother."

Her father gave him a grim smile at the insult. "You rather she take after her mother than me?" He gave a sarcastic laugh. "You're right; she does." His head fell back onto the pillow. "You're fucked and don't even know you're fucked."

"What does that mean?" Doom's jaw clenched. If her father wasn't already at death's door, Doom would put him there.

"You figure it out. You said stupidity wasn't your problem."

Having had enough, he went to the door. If he stayed any longer, he would hasten the fucker's death.

"Send Arden a postcard when you get to where you're going. She can put it in a scrapbook."

I will not kill the fucker. Does he want to die so bad he's trying to push me?

The thought had Doom turning around to stare at him. Taken off guard, he caught an unexpected expression on the man's face. Doom's jaw clenched not in anger but in another emotion he didn't want to admit to.

Tink's father was goading him into recognizing he was in love with Arden. Confined to the bed, he was fighting for his daughter's happiness the only way left for him.

Doom looked at the picture with them sitting on the motorcycle. The adoration was visible on both of their faces.

"Can I get you anything before I leave?" he asked begrudgingly.

Surprise glinted in Tink's father's eyes. "You could sneak into the kitchen and grab me a beer."

"Are you allowed to have it?"

"No, which is why you need to put it in my tumbler." He gestured to the large tumbler sitting next to his bed. "You need to hurry; the nurse should be here any minute. Arden hides them behind the yogurts."

"Where's the kitchen?"

"You're the Navy SEAL; find it."

Getting the tumbler, Doom left the bedroom. Asking himself why, Doom made sure not to make any noise as he went behind Tink's mother's chair. He took a silent breath and made it to the entryway, past the dining room, to where he saw an archway. He walked through it and found the kitchen. Quickly, he located the beer and poured it into the tumbler. After hiding the empty beer bottle in the trash can, he went back through the archway, peeked around the wall, and saw Tink's mother had fallen asleep.

Quietly, he maneuvered behind her chair to make it back out of sight.

When he set the tumbler back down, he saw her father was attempting to raise his bed. Reaching for the control, which had dropped below his reach, Doom raised the bed. Once he was situated, Doom handed him the tumbler.

"You good?"

"Yes, thank you for the beer. A Marine would have done it quicker. At least you beat the nurse getting here."

Leaving before he coldcocked him with the tumbler, Doom tried to pass the chair as silently as before.

"You get him his beer?"

Startled, Doom paused in front of the chair. "What beer?"

Smiling, she adjusted the oxygen tubing under her nose. "The beer he asked you for. I must have dozed off. I didn't see you go past me."

"How did you know?"

"He asked for a beer?" Her hand went to the side table to pick up a small monitor. "Arden makes sure I have this when there is a gap before the nurse gets here. She doesn't tell her father I have it. She doesn't want to hurt his pride."

"I guess it would be useless for me to lie about it then, wouldn't it?"

"I'm amazed you would make the effort with how rude he was to you."

"Can't blame a father for protecting his daughter."

"Are you going to tell Arden?"

"No."

She gave him an approving smile. "I like you."

Doom smiled back. "The feeling is mutual. Can I get you anything?"

"No, thank you. I have everything I need."

"All right, I'll be leaving then. It was nice meeting you."

"It was nice meeting you, Karson."

A question came to his mind, which he had no intention of asking, but she must have seen the indecision on his face.

She had picked up a magazine, turned to a crossword puzzle, and was lifting a pencil when her gaze turned back to him. "You have a question?"

"Did you know about the texts?"

"Ah... You're wondering if I was aware what my husband was doing or if I was in on it with him?"

Feeling an unexplainable closeness to Tink's mother, he really hoped she hadn't participated in the plan.

"I didn't. My husband can be impulsive sometimes. Arden may be like me, but she does share that characteristic with her father." Her gaze didn't detour away from his when his sharpened.

"When he makes these mistakes, what do you do?"

"Depends on how bad it is. Usually, the mistakes work

for the better. Would I have had the opportunity to meet you if Carter hadn't sent the texts?"

"Probably not."

"I like having a face to put to the man my daughter has been telling me about. You're aware Arden is in love with you?"

Doom looked toward a family photo sitting next to her chair.

"Yes, you know." She gave a soft sigh, drawing his gaze back. "Don't worry; Arden is very cognizant of the fact you don't return her feelings. She may have inherited Carter's impulsiveness, but she did my common sense. Usually, it keeps her from jumping headfirst. I can see why she couldn't resist you. Unfortunately, my common sense didn't prevent me from falling in love with Carter. I knew we were too young to get married. The statistics were against us from the get-go, especially with him going into the service and me determined to go to college. I let Carter convince me to marry him. That was before I realized he had a habit of being impulsive." Soft laughter hit him in the chest, seeing the bittersweet pain in Arden's mother's face. "I convinced myself love could conquer all our problems, so I went ahead and married him."

Doom expected her to say more, so when she went back to working on her crossword puzzle, he didn't leave.

"Yes?"

"That's it?"

"What else should I have said? Love did conquer our problems."

"But..." Doom broke off. If she had dozed off during the part when Arden's father had talked about cheating on her, he damn sure didn't want to bring it up.

"Carter cheated on me. Is that what you're being too polite to say?"

"Yes."

"I didn't say our marriage hasn't been without our share of problems, only that we had to work through them."

"How did you find out?"

She gave him a wry smile. "Most women know. They may lie about it to themselves because it's too painful to acknowledge, but I've never been good at lying to myself. The pain was intangible."

"Yet, you didn't leave him," Doom stated.

"Why? Because he made a mistake? I could tell he was just in as much pain as I was. I think it surprised him how much breaking his vows shook him. I came to the conclusion he punished himself more than I could have guilted him into. I never wanted to marry a man I could put on a pedestal. I wanted a man who stayed through the good and bad times. If I couldn't stick with him when he had a lapse of judgment, how could I expect the same in return? Marriage is about give and take. At this point in your life, you want to take, but you're not ready to give your heart.

"Arden is smart enough to recognize that you're not at the point when you're ready to settle down. Once you're gone, her heart will take time to recover, but she *will* find someone at the same place, at the same time in life, and what she feels for you will turn into a memory that dies as surely as I will."

The atmosphere in the room became claustrophobic. With a polite goodbye, Doom left, regretting he had ever stepped foot inside the house. He had been prepared for dealing with a protective father, but Tink's mother had given him the willies. She was as gracious as a lace doily that lulled you into missing the fact that you had a knife pointed at your nuts.

Rubbing the back of his neck, he was determined to wake Train from his nap and put Ohio in the dust. He didn't need or want a going away party. Planning to stay until the church meeting was over to discuss whether Tink, Puck, and Buck had lied made it feel like he was one snare away from never leaving.

He got on his motorcycle and started zipping up his jacket but stopped when the zipper became entangled with the necklace. He untangled the cord, and the words hit hard, as if someone had piledriven him from behind. Tucking the necklace under his T-shirt, he finished zipping his jacket.

Andy's gift couldn't have come at a better time. It only served to reinforce what he already knew.

To Thine Own Self Be True.

Doom was going to do exactly that.

CHAPTER 56

THE SWITCH

Arden stood nervously in front of the stern-faced members of The Last Riders. Afraid any nervous movement would be a dead giveaway to her guilt, she remained motionless.

"How did you earn your votes from Puck and Buck?" Wizard asked.

"Exactly how did they say I earned them?" she hedged.

Dourly, Wizard unwrapped a sucker he had removed from a cellophane bag to place in his mouth. Arden was sure he was doing it to prevent himself grinding his teeth together. She could tell from the moment she had walked into the club that Wizard was in a foul mood. Andy had told her The Last Riders were throwing Doom a going away party. From Wizard's appearance and the state of the bar, there must have been a free-for-all at the end. Bluish, purple swelling surrounded his left eye, and Wizard had tissues poking out of his nostrils.

"Did Puck and Buck lie when they said you earned their vote, or did you buy them by giving them Super Bowl tickets?"

"I was going to give them the tickets regardless."

Her knees started shaking inside the slacks she was wearing at the way Wizard glared at her.

"Which still doesn't answer my fucking question." Taking the sucker out of his mouth, he used it to point at her. "Go sit your ass down. Buck, front and center," Wizard ordered sharply.

As Buck got off the stool, Arden knew he was going to maintain their lie. Puck didn't even glance as his brother when he got up. He was going to lie too, when his time came.

"Wait." Arden remained where she was. "I begged them to give me their votes. They didn't want to lie to any of you, but I begged them. Don't be mad at them. It's *all* my fault. I'll take any punishment you want to give them. You can even take back all the votes you have given me and throw me out of the club if you want."

With Doom leaving this morning, it was hard being here, anyway. She kept looking around for his face in the bar, and each time the door opened, she felt a piece of her heart die when it wasn't him coming inside.

"You're willing take the punishment I would have given Buck and Puck?"

"Yes." God, she hoped it wasn't too bad.

"At least you didn't make it worse by lying to me, I'll give you that." Wizard drummed his fingers on the table. "Concerning your punishment, I have a question."

Arden stared at him questioningly.

"Were these knuckleheads worried about us finding out they lied for you?"

Arden felt the color drain out of her cheeks. "Yes. They knew I would be the weak link."

Wizard rolled his eyes at her then grimaced. "Don't give

them so much credit. If they were so fucking worried, they shouldn't have fucking accepted the tickets!"

"They had me agree to a stipulation."

Wizard's interest piqued, and his jaw punched out with the sucker. Well, either it was the sucker, or he was furious. Arden really wanted to sit before she fell.

"What was the stipulation?"

"That I couldn't ever tell how they gave me their vote."

Folding one leg over the other, Wizard folded his hands on his stomach to stare over her head at the two men who had come to stand behind her. She couldn't tell if it was to show their support or to strangle her.

"What if she told?" Wizard asked them.

"We told Tink that we would expect her to earn our vote the way we said she did," Puck spoke up.

"Hmm..." Wizard nodded. "Technically, the votes wouldn't be a lie if you three have sex. We could say the votes were a loan until you were ready to earn them. There, problem solved. You three get busy." Wizard reached for another sucker.

"Celeste, bring me a fucking beer. Church over."

"Wait!" Arden objected loudly. "I don't understand."

Wizard gave a loud groan, staring up at the ceiling as if his patience was exhausted. "What's so fucking hard to understand? I'm trying to be *fucking nice*," he snarled. "Save two knuckleheads from being thrown out of the club because they misguidedly got a fucking hard-on and lost their judgment when you dangled those tickets in front of them instead of your tits and *fucking lied to us*!"

Arden winced as Wizard's voice rose in volume to a shout.

"You can throw me out of the club—"

"Did I fucking ask your permission as to what I can do?" Wizard looked as if he was about to strangle on his sucker.

"No..." Arden took a step back to save her hearing.

"I was beginning to fucking wonder if the brothers voted you in while I was fucking sleeping. Did you, fuckers?"

"No, brother," The Last Riders chorused. "You're the president."

"Good, now that's settled, are you prepared to repair the damage you've done to Buck's and Puck's loyalty where the club is concerned, or are they saying their goodbyes?"

What was she supposed to do? She couldn't have sex with them, but she didn't want them thrown out of the club either. Luc would lose their friendship too...

"I'll do it." Arden couldn't believe the words came out of her mouth.

"Don't sound so excited," she heard Buck say sarcastically from behind her.

Arden turned her head to the side. "You want me to be excited? Try showering." She wrinkled her nose at him. "I smell at least five women on you. Must have been a hell of a party last night."

"It was," Puck said, winking at her. "Don't worry; I showered. Buck can shower while I get you warmed up."

Arden turned forward again, trying not to cry. Her heart was breaking just thinking how many women Doom had been with before saying his goodbyes this morning. Then she wanted to smack herself for even thinking of crying. He had left her to face the club alone. She had gotten herself in this mess, but would it have killed him to stay until after the club meeting?

She regretted every instance of having sex with him, especially the blowjobs. He had enjoyed them too much. If by some miracle she could do it over, she wouldn't have been so careful with her teeth.

"Glad that's sorted." Wizard yawned and got out of the chair. "I can get some sleep. Puck and Buck, keep the noise down. I need my beauty sleep."

Wizard stiffly began walking around the table he had been sitting behind, while the rest of The Last Riders used the opportunity to flee until Wizard was in a better mood.

Was he limping?

Arden bit her lip, trying to come up with an idea to get out of the inevitable without raising his ire again.

"I wouldn't want to wake you. I can get a little loud. I'll just clean up in here. We can do it later when you wake."

Buck and Puck simultaneously shook their heads.

"Nope. Wizard has it arranged for the prospects to clean. We're good to go." Puck ran a seductive hand down the arch of her back. "Buck can take a shower while I go change the sheets. You mind making me a sandwich? I'm running on empty. I'm going to need all my strength. Don't want you saying later I couldn't get you to the finish line."

Witheringly, she shoved his hand away from her. "You want me to make you a sandwich?"

"Please," he said pitiably. "Unless you want to help me make the bed?"

"I'll make the sandwich," she said numbly, already deciding to do what she had to do to keep the men in the club then never step foot in it ever, ever again.

Stiltedly walking toward the kitchen, she planned to make the grossest sandwich imaginable. Should she make one for Buck? Yes, that way, they would both be in the bathroom, vomiting it out. She would have to remind them not to wake Wizard, she thought snidely.

"You do remember which room is mine?" Buck called out.

"How could I forget?" Sarcasm dripped off her tongue as she went through the doorway, remembering when Doom had carried her down the hall and Buck had opened his door naked.

As she made the sandwiches, Arden put enough peanut butter and jelly on them to make a dozen, hoping to glue their tongues to the rooves of their mouths. Feeling guilty at the thought, she poured them a large glass of milk to drink with it. Doom was pretty much the only one who drank it.

Blinking back tears, she put the remaining milk back in the refrigerator. The rest was going to spoil without him to finish it off.

With leaden footsteps, she came out of the kitchen, aware none of The Last Riders were meeting her eyes. She walked down the hallway and paused outside the door. Should she knock? She didn't.

Opening the door, she saw Puck sitting on the bed in the dark room. With the hallway dark, all she could see was his shadowy body.

She closed the door with her hip but regretted it instantly. She should have turned the light on before closing the door.

Immediately, she knew why she hadn't. What had to be said would be easier in the dark.

"I'm sorry, Puck. I can't do this even to keep you and Buck in the club." The tears she had promised she wouldn't cry started sliding from her eyes. "Not even for Luc..." she choked out. "I love Doom. I wish I didn't, but I do."

Arden heard the sound of Puck getting off the bed, and then the milk and sandwich were taken from her hands. The rattle of the dishes being placed on furniture had her hand reaching for the doorknob. The door didn't budge when she turned it.

Warm breath warned her as a mouth settled on the curve of her jaw.

"I love you too," he said huskily.

Shocked to hear Doom's voice, she pivoted into his waiting arms.

"Doom?" she asked uncertainly.

There was a movement at her side, then light filled the room.

"Who else would be telling you they love you?" he asked sternly yet with a gentle expression.

Arden had to run her hands over his chest to make sure he was really there.

"No one." Happiness exploded in her chest. "You didn't leave!" Jumping toward him, she grabbed him by the neck to kiss him. "I'm so happy!"

"Tink..."

Suddenly, the happiness vanished just as quickly as it had struck. Jerking her arms back, Arden stepped away from him.

"I didn't mean to jump to conclusions. Are you here to say goodbye to me? Please don't expect me to wave you off like I said I would—"

"Honey—I'm not going anywhere yet."

"Yet?" she interrupted.

"I had a talk with Train last night. I told him I couldn't join his team. I would have to be undercover for at least six months. I can't leave you when you're so close to losing your parents. Nor did I want to leave you for that long of a period of time regardless. Train said he understood and still offered me a part-time team position. I'll be gone a couple of days at a time and be on call when the team's deployed. The job is still dangerous, and one day, I might not be able to come home to you, but it won't because I don't want to. Will you be able to deal with me possibly having to leave without a minute's notice, during birthday parties, holidays if I'm called in?"

"You'd come back in a few days?" Arden buried her nose in his neck as she wrapped her arms around him.

"Barring death, yes."

Could she live her life with Doom constantly risking his life? Yes, she could. He would be risking it regardless of if he was with her or not.

The last week she had spent without him had given her a brief glimpse at what it would be like. All he was asking of her was to accept a job that was so important to him, perceiving it would feed a need in him that she would never be able to fill.

"Doom, I don't have to be your whole world; I just want to be a part of it."

"Honey—you've been my whole world since the moment I saw you. When I'm not here, that doesn't mean my heart isn't."

Arden gave a shuddering cry at him baring his soul. Doom was a man of few words. That he was being so open about his emotions had her holding him tighter.

"I thought I'd never see you again. What changed your mind?"

Doom made a face at her. "I kept telling myself all week I was going, but I never could come up with a price to sell my furniture. I put it in a storage unit instead. Then I told myself I'd rent an apartment when I came off assignment, but I realized for sure I wasn't going to leave you when you dropped Andy off the club yesterday."

Arden frowned. "I didn't see you."

"You couldn't. I was on the roof, trying to fix Wizard's fucking air conditioner."

"You know how to fix an air conditioner?" she asked in surprise. Doom was the least mechanical person she knew. His skills ran to plugging electric cords in the socket.

"I don't know jack shit about fixing an air conditioner."

"Then why were you trying to?"

"Because Wizard was going to ask you to fix it when you came in today."

Warmth at his concern had her smiling mistily at him. "Awe, that's so sweet. You didn't want me on the roof."

"Shit." Doom grimaced. "I wasn't worried about you being on the roof. Knowing you, your old man taught you how to walk a tightrope."

"Then I don't understand why Wizard asking me to fix his air conditioner influenced you to stay?"

"The son of a bitch told me if you fixed it, he was going to marry you right after he got you drunk enough to accept." Doom looked as if he was in pain at his admission. "I think the fucker was deliberately making me jealous to make me stay, which was how a fight started."

"Who started a fight?" Confused, she leaned her head back to see his face.

"I did."

Arden couldn't help but wrap her arms around his waist to hug him.

"I'm just curious." Doom's hands went to her bottom to pick up her, his pelvis suggestively rubbing against hers. "Not that it really matters, of course, but would you have been able to fix the fucking thing?"

"Sweetie—" Arden gave him a loving pat on his cheek, "air conditioners are my specialty."

EPILOGUE ONE

Coming downstairs, Doom was surprised to see Tink and Carter's nurse about to wheel her father out the front door.

"Dad woke up feeling good today," Tink explained. "He wants to sit outside."

"Let me." Doom took the handles and carefully maneuvered the wheelchair through the doorway outside. Locking the brakes, he moved to stand in front of his father-in-law. "Looking good today, Carter," Doom complimented the ill man.

Carter didn't bother to smile. Doom didn't take it personally. His father-in-law didn't have much to smile about anymore. His illness had become worse in the last three months since Tink and he got married.

He had asked Tink to marry him before he let her near Wizard's air conditioner. Not wanting to take any chances that one of the brothers would steal her away from him, he used her parents' health to convince her to marry him in a private ceremony with them and Blue. Tink's mother had passed away a month later.

Living with Tink's family hadn't been the adjustment he had expected. Blue and he got along well, and before Tink's mother passed, he enjoyed spending the night watching television with her as she reminisced about Tink's and Blue's childhoods.

"I feel good. I might do some piddling around the house today."

"Might have trouble finding something to fix; Tink was trying to find something yesterday."

Carter gave her a baleful look.

"Sorry, Dad," she apologized.

Kissing her despite the irritated glare she gave him for telling on her, he decided it was a good time to leave.

"I'm going to head on to the club. I'll be back in an hour."

"Take your time. We can get Dad back inside by ourselves."

Getting on his bike, Doom noticed Carter staring at him wistfully.

When he arrived at the club, he headed straight to Wizard's room. He didn't have to knock since the door stood wide open, Wizard sprawled naked with Celeste lying partially over him and Kat curled to his side. All of them were blissfully asleep.

"Wake up, brother. We have shit to do!"

"Fuck off," Wizard groaned.

"Can't today. Get your ass out of bed. We're going for a ride."

TINK AND CARTER were still sitting outside when he returned.

Tink stood up when row after row of motorcycles started lining up in the street.

Getting off his bike, Doom walked up the driveway to where Carter was sitting. "You up to a ride, old man?"

Carter's eyes filled with tears. "Hell yeah."

"Dad..." Tink gave her dad a concerned look before throwing him a reprimanding glare. "I don't think that's a good idea—"

"He can wear his portable oxygen. I checked to make sure it's safe. He's going to ride with me."

Seeing how happy her dad was, she caved. "I'm coming too."

"Thought you would. You and Blue can follow in the car."

Doom saw her disappointment that she wouldn't be riding on a motorcycle, but Carter was riding with him, and Tink's ass wasn't getting on another brother's bike.

He rolled Carter's wheelchair down the driveway, then helped him onto the bike. Then, pulling out a specialty backpack designed to carry the portable oxygen, Doom placed it inside and helped Carter slide it on his back.

"You ready?" Doom asked.

"Been ready." Carter adjusted the nasal tubing more comfortably. As he gawked at all the bikes, Doom saw him go misty-eyed again. "They're all veterans?"

"Every last one of them." Doom pointed at the two bikers who would ride next to them. "Rhodes and Nashville were in the Marines."

"I haven't been on a motorcycle since I sold mine."

"That's what Tink told me. I'll make sure not to go too fast, so you won't fall off," Doom teased him.

Carter's happy expression deflated, believing he was serious.

"Brother, I'm joking. I've got you. Tink is going to have a hell of time catching up." He stared his motorcycle, then signaled to Wizard that they were ready.

"Brothers!" Wizard bellowed out. "Let's ride!"

The motorcycles kept to the speed limit until they hit the road leading to the club then gradually picked up speed. As they reached the club, the bikers all parked to go inside. Doom didn't miss the disappointment on Carter's face when he got off.

"I thought we'd grab a beer."

Joy lit his father-in-law's face.

Lifting Carter into his arms, Doom carried him inside to place him on a stool at the bar.

"Kat, give this Marine a beer." Doom sat down next to Carter.

Kat had just placed the beer down when Tink and Blue walked through the door. Motioning for Blue, Doom stood up and let son and father sit together.

Going behind the bar, he poured a beer from the tap then set it down in front of Blue. "Enjoy a beer with your old man."

Blue stared down at the beer then back at him. Doom knew the composed expression on Blue's face was a façade. He could see the depths of anguish Blue was hiding from his father.

"Thanks, Doom," he said in a thick voice.

Pouring himself a beer, he stood, listening as Carter talked about a road trip he had taken when he was eighteen.

He was lifting the beer to his mouth when feminine arms slid around his waist from behind, and he could feel Tink pressing her body against his back.

"I love you."

Unlike her brother, Tink wasn't able to keep her tears at

bay, using his body to hide the emotions she didn't want her dad to see.

His free hand went to one of hers to link their fingers together.

"Won't you get in trouble for giving Blue a beer?"

"Not if we don't get caught." Doom shrugged uncaringly. "Every father deserves to have at least one beer with his son at a bar."

"You didn't want Dad to miss out," Tink stated.

"I didn't want Blue to miss out," Doom corrected her.

"He seems so much better today. He's been so sick for the last few days that I was starting to get scared..."

Doom didn't want to give her false hope. "It's called the rally time." He had noticed how ill Carter had become, and he had been carefully watching for his father-in-law to exhibit the signs of rallying, which certain terminal patients experience a day or two before dying. "My mom did the same before she died."

Tightening his hand over hers, Doom shielded Tink from her father's and brother's eyes.

Several minutes passed before she was able to gather enough control for her to move to the side and participate in the conversations going on with and around her father.

When Doom caught sight of Carter growing tired an hour later, he made his way back around the bar to place a steadying hand on his shoulder. "We should leave before you get too tired to ride back."

Carter nodded gratefully. "I don't want to miss that."

Picking Carter back up, he carried him back outside with all the vets they had asked to come and The Last Riders following closely behind. Several Last Riders had arrived after they had come but had remained outside and were standing in a group in the middle of the parking lot.

Carrying Carter toward them instead of his bike, Doom stopped in front of them to nod his head. The Last Riders moved aside, showing the motorcycle hidden from view.

Carter stared at the bike in astonishment. "Is that—" he had to stop before he was able to continue, "my old bike?"

Lucky grinned. "Yes, we had a hell of a time finding it." Lucky used his chin to point at Rider, who was standing next him. "Rider just finished the repairs a couple of days ago. It's all yours."

"I can't—accept."

Doom sat his father-in-law down on the motorcycle.

"You have to." Lucky grinned at Carter. "Tink took care of Andy when I lost contact with him. I have to pay back my debts."

Carter lovingly touched the handles and started laughing.

Everyone looked at Carter in concern when he used his hand to wipe the tears away.

"It's funny how life comes around."

"What do you mean, Dad?" Tink asked, handing her father some tissues.

"I always planned to leave this bike for my kid. I can't refuse it if it was meant for Arden. I would have left it to her when I died anyway."

Doom didn't miss the crushed expression on Blue's face. Carter didn't miss it, either.

"I was going to leave it to Arden, because I taught her to ride on this motorcycle."

Doom looked at his wife in astonishment. "You know how to ride a motorcycle?"

Arden nodded as her hand familiarly grabbed the handle. "Yes."

"Why did you stop?" Doom asked Arden.

"I sold the motorcycle," Carter provided the answer. "I needed the money to pay for medical bills for her mother."

Doom could hear the pride in Carter's voice.

"I was going to buy another motorcycle, a less expensive one, when I got back on my feet financially and teach Luc. A few times, I was ready to buy, but Luc's mother talked me out of it. She was overprotective because we almost lost him a few times when he was a baby. I let her talk me out of it. Arden and I have been on the lookout for one for Luc, but every time I get close to buying him one, something comes up, and the money gets spent. Arden has offered to give me the money, but if I couldn't buy her one, I didn't think it was fair to take her money."

"You wanted to buy me a motorcycle?" Luc eyed his sister.

"Yes."

"You said they aren't safe."

"You talked about it in front of Mom. I didn't want her upset. When I tried to discuss it with you when she or Dad weren't around, you wouldn't listen."

"Because I was angry." Luc's voice started to rise.

"I, um—Doom!"

Doom ignored Tink's shocked yell. "Apologize. Now."

"Doom, let my brother go."

"You raise your voice to my wife again, you and I are going to have problems. I don't give a rat's ass you're resentful of your sister. Man up!"

"I'm not resentful of my sister," Luc argued.

"I love both children exactly the same," Carter asserted.

"I know you do. Tink and Blue know you do. The problem is Blue can't compete with what Tink can do. Shit, I wish I had half the know-how to repair some of the stuff she can. You know how I know you're resentful? There isn't a brother—"

Doom accented his anger by giving Blue another shake, "here who wouldn't take their eye teeth to have the natural ability she does. The way your mind works for science and math is the way her mind troubleshoots what she's working on. When you're some big-time doctor, making a couple hundred grand a year, I'd kiss your fucking ass if all that fucking resentment goes down the drain when your name-brand dishwasher goes on the fritz." Doom gave Blue another shake to emphasize his point.

"Doom, will you please let my brother out of the headlock?"

Doom released Blue with a final shake.

Blue gave his sister an apologetic look. "I'm sorry."

"It's okay. You don't know how many times I wish I were as smart as you."

"I'm sorry if you felt I thought differently for you and Arden." Carter caught his son's hand.

"You didn't, Dad. Doom is right. You tried to teach me the same things you taught Arden, but to tell you the truth, it was easier to resent Arden than having to admit that we don't share the same interests," he admitted then hastily added, "other than motorcycles."

"Can't blame you there. I hate fixing shit too," Buck said from the side.

"We should be getting back." Tink smiled at Lucky and Rider. "Thank you for getting and repairing the bike."

Carter gave his thanks, shaking The Last Riders' hands.

Doom got on the motorcycle. "Here, Tink."

She turned, and Doom tossed his wife the keys to his bike.

"You can ride it back home for me."

"You trust me to ride your bike?" Disbelieving, she stared at the keys.

"Of course."

Doom had to brace his feet to keep Tink from tilting her dad's bike when she threw her arms around his neck to kiss him.

"You can ride next to us," Doom said.

She gave Blue a hesitant smile. "Do you want to ride with me or drive my car back?"

"I'll ride with you."

"Just leave the keys in the car. One of the brothers will drive it back," Doom told her.

Excited, Arden and Blue got on the motorcycle.

Doom looked around, searching for Wizard as president. They couldn't leave without him in the lead.

"Burn, where's Wizard?" Doom yelled out.

Burn rolled his motorcycle forward next to his. "He went inside to ask if anyone had any cigarettes."

Doom frowned. "Wizard quit smoking. He hasn't smoked in months."

"Yeah, well..." Burn grinned. "He's pretty pissed off right now."

"About what?"

"He was complaining about how you stole Tink right out from under his nose. He said it isn't fair you nabbed the only woman in the state of Ohio who doesn't mind plunging a toilet. But I think her being able to ride a motorcycle was too much for him. He needs a cigarette to calm down. He went back inside, hoping one of the older veterans might have one."

Doom snorted. "Most of them are on oxygen. He'll blow the club sky high."

Burn took a pack of cigarettes out of his jacket pocket and pulled one out. "I don't think he cares."

Doom heard Tink's laughter at Wizard's sour complaints.

"Why are you laughing?"

She made a face at him. "Well, you kind of did, remember?"

Damn, he had. Tink hadn't been in the club three minutes before he had scooped her up to take her to the office. Doom couldn't help but appreciate how fucking hot his wife looked on the motorcycle.

Kicking down his kickstand, he got of the motorcycle to wrap a hand around the nape of Tink's neck, giving his wife a passionate kiss. Raising his lips to admire her rosy-red ones, he gave her a predatory smile.

"Honey, I've never been accused of being a stupid man."

The ride back was one he would always remember for the sheer happiness on Carter's face when they arrived back home.

As he got off the motorcycle, his father-in-law grabbed the sleeve of his jacket.

"Could someone take a picture of us together before you take me inside?" Carter asked.

"Of course."

Wizard took several pictures of Carter with Tink, Blue, and several of them all together. Doom especially liked the one where Tink sat on the motorcycle, with her dad behind her and Luc's arm around his father's shoulders. Doom promised himself he would get it printed tomorrow.

Wizard showed Carter all the pictures before Doom carried him inside and put him on his bed. Then the nurse bustled around Carter, getting him changed into pajamas, while Tink made a plate of sandwiches she brought to the room. They all spent a couple of hours just sitting around his room with the television playing in the background as they talked.

When the nurse gave Carter his night medicine, Tink and Luc took it as a sign that Carter needed his rest. They kissed their father before leaving, but Doom lagged behind. He had gotten into the habit of double-checking if Carter needed anything that he didn't want to ask his children for.

"You good?"

Noticing his embarrassment, Doom carried him to the bathroom and watched television until he heard Carter calling out to him when he was ready. He took him back to bed and placed the covers back over him.

"Thank you for today, Doom."

"No thanks needed. I enjoyed it as much as you."

"Doubtful." Carter gave him a tired smile. "I thought I'd never sit on a motorcycle again before I died. Thank you for making that possible."

Doom gave him an encouraging pat on the arm. "There's no reason we can't do it again."

He still didn't leave, sensing there was something else Carter wanted to say. The nurse must have felt the same, making an excuse to leave to make herself a snack.

"Your friend put the motorcycle I bought off him for Luc in the garage?"

"Burn did. It's there until you're ready to give it to him."

"I'll give it to him in the morning."

Doom noticed the worried frown on Carter's forehead. "Anything wrong?"

"You ever disappoint anyone?" Carter asked.

He nodded. "Once, when I didn't take the job I was supposed to take."

"Do you regret not taking it?"

"No. I don't do regrets. They're a waste of emotions. I didn't take the job; I got married to your daughter instead. It all evened out."

"I have two regrets. I cheated on my wife, and I sent Arden those text messages."

"Your wife knew. She forgave you for your mistake. Arden knows about the text messages, and she forgave you too."

"How do you know?"

"They both told me. Your wife and I talked after the first time I came here. I hate to tell you, but she listened in on our conversation with a monitor. She knew you regretted your mistake and forgave you."

"Did you tell Arden I was the one who was texting her?"

"No. Her mother accidently did when she was on pain medication. Tink knew you were just concerned for her. She totally forgave you. Regrets will fuck with your mind. Don't give them the time of day, okay?"

"Okay. I'm glad you decided to stay."

"Me too. Night, Carter."

"Doom, take care of my children when I'm gone."

He placed his hand over Carter's heart. "Rest easy, brother. I've got you covered."

Carter gave him a weary nod. "Night, Doom.

A KNOCK EARLY the next morning woke Tink and him from sleep. Doom went to the bedroom door and quietly talking to Carter's nurse, before he told her they would come downstairs. He closed the door and turned to see Tink sitting up in bed.

"Dad?" she asked tearfully.

"He's gone. The nurse called the doctor. He's on his way."

"I'll get dressed." Tink started to get off the bed then sat back down, bursting into tears. "I'm going to miss him so bad."

"I know, honey." Doom sat down next to her and pulled her into his arms.

"The angels will be giving him his wings," she sobbed.

Doom hated to disabuse her, but her dad might not have belonged to a motorcycle club, yet he had the heart of a biker. He damn sure didn't want her saying that when it was his turn to bite the dust.

"Honey... Bikers aren't about the wings unless they're patched onto their jackets. Bikers go to biker heaven, where we're given a Harley, a glass of beer, and can ride to their heart's content."

Tink used the corner of the sheet to wipe at her tears. "I can't believe you're making jokes."

"I'm not joking. You have your idea of heaven; bikers have theirs."

"My dad was not a biker."

"Take it from me—he was a biker."

"You only knew my dad for a few months, and you think you know him better than me?"

"Let me ask you a question."

Tink jerked herself out of his arms to start grabbing clothes. "What?" she snapped.

"Have you never seen your dad's naked ass?"

EPILOGUE TWO

MANY, MANY, MANY YEARS LATER...

"Blow out the candles, Grandpa!" a chorus of childish voices yelled out.

Pressing his necklace to his chest, Doom leaned over the table to blow out his candles. Thankfully, Tink had bought the number candles for 84 instead of the dozens she had last year.

"Happy birthday!" Tink pressed a kiss to my cheek. "Who all wants a piece of cake?"

"I do!" A little girl sitting on her knees on the chair next to the cake bounced up and down in excitement.

"Mine first!" another little girl sitting across the table spoke louder, trying to overrule her sister.

"Grandpa gets the first slice, and then I'll cut you each a piece and give it to you at the same time," Tink told them placatingly.

Taking his cake from Tink, he walked around the room, mingling with his guests and family members. When he was finished with the cake, he threw the paper plate away and made his way to his office, where he turned on the light before closing the door. Sitting behind the desk, he opened a drawer to take out an empty jewelry box. As he was closing the drawer, Doom heard a knock on the door.

"Come in," he called out.

His son stuck his head in the door. "I wondered where you had gone off to."

"I just wanted to get this package ready for you to mail for me in the morning, if you wouldn't mind?"

"Not at all." Carter came further into the room to stand in front of his desk.

Doom took off the corded necklace he hadn't taken off since he had put it on all those years ago. Some days, like today, it lay loose on his chest; other days, it was a choker, the tight length leaving an imprint in his flesh.

Gently, he slowly put the necklace in the box then snapped the lid closed. Reaching for an envelope, Doom put the box inside with the letter he had written last night before sealing it closed.

He raised his eyes when he was finished and saw the stunned expression on his son's face.

"You're giving your necklace away?"

"Yes."

"I always thought you would hand it down to me after..."

"I died?" Doom shook his head. "No. This necklace wasn't meant for you. It's not meant as a keepsake. You don't live the type of life that a man who would benefit from wearing this necklace needs. I doubt you had a moral dilemma your whole life. You've never veered from the straight and narrow. You don't need the necklace to remind you of what's in here." He placed his hand over his heart. "You've got your mom's heart. You always listen to that, you'll be good. The man who gave me the necklace thought

I was who it was meant for. I wasn't. It's time it went to who it really belongs to."

"Why now?"

Doom stood up to come around the desk and shut the door. "Yesterday, my doctor told me I'm dying. He gave me a year to live." Then Doom strode over to his son to push a chair behind his legs. "Sit down."

Carter sat down, visibly shaken.

"Son." He tried to lighten the atmosphere from the grim news. "I'm eighty-four; you should have been expecting me to bite the dust every day. Hell, at my age, me eating a taco could take me out."

Carter lifted his face. "That's not funny!"

Doom stood closer to the chair, giving his son a side hug. "Listen, there's no need to get upset. When are doctors ever right?" He gave a sarcastic snort. "I'll probably be alive and kicking five years from now."

"Have you told Mom?"

"No. I'm going to tomorrow. I didn't want her upset before everyone came over."

"She's going to take it bad, Dad."

"She will, but she knows I'm a fighter, so she really won't start worrying for a couple of years."

"How are you not upset? Aren't you scared?"

"You were raised around bikers. I've told you about biker heaven. Bikers aren't afraid of shit. Besides, there is something about marriage I didn't warn you about. Your mother and I have been married a *long* time," Doom drawled out. "The last ten years' blowjobs have gone from few to far between, like non-existent. The idea of biker heaven is the only thing tiding me over."

Carter looked as if he didn't know whether to laugh or cry. "You're going to cheat on Mom in heaven?"

"Son, your mother and I came to an agreement a long time ago. I can do anything I want with her full approval when I get to biker heaven. She's already given me permission, so I'm good to go."

Carter didn't seem convinced. "Mom gave you permission to get blowjobs every ninety minutes?"

"She sure did." Doom nodded. "The only stipulation is when Tink gets there, I have to go back to being faithful. *So*, there is something else I need you to do for me."

"Of course, what is it?"

"Make sure your mother outlives me for at least eleven years."

FOUR DAYS LATER...

A postal carrier drove into a parking lot. Getting out of the van, the postman silently cursed as he climbed the mountain of steps to the front door. Fearful, he approached a man standing at the front door.

"I have a package that requires a signature." The carrier did his best not to piss in his pressed shorts when dead blue eyes met his.

"Who's the package for?"

Made in the USA
Monee, IL
29 July 2023